SYNTHETIC

A Dystopian Sci-fi Novel

CAT THOMAS

Gwillion Press

A CIP catalogue record for this title is available from the British Library
ISBN 978-1-9160251-9-6
Gwillion Press

For Paul, with love

ONE

Lona and the electric wolf

I was sitting on the head of John the Baptist, looking at a knitted model of Jesus casting demons into a herd of swine. Tiny, ribbed, pink pigs threw themselves into a bright blue sea on a corner of Yvonne's desk.

'Only another five forms to fill in.' Yvonne peered in front of her at a screen invisible to me. 'Won't take long, Lona. Now … religion. Shinto, yes?'

I shifted uncomfortably on the embroidered cushion. Cross-stitched prophets stared at me suspiciously from the other chairs.

'Yeah.'

'And you'll be attending the shrine at Abergavenny, or going down to the big one in Newport?'

'Ah, not sure yet. I've set up my travel shrine in my rooms. Combining work and faith, you know.' I nodded at the Christian craft objects illuminating Yvonne's office.

She gave a rabbity smile as she tapped the air, selecting the invisible option on the invisible form. 'Oh, I understand. It's enriching. Even our Corporate Director, James Fish, has one of my tapestry Bible texts in his office and he's *very* austere. Now, education. It says here you attended St Expiditus Roman Catholic Girls' School in Cardiff?'

The embroidered prophets looked at me beadily as I nodded.

'You're from South Cymru, then? I had you down as a Londoner, Lona, with the World Citizen accent implant and all. Luminos isn't a Welsh name, is it?'

'Well, I *am* here to translate an Old Welsh text, so …'

'Silly me. Says it here. *Nationality: Cymraeg.* That's a lot of languages you speak, besides Welsh and Old Welsh. Ogham. I'll be honest with you Lona, I don't even know what that is.'

'The runes in the Pryddych tomb. They're in Ogham.'

'Are they now? There's obscure, even for St Cadog's.' She gave a little laugh. 'Fluency in Spanish, Russian, Mandarin, Arabic, Japanese, Portuguese, Italian, French … They're a bit more modern aren't they? *Master* of the Guild of Translators.' Her shoulders tensed and her bright little eyes looked at me with something that might have been respect. Or discomfort. I wasn't sure. Either was good. 'I do beg your pardon. Didn't realise without the Guild robe or insignia. Do you prefer Master Luminos?'

'Lona's fine,' I said, and her shoulders relaxed. 'Do Guild members normally wear robes here?' I'd noticed as I made my way through the old college to the admin block that the academic staff wore informal robes, and even the students milling about in the corridors had dark red gowns over their jeans and trainers.

'Well … academic staff. And students. Clergy, too, naturally, but they're mostly academic. The rest of the staff are a bit more up-to-date. We only "robe up" for ceremonies. Though some of us wear our insignia.' Yvonne tapped her chest. Among the litter of appliqué and brooches, half hidden by a scarf, I could just about make out the crossed pens insignia of an ordinary member of the Guild of Administrators. On the other side of her chest she wore a Methodist cross-and-flame Flogo.

I sighed inaudibly. I'd have to come up with some badging if I was going to fit in at all here. In my normal life I didn't need it. My ability to do the job as anonymously and neutrally as possible was all that mattered. Well, being able to hold my nerve too. I'd got a bit shaky at that bit, though, lately.

'Now, next of kin.'

I gave her M's details.

'Kyoto, eh?' She entered the comms details. 'That's a distance.'

It was. It was too much of a distance. Hardly ever seeing M hadn't been helping me cope with the relentlessness of the day-to-day. But what could you do? We both had to work.

'Right, I think that's all the personal information. I can always get back to your agency if we need anything more. If you'll just look at the camera and put your hand on the touchpad, I'll start the security clearance.'

Normally I do business translation. High-level meetings between questionable clients on neutral territory – high stakes, high pressure, tight security – but I'd never been put through a drill like this before. And I came here for a bit of a rural working holiday.

As the TransBub had touched down in the rooftop garage the previous night – and said 'Arriving at St Cadog's, a partner college of Synthesis Edutainment,' in its calm Bubble voice – I'd got that cheerful, stretchy sort of feeling that you have at the beginning of something you know is going to be quietly satisfying, in a low-stress kind of way. I'd followed the trolleybot through the sort of 'welcome' arch William Morris would have designed if he'd designed welcome arches, apart from the familiar minimalism of the *Synthesis* logo shimmering brightly over it. Underneath, a sign in gothic lettering read: *St Cadog's Methodist College, founded 1866.*

'Hi there, Lona and Dodo,' the arch had said. 'Here at St

Cadog's Edutainment Experience we're bringing heritage to life and keeping religion real. Get ready to enjoy your adventure!' And we'd followed the trolleybot along what felt like the corridor of an ancient monastery overlaid with splashes of advanced tech, to the faux-medieval splendour of my rooms, the Gawain Suite.

Okay, it would be an institution I was working in, and I'd never been good with those, but I was a contractor and the project I was working on was kind of free-standing, so it wouldn't be too regi-mented. Yvonne was just a personnel hurdle.

She swiped her invisible screen. 'While that's running I'll do your health and safety induction. Particularly important at present, with all these godless hippies camping all over the place. Now—'

She took me on a dizzying tour of what-not-to-do, covering so many aspects of physical, mental and spiritual hygiene that even my high-spec memory enhancements only just managed to take in:

- If a colleague shows signs of Satanic possession, do NOT attempt any kind of exorcism; report to an accredited Demonic Possession Specialist,
- If you find an incubus or succubus on the premises, do NOT attempt to tackle it yourself; call in the Satanic Cleansing Department,
- If you encounter signs of anti-religious activity, do NOT argue, debate or wrangle; alert the local Faith Protection Alliance unit.

'Right, that's all downloaded to your outerbody system,' she said, with a gesture at her data.

Where I would never so much as glance at it. I'd maintained a poker face as Yvonne asked all her intrusive questions – not so easy now I'd cut down on my calm meds, but, *please*. I didn't need useless advice about dealing with imaginary beings. And I was as likely to contact the Faith Police as I was to start saying Hail Marys.

'You use Synthesis vOutside. There's handy. And all your self-ware's Synthesis, is it? Not just your outerbody dataware?'

I nodded.

'We're trying to get everyone to upgrade here, we've got a special deal, being a Synthesis partner college, but people are a bit stick-in-the-mud.' She smiled at me, conspiratorially. 'Academics, you know.'

'Your tech here's quite advanced, isn't it?' All the ambient tech in my rooms, from the door that greeted me to the drinks dispenser in my kitchenette, were high-end business hotel grade, which was at odds with the general ancient appearance of the place.

'Down to James Fish, that is.' Her smile was proud now. 'He's turned us into a smart university.'

'It's not because of Synthesis, then?'

'Partly, but that was Fish's idea too. He set up the partnership.'

'But Delauney's the Synthesis lead now, isn't he?'

Yvonne pursed her lips when I mentioned my new boss.

'The *academic* lead. Lot more to a partnership than that, Lona.' Yvonne seemed about to say something else, but changed her mind. Instead, she looked at Dodo as he lay meekly on her cross-and-flame rag-rug, his head between his paws.

'Let's move on to your, ah, friend. Now then, DigiPal have corroborated the security details you sent over. Let's see. Companion animal model Lupus W34.6. Yes, that's all in order. He's quite a size, isn't he?'

Dodo looked at her with his head on one side and gave his tail a cautious wag. I bent down to rub his ears, avoiding the gaze of the prophets.

'He's a big softie, really.' My stock phrase usually worked with people who didn't know better.

'I'm sure he is.' She looked anything but sure. 'But, thing is, Lona, we don't normally allow pets on campus. Health and safety, you understand.'

'Delauney's already agreed to Dodo being with me on this assignment.'

Yvonne bridled slightly. 'He has? On standby, in your rooms, I expect.'

'Active and with me.'

Yvonne made an effort to sound reasonable. 'If that's your

agreement with Professor Delauney then I suppose we have to honour it, Lona.' Her body language, if I was reading it right, said she was exasperated. Or maybe frustrated. My system wasn't entirely accurate. 'But your insurance would have to cover it.'

Access to Dodo's insurance documents calmed her down a bit. 'Personal *and* third party, even though he's a DigiPal pet. Always best to be on the safe side, eh? I always—'

Yvonne's office door interrupted her. 'Sister Continence for you, Yvonne,' it said. 'She *says* it's an emergency.'

'Excuse me a second, Lona.' Yvonne nodded to the door.

A nun rushed in, the cross-and-pen insignia of an admin order heaving on her bosom next to her Methodist Flogo as she struggled for breath.

'Yvonne, it's the Pagans,' she gasped.

'What have they done now?' Yvonne asked.

'Fish. They've kidnapped Fish,' Sister Continence said. 'They're holding him hostage. In the tomb.'

Naz: A Journal of Unnatural Thoughts

Tuesday 20 October 2071

7am

My first entry since last week's events, this. Bit undisciplined. But being attacked by a madwoman can get you like that.

She just appeared in front of me, brandishing a screwdriver, screaming that I was the instrument of evil. That I had to be stopped. Luckily, Owen and Fish restrained her before she got physical, so I didn't have to use force.

I was just in the middle of designing a talking deer, too. Subtle, complicated work that – because you want to make it engaging, but all the time you're haunted by the ghost of Bambi. I've had to shelve it until I'm feeling a bit better. Been getting on with some bird flight instead – complex mathematically, but not so creatively demanding.

Naturally, Delauney offered me counselling, but I'd rather not subject myself to the homespun, mystical wisdom of the Little Sisters of St Brynach. Recording this private journal's the best therapeutic tool for someone like me anyway. Kept as a standalone, in one of my safe drawers, so I can be honest.

I'll recover from the trauma, I'm too psychologically well-balanced for it to make a permanent mark.

Meanwhile … meanwhile, it's time for my daily check-in and testing with PsychLabs. And then. Then her replacement starts today.

I'll get on with designing some more kestrels. Or maybe red kites.

TWO

What would Eirrod do?

The Faith Protection Alliance was formed in 2050 as a broad-based coalition of religious, peacekeeping and law enforcement professionals. Our mission of 'facilitating hope and preventing despair' is driven forward by a staff dedicated to opposing both religious prejudice and godlessness. Backed by military know-how, and working in harmony with all recognised religions, the Alliance spreads the light of faith into some of the darkest corners of the United Nations of Britain.

Alliance Field Manual, Chapter 1: Verse 1

Yvonne seemed a bit reluctant to let me come with her to their hostage situation. I pointed out that I needed to know where the tomb was if I was going to translate the carvings on its walls. She could think of it as part of my induction.

'Just keep out of harm's way, Lona.' She nodded towards Dodo. ''Specially him.'

Dodo and I exchanged glances as we made our way out of the

blue glass and glinting steel of admin block; a new extension, bolted onto the back of the old Victorian building. A bruised sky hung low over us as we made our way across a rugby pitch, and towards the small crowd that was gathering near a wood. In the distance I could see what looked like a campsite on the edge of the woodland.

Yvonne bustled to the front of the crowd and we followed. I found myself looking at a circle of people who stood shoulder to shoulder, facing outwards around what looked like a hole in the ground. They were a mixed bag, hippyish types in cloaks fastened with Tree of Life Flogos, ecopunks and a sprinkling of urban warriors. They all looked excited, determined.

A large fair-haired man, respectably tweedy under his professorial robe, approached Yvonne.

'They've got your boss in the tomb.'

Despite his crucifix Flogo he looked almost amused. Even a little excited.

'Well they'll regret it, Delauney,' muttered Yvonne. 'The police are here now, look. And not just the Civil Police.'

Two police vans nee-nawed to a halt near us, followed by a blue-lit car with law enforcement number plates. A dark van with tinted windows glided up to park next to them. Its anonymous number plates spoke of the Faith Protection Alliance. Faith Police. The studenty Pagan who was recording the event pointed her lens studiously away from it.

'And Lona, hey,' Delauney hailed me. 'Great to see you. Welcome to St Cadog's.'

I hadn't recognised my new boss's World Citizen accent and practised white smile from our holointerview. 'Delauney. Hi. Sorry, you look more … alive. In the flesh.' And he did, he was somehow hyperphysical.

'Guess that's good.' He looked amused.

I retrieved my hand from an energetic shaking and realised I'd said something a bit wrong. Delauney was welcoming Dodo now, who responded with equal enthusiasm. That usually helps to deflect attention. One of Dodo's many good points.

I nodded towards the Pagans. 'They're signed up to this new idea that Eirrod was a Pagan king, then?'

'Yeah,' he gestured towards the ramshackle tents, 'they've been camped near his tomb since the news was leaked. Mainly to own him, pay homage, raise the profile of their cause. This stuff today's about them thinking the College plans to sell the manuscript and the other tomb artefacts, though.'

'And does it?'

'Not exactly. Synthesis will keep the originals safe at the Celtic Culture Centre back in the US, but a copy of everything will stay here, so no one will know the difference. And the College gets a big wodge of cash from Synthesis so everyone's happy.'

'Except the Pagans.'

'Ah, this stunt's been orchestrated by the hardcore fringe. They're mostly Cymru Liberation Front – more about politics than religion. The rest of them are more sensible, but their leader, Rowan, is away for the day and looks like CymLib just seized their opportunity.'

He still seemed excited by it all.

'You're not … annoyed with them?' I asked.

'All publicity for our manuscript.' He smiled. '*Your* manuscript.'

Police had emerged from their vehicles and were all over the grass near the circled Pagans now. The doors of the Faith Police van stayed ominously shut.

Yvonne collared a sharp-featured, sandy-haired woman who looked vaguely familiar to me.

'A serious matter, DI Driscoll,' we could hear Yvonne saying to her.

Delauney winked at me and said quietly, 'Let's see if I can't sort this out.' He went over and put a companionable arm round each of the women.

Two of the kidnappers facing us – a big lad with a shock of curly, dark hair and a tough-looking man dressed in black combat gear – conferred. The boy spoke out.

'We have James Fish – who's leading the conspiracy to sell Eirrod's body, the Pryddych Cycle manuscript, and the grave artefacts to a foreign company – here in the tomb. He's unharmed. We'll let him go when the College pledges publicly that they won't sell our heritage.'

There were gasps and the odd cheer from the crowd around me, which had grown larger since we'd got there. Students, college staff. Pagans.

The buzz of excited chatter from the crowd got louder and DI Driscoll stepped forward, away from Delauney's placatory arm. 'We can't talk while you've got a hostage, Owen,' she said, with weary patience. 'Let Fish go and we can discuss it.'

Looking down, I noticed an angel peering at me through the grass. Dodo looked up at me, pleased with himself, then he picked up the papier mâché figure in his mouth. It was a strangely plain angel; more like an insurance salesman with wings. Better make sure I returned this one. Dodo wasn't too popular with Yvonne as it was.

The tough man whispered something to Owen.

'It's Britain's oldest book we're talking about,' Owen said. 'All this is our history. It belongs to us, the people of Pryddych, and we *won't* sell it.'

More cheers from the crowd.

Delauney stepped towards him now. 'You won't get what you want by this kind of prank, Owen. What you *will* get is expelled. But no damage done yet. Come on, let's all sit down and discuss it like adults. Like Eirrod would have done.'

Owen looked unsure. A small girl with candy pink hair standing next to him spoke.

'But it's Eirrod's body you're trafficking in, isn't it? That's created trouble already, look at what's happened to poor Elaine and all she did was start to read the sacred book. Let us bury our king in peace, Delauney, for everyone's sake.'

The crowd murmured and whispered around me.

'Oh come on, River,' Delauney said. 'You don't really believe all that curse stuff. You're an historian, we deal in facts. And Eirrod wasn't a mystic, he would have been pragmatic, done what was best for Pryddych.'

'Eirrod was a warrior.' The tough man spoke slowly, looking

round at everyone, making the most of every word. 'He would have fought for his people's rights.' He was very convincing. Even I was a bit convinced.

When the shouts of encouragement from the crowd had died down, Delauney said:

'By negotiation, Kite, not by force. Eirrod was—' but his voice was drowned out as the noise started. It was a heart-freezing sound. A kind of high keening wail, or a very pure humming sound, it grew gradually louder. And it came from the direction of the tomb. It continued, reaching an almost deafening pitch, and a woman appeared out of the crowd. A large woman, moving with focussed energy. When she stood in front of Owen, the energy coalesced as the sound grew louder still. Her peroxide hair shone with it. Her round cheeks glowed with it. She stared at Owen and he dropped his gaze and let her through.

The woman grabbed the ladder that lay on the ground inside the ring of Pagans and lowered it into the tomb. There was some muttering from them but no one tried to stop her. Gradually, a man emerged from the depths of the burial chamber. Tall, spare, far from happy. He stepped onto the grass, next to the woman, and looked round at his former captors. The keening noise stopped.

The complete silence that the wailing sound left when it disappeared was cavernous.

'Owen Gryffydd,' the woman said slowly, into that silence. She stared Owen full in the face. 'You are *so* grounded.'

DI Driscoll walked up to them. 'He's more than grounded this time, Gwenda.'

'Oh, nonsense Faye, Fish won't be pressing charges.'

DI Driscoll looked questioningly at the un-entombed Fish.

'Er, not against Owen. No.' Gwenda squeezed Fish's arm. He smiled. A thin smile, but even I could see he was trying.

'Hum,' DI Driscoll said. Darkly. 'The College will want to take disciplinary action, anyway.'

Delauney came forward. 'Ah, student prank, no real harm done. Fish is okay.'

Gwenda beamed at Delauney. He smiled, too, but then it came easily to him.

DI Driscoll shook her head in disbelief. 'The rest of you aren't going to be so fucking lucky,' she called out to the other Pagans and waved the waiting uniforms forward. 'Get this lot in the vans. Not Gwenda's little prince. This time.'

I

She's arrived, the new translator. A hard-boiled city type, nothing like Elaine. Bit of a shock to sleepy Pryddych. She'll want to succeed, though, and that's what we all want. One way or another.

I've not been myself lately. Since the excavation I've felt more alive. As if I've become real. As if life's changed from black and white to Technicolor. Exciting. But a bit much.

Because if I'm not myself, then who am I?

THREE

A long way from Kansas

The tomb was deep. Very deep. Once I was inside it everything went quiet. The outside noise of the crowd dispersing and the police vans leaving was more or less swallowed up by ancient silence. I could just about hear Delauney's end of a comms call before he climbed down the ladder to join me, his fair hair flopping over his forehead.

Yvonne had reluctantly given me into my new boss's care with the proviso that he should follow the set protocols in the new staff orientation handbook and complete the institutional induction checklist. All three of us knew he wouldn't.

'Thought I'd better give Rowan a quick call,' Delauney said. 'Get the lawyers alerted. Don't want my students missing lectures because they've been arrested. It was just a stunt.'

'The man they kidnapped – Fish – he'll press charges?' I asked.

'No. Bad publicity for the College.'

'Right.' Had it all been play-acting, then, I wondered? 'So, anyway, what in the name of all the ancestors was that wailing noise?'

'Creepy, huh?' He flicked his hair back from his forehead and smiled. 'But it's just an effect of the wind from the mountains howling through the underground chamber.' Delauney gestured expansively at the bleak hills as if he was introducing me to them.

In fact, they'd been an oppressive backdrop to much of my childhood. Having them tower over me again brought a muffled sense of longing and dread. I'd chosen this assignment to recuperate from the day-to-day of my normal working life but it hadn't occurred to me that my own ghosts would be waiting for me here. I shivered, slightly. Luckily, Delauney was too focussed on his topic to notice.

'The wailing was the main clue that the tomb was there at all,' he went on. 'It's been heard for centuries. People used to think that it was the voice of the Seeing Stone, protecting Pryddych from evil.'

'That's from the *Green Book of Fwddog* isn't it? Something to do with a prophesy?'

'It's from the *Green Book*, yeah.' He looked up at Dodo, who was peering over the edge of the tomb, and laughed. 'Having a wolf looking down at us seems totally the right thing. So, what do you think of the tomb, Lona? You can really feel it when you're here, with the mountains and the trees all around us. You get a sense of what they believed in – what they worshipped. Magical, huh?' His face glowed with an enthusiasm that was almost infectious.

The tomb was atmospheric, I had to admit. It was circular, its walls formed of engraved slabs of stone, and it was empty now that Eirrod and his gifts had been taken away. There was an odd quality of soothing peace and alien strangeness that calmed me. I ran my fingers over the Ogham carvings that covered the walls.

'We've recorded all those.' He gazed at them, eagerly. 'But Elaine didn't know much Ogham. I understand a little; enough to tell, along with all the symbolism of the grave goods, that it's probably not a Christian tomb. But you'll be the first to read the inscription properly in sixteen hundred years. Think of that.' He seemed awed at the idea. Sixteen hundred years.

I touched the Ogham hieroglyphs next to me. *We are the stories*, they said.

'So, Elaine?' I asked. We were walking back to the university, the grey bulk of the main building looming ahead of us. It had been built by Victorian Methodists to look like a dour version of an Oxford college. The overall effect, set against the cheerless landscape of dark cloud and darker hills, suggested a medieval monastery. Strangely well preserved and probably haunted.

'Ah, yes. Elaine Bowen. Your predecessor. Old Welsh language and literature scholar, the College Principal's research assistant, before he gave her the translation job. She's... uh... She became ill.'

'Cursed, apparently.'

'Oh come on, Lona. I know you won't be taken in by that mythical twaddle. You're more rational, I can tell.'

After scanning us thoroughly, the heavy oak back doors to the campus opened, just as the rain began.

'So she's not cursed?' I asked, as we turned down a corridor with stone walls and floor, illuminated by mullioned windows. 'Just sick?' The monastic feeling persisted inside the College, except that the occasional student who flitted past was in an academic gown not an ecclesiastical one. The tech embedded everywhere made it feel more haunted than smart, I thought, as, one by one, the line of mullioned windows along the corridor creaked shut, sensing rain.

'Equally cursed and blessed,' he said. 'She's a visionary. That didn't make her ill, but mystics are never robust.' There was something about his body language that said something else, though. Irritation, maybe? Dislike? But my system was probably at fault. You wouldn't dislike someone just for being sick; and Delauney was a Catholic, they loved their visionaries.

Delauney ushered me through one of the arched oak doors that lined the corridor and into his office. After the austere, monastic hallway, his room came as a bit of a shock. It was crammed with ornaments, rugs, and furnishings from all over the world, with clashing styles and colours that made my head spin. More was clearly more, where Delauney was concerned.

Over the coffee that his office made us, I tried to adjust to the sensory overload. Delauney drank his cappuccino and told me about the excavation of the tomb, and their excitement at finding the *Pryddych Cycle*.

'This is going to be huge, Lona. Massive. The archaeologists used a totally new technique to reconstruct the manuscript – took them months. So not only is it Britain's oldest book, but if it suggests the tomb was Pagan, then well. We're rewriting history.'

Delauney had been here six months already, he told me. He was brought in by Synthesis as the lead historian once it was clear that the dig was going to be something special.

'And this virtual reality environment that's going to be created out of the manuscript?' I asked.

'The OtherWorld. Synthetic reality, it's called now. I've got a top-class developer on that. Naz – you'll meet him soon. We've used the existing Early Welsh texts – the *Mabinogion*, *Green Book of Fwddog*, and so on – to create the OtherWorld, so the framework's there.

When you've translated our manuscript, which is likely a collection of stories, like the others, Naz will feed it in and bring it to life. You'll advise on that, while he's doing it.'

'So the OtherWorld's kind of a virtual, sorry, synthetic, teaching environment?'

'That's right. Students learn about Early Welsh history and literature by having guided experiences in the synthetic world. Groundbreaking. They can use it to teach other subjects, too, later on.'

'But they'll have to be here to do that?'

'At the moment, yes. We've got a big, empty room next to Naz's lab we use as the OtherWorld studio. But in future, students will be able to port in from anywhere in the world. Like they do now with the old system, most of St Cadog's students are overseas.'

'Old system?'

'They've got a clunky old educational environment that uses avatars and holos to teach groups of distant students. The same one as every other college uses. But the OtherWorld will leave that standing.'

For St Cadog's it might be inspired business development, and for Delauney it might be career-making, but for me all this still sounded like a holiday. With dragons and talking sheep. A holiday I badly needed. I'd been working too hard for too long. Sorcerers, riddles and a fantasy world sounded like a perfect rest cure. I loved stories. I'd always loved stories. The more unlikely, the better. For a few months I could just relax into them, enjoy them and then live them in a virtual world. And get paid for the pleasure.

'Now let's get some lunch,' Delauney said. 'The food's one of the best things about St Cadog's. Gwenda – you saw her earlier? Gwenda's in charge of that and she's a star.'

As we left, the boy called Owen emerged from the Principal's room opposite Delauney's office. He looked sheepish.

'Hope Benedict read you the riot act, Owen,' Delauney said.

'Fish did,' Owen said, ruefully.

'False imprisonment,' Delauney went on. 'That would have been major if we'd taken it seriously.'

'Fish said. Spiritual reprogramming and ten years forced labour. I just … I didn't think. I was trying to do what's right.'

The Principal's door opened again and Owen disappeared speedily down the corridor muttering something about checking on his arrested comrades.

Two men emerged from the Principal's office. One was a slight figure in academic robes, whose white hair created a kind of halo effect against the morning light streaming in through the window behind him. And the second was the man I'd seen emerging from the tomb, the College Corporate Director, James Fish.

'Guys, let me introduce our new translator, Lona Luminos,' Delauney said. 'Lona, this is Benedict Pleasance, the College Principal. And Fish, who organises everything for him.'

'My dear, I believe you come to us from east London, an area I knew so well before the wars.' Benedict took my hand in both of his, in a vicarly manner. 'You are so very welcome to our little community.'

'Delighted that you're joining us, Lona,' Fish said. The smile on his gaunt, mobile face was unexpectedly genuine, if I was reading it right. 'Just what this project needs.'

Delauney gave him a sideways glance at this. I busied myself with Dodo, who had offered Benedict his paw (he's good at sucking up to people in authority) and was bemused at how long it was being captured and gently patted.

'You okay now, Fish?' Delauney asked. 'No bones broken?'

'As you said, Delauney, it wasn't much more than an ill-advised student prank. The Pagans needed reining in, though.' Fish's mouth hardened. 'But DI Driscoll's dealing with that now. So that's a positive outcome.'

'Humph,' Delauney muttered, as we left them and went out through another door onto a paved courtyard, open to the cloudy sky. 'Reining in. This place is supposed to be all about religious tolerance.'

'Paganism's still illegal though?'

'Christianity was illegal once,' he said. 'Anyway, this bit's the

quad, Lona, the old college is built around it. And, more importantly, it's the shortcut from my office to the refectory.'

I looked round at the medieval-effect quadrangle I'd seen from
my window earlier this morning. A couple of clerics, deep in conversation, walked along the cloisters that bordered it and disappeared
through a door that opened silently for them. We could have been in
the twelfth century. Well, a haunted twelfth century.

This place was different to any of the universities I'd visited
before, to do translating tests or the odd short course. For one thing,
they'd been busier, crowded with a lot more students. Here, most of
the students weren't actually on campus, they were miles away,
attending synthetic seminars in virtual classrooms. For another, they'd
been more modern, much tattier and substantially less tech-enabled.
This place was like going forward in time to a well-heeled past.

The door out of the quad refused to open for us.

'I can let you in Professor Delauney, and Master Luminos, but
the wolf isn't registered.'

'I think you'll find he is,' Delauney said. 'Reload your data.'

After a few seconds the door opened for us, very slowly, and
closed with a peevish slam.

'My room door calls me Lona,' I said, as we crossed the corridor
to the refectory. Students and staff sat on benches at long, rough-
hewn oak tables, eating and talking and under a vaulted ceiling. A
huge, plain cross hung on one wall.

'Those quad doors are more formal.' Delauney steered me over
to a quiet corner of the big room. 'And that one's a prototype of a
new, more capable kind of door, so it's got the odd bug as well as a
bit of an attitude. Elaine makes a point of being polite to it – says it
feels undervalued. Maybe it's being a little uppity because you're
replacing her.'

'How ill is she, this Elaine? Can I talk to her?'

Gwenda bustled up to us, saying, 'You won't get much sense
from Elaine at the moment, my lovely, raving she was last week,
poor girl, thought she was being persecuted by monsters and things
from the old stories.'

Owen, reappeared in her wake and chipped in, 'Oh, aye, she thought Naz was going to let loose evil upon the world and she tried to take a screwdriver to him. That's when they put her away in St Brynach's. Shame, it was, but a bit scary.'

'Right. A screwdriver?'

'He's an android supertechie.' Owen rough-and-tumbled Dodo enthusiastically and tried to persuade him to give paw. 'He's brilliant, NZ 300 series.'

Delauney shot Owen a frown, but he was too busy with Dodo to notice.

'Um, that thing in the shopping mall in Kansas, wasn't that an NZ 300?' I asked. 'You know, the twenty-seven fatalities with fifteen shots incident? That one?'

Delauney looked carefully round our empty corner of the room and lowered his voice. 'That was the original NZ 300. An earlier model. No conscience or sense of self-protection; they were all withdrawn. We're a long way from Kansas with Naz, he's so much more sophisticated than that. He, um ...'

Delauney paused.

'I've signed the non-disclosure agreement,' I said.

'Well, very exciting, Lona, but highly confidential. Only a handful of people at St Cadog's know about this. I mean, everyone knows Naz is an artificial human, but they assume he's a standard 200 series model. But Naz is an NZ 300.37. The prototype for the next generation of synthetic humans.'

'And this new model, then... He's being trialled here?'

'Wonderful, isn't it? We have to keep it a secret, otherwise we wouldn't be able to move for the media. I had to fight hard to get him, believe me,' Delauney said.

'You're looking a bit weak, my lovely, I'll have of my girls bring you some food, need to keep your strength up.' Gwenda sailed off to the servery.

In fact, despite the shock, the Bard Burgers and Seer's Salad did revive me a bit.

'Good aren't they? I thought of the names,' Owen said, through a mouthful of Phantasy Fries. 'The Caradoc cake's lush, you've got to try it.'

'You checked on your comrades then, Owen?' Delauney asked as he tucked enthusiastically into a plateful of Druid's Delight.

'Yeah, the police aren't charging them, they should be back soon, so—' he was interrupted by a call on his comms and, gesturing an apology, moved over to the next table to talk.

'He's all about the *Mabinogion*, then?' I said.

'He'll be even more about the *Pryddych Cycle*,' Delauney put down his fork. 'And so will everyone.' He waved his arms, expansively at the refectory, throwing one of his sparkling smiles out to Gwenda at the servery as he did so.

Owen returned, looking a bit confused.

'That was Elaine.'

'Still a bit scary?' I asked.

'Ach, no, I'm not scared of Elaine, I've known her since I was a kid. Well, as much as anyone ever knows Elaine. She just... *She's* scared. And she wants to talk to you, Lona, says it's urgent.'

I looked at Delauney. He shrugged.

'Bit of a crazy handover but I've no real objection. Just don't let it distract you from the real work. I know you won't, Lona, you're more robust.'

'Right.' Good that I'd managed to convince Delauney, anyway. 'How do I get there?'

'Gwenda's going over there in a little while, go with her. Better leave Dodo here though, don't think Mother Zachariah'd approve of a wolf on her premises.'

'I'll look after Dodo for you, if you like,' Owen volunteered. 'Take him out for a run.'

'Do you know how much a pet like that's worth, Owen?' Delauney asked. 'Lona's not going to let you run off with him.'

But Owen seemed harmless, despite his earlier antics, and Dodo loved a run. Anyway, Dodo thumped his tail on the floor and gave paw, so it looked like the deal had been struck.

FOUR

A few bits of jewellery and a storybook

The Healing Sanctuary of St Brynach's: health and wholeness through the loving spirit

Is someone close to you troubled? In need of intensive spiritual help and support? At St Brynach's we provide a tranquil environment, away from worldly pressures and negative influences. Here, those seeking respite from psychological ill-health can be gently guided back to wellness by our healers.

When they have completed their journey of the soul, most seekers are ready to rejoin the outside world. Alternatively, they may enter our long-term healing facility, which offers sanctuary and safety for those who need to continue their sacred quest.

If someone you love is suffering psychic pain and spiritual emptiness, then call us for a free, confidential consultation.

St Brynach's is a registered charity, endorsed by the Ministry of Faith and the Faith Protection Alliance.

I just had time to return Yvonne's angel before we drove the couple of miles to St Brynach's. As the quad door opened for me, begrudgingly, I said: 'I'm going to see Elaine in a minute. She invited me.'

'Send her my best wishes,' the door said. A bit stiffly, but it didn't slam behind me.

The quad had less of a monastic look now it was lunchtime, with students milling around in their jeans and scholar's gowns. Back along the executive corridor I went, past Delauney and Benedict's offices, and through the plate glass door of the admin block, carrying an angel and a packed lunch for Fish from Gwenda.

'He never stops to eat, he'll make himself ill how hard he works,' she'd said.

Apart from Yvonne's sampler, Fish's room was like a regular office, which I was beginning to think was unusual at St Cadog's. He was grateful for the food.

'So much to do, Lona, it's hard to find time to stop. But your being here is a relief.' Light glinted off the Guild insignia on Fish's lapel. Presidential rank. Class.

I looked at him, quizzically.

'A professional business translator, someone organised and efficient. You'll be a huge benefit to the whole project. Between you and Naz, I can see it will run smoothly now. It's a load off my mind.'

'Delauney's leading it, Fish. We're just the troops.'

Fish gave a tired smile. 'Delauney may be a brilliant scholar and a prominent public intellectual in his field but – well – organisation is not his strongest suite.'

'You mean you have to sweep up after him?'

'I wouldn't quite put it *quite* like that, Lona.' He smiled. 'God gives us all different skills. But the whole of this project is business critical for all of St Cadog's work. Your Pryddych Cycle will raise our profile internationally, and having the best synthetic educational environment in the world will put us ahead of our international competitors. It's all much bigger than Delauney's private research project.'

'So it's about the survival of St Cadog's in the international higher education market?'

'Exactly. I can't tell you how good it is to hear someone on the project talk like that.'

'And you need it to be properly organised and delivered on time.'

'For next autumn, yes. Which Delauney has promised, but there's already been one setback, with poor Elaine's illness. I'm not convinced he's factored in any unexpected glitches into the project plan.'

Poor Fish. I knew this was the organisational politics I always kept out of, as a contractor, but I felt sorry for him. He was just trying to keep the ship afloat in some pretty eccentric seas.

'If you need to know how the translation's coming along I suppose you can just ask me,' I said. 'I mean, it's not a secret, is it, inside the university? Delauney wouldn't mind.'

'I'd appreciate that, Lona. I do need to manage market expectations. International education's a cut-throat world.'

'REALLY SORRY ABOUT THAT.' NEXT DOOR, IN YVONNE'S OFFICE, I handed the slightly soggy angel back to her. 'It's a thing Dodo does when he likes people.'

She simpered. Which was a relief. In fact, it was something Dodo did when he was under stress or felt threatened. But M had taught me not to say that.

'Maybe I could make him a little toy,' she said. 'Then he wouldn't need to steal things.'

'It's a feature, not a bug. His unique personality trait. DigiPal think it gives pets individuality. But,' I remembered to add, 'thank you.'

'It's not godly, though, is it, stealing?' She considered for a moment. 'Unless it's different in Shinto?'

I nodded, inscrutably. I had no idea how Shinto regarded theft, or pretty much anything else. But then, neither did anyone else here. That's why it's a good screen religion. And if you get things wrong in Japan people just assume you're a clueless convert.

'Oh, Lona,' Yvonne stopped me as I was leaving her office. 'You'll be seeing Naz later, won't you? Could you give him this Ganesha?' Blushing slightly, she handed me a large, knitted elephant god.

I was so bemused I took it from her. I wasn't due to see this Naz till tomorrow morning but once I had my arms full of woolly icon I thought it might seem a bit irreligious to hand it back. You have to be careful about these sorts of things. So, feeling like a fool, I carried it across the quad, getting one or two amused looks, then made a quick detour to dump it up in my rooms. The Gawain Suite. Opposite the Launcelot Suite. They liked a theme at St Cadog's.

I left Ganesha enthroned on the green and gold velvet sofa, staring pensively at Sir Gawain's coat of arms on the opposite wall.

As the car drove us to our destination, Gwenda kept up a lively monologue.

'Bit more complicated, my St Brynach's contract, seekers can be particular about what they'll eat. And we can't use Owen's menu names, it sets some of them off. I've had to find more reassuring titles.'

'Is everything okay with Owen?' I asked. 'After this morning.'

Gwenda sighed. 'He's good boy really. You can see that, Lona, you've trusted him with Dodo. And his faith is strong. Chapel, no problem there. But …' she shook her head. 'His dad worked on the big merchant ships, the ones that fly out to the colonies in the New Worlds. He was away a lot, Glyn, when Owen was growing up, so... you know...'

'Difficult,' I said, selecting a context-appropriate word from my stock.

'It was, Lona. And Owen idolised him. Anyway, one of Glyn's mates got caught in some kind of smuggling racket and Glyn covered up for him. Got ten years down the lunar mines for his trouble. Died a year in, like most people.'

'I'm sorry,' I selected.

'Thing is, Lona, Owen saw his father as a loyal hero, wronged by the law. It was all happening so far away it was almost like a holo-movie to him. A heroic story. But he thinks life's some kind of heroic story too. I mean, studying Welsh History, where's that going to get him? I wanted him to do Ethical Business Studies, or Creative Accountancy – something practical. Then all that stuff this morning about those old relics, I mean, it's just a few bits of jewellery and a storybook isn't it? No offence, mind.'

The door to St Brynach's Healing Sanctuary let us in after Yvonne-level security checks, promising us 'Health and Wholeness through the loving spirit'. We were greeted by the scent of incense, and then by a woman in flowing yellow robes.

'Peace to you, Gwenda. And you must be Lona. Welcome. I'm Sister Agape, Elaine's primary healer.'

Gwenda went off to the Mother Superior's office to discuss menus for spiritual health and Sister Agape swept me off down a hallway painted with muted, but cheerful, colours.

'It will be good for Elaine to have a visitor, Lona. She's been rather excitable today and the distraction may help. But overall, Elaine's strong spirituality is helping her regenerate.'

'Right.' I was having a hard time controlling the feeling of hostility I get around these healing nuns.

We passed a doorway through which people in dark green robes stood sketching at easels, and turned down a corridor decorated with sacred images from different religions. Whale music played in the background.

'It's much easier for seekers who come to us with faith,' she twittered on.

'But, ironically, it's the initially faithless seekers who gain the most from their stay. They replace their inner emptiness with spiritual peace. That's so rewarding for us, as healers.'

Twenty years ago. One of these nuns trying to get me to talk about my 'trauma'. Promising me spiritual peace if I did, incarceration if I didn't.

I took a deep breath to control the fireball of anger inside me. 'And if they don't become spiritual?'

We stopped at a door with Elaine's name on it.

'Oh, all our seekers become enlightened sooner or later, Lona.' Sister Agape gave me a pious smile.

I felt like punching her.

She tapped on the door and opened it.

The room was empty and cold. Sister Agape's spiritual peace took a bit of a knock as she noticed the wide-open window. She groaned. 'Mother Zachariah'll kill me,' she muttered and hurriedly activated her comms.

FIVE

The scream

Bringing the Celtic Otherworld to life

(St Cadog's College Press Release, 10 October, 2071)

St Cadog's College will soon launch the 'OtherWorld', an exciting edutainment AlterVerse.

The OtherWorld brings to life our historic, newly discovered *Pryddych Cycle*, as an immersive experience for you to explore. It also recreates the magical storyworld of all Early Welsh literature, including the *Mabinogion*.

Offering an innovative step-up in virtual reality with Synthesis *Liberation*™ technology, the OtherWorld feels just like real life! Ideal for Celtic studies students, for history enthusiasts, for gamers or just for lovers of a good interactive story. The OtherWorld will whisk you off to a misty Celtic hinterland for a breathtaking experience you'll never forget.

St Cadog's – *The University of the Spirit*

Synthesis Edutainment – *making learning effortless*

'I'll bet they'll find her off somewhere talking to a standing stone.' Delauney looked more irritated than concerned when we got back to St Cadog's. Mother Zachariah and DI Driscoll's respective troops were searching the area.

'That's harsh, my lovely. If she hasn't come back by teatime we'll all go and help look. I know you'll come with us.' Gwenda squeezed Delauney's arm before disappearing into Fish's office.

'Why do you think Elaine wanted to talk to me, Delauney?' I asked.

'Who knows?' Delauney was still looking at the door that had closed behind Gwenda, for some reason. 'She'd only been working with us for a couple of weeks and she stopped making sense pretty quickly. And, well, she was Benedict's appointment, not mine. Might be brilliant at Pagan and Roman religious narrative, but she isn't a proper professional zlator.'

'Mmm, look, I hope they find Elaine and everything, but is there any reason why I can't make a start with the translation?'

'No reason at all.' He turned back to me with renewed interest. 'High time you saw the artefact centre.'

We left the busy buzz of the admin block and the twenty-first century and went back across the quad which was quieter now lunchtime was over. Dodo was still with Owen, so the door didn't complain when we reentered the building. Delauney ushered me down the stairs near the main entrance and along a gloomy, low-ceilinged basement corridor. It felt like a dungeon. We stopped at a heavy metal door; more or less in the same place as my rooms were, three storeys above. He keyed in codes and we were biologically and electronically scanned. The sacred temple of Eirrod's artefacts opened to us with a faint click.

We entered the domain of the manuscript.

It was silent, windowless, cold. Delauney showed me how to manipulate the various environmental controls, and I took his instructions in without really listening. I was too overwhelmed by the eerie atmosphere of the room.

Several glass cases around the walls contained Eirrod's ancient relics: weapons and jewellery intricately wrought from precious metals, studded with glittering stones. The case ahead of us contained Eirrod, a weathered skeleton on a stone slab. I walked up to the case and looked down at the bones of the man whose story I was going to bring back to life.

'That's our boy,' Delauney broke my reverie. 'But the manuscript's in here.'

I turned away from Eirrod, towards the table in the middle of the room. On it was a metal case. Delauney carefully opened the seals and there it was, under glass. The manuscript.

I was surprised how excited and apprehensive I was about seeing it. What would it say, this book that no one had read for hundreds of years? The last person who tried to read it had gone mad. Mad even by St Cadog's standards. Was that coincidence? I realised, then, how badly I needed to succeed in this simple thing. A bit of professional pride, of course, but more for my own burned-out sanity.

Ancient, brown and frail, the object of everyone's interest lay modestly in its case. The first page wasn't a cover, it was the beginning of the stories. Undecorated, nothing but faded brown words on a yellowed background. I'd expected something larger, fancier. Illuminated, maybe. Glamorous.

When I looked at it properly, though, I could make out quite a lot of the words and understand most of them and I began to feel a slow, warm thrill of excitement. I nodded, slowly, staring at the text.

'*The realm of Pryddych was a wild and beautiful land. Among its ancient, Black Mountains, in its pure, silver streams and within its verdant valleys lived many creatures, both of this world and the Otherworld,*' I said.

That was my on-the-hoof translation, at any rate. The streams might have been making a silvery noise and the valleys deep rather than verdant, but you get the picture.

Delauney certainly got the picture. He stared at me for a second with something close to awe. 'Impressive, Lona.' And he carried on staring at the text.

I wondered what he was seeing. His place in history?

33

After a while, Delauney reluctantly sealed the manuscript away again, despatching it back to the safety of darkness and obscurity.

'Here's the version you'll be working with.' He gestured and it appeared on the sharescreen. 'We've cleaned it up 'tronically to make it more legible. It's linked to your outerbody files but the only place you can access it is in here. The security measures on this, well, I'm sure you understand.'

I indicated I was used to tight security.

'Of course you are. And, ah, your Synthesis selfware? You keep the reporting to Synthesis turned off, don't you?'

I nodded.

'Good, I need to manage what we tell them about all this. So – all yours, Lona. Benedict can help you with any literary stuff; make sure your dragons have the right number of heads, that kind of thing. Come to me with more serious historical questions. Then when it's translated, Naz will do all the technical stuff.'

'And Elaine's transcript?'

'She didn't exactly get that far,' Delauney said. 'I'll let you have the notes she made, later, but you'll have a hard time making sense of them. Better just start with a blank sheet, for now.'

The door clanged shut behind Delauney and I sat back and looked at the text on the sharescreen. Dark brown characters on a light-brown background. Simple, unadorned. Then I looked past it at the chieftain on his stone bed. At the weapons and ornaments he took with him on his journey to the Otherworld.

A long-dead ancient from an unknown land.

But not for much longer.

Taking a deep breath, I began. 'The realm of Pryddych was a wild and beautiful land,' and the words appeared, hard black on the pure white of my personal vision.

A while later, I'd done the first block of translation and looked through the rest of the stories. The room was beginning to fill up. I could feel the characters from the story materialising, jostling for space and peering over my shoulder, curious and sceptical, as I wrote their lives and deeds.

I began to have that sense of cautious excitement that comes when you're just starting to do something that you know you can do superbly, in ways that will be unexpectedly impressive, even to yourself. Like a diver on the high board, I could smell the chlorine, see the glint of the distant water and I knew that what I could perform in that space would be exceptional. I measured the distance, planned the dive, adjusted my goggles.

That was when I heard the scream. It was loud and lost. But not long.

SIX

This cosy Tudor room

Some 'faux religieuse' freely confess their faithlessness to one another. Within their deviant subculture, they use the term 'faux' or 'foe' to describe themselves. They also use the word 'foedar' to describe their ability to spot other godless individuals. The cunning of the faux religieuse means that this foedar ability is stronger in them than it is in the faithful. That is one of the many aspects of our work that makes the Alliance mission such a joyous challenge.

Alliance Field Manual, Chapter 3: Verse 2

I sprinted out of the artefact centre, along the dark corridor and up the stone stairs, towards the direction of the scream. The quad door was open, shivering slightly. Through the doorway I could see Gwenda running across the quad towards a woman who lay face down on the ground, her arms stretched out in a cross shape. As I got nearer I recognised the green robes worn by St Brynach's seekers. The dying rays of weak autumn sun gilded the vast quantities of red hair that flowed from the woman's head, and small quantity of red liquid that flowed from the woman's body, as it lay on the grey stone floor.

Gwenda bent down and felt for a pulse on the white neck. She straightened up slowly, her face sombre.

I stared at her for what felt like a long time, then at the body for even longer. The hair was too bright, the blood too red, the body too still. The solid granite of the College walls, of the flag-stones, appeared to shift, tilt. The shafts of sunlight appeared to bend, shatter, disperse. I thought of another time, a woman's body on the ground – blood, too much blood – and Lyneth howling for revenge.

Breathe, Lona, M would say. Breathe. In, out.

Then other people were there: Delauney, Benedict, Fish, Yvonne, Owen and Dodo – very muddy. More people, students, staff – too many people, pressing towards us. Benedict gently gathered me and Gwenda up, ushering us away from the horrible scene and into a room full of dusty tapestries and dark oak panelling. The Principal's office. Delauney, who'd had his arm around Gwenda ever since he turned up, was with us.

'Poor, poor Elaine. What a terrible thing, what a dreadful waste.' Benedict's hand shook as he stood behind his great carved oak desk pouring the emergency brandy. 'She was the most talented PhD student I've ever had. Pagan and Roman religious narrative, you know. Most insightful. Heavens, how I'm babbling on – the shock, you know.'

Gwenda accepted a glass of brandy gratefully.

'There, Benedict, we're all feeling it.' She shivered. 'A highly strung girl, she was, Elaine, God rest her soul, but this?' She shook her head.

'I know, Gwenda. Elaine was a sensitive spirit, I'm not sure any of us understood her, or—' Benedict's voice began to crack, 'or what she was going through.'

'Elaine was a mystic, you see, Lona,' Gwenda turned to me, wiping tears from her eyes. 'Been seeing angels since she was a child, but lately … lately maybe she was seeing other things. The poor girl, we just didn't realise how much she was suffering, I wish we had. I wish we'd helped her.'

Delauney bent his head down to her. 'We couldn't know, Gwenda.'

'And you my dear,' Benedict turned his pale blue gaze to me. 'What a terrible beginning to your time with us.'

'Lona's not easily fazed.' Delauney patted my shoulder with his free hand and I spilled some brandy.

'She – Elaine – she wanted to talk to me.' I stared at the tawny liquid in my glass and the gilded droplets on the dark oak floor. What had Elaine wanted to tell me and why had it been so urgent?

'Professor Pleasance,' the door said, 'James Fish to see you.'

Fish looked out as of place in the muddled faux-Elizabethan room full of shocked, tearful people as he had in a field surrounded by Pagans.

'I'm trying to keep everyone calm, Benedict, at this terrible time. We're arranging counselling for anyone who needs it. St Brynach's flying squad should be here within the hour.'

I shuddered.

'Such an appalling tragedy, Fish,' Benedict said. 'But counselling, of course, yes. How thoughtful of you.'

Fish looked sad. Haunted. 'I can hardly take it in, Benedict. It makes no sense. Elaine was making good progress at St Brynach's.'

'Are the police here, yet?' Delauney asked.

Fish nodded. 'DI Driscoll's insisting on total lockdown, Benedict. She wants to interview everyone on campus at the time. I'm setting her up with a room they can use for a few days as an ops hub. And – sorry, Lona – the Gawain Suite's cordoned off for the present. Along with the other rooms directly above where Elaine... was found.'

'Lona's rooms?' Gwenda shook her head. 'Ah, no. You don't mean …'

'Is that what DI Driscoll thinks, Fish?' Delauney asked. 'That Elaine might have jumped from Lona's window?'

'Not necessarily.' Fish bit his lip.

'So, she wants to interview everyone because?' Delauney persisted.

'In case someone saw something, or …' Fish looked cornered.

'Or?'

'Did something.'

'MASTER LUMINOS.' DI DRISCOLL, EYED ME NARROWLY FROM THE other side of the desk. I still couldn't shake the feeling that her thin, freckled face looked familiar. 'Mind if I call you Lona? You were at the Pagan protest this morning. An eventful first day at work.'

Fish had given the police an office in the gloomy basement, uncomfortably near the artefact centre. Or comfortably far away from the executive offices, depending on your perspective.

'I came here for some peace.'

'From Columbia, where you were working for Vasily Zhidkov. Can't have been very peaceful, that.'

'I'm just a zlator.'

'But somehow trouble followed you here. Like a robot wolf.' She looked at Dodo, who thumped his tail on the ground. He offered her his paw. She tried to look stern, but scratched his head. She leaned back and sighed.

'I *do* know who you are.' She looked at me steadily. 'Lona Luminos.'

I waited.

'Lumo and Mab's daughter? We all knew Queen Mab.'

I was back in 2051 again. I saw the sandy-haired girl in the courtroom, looking blank as her father was sent down.

'Driscoll,' I said, slowly. 'You're his daughter. Alan Driscoll's daughter.' I hadn't made the connection, despite her name. Because I didn't want to. I didn't want to think about it.

She paused. 'I'm nothing like him.'

'You're a copper.'

'A straight one. A sober one.'

I stared at her. Her pinched face looked strained, her shoulders were tense.

'See much of your family, do you, Lona?'

'I'm nothing like them,' I said.

She made a small sound that might have been a laugh.

'You must feel right at home with all this Pagan stuff, though.'

'What? I'm Shinto now. And it's not like Zanegells are exactly ...'

'Devout? No. Not like Shintoists.'

'You're the Faith Police now, then?'

'Lucky for you, no. But watch yourself, Lona, they'll be sniffing around. You don't want them to think you're faux.'

DI Driscoll's Flogo was Methodist, like most people round here. But her warning might be partly genuine. There wasn't usually much love lost between the Civil Police and the Faith Protection Alliance, and she wouldn't want them interfering in her investigation.

'What made you go to St Brynach's to see Elaine Bowen, then?'

'She called Owen. She wanted to speak to me.'

'According to Owen Gryffydd?'

'Well, yes.'

'And who does the door of your rooms let in, apart from you?'

'You'd have to ask the College. Housekeeping bots, I suppose.'

'Dodo?'

I nodded

'And when you heard the scream, Dodo was..?'

'Well, yeah, with Owen. But they went for a run. He was muddy.'

'There's a lot of mud round here, Lona. And much of it sticky.'

SEVEN

Not much that's normal

Your New Ideal Colleague

(PsychLabs Press Release, 15 September 2071)

A totally new kind of synthetic human is in the last stage of testing at PsychLabs. These new humans have implanted memories (synthesised from actual human experience) of growing in the womb, being born and raised.

These memories of a loving, stable upbringing are tailored to create the most well-balanced personality possible. They provide our new humans with an unconscious mind, so they think and behave just like naturals. Additionally, their prime directive towards natural humans, *always help and never harm*, gives them a peaceful and kind approach to all.

PsychLabs' new NZs are empathic, with an evolved conscience and a marked duty of self care. Just like us. Marry that with their intellect and sensitivity and the NZ 300.37 is set to become everyone's ideal colleague and best friend!

'**G**ood and bad news, Lona.' Delauney said when he called me the next morning. I was on my way to meet this 'Naz' PsychLabs were trialling on us. He was only a few steps down the creepy corridor from the artefact centre, a bit closer than I would have preferred. 'Good news is that you won't have to spend another night in the student block. You can have your rooms back today, the police have finished with them.'

'And the bad news?' I paused in the corridor. The flame-effect sconces on the walls dimmed a little.

'Ah. Elaine did fall from your living room.'

'Fall? She didn't jump?' I imagined the green seeker robes billowing out as she plummeted downwards. The loud, lost scream.

'They've ruled that out now. They … found signs of a scuffle.'

'So my living room's a murder site?' Something else I should avoid mentioning to M. Who, six thousand miles away, had seen the recording of Fish's kidnap before going to bed and had woken up to my predecessor's suspicious death. Tried to get me to go home. I was meant to be here for a rest, M had pointed out, last night. I'd sat in the anonymous student room and looked at the familiar face on the screen. Even I could tell M looked concerned, worried. A student prank, an unhappy young woman, I'd told M. Nothing compared to what I was used to.

Because what was the point in worrying someone who was six thousand miles away?

'We can sort you out another room,' Delauney offered. 'Won't be as good as the Gawain Suite, though.'

I'd have preferred a broom cupboard to the Gawain Suite, under the circumstances.

'No need, thanks.' I shifted the stuffed Ganesha to the other arm and kept on walking.

'Thought you'd see it like that, Lona.'

'So, who pushed her?' I asked.

'Ahem.' He sounded taken aback. I must have done the over-direct thing, M's always telling me about that. 'Apparently, it has to be someone inside the College. Fish's security's too good for anyone to slip in. But that's 900 people.'

'But who does DI Driscoll suspect?' That was probably over-direct, too, but I needed to know.

'They've talked to Owen at length. They usually do. And the Pagans who have access to the building are all under suspicion. St Cadog's doesn't do much surveillance once people are on campus. They grilled Naz, made me show them all his credentials, contacted PsychLabs. But apart from the ones who were teaching or in meet-ings, or the students who were in lectures, plenty of Elaine's colleagues weren't with anyone when she ... fell. Owen and Naz weren't but neither were Benedict or Fish or Yvonne. Or Gwenda. Even I don't have an alibi.'

'Or me, I suppose.' I'd reached the door to Naz's lab now. I wasn't in a hurry to go in. 'They didn't find anything else?'

'They've got no unaccounted fingerprints or DNA from your lounge or from her body. So I'd be surprised if their other tests come up with anything. They don't even know why she was in your rooms.'

'She wanted to talk to me, Delauney.'

THE PLATE ON THE OAK DOOR OF THE LAB SAID 'OTHERWORLD Development Team'. Underneath was pinned a cartoon drawing of a wizard waving a wand to produce the words 'Reality under construction'. I steeled myself and opened it.

A big, open plan office, the sheen of classy tech lit by high-end ambient lighting. I looked around for the NZ 300.37. Most of the people in the room were youngish, techie scruffy, with that slightly dreamy quality about the eyes, always envisioning code. Some were sitting on their own, manipulating invisible displays. Others were gathered round a massive sharescreen in intense, caffeine-fuelled discussion.

None of them looked dangerous. I walked in carrying a big, multi-coloured elephant god and they barely looked round.

A slight, dark, androgynous-looking person shimmied up to me. Wary green eyes in a light-brown face, steel handshake.

'Thanks for coming here, Lona,' Naz ushered me into his glass-walled inner sanctum, moving softly, elegant as a cat. 'I'm not over keen on the artefact centre. It's designed for those old organic objects, last time I spent more than ten minutes in there I had to reset all my temperature and humidity controls.' He shook his immaculately groomed head and made a graceful gesture towards the walls of his office to render them opaque.

I handed him the knitted Ganesha.

'From Yvonne?' His soft voice had a faint northern English intonation.

I nodded. Sighing, he placed it on a chair next to him.

'You must be wondering what you've walked into, though? Terrible news about Elaine and – well – the implications are pretty unsettling.'

'I'm not easily unsettled,' I said, gratefully gulping down the double Cubano Espresso he provided me with.

'Don't suppose you slept much, though, all things considered.'

'Worked till three then took a pill. Four hours is plenty.' Or would have been if they hadn't been filled with loud, lost screams echoing down haunted corridors.

He looked at me shrewdly. 'You're keen to finish the translation before someone pushes you out of a window?'

I stared at him trying to work this one out. I could deduce that he was being inappropriately callous, but I couldn't work out why. And the translation?

'Hadn't exactly made that connection, Naz. Just a hard-working zlator doing my job. I've finished the tomb carvings already.'

Naz's glance flicked to the Guild insignia I'd somewhat unwillingly pinned onto my jacket that morning.

'Speedy. Even for a master zlator. Anything interesting?'

'Funeral text mainly, referring to the stories. Which I've made a start on, too.' I hesitated, a second, then asked. 'Naz, what's happening about the manuscript, exactly? And the other artefacts?'

'Welsh Heritage are contesting the College's right to transfer it all to their parent company. That's what Synthesis are, by the way, don't be fooled by all this 'valued partner' stuff. Silicon Valley owns all our arses round here, not just mine. Anyway, loads of people are getting all Cymru pride about the sale. The Pagans say their gods are angry. Proper fuss all round.'

'So the College are selling it because...?'

'The payment from Synthesis'll make a big difference to St Cadog's. It means they can stay pure, become an international leader in Welsh language and culture, build on their research profile in non-conformist theology and Early Welsh History. Leverage the advantage the OtherWorld is going to give them.'

'So it's a cash injection they need to capitalise on their business strengths and protect their brand?'

He looked amused. 'That's how Fish would put it. The academics would call it being a properly funded university. Either way, if they don't get it they'll end up running "Implementing Spiritual Realignment" training sessions for the Prison Service and "Identifying the Faithless" seminars for the Alliance, to make ends meet, like every other college.'

'Then it's just the Pagans who don't want the manuscript translated?'

'No, you're wrong there, Lona. If the stories turn out to be Pagan, they want them translated more than anyone. It helps their cause. To become a recognised religion, that is. The police went down that dead end yesterday with all the Pagans who are registered as students, but they let them all go in the end.'

'Are a lot of them students?'

'Fair number of them are doing extra-mural courses, a few of them are undergraduates. Their leader, Rowan, is doing a Doctorate here. Does a bit of teaching.'

'So who doesn't want it translated, then?'

He shook his head. 'Everyone's got a stake in it. We're all behind you, Lona. Not in a defenestration sort of way, though.'

I stared at him again. I was fairly sure this was emotionally inappropriate, but I didn't always get these things right. Maybe it was just college humour. Then I realised I'd been staring too long. M was always telling me about that.

'Thanks for that thought, Naz. DI Driscoll couldn't, or wouldn't, tell me how Elaine and the murderer got into my rooms.'

'Someone over-rode the security protocols. The interior locks aren't hugely sophisticated because the main doors have such high security, so it wouldn't be impossible.'

'For someone techie.'

'And the police have questioned me pretty closely about that, Lona. Someone with reasonable tech skills. So not Elaine.'

I got it now, the way Naz was talking about Elaine. He really hadn't liked her. What was it Owen had said about Elaine attacking Naz? Was that enough to bring on a Kansas shopping mall event? Only a bit more subtle this time?

The lab door said 'Owen Gryffydd to see you, Naz,' and Naz nodded.

'Alright, Lona?' Owen looked subdued. 'Naz, I can't go on our OtherWorld trip today, sorry and everything, I know the upgrades need trialling. But we're helping Yvonne with Elaine's remembrance service now. Me and River.'

'Of course you are,' Naz said. 'And we'll be there this evening, all of us. Owen's our superuser, Lona. He's helping us trial our Other-World. You go on a trip most days, normally, don't you, Owen.'

'Aye, but there's not much that's normal round here at the moment, Naz.' He looked at the elephant god and his sad eyes twinkled a bit.

'Didn't know Yvonne was one of the fan club, mun.'

Naz looked resigned.

'Fan club?' I asked.

'Oh aye, Naz has quite a few admirers at St Cadog's.'

'Whom I handle with absolute professionalism.' Naz pursed his exquisitely shaped mouth, primly.

Owen looked round. 'Where's Dodo?'

'In my rooms, on standby.' A precaution, just for this morning. One I really hadn't wanted to take, all things considered, but I suspected Dodo might be uncomfortable around Naz and I didn't want him confined to rooms permanently.

Owen perked up a bit.

'Have you got one of them whistles?'

I held up my pendant.

'Owen, no, don't press it!'

'Sorry,' Owen said. 'Will it matter?'

I groaned. 'A wolf running through a university campus? When everyone's looking over their shoulder for a murderer?'

I went out to find Dodo and limit the damage. When he came lolloping through the door into the main lab, I called out:

'It's okay, he's a synthetic pet.'

'What about the wolf?' someone sniggered.

Back in Naz's office I said, 'Never touch that pendant again, Owen, or I'll make Dodo bite you.'

But it wasn't Owen that Dodo was planning to bite. He was staring at Naz with his ears back and his teeth bared. He began to growl.

'No, Dodo. Naz is a friend. See?' I put my hand on Naz's shoulder and Dodo reverted to calm mode.

'Sorry, Naz. His last experience of a synthetic human wasn't good and he's stored that. He'll be okay with you now.'

'You mean the bodyguard in Los Angeles?' Naz asked, brushing an invisible speck of dust from his sleeve.

'Ah, you heard about that. Bit scary.' My last experience of someone being killed in my place of work had been a shooting during a face-to-face. I was still hoping meetings here would be safer.

'He was a 200 series. With an illegal assassin override.' Naz looked pointedly at Dodo.

There would have been an awkward silence, but Owen perked up at the idea of psychopathic android bodyguards. 'There's a bit like that in *Grand Theft Auto 17*—' he began, then he saw our expressions.

'Anyway, I'd best be off. You coming tonight, Lona? It was going to be an Interfaith Harvest Festival but Benedict's made it a memorial for Elaine as well.'

'Owen, what did Elaine say yesterday, exactly?' I asked. 'About wanting to talk to me?'

Owen ran a hand through his hair. 'Been up half the night going over and over this with the police. All she said was something about someone coming into the stories or coming out of the stories and she had to warn you. And he was channelling and the sorrow and mystery was coming.'

'Sorrow and mystery?' I asked. 'Was she a Catholic?'

'No. Chapel, like me. Said it was something to do with the prophesy, she did, and that you had to stop it.'

'*I* had to stop it?'

'Because you'd taken over from her as the storyteller and it was your destiny. But she said a load of other stuff, too that didn't make sense, about how she'd been wrong about shooting the messenger or the maker of the message machine. Then she went on about people having their souls sucked out.'

'Just to put this into perspective,' Naz said 'Elaine, may her spirit find peace on its journey, was extremely disturbed at the time, so I wouldn't take that burden too seriously.'

'Well, she was pretty muddled,' Owen said. 'Oh aye, she said it all came back to the stories. You have to listen to the stories.'

'Why would anyone kill her, Owen?'

'Maybe she knew something. Maybe she'd found something out about the manuscript.' He looked sad. Angry. 'Maybe Synthesis wanted to shut her up. Or the College. Maybe the Faith Police. We should have protected her. We shouldn't have let them.' But I could tell from my system there was something he wasn't being upfront about. I just wasn't sure what.

'You couldn't know, Owen.' Naz put his hand on Owen's arm. 'No one thought she was in danger. And it could have been personal, or even random. A psychopath, that's what most people here seem to think.'

'Did she have friends?' I asked. 'Partner? Ex-partner?'

'Everyone knew Elaine,' Owen stood up to go. 'But she was sort of private. You didn't know what was going on with her. She was in another world half the time.'

After Owen left, Naz said. 'If Owen's conspiracy theories are true, stick anything you find out down on the sharescreen in the artefact centre. Then either you'll be safe or me, Delauney and Benedict'll be in danger, too.'

I got it now. Naz hadn't liked Elaine and he thought I wouldn't care about her either. I was surprised to find he was wrong.

'Happy to share my peril with you, Naz. But I'm not really worried for myself.'

'Yeah, you're probably less pushable. And you've got a guardwolf.'

'Companion animal,' I said.

As I walked back down the silent hall to the artefact centre, I heard footsteps. I looked round to see an empty corridor stretching out behind me. Nothing moved but the dust motes in the pools of artificial candlelight.

For a moment I stood still, staring at the emptiness. Dodo looked at me, his head on one side. I shook myself and opened the door to the stories.

EIGHT

Harvest

Since 2034, intersex citizens have been legally recognised in the UK. There is no evidence that they are any less pious than men or women, and some faiths permit them to hold religious office. Intersex individuals have been accepted into the Alliance since 2063; discrimination against them is discouraged. Correct ways of referring to such a person are *intersex* or *third sex*; *they* rather than *he/she*; and *their* rather than *his/her*. The term 'it' is not an appropriate way to describe an intersex individual and is considered offensive, as is the term 'ladyboy'.

Alliance Field Manual, Chapter 6: Verse 11

Everyone has to have a religion, nowadays. The Faith Wars saw to that. It would be obscene to think that all those people who died fighting for their gods died for nothing.

So I dusted off my Shinto Flogo, pinned it onto my Guild robes and went to their Interfaith Harvest Memorial. I took sake and edamame.

'Do you think we'll have a miracle?' Gwenda sat down next to me. 'It would be fitting; poor Elaine having been such a mystic.' She looked wistful.

We sat round on our squashy yet supportive cushions in the circle of life. Offerings were piled up in the middle of the circle. Knobbly green and gold pumpkins, frilly purple cabbages, baskets of polished apples and armfuls of autumn flowers. My edamame and sake sat looking minimal next to all the Harvest excess. Vidloops showed Elaine looking otherworldly, her amber eyes wide with surprise at finding herself there in the middle of it all. We sat and waited for a miracle. Or just a way of making sense of what had happened.

'We might; it being the Autumn Equinox, and the Harvest moon too, and the feast of St Hedwig and – well – it is St Cadog's,' Gwenda continued.

'Tsukimi. It's Tsukimi too.' I said. 'Feast of the moon spirit.'

'That sounds auspicious.'

'St Cadog's is known for miracles, then?' I asked.

'Oh yes, thick with them it is, always has been, even before they got so popular. Never when I'm around though. But Rowan,' she nodded to a figure sitting cross-legged on the other side of the room, 'thinks it might happen. They say the spirits are angry.'

Rowan, the chief Pagan – a quietly authoritative, intersex Druid – was calm and silent in the midst of all the anxious chatter. Above them, the full moon shone through the red stained-glass window. It looked huge, magnified by the glass, a great red globe hanging over Rowan's head. Wolf moon. Tsukimi.

Fish and Yvonne came in and surveyed the crowd, a couple of their admin nuns fluttering round them like pale blue moths. There were hundreds of people crowded into the chapel for the ceremony, many from the Pagan camp. Everyone who was a Guild member was wearing their robes and the academics had fancy caps or mortar boards as well. The only person who wasn't in their uniform was DI Driscoll, who was sitting on the outside of the circle, trying to keep a low profile. Even Naz, who hadn't even been wearing any badges earlier, had his Engineering Guild robes on. Master grade, naturally. Many of the Pagans dressed in robes as a matter of course, but theirs were wide-sleeved cassocks topped off with capes, rather than the kimono-type things that the rest of us shrugged on over our normal clothes.

Fish, his Presidential Guild robes quite subdued compared to some of the academic gear, went over and spoke to Benedict. The Principal stood up and straightened his tasselled velvet cap and faux ermine hood.

Benedict took his place at the pulpit and looked around the room. Gradually everyone fell silent. He spread his arms in greeting. The Pagan girl with the camera stopped scanning the audience and pointed it at him.

'Welcome, everyone. We meet today to remember Elaine and mourn the loss of a brilliant scholar and a dear colleague. Like too many of her generation, Elaine was an orphan of the Faith Wars and had no other family. We at St Cadog's were her family. And it's fitting that we should celebrate her life, as we celebrate the Harvest, in our interfaith ceremony.' Benedict was a surprisingly capable and engaging speaker, once he was at the lectern. Bit like a mild-mannered vicar who gave a cracking Sunday sermon. 'Our little community is still stunned at our loss and at the evil that has been perpetrated in its midst. Now, more than ever, we need to join together and offer each other support and understanding. So I begin by passing round the Loving Cup for us all to share, to observe and honour the coming together in religious ritual of our different faiths.'

While the chalice of smartwine was going round, Gwenda decamped to the organ and struck up a rousing version of 'Harvest for the World', which was led by a man with a voice that could have filled a cathedral, and everyone jumped to their feet and sang, swaying to the music. Some joined hands. Opposite me, Fish gave voice enthusiastically, hand in hand with Yvonne (who kept trying to catch Naz's eye) and the pink-haired Pagan girl from yesterday. Even Naz, next to me, joined in the singing and loosened up a bit.

'That girl,' I whispered to Naz. 'River. Wasn't she involved in the kidnapping stunt?'

'Delauney's star undergraduate? Maybe – but normally River's one of the more sensible Pagans.' He looked at Fish, then at River. 'Perhaps Fish is reaching out,' he said, carefully avoiding eye contact with Yvonne.

I looked around at the significant Pagan presence.

'Naz, all the Pagans from yesterday are here. The ones that got arrested.'

'Yeah, they were all back in a couple of hours. Not that bothered about Paganism, the local police. DI Driscoll just wanted to give them a scare. And Benedict's pretty pro-Pagan. Rowan's an old mate of his, they go back years. So Fish won't be pressing charges.'

So. The Pagans were all here in plenty of time to be suspects in Elaine's murder, then.

Before I'd come to the ceremony I'd talked to M for a bit, then wandered restlessly round my rooms, missing M and wondering what I was doing there. Thinking about why I'd come back to the Welsh Marches after all this time. Back to the borderlands. I guess I'd wanted to re-experience it as calm, stable. Safe. And had found that it was the same old same old.

To distract myself from the knot of unwelcome feelings lodged inside my ribcage, I tried focussing on my rooms, finding out how everything worked. The small bedroom wasn't too busy with overblown medievalism, apart from the odd dragon's head door handle, so once I toned down the colour controls of the lighting and got rid of the 'relaxing' room scent it was okay. The tiny bathroom off it was relatively normal. The living room was another matter. It was over-decorated with hangings and throws and pictures and there wasn't much I could do about all that. I'd just have to try and screen it out. There was a kitchenette at one end and a murder scene at the other. I stared at the mullioned window that Elaine had fallen from and saw my ghostly image reflected. It looked capable, strong. Nothing like Elaine. Less pushable. I told the curtains to close. But there were some things they, like me, couldn't screen out.

So I'd occupied myself with Netting my new colleagues. Potential new friends. Potential murderers.

I looked over at Fish, as he drank from the Loving Cup. I'd

discovered in my Netting that he'd been in the army during the Faith Wars. He was also as busy outside the University as he was in it, volunteering as a Methodist lay preacher as well as leading the UK Guild of University Administrators. In the vid of his presidential address he'd announced: 'We must sweep away this dated muddle of cronyism and old-boy networks and replace it with an organised, meritocratic, information-based approach to higher education.'

He passed the Loving Cup on to River who accepted with a sweet, crooked smile, while Owen, on her other side, glowered at him.

Owen's WorldNet profile had told me he was on an Abergavenny Eagles rugby scholarship and was a Celtic warlord in the Battle for Britain multi-user game. SubNet revealed he had form. Just bar brawls, by the sound of it, but he'd been detained for spiritual reprogramming at a corrective institution in Pontypool, where he'd spent six weeks working on his consequential thinking skills and impulse control. I could see why Gwenda was concerned.

Owen, smart in his club tie and blazer under his student gown, passed the Loving Cup to the Pagan called Kite. He looked straight at me as he drank a draft, then wiped his mouth with the back of a scarred and beringed hand. I looked away. Too much about him reminded me of the home I'd never been sick for.

When the Loving Cup made its way round to us, Naz took it, made a show of drinking from it without actually doing so, and passed it on to me.

'No stimulants?' I asked.

'No hygiene.'

Wanting to be in control of my meds, I copied him and passed it on. My Netting of Naz had told me everything and nothing. The PsychLabs blurb said that NZ 300.37s were in the last stage of lab-testing but didn't mention that St Cadog's was the lab. It told me they were individual personalities and were everyone's ideal colleague and best friend, but said nothing about the particular individual personality next to me.

At the pulpit, Benedict was talking about Elaine. About her

quiet gentleness and sensitivity, her academic abilities, her diligence as his research assistant, her excitement about the manuscript. Her delicate face on the vidloop looked like she was listening to every word. He talked about her religious devotion and her strong belief in the power of goodness as a weapon in the battle against evil. Sadly, during her period of illness, Elaine had felt that those that evil forces were controlling those around her. But we must remember that this was just a temporary distortion of a pure and ethical spirituality.

My ideal colleague shifted slightly on his squashy purple cushion.

Then Owen and River stood up. Elaine had been their tutor, they said. They wanted to honour her by reading a funeral poem.

'Fear no more the heat o' the sun,' Owen began. He read with surprising command and, as he continued, the room went completely silent.

'Fear no more the frown o' the great, thou art past the tyrant's stroke,' River continued in a gentle, low voice.

'No exorciser harm thee! Nor no witchcraft charm thee!' they chanted together. 'Ghost unlaid forbear thee! Nothing ill come near thee!'

Delauney took the floor next, with his usual easy confidence, making connections between Elaine's death, though tragic and untimely (he looked solemnly into the camera at this point), and the sacred circle of life; then moving on to the links between the Christian celebration of Harvest and the Pagan one, the Autumn Equinox.

In my Netting of Delauney I'd turned up lots of WorldNet intel about his glittering academic career and many references to his research on SubNet Pagan sites. I also found a photo of his interdenominational wedding, seven years ago, to a skinny blonde corporate lawyer with a face too regular for nature and a smile too bright for normality. There was little information about the divorce, which had been finalised four years later.

None of my Netting had uncovered anything that might suggest murderous tendencies in anyone. I'd have to chase up one of my contacts who could dig a little deeper. Without legal constraint.

We were invited by Delauney to say a few private words of our own in prayer and my ideal colleague muttered some words in rusty Sanskrit. My foedar woke up.

'Now, on the Pagan feast of the Autumn Equinox, I'd like to welcome Rowan who will tell us about their celebration.' Delauney extended a hand towards the chief Druid.

Rowan made an imposing figure in the pulpit, with a calm but piercing gaze and grave expressive face. And truckloads of gravitas. The other speakers had all been good in their different ways but you could see that Rowan was a national religious leader. Rowan spoke earnestly, in their quiet serious manner, about the loss of Elaine, describing her a person with a deep feeling for the sacred, sensitive to the spirituality of others.

It occurred to me that everything the speakers had said about Elaine was kind of impersonal. No one had called her their friend or told anecdotes about things they'd done together. No one had smiled through their tears about her little foibles. St Cadog's may have been her family but no one seemed to really know her.

Rowan was now talking about the Equinox celebration and then they, River, and a couple of the other Pagans, started a ritual chant. One of them beat out a rhythm on some kind of drum and they all began to dance in the circle. Gradually, other people joined in, until most of the people in the room were dancing. And chanting. The great red wolf moon hung above them as they whooped and swooped, and I thought I saw other indistinct forms joining in. I wasn't sure who or what they were and when I tried to focus properly on one, it slipped away past the edge of my vision. I tried again. Again, it escaped from my gaze into the shadows. Gwenda grabbed my arm.

'A miracle,' she whispered, and then she was off dancing with the others.

ON THE WAY BACK TO MY ROOMS, STILL A BIT DAZED FROM THE service, I saw a woman through a window in the corridor. She had long silvery-white hair and a circlet round her forehead and she looked at me, speculatively.

'Listen to the stories,' she said. 'They'll tell you what to do. Only you can understand them, storyteller.'

I stared through the window. The woman stared back at me under a tangle of short, dark hair which fell over a forehead that wore only a puzzled frown. Because I was looking into a mirror.

'YEAH, MAYBE THERE WAS SOMETHING IN THE WINE,' OWEN SAID THE next day. 'Everyone saw things.'

'What things?' I asked.

'Oh, Otherworld creatures. Spirits. That sort of thing. Everyone. Even Mam. Even Delauney.'

Like I had. But I hadn't had any wine.

II

There are problems again. The new translator's been contacted, too. What are they doing? Look how Elaine ended up. I mean, before … what happened.

They should know this one won't take any notice, anyway. She's a hard-boiled rationalist, not a spiritual bone in her body. She won't believe them. She'll think something went wrong with her sleepmeds and it's warping her perceptions. I hope so anyway. Because I really don't want to have to intervene again.

NINE

The purveyor of dreams

Gaming Tomorrow Advertorial, 10th October, 2071

Liberating the AlterVerse

An exciting new generation of AlterVerses will soon be available from selfware giant, Synthesis. No headsets or datasuits – you just walk in through the AlterVerse doors and begin your adventure. Inworld, their *Liberation*™ software connects up with your implants so that you seamlessly feel, see, hear, smell and even taste the experiences – as if they're real.

First off the blocks is an edutainment offer, the *OtherWorld*. Synthesis CEO, Chip Barber, says their move into the virtual reality market complements their distance learning partnerships. 'Make no mistake, this is a revolution,' Chip says. 'We're storming the Winter Palace of virtual reality and disrupting conventional ideas about education. Get ready for fun, friction-free synthetic learning!'

'Where do you come from?' The many-tentacled purple monster lolled on a stone in the middle of the grey-green river. 'Tell Cawl truthfully and you will cross the river.'

Owen stepped forward. 'Pryddych,' he said. 'I'm a son of Pryddych, Cawl.'

'Through and through, Owen Gryffydd?' asked the monster.

'In my soul, yes. My ancestry … well, mostly.'

My first OtherWorld trip, and I had a lot of company. Apart from Naz, Owen and Delauney, half a dozen people had volunteered to come and trial Naz's latest upgrades. We were all, to different degrees, escaping from our fear, grief and trauma to a safer world where you knew who the monsters were. Probably. And, for some of us, it was work. I needed to understand this new synthetic world that my translation would reshape, and Naz had to monitor the user experience.

Cawl waved a graceful, mauve tendril and Owen appeared on the other side of the river. Like most of us on the trip, he was dressed as an early medieval peasant. Unlike most of us, he had an enormous broadsword, which he'd brought in with him, tucked into his leather belt.

Gwenda went next, voluptuous and somehow more magnetic in her modest peasant dress.

'Pryddych for me, too, Cawl. Wish I could say otherwise, but I've barely left it,' and she joined her son on the far bank.

Naz stepped forward, his fifth-century clothes elegant, brightly coloured. 'In my body, PsychLabs, San Jose, California.' He looked thoughtful. A bit sad. And stayed on the bank.

'In my mind, from Manchester, Britain,' he added. 'That's my memory.'

Naz was whisked across the water, which seemed to cheer him up, leaving the rest of us on the opposite bank.

Naz had fussed around me like a solicitous host when I went into the OtherWorld for the first time, a few minutes earlier. He'd escorted me into the departure lounge, a room next door to his lab which, inevitably, his team nicknamed the wardrobe. It was another faux-medieval room with tapestried walls and uncomfortable seating. He'd set me up as a user, with Dodo added to my account, and let me choose a safeword and a default clothing style. Then, when the others joined us, he'd led us through the metal-studded oak doors that dominated the room. We emerged onto a riverbank, dressed as early medieval people. That's what the OtherWorld software told us we were seeing when it connected with our implants, he'd told me. It was astonishingly realistic, much more so than the traditional headset and datasuit virtual reality.

Owen, Gwenda and Naz looked across the river at the rest of us, where we stood around like extras from a sword and sorcery movie, waiting for a cue. Delauney, Fish, Benedict and Owen's Pagan friends, Kite and River. And me and Dodo.

'Dodo comes from DigiPal,' I said to Cawl.

Cawl raised a monsterly eyebrow.

'He's … had some mods … from another lab,' I added.

'That's his memory, too,' Cawl said and let him across.

Dodo looked back at me and whined.

'What about you, Lona Luminos?' the monster asked.

'Er, the Welsh Marches once. Whitechapel now.'

Cawl waited. My points dropped to minus numbers.

'My tribe. Are warriors. I come from nowhere, Cawl. From everywhere.' And I was standing next to Dodo.

'Boston, Cawl.' Delauney.

He remained on the bank.

'My heart's in Celtic Britain,' and he joined us, looking majorly chuffed.

'You've a heart?' Naz asked.

'And it's in the right place,' Gwenda beamed. But not as much as Delauney. Owen and Naz exchanged glances.

River stepped forward, looking more or less the same as usual except for the kerchief covering her hair.

'I'm from the hills and the lakes and the seas, Cawl,' she announced.

'Specifically?' Cawl looked amused.

'Colwyn Bay,' she muttered and joined us.

That left just Benedict, Fish and Kite.

'I'd like to think I came from faith and belief,' Benedict looked at home in his medieval monk's habit. 'From knowledge.' He remained on the bank. 'But lately, Cawl, I feel I come from a place of uncertainty, ignorance and doubt,' and he was over.

'I am from a place of right.' Kite stood with his feet apart and his hand on the hilt of his sword. Kite had been a soldier in the Faith Wars before converting to Paganism, Owen had told me. He certainly looked combat-ready.

'Well, we'd all say that, wouldn't we, Kite? And is your place of right a place of truth?'

'I would never let righting wrongs be a slave to truth,' he replied.

'You'll get along well here then.' Cawl waved him across.

'Norwich,' Fish said. 'It's that simple, Cawl.'

'Norwich?' I said as Fish materialised next to me. 'How did you get away with that?'

'My family's lived there for generations,' Fish apologised. 'Not as exciting as coming from a military family like yours. But it's who I am.'

PEOPLE HAD BEEN KEEN TO JOIN OUR AWAY TEAM FOR MY FIRST TRIP that morning. The current reality in the College was sombre. No one had been arrested for Elaine's murder and, according to Delauney, the police had no real suspects. Although the memorial had provided some release, at breakfast in the busy refectory the atmosphere was tense and confused, as everyone tried to come to terms with a St Cadog's where there was no trust, no safety, no normality.

For my part, I was fine in the stories. It was only when I emerged into the twenty-first century that the knot in my ribcage came back. I remembered the lost scream and the lurking murderer. And I started remembering local histories that I'd spent the last twenty years trying to erase. So, like everybody else, I was up for an Early Welsh wedding feast with the likelihood of a bit of riddling and mindless swordplay thrown in. What's not to like?

We followed the sound of voices through the woodland on the riverbank until we emerged into a huge forest glade with a massive oak, half blackened by lightning and half green with spring growth, at one end. Hundreds of people were milling about the lightning-tree glade. There were local people of varied social standing, all in their Sunday best; clusters of fair-haired people, their smart dress ornamented with gold brooches and embroidered belts, who I thought were high ranking Saxons; and people in more foreign clothing, bright colours, long tunics, even in silk.

Three figures appeared from among the trees, hand in hand, the middle one leading them to the centre of the glade. The crowd fell back. The tall man in the middle I thought was Dorath, the Green Druid. On his left was a delicate girl with a wreath of leaves around her head, and on his right a sturdy blond boy.

Dorath raised the youngsters' arms as if they were boxers and he the referee. Everyone went quiet.

'Today,' Dorath announced, 'Megan, daughter of Eirrod of Pryddych is married to Wolfric of Edwin's tribe. Let these young people be happy and have many children who will rule our two kingdoms, together.'

Two older couples joined them – one of the men stately, charismatic, in a rough and ready sort of way. Eirrod. It was Eirrod.

I watched the king kiss his daughter, embrace his new son.

'This is all from *The Chronicles of Caradoc*, right?'

'More or less,' Benedict's eyes were on Eirrod too. Everyone's were. 'That and the *Green Book of Fwddog*. Stories gain their own momentum once they are fed into the OtherWorld. They mix and mingle, and the characters can improvise.' He watched Eirrod and his queen, Merry Nerys, move to the tables at the edge of the clearing, with Megan and their new Saxon family, then he turned to me. 'Cawl, for example, has a minor part in the *Chronicles* but he seems to have come into his own here. That's why it's so exciting.'

'Awesome, huh?' Delauney regarded the royal party with pride.

'We think the more recently discovered texts, *Caradoc* and the *Green Book*, that is, will have the most in common with our new stories. Eirrod and his court are in those already but they aren't in the *Mabinogion*. The *Mabinogion*'s likely set later, we don't really—'

Shouts and screaming broke into Delauney's history lesson. Everyone jumped. Even Owen and Kite. Then we relaxed.

A band of dangerous looking Saxon warriors had gatecrashed the party. That was all. They stood in the clearing, swords drawn. Looked like their tribe didn't approve of mixed marriages.

Owen drew his sword and stepped forward. Kite was close behind. I felt Dodo alert at my side and signed to him to stay. He wasn't really getting the 'virtual' thing.

Most of the partygoers had drawn back in horror, but a few of Eirrod's soldiers emerged from the wood and moved towards the stand-off. After conferring with a hawklike man next him, Eirrod gestured to them to fall back. Owen and Kite were on their own.

Owen locked eyes with the leader. Then with a warlike yowl he and Kite threw themselves at the warriors.

'Hmm, that light on metal effect's improved.' Naz winced as Owen hacked off a man's arm and blood spurted out over a patch of snowdrops. 'What do you think of Owen's sword? First successful thing we've made with the matter replicator, that. It's real. Reproduction of Owain Glyn Dwr's.'

'Looks, uh, authentic.' It was all too authentic. Blood dripped from the snowdrops. I felt a sick sense of horror at the sight. Trying to get a grip, I told myself that none of this was real. Even our clothes weren't real. We were actually standing around in a huge, empty room watching Owen and Kite fight an invisible foe. The Otherworld was connecting up with our implants and making us *think* we saw these early medieval people, that monster and river. These snowdrops. That blood. It was an illusion.

Settled a bit by that thought, I noticed that Owen and Kite seemed to be winning. I watched Kite's tactical, skilful swordplay as he cornered one of the attackers. Owen had more guts though. 'What happens if they get hurt?'

'They lose points. When the software connects up with your

implants – and naturally, it works best with Synthesis's vPlants – it gives you the sense that you're physically feeling something, although you're not. But that only goes as far as touch, not pain. In this AlterVerse.'

'And if they get … killed?' With a roar, Owen finished off one of the Saxons. The man lay bleeding against the rock he'd fallen onto. Red blood on grey stone. I remembered the red pool spreading slowly over the quad and felt a little ill. Then the memory came back to me of standing staring at a blood-soaked barn floor as the world suddenly stopped. I shook myself. Those horrors might have been real, but this wasn't. None of this was real.

'Are you okay?' Naz asked. 'Maybe this was a bit soon.'

'No, I'm fine. Just a bit of virtual reality nausea,' I lied. Fish was looking a bit sick and Gwenda, too, but everyone else seemed alright. 'Go on, what happens if they die?'

'They lose loads of points,' Naz looked at me carefully. 'And are spat back outworld into the OtherWorld studio. Which they'd see as a big empty room, not the woods and river you saw when you walked into it today. Then they can watch us moving around like idiots and talking to imaginary people. Or go back through the wardrobe doors once that loses its novelty.'

The fallen Saxon slowly disintegrated and disappeared. Seeing him defeated, the other men took flight into the forest. Owen and Kite slapped each other on the back and crowed. Fish and Gwenda looked relieved it was over.

'Life's pretty cheap in the fifth century,' Naz said, as Owen approached us.

'That's fifty more points, so I'm at sorcerer level now. Ace.' Owen was still a bit out of breath. 'So, how do I do this shapeshifting thing, Naz? Now I'm a sorcerer?'

'You raise your arms above your head and say what you want to turn into.' Owen raised his arms above his head and muttered something. Naz watched him intently, through narrowed eyes. The next moment, Owen had disappeared and in his place a glossy-coated young wolf stood in front of us. He looked round at Dodo, who mutely asked me if he could join his new companion.

I nodded and he loped towards Owen. They sniffed each other a bit. The two wolves started to race each other round the clearing in a game of lupine tag, the rules known only to themselves. The guests laughed, clapped and cheered as they watched them running nimbly round, in between the people, the tables, the trees.

Finally, they returned to us, panting hard, their pink tongues lolling out of their mouths. The Owen-wolf stretched out his forelimbs, downward-dog style and barked. And Owen was back before us, looking almost as delighted as Naz.

'Perfect,' Naz muttered, as Owen went back over to Kite. 'Perfect.'

THE HAWKLIKE MAN USHERED OWEN AND KITE OVER TOWARDS KING Eirrod and we watched the crowd drift to the edges of the glade where the great circle of tables were laid. Musicians moved in to occupy the centre; food and drink were brought in.

I made a fuss of Dodo, who was bemused at the disappearance of his new friend, and we followed Delauney to the posh end of the tables where Fish was deep in conversation with Dorath, Eirrod was congratulating Owen and Kite, and the rest of our party were sitting round chatting with their new friends. The tables, strewn with flowers and greenery, were heavy with food and drink. We sat down opposite Gwenda and a dark-skinned man who seemed to be discussing catering, and Dorath, who appeared to be talking to Fish in riddles.

'Fish is the master of the "why has the White Spring run backwards since the mayflowers blossomed?" problem.' Naz poured me some wine out of a flagon. 'Can't stand that sort of thing, me.'

'Me neither.' I stared at my blood-red drink. 'Too illogical.'

Naz laughed. 'It's the triviality I can't hack. But Fish likes to solve problems. He's Benedict's fixer, I suppose you've realised?'

I hadn't, exactly. I'd spent most of my time here in the fifth century. Or in nightmares.

'Welcome, my friends.' Dorath gestured expansively at us. 'And Lona, it's good that you've come to help us. You and your magical beast.' My magical beast put his paws up on the table and wagged his tail.

'An important day for Pryddych, Dorath,' Delauney said.

'We hope this will bring about many years of peace in my homeland. Your home too, Lona, I believe?'

'It … Sort of. I'm not sure where my home is any more.'

'Ah, you modern Cymry.' Dorath shook his head. '*Our* problems are feeding our people and staying alive. We know where our home is.'

'We've got new ways of feeding people, Dorath,' Gwenda said. 'We're big in the gaming industry round here. Synthetic reality's our main export.'

'You trade realities? Games?'

'Dreams,' Naz said.

The man sitting next to Gwenda laughed. 'I trade dreams and realities, too. But only good ones.'

Dorath laughed and raised his goblet. 'We'll find out today, Zeno.'

Zeno raised his drink. 'Constantinople's best red wine, Dorath, I assure you.'

The musicians had started playing and people were twirling around in the middle of the glade. One of the dancers was a familiar purple figure.

'Cawl's cutting some serious shapes,' Naz said.

'He really can adapt to any narrative, can't he?' Benedict looked at the dancing monster intently.

'Why don't we join him?' Delauney stood up. 'Gwenda?'

Gwenda came round and took Delauney's hand. Naz looked over at Owen, who, from the gesticulations that were going on, was trading battle stories with Eirrod and his posse. Owen noticed Delauney and Gwenda on the dance floor, grinned slightly at Naz, licked his finger and drew a figure '1' in the air.

'Is Gwenda—? And are you two—?' I asked.

'Is she dangling them both on strings, like helpless puppets?' Naz said. 'Yeah. Pitiful to see. Might seem a bit callous under the circumstances, but yes, we're gambling on the outcome of their suffering and my money's on Fish. Have to make your own amusement in a place like this. You dancing?'

I can't dance, even M's never been able to persuade me to do it in public, but the fifth century version seemed to be mainly skipping, so I gave it a go. Dodo sat at the side looking disdainful.

We skipped and hopped and twirled around. One moment my partner was Naz, the next moment I was hand in hand with Kite. He smelt pungently of thyme, a warm organic scent.

'So.' He looked me directly in the eye. 'Lona. You're joining our struggle.'

'Translating can be a bit of a struggle, Kite. But mine and mine alone.'

'You're not alone now, though, Lona. You've got us on your side.' He squeezed my hand, disappeared and was replaced by Cawl.

'Are you enjoying the party, Lona?'

I could still feel the pressure from Kite's hand.

'What happens if I get your question wrong, Cawl?' Behind Cawl's back I could see River talking to a tall silver-haired woman wearing a circlet round her head. The woman had her eyes fixed on Dorath but didn't approach him.

'I recognise her.'

'You should do, you're writing her.'

'No, I saw her in the corridor, how did—?'

But Cawl had skipped sideways and I was dancing with Fish.

'How's the translation going, Lona?' he asked.

'It's definitely a collection of stories. I'll be able to show Delauney and Benedict a draft of one soon.'

He smiled, sadly. 'They'll be pleased to have some good news.' Then the hawklike man replaced him.

'Welcome, Lona. We've waited a long time for you.'

'Uh, a few days while I finished up my last contract.'

He smiled. Wolf smile. 'Sixteen hundred years. We knew you'd return.'

'You're Anwhyn, aren't you?'

He inclined his head.

'And that's your twin sister—'

But Anwhyn had disappeared and I was dancing now with Zeno, the purveyor of dreams.

TEN

Dark twin rising

'Lona, I've got something for you.' Delauney placed an old-fashioned paper notebook on my desk. On the mottled cover, Elaine's initials, E.B., were illuminated like a medieval manuscript with fantastical snakes twisted through them. I'd only got back from my first OtherWorld trip half an hour ago, so my senses were slightly disorientated. It seemed to me that the snakes were moving.

'Retro.' I looked at the dead woman's notebook for a few seconds. Then I picked it up and flicked through the pages. All that was in it was a jumble of odd phrases and nasty scribbled pictures.

'Muddled, like I said.' Delauney sank into a chair. 'She was not well.'

'I've got something for you, too. Rough translation of the first tale.'

For a horrible moment I thought he was going to kiss me.

'Great news, Lona. And I certainly need some.' He was looking tired, his usual energy a bit toned down. 'Synthesis have been riding my ass since they heard about Elaine's death. They think the place is wild. Unstable.'

'Thought they were keen on wildness and disruption?'

'Only if they can tame it enough to make it pay.'

'Suppose the Pagan camp doesn't help?'

'Ah, they're okay with that, bit of cool local colour, good for the company image. As long as the Pagans don't protest too loud.'

I eyed Delauney's crucifix Flogo. 'The Vatican's not pro-Pagan though, is it?'

'Mmm, Pope Theresa's a little hardline about it, but most of our cardinals are more liberal. Not expecting a papal bull nailed to my office door or anything. You should go down to the camp, Lona, talk to Rowan, get a feel for the modern Pagan movement. Why not go down now, while I round up Benedict so you can read us the first story? Think of it as part of Yvonne's staff induction.'

ROWAN HAD RECITED A VERSE AS I SAT WITH RIVER IN THE CHIEF Druid's tent.

If Eirrod's book and Eirrod's bones
Leave the realm of the Seeing Stone
Then strife and doom will be at hand
A foul thing, loosed, will stalk the land
And haunt the people of the realm.

'The prophesy, right?' I said. 'From the *Green Book of Fwddog*?' The so-called curse of Eirrod's books.

'You have to understand that this is a sacred place for us.' Rowan looked at me calmly, from between long curtains of hair. 'A holy place. Magical things happen here. Perhaps you've felt it?'

'What … sort of things?' I asked.

'It's close to the Otherworld,' Rowan leaned forward, intently, their fingers combing back greying hair from their temples. 'The real, ancient Otherworld. This is where the veil between the two becomes thin. A borderland. Eirrod brought the Old Religion back to life here and if his book and his bones are taken away, Pryddych and Cymru will be cursed.'

'If we were an accepted religion, the College wouldn't be able to sell the artefacts,' River chimed in. 'They'd be protected, as our sacred relics. Like the Turin shroud. Only more historically authentic.'

Rowan shot her a look.

'It's okay, I'm Shinto,' I said.

Rowan's face relaxed. 'Not so far removed from us.'

'Yeah, maybe. Elaine was worried about the prophecy, though. She wanted to talk to me about it. That has to be why she went to my rooms. And Owen thinks that Elaine was murdered because she found something out. About Eirrod's book, the prophesy. I don't know … something.'

'A curse begins somewhere. Tragically it may have begun with Elaine,' Rowan said.

'Otherworld spirits don't go round pushing people out of windows, Rowan,' I said.

'When you pray to your ancestors, Lona, do you expect them to intervene?'

'Not ... no.' I paused. 'Perhaps to influence?'

'Sometimes influence is all that's needed,' Rowan said.

BACK IN THE DUNGEON THAT WAS MY WORKROOM, I TOOK OUT Elaine's book. I ran my fingers over the decorated E and B on the cover. 'What did you find out, Elaine?' I asked. 'Why were you cursed?'

I opened the book. The first thing that struck me were the pictures. Crude, but executed with a degree of raw talent. Disturbing. They were scattered through the book, jumbled amongst the text.

There were pictures of people, animals and everything in between. All of them leered malevolently from the pages of the book. Grinning robots carried out mysterious, but clearly malicious, activities. One of them stood on a mountain and manipulated a huge machine, all levers and flashing lights, that spewed out jagged lines into the heads of people innocently walking around below. Another slyly opened a door to let in a hoard of vicious, half-human creatures.

I shivered; and reminded myself that this was the way Elaine had interpreted the world of St Cadog's and the stories. It wasn't real. None of this was real. I shook myself, to shake off the spell of those troubled images, and Dodo looked up, sensing action.

'Poor, crazy lady.' I scratched his ears. 'Mustn't let the crazy lady take over our heads, eh, Dodo?'

But I felt a sudden, deep, pang of sympathy for Elaine. She'd been here, in this creepy room, like I was, sitting here surrounded by grave goods and an ancient skeleton. Doing this job. But she'd been alone. Alone with this terrifying view of the world. She had no family, partner or lover. As far as I could make out, although most people had liked her, she had no close friends, just people she knew from work. And they'd thought she was a bit odd.

Being alone, she'd been isolated, vulnerable. I thought of the green-robed figure on the grey stones, thrown down like a discarded doll. A wave of anger hit me at the cruelty, the injustice of it.

Someone had valued her life at nothing, compared to their need. Their need to keep her quiet, maybe? Their need to send a message? A message to who? To me? Who did this scumbag think they were? There was one value from my upbringing that I hung onto, still.

I believed in getting the bastards.

Once the anger cooled to resolution, I turned my attention back to Elaine's book and looked at the text itself. Looking for clues. The handwriting was hard to read and there didn't seem to be any logical organisation. There were snatches of transcription of original passages from the book and pieces of translated text which didn't marry up with them. Then, what was this? Something headed, in the language, 'Forbidden Incantation,' and underneath some text in Old Welsh, followed by a few badly executed Ogham hieroglyphs.

It was all difficult to read because the words were sketched around with, and tangled up in, more of Elaine's illustrations. They were sketches of leering twin figures, in what looked like Roman dress, holding torches. One held his torch upside down and underneath Elaine had scribbled, in Old Welsh, 'The Mystery Cult. Dark twin. RISING.'

ELEVEN

The sorrow and the mystery

Dragons, Dreams and Drugs: narrative in Pagan ritual
by Benedict Pleasance and Elaine Bowen

This lively and readable work explores the role of stories in early British Pagan ritual and how Roman religious practice influenced this. Pleasance and Bowen show how fiction had a magical power for early Britons, weaving together the real and the Otherworld; the past, present and future; the living and the dead.

Non-fiction book of the year, US Celtic Culture Awards

Over 2 million copies sold worldwide!

Faith Protection Alliance warning: *the belief systems discussed in this book do not constitute religions in the United Kingdoms of Britain. Any persons practising them may be liable to prosecution. This book is not recommended for the spiritually challenged or those of weak faith.*

F ive minutes later, Delauney and Benedict had joined me to read the first draft of one of the stories. They were visibly tense with excitement. Delauney had his normal animation back and Benedict kept blinking his pale eyes.

They looked at me expectantly.

'Before I start,' I said, 'I've found something in Elaine's notebook. It might have something to do with … with what she wanted to tell me, just before she was killed. It sounds like your kind of stuff – ancient cults and rituals.'

The sorrow and the mystery were coming, Elaine had said to Owen. I'd thought she'd meant the sorrows of Mary and the mysteries of the Rosary. I was used to all that stuff, M was officially a Catholic. But Elaine wasn't. Then this mystery cult stuff in her notebook. I looked down at the malevolent Roman figures.

'But, my dear, surely you should go to the police if you have something that might help them? After all, whilst I'm sure both myself and Delauney are blameless in the matter,' Benedict paused, looking flustered, embarrassed, 'you really are being … rather trusting.'

'That's why she's asking us both together, Benedict.' Delauney attempted to sound patient. 'So we'll tell her the truth even if we're guilty.'

I looked at them both. 'It seemed like the logical thing to do.'

'Perfectly reasonable, Lona,' Delauney smiled slightly. 'Let's see what you've got.'

I showed them the first passage I'd found in Elaine's book.

'The Forbidden Incantation, sure.' Delauney looked up from the text. 'You've probably heard about that before? The myth that the skies will fall if you read out an Ogham text? Which I've done plenty of times in translation, and they didn't.'

'But here I think it might be tied up with the prophesy from the *Green Book of Fwddog*? That if Eirrod's books and bones are taken away from Pryddych then it will be cursed.'

'That's a popular Pagan belief.' Benedict cast an apologetic glance at Eirrod's remains. 'That the mortal remains of a leader have protective power. And that the tales about them animate that.'

'Yes, but then this stuff further down.' I pointed at the rest of the text and the drawings. 'It translates as "The Mystery Cult. Dark twin. RISING." She'd been talking about that. The mystery.'

'Well a mystery cult was a Roman religious sect,' Delauney said.

'Yes, and these twins were part of the Mithraic mystery cult,' Benedict looked intently at the drawing. 'Cautes and Cautopates.'

'In the temples, Mithras was always flanked by the twins,' Delauney said.

'Who represent light and dark,' Benedict added.

'So the dark twin she says is rising, is that Cautopates?' I asked.

'Rising, hmm. Yes, he stands in for darkness, winter, death. But I seem to remember …' Benedict broke off, frowning. 'Now I should know this. It's in our book, *Dragons, Dreams and Drugs*, a footnote, I believe, some of Elaine's research.' He shook his head. 'No, it's gone. But I can show you, perhaps when we've finished?'

'Thanks, yes,' I said. 'Why mystery, though?'

'They were closed to outsiders,' Delauney said, 'and cult members were sworn to secrecy. The temples – Mithraia, they're called – were, literally, underground. They were cellars. Naturally, there was a lot of speculation about what they did in them. Still is.'

'It's really not my area, I'm afraid, but isn't there a Mithraia excavation going on at Caerwent, Delauney?' Benedict asked.

'Sure, we could go take a look if there's some bearing on the stories. Not exactly my area either, so could be useful to talk to their guys. I'll give them a call.'

I nodded, absently. The sorrow and the mystery were coming. Is that what Elaine meant, some kind of mysterious religious cult? Somehow linked to the stories in Eirrod's book? I couldn't see it. But maybe I wasn't looking properly.

I gazed around the room at the grave goods, ranged around the walls in their glass cases. Did they have stories, too? Ones I was supposed to listen to? That dagger, made of entwined gold and silver snakes with emerald eyes that looked back at me; the heavy golden torque with ends shaped like wolf heads. Had Eirrod, or maybe his one of his druids, carried that silver spear, worn that heavy silver ring with those runic inscriptions carved into them? And that delicate circlet with a green stone at its centre, wasn't that what the woman was wearing last night? The one I didn't see in the mirror?

'Lona?' Delauney's voice broke into my reverie.

'Yes. Sorry. Just these things,' I motioned towards the grave goods. 'What do you know about them?'

'The artefacts? The good stuff is the jewellery and weapons. They probably belonged to Eirrod's followers. All the plate,' Delauney gestured at jewelled chalices and ornately decorated platters, 'is less interesting.'

'The weapons and the jewellery were thought to have magical properties.' Benedict looked at them thoughtfully. 'Which is partly why they were given to him for his journey to the Otherworld. Along with the stories.'

'Speaking of which?' Delauney said.

'Okay, yes.' I sat up straight. 'The story. It's about Anwhyn mostly. We know him a little bit from the *Green Book of Fwddog*. I danced with him on our OtherWorld trip this morning, in fact. But here he's more … well, you'll see.'

I mapped to the sharescreen and the system read out:

The Pryddych Cycle: Anwhyn and Anghared

The realm of Pryddych was a wild and beautiful land. Among its ancient Black Mountains, in its pure silver streams, and within its verdant valleys, lived many creatures, both of this world and the Otherworld. The Otherworld was strong in Pryddych and all those in the lands around the realm thought it to be a magical place; a land of sorcery and strangeness.

But, in the time that our fathers can tell of, the once-free land of Pryddych went through many troubled years. Invaders came from the sea, with mighty armies, and enslaved the people of this fair land. These invaders were cruel people who would not permit the proud folk of Pryddych to have their own ruler, follow their own customs, and worship their own gods. They violated the sacred shrines of the native gods and punished the people cruelly for worshipping them. They forced upon them a foreign ruler, unfamiliar foreign customs and strange foreign gods.

The spirits of the mountains and the trees and the rivers grew restive at their neglect and maltreatment, and they conjured up a whirlwind. When the whirlwind stopped, in the centre of it were two infants.

'These twins will grow to be the saviours of the realm,' said the mountains.

'Their names will be Anwhyn, Prince of Stones, Lord of the Seeing Stone, and the Lady Anghared, Sorceress of the Silver Pool,' said the West Wind.

'A boy lives in the village of Fwddog. That boy is called Eirrod, son of Bryn, whose mother Bethan was the daughter of the noble princess Esta from far lands across the seas,' said the river.

'That boy will be called Eirrod the Fair. With the aid of Lord Anwhyn and the Lady Anghared, Eirrod will become King of Pryddych, driving out the invaders and their foreign gods,' the mistletoe said.

And so it came to pass.

The twins from the Otherworld were raised by an ancient woman, the witch of the dark woods, and learned much from this venerable sorceress about magical lore.

At fourteen years old, Anwhyn went to join the rebel warriors in the mountains. The young Eirrod came to trust this clever, quick and wily boy, with his strange dark looks and his unsettling powers. But others close to the leader were suspicious of him, thinking him an emissary from a dark and terrible god. They persuaded Eirrod that the boy should be sent to far foreign lands, to uncover the secret of what was troubling the realm and learn how it could be restored to its happy state under the rule of its native people.

So the boy, Anwhyn, was sent off in search of the answer to this question. He travelled amongst many far-off lands and had many adventures amongst their people. Finally, after three years and three days of his quest, he returned triumphant to Pryddych with the answer.

Eirrod was delighted to have his friend back and gave a great feast in his honour. At the feast, he turned to Anwhyn and said: 'Anwhyn, who left us three years and three days hence as a boy and returned in the season of the mistletoe berry as a man, answer our question. What is the reason for Pryddych's misfortunes and how might they be mended?'

The whole room went quiet. Anwhyn spoke: 'My king, I have

travelled through many countries and seen many things. I have learned the ways of the peoples of other lands. What I have to say is foreign to our way of thinking, but pray, hear me out. The realm has not suffered for the reasons we would normally assume. There are no dragons fighting underground, no curse has been put on us by a powerful witch. Rather, there is a bloodsucking ogre in Rome, who has many sons and has sent his sons to subdue half the world. He rules by fear and brutality, that none dare disobey him. What we have suffered is what peoples of other lands have suffered at his hand. For hundreds of years his sons have sucked out our lifeforce, stolen the gold from our hills, taken our fairest womenfolk for their brides, mocked at our gods and outlawed our ways. Since they left, their half-breed sons live here still and make pacts with these new invaders – yellow-haired thugs from the place they call Saxony.

'It is men, my Lord, who are the curse of Pryddych. Greedy, brutal men, who invade our quiet and beautiful realm. These men bring their own gods and magic, which they use against us. But it is the men who are the origins of our plight.'

There was a murmur round the hall.

'And how are we to fight these men?' a voice from the crowd asked.

'It is as the old gods prophesied. The bravery and leadership of Eirrod the Fair will triumph, liberating the land from foreign tyranny. Our king will accomplish this with the aid of the magic of my twin, Anghared, the Lady of the Silver Pool and of the wisdom I, Anwhyn, Prince of Stones, bring to his court. Eirrod will make pacts with tribes where it benefits us to make pacts, and will out-manoeuvre our enemies to gain back control of our lands. The strength of their evil magic we will fight, Anghared and myself together. We will tame it and bind it up in the Seeing Stone, to protect Pryddych forever. The old gods speak true and they have spoken to me in many lands. This will come to pass.'

And the company cheered, that their land would be once more free.

TWELVE

Magical materialism

'Good heavens.' Benedict looked astonished.

'Strong stuff,' Delauney's eyes sparkled. 'And unquestionably Pagan. This is revolutionary, Lona.'

'Rebel warriors in the Black Mountains,' Benedict shook his head. 'Good Lord.'

'Pagan anti-colonialists,' Delauney said happily. 'Magical materialism. Oh, we are going to have fun with this. Great stuff, Lona.'

'Yes, very good, my dear,' Benedict said. 'An elegant translation.'

'We'll get that straight out on our site,' Delauney said. 'The publicity will be massive. And we badly need some good press at the moment. The police aren't getting anywhere with finding out who killed Elaine.'

'Have patience, Delauney,' Benedict said. 'We all want an end to this.'

'I thought you were keeping it under lock and key?' I said. 'The manuscript. All this security?'

'That's just for the original, different thing altogether.' Delauney seemed to have got his vitality back completely. Maybe the stories were magic, then. 'We want the world to know about this. What's the next one?'

'It's about Anghared. The Lady of the Silver Pool. I've translated maybe half of it.'

'Any chance of a preview?' Delauney asked. 'After this afternoon's reading?'

'Anghared, from the *Green Book of Fwddog*. She was a favourite of Elaine's.' Benedict smiled, sadly. 'This will be more familiar territory for us, I expect.'

Dragons, Dreams and Drugs?

'I expect so,' I said.

III

——————

It's harder than I thought it would be. Than I was promised. Elaine's memorial was painful – made me question what happened – and since then I've struggled. I'm trying to follow the right path – the dark light – but I can't pretend I've got no doubts. But that's what faith is, I suppose.

I never wanted to harm Elaine. In fact, thought she might be an ally. Which would have been good because I'm on my own here. The right path is a lonely place.

All I did was try to show her the truth. She seemed to be taking it in at first, she was always very spiritual. But first there was what she thought she learned from the stories, after that there was some interference and then, well, maybe I got over-confident, took it too fast for her. She wasn't ready to see the true face of righteousness. She went haywire. Started making crazy accusations, said she had to tell everyone.

So I had no alternative.

She made me do it.

Naz: A Journal of Unnatural Thoughts

Thursday 22 October, 2071

2pm

My day started with a purple monster asking me impossible questions. That's been the most normal part of it so far. After I came back from our OtherWorld trip, I got the confessions of a love-sick Fish and then things just carried on getting weirder.

I went round to talk to Fish about security protocols and he started banging on about the meaning of life and the importance of love. Because having a murder on campus made him realise how fragile life was and what it was that really mattered. Apparently.

' "What remains of us is love", isn't that what they say, Naz?'

I told him that's what Phillip Larkin had said and he seemed to think that validated his view. Obviously doesn't know much about Phillip Larkin.

I sat there thinking that it was an oddly philosophical conversation to be having in Fish's plain, businesslike room. Nothing in it but anonymous office furnishings, with only one of Yvonne's biblical samplers, above his desk, for decoration. *Blessed are the Pure in Heart for they shall see God,* the text says. It felt like the sort of discussion you'd expect to have in, say, Benedict's dusty old Tudor room or Delauney's den of international loot. Not that Delauney would ever talk about something like love.

Fish sighed and stretched out his long arms above him, as if he was trying to reach the text. His fingers were interlocked, exposing his bony wrists. Fish's suits always seem to be too short for his arms and legs, somehow. They're smart, well-cut, but he favours that tight look, like a 1960s mod. With his buzz cut and bony face it all makes him look a bit undernourished.

Then he dropped the bomb. Suicide bomb, to be more precise.

'It's over twenty years since I lost my wife to a suicide bomber attack in Cardiff, Naz.'

I told him how sorry I was – and I really was. Poor Fish. And that I had no idea – and I really hadn't, College gossip had let me down there.

But Fish should be married, he's made for it. And Gwenda would be ideal.

With that kind of resignation people have when they talk about the Faith Wars, he said that everyone lost loved ones. He'd been through a dark time after her death, but he wasn't special.

'We're all scarred,' he said. True enough, even I'm a bit scarred by losing a cousin in a Manchester bomb when I was a child. Psych-Labs put that in for psychological texture, I know, but it feels real.

Fish said he'd never thought there'd be anyone else for him, but when he came here five years ago and experienced Gwenda's prowess at the chapel organ, well... And when he got to know her, his admiration became more than organ-based. 'I could see she was the most effective person here, Naz. She shone.'

Unusual reasons for falling in love, those, but there's worse. And to be fair she does shine, Gwenda.

Had he told her how he felt? I asked him. I'm backing Fish against Delauney in my bet with Owen because Gwenda's too sensible to choose charisma over reliability. But he's never going to get anywhere if he doesn't make an effort.

He said that when he first arrived it was too soon after her husband's death for Gwenda to consider romance. He'd tried to be a friend to her – a support, particularly through the times when Owen was troubled. But as Owen had matured, Fish's friendship with Gwenda started developing into something more meaningful. He smiled when he said this, his eyes going a bit misty. The mist became a cloud.

'Then Delauney showed up and everything's stalled since then.'

Glamorous, amorous Delauney.

Fish said that a wonderful woman like Gwenda deserved better. Delauney would be back in New England when the OtherWorld was up and running, and where would that leave her?

Then he asked me, looking even more hungry than usual, if I knew what was going on between them.

I stared at the embroidered text above him in a way that was worthy of Lona. *The heart is deceitful above all things and beyond cure* might have been a better epigram.

But Fish was still waiting for my answer, a touchingly eager look on his bony face. So I told him not to give up hope.

' "At the proper time we will reap a harvest if we do not give up," Naz? Wise counsel indeed.' He nodded thoughtfully.

Maybe he's going to get Yvonne to put it on a sampler for him.

Next I got an admission of fauxness from Lona Luminos. Not religious fauxness, though I'm becoming convinced about that, too. Empathic fauxness.

Fish was still talking about Gwenda when Lona joined us.

'I don't suppose you know anything, Lona?' he asked.

And there was something about the way she looked at him, a fraction too analytical, maybe, before her slightly stock sympathetic response, that made me wonder.

Afterwards, on our way back down to the basement, I asked her if she thought there was anything going on with Gwenda and Delauney and she ummed and ahhed a bit and said it was hard to tell.

'Emotional literacy not one of your enhancements?' I ventured, and she laughed and admitted that understanding people's feelings wasn't very instinctive for her.

'I've learned to work it out from de-coding body language, voice tone, that sort of thing.' She kept her voice low as we crossed the quad.

I told her I was impressed that she had a system and she said that it served her pretty well most of the time but when it came to romance and stuff, people were so contradictory that logical analysis didn't work properly. She shook her head over the illogicality of natural humans as we descended to our offices in the dungeon.

I told her I'd only rumbled her because of my enhanced empathic capabilities; it wouldn't be obvious to anyone else.

'It's not a secret, exactly.' She looked down at Dodo and scratched his neck, which she does when she's having to think about what to say. Once she's stopped staring at people to de-code their body language. 'But I've only told only M and one or two other people. Generally in life, I pass for normal.'

It must be a useful skill to have, I said to her. She couldn't do her job without it, she told me, it was invaluable. But there was a lot she couldn't make sense of here at St Cadog's. Nearly everyone seemed to be giving out contradictory messages. It couldn't all be about romance, could it? she asked. Everyone here seemed, to her, to have secrets.

'Not me,' I said.

She looked pointedly at the Hindu Flogo I'd put on this morning and gave me an old-fashioned look, before disappearing into the artefact centre.

Then we had the announcement about the first story. Eirrod and Pryddych were Pagan in the fifth century, apparently and Anwhyn was some kind of Early Welsh Che Guevara. The Pagans are going mad. Here and round the world.

So Lona's well popular with them. Don't know how she feels about that, but then neither does she, presumably. Unless she can read her own body language.

After that, over lunch, I got Owen's philosophical problems. He wanted to know whether, after the news that Eirrod and Anwhyn and were anti-colonialist fighters, I thought violence was ever justified. I told him the only suitable answer from an NZ 300.37 was 'no.' Particularly in our current circumstances.

He persisted. What if it was a situation like in *Correbor and the Monster of the Deep*? One of Owen's favourite holos, *Correbor*: high romance, heroism, battles, sacrifice and more battles. Twenty-three times, he's seen it.

What if it was like when Correbor has to choose between the greater good and his treacherous brother, Branwyn? Owen wanted to know. Where he sacrifices Branwyn to the monster, even though it breaks his heart and means that the Lady Freya, whom he loves more than life itself, deserts him, because he can't tell her the truth.

He asked me if I thought what Correbor had done was right and I suggested he might have sought a diplomatic solution rather than letting Branwyn die.

'Oh, come on, mun, then the monster would have raged against the whole village and eaten everyone,' Owen said.

So I asked him what it was really all about and he told me River had asked him to join CymLib.

'River? I thought she was one of the sensible ones? And you're a Methodist,' I said.

He told me that CymLib weren't all Pagan and they weren't what I thought. They'd done some serious stuff. It had been them behind the exposé of the Prince of Wales in the 20s, all that weird stuff with the organic leeks that'd ended the hereditary British monarchy.

Leekgate. I admit I was surprised.

Lowering his voice, he told me that CymLib were loosely connected to the mega-respectable Welsh Heritage. Their military wing, some thought.

So I had to point out that his friend Kite, who thought that people like me should be de-commissioned, was a CymLib member, too. He insisted that no one in CymLib or at the camp agreed with

Kite, it was a really old-fashioned Pagan view. And weird, seeing as Kite was techie himself; a hacker and everything.

'Anyway, River's just joined,' he said. 'She wouldn't believe in anything that's wrong, though Naz. She's very high minded. Like the Lady Freya.'

I reminded him that the Lady Freya believed that Correbor shouldn't sacrifice Branwyn.

'Fair play,' he said and headed for the crowded servery, in search of more food, looking even more confused than before.

IV

I didn't want to intervene last time. I tried to stop it happening, I tried to get Elaine to see the true path of righteousness. But she couldn't, or wouldn't make the leap and in the end there was no option.

But I dread being called to act again. Lord, please don't ask it of me.

THIRTEEN

Unspeakable writing

Gaming Tomorrow Advertorial, 18th October, 2071

Beyond the OtherWorld

Selfware colossus, Synthesis, have revealed plans for two new *Liberation*™ AlterVerses, following on from their announcement of their edutainment offer, the *OtherWorld*.

Playing to their selfware strengths, the second of the trio is *Virtual Valhalla*, a self-storage environment which some hope will be the 'death of death'. It allows users to interact with loved ones who left their imprint on the AlterVerse before they passed away. And third is *Virtual Love*, a dating environment where 'anything' goes.

'Synthesis's disruptive technology will not only revolutionise the way we learn, live and love,' says CEO, Chip Barber, 'It will allow us all to manage learning, living and loving much more effectively and efficiently in the future.'

'I'm sorry my dear, I just can't seem to find it.' Benedict had been searching through *Dragons, Dreams and Drugs* since Delauney left us. 'And now we've a holomeeting with Synthesis, they're getting very anxious for some ... some *resolution* to this terrible tragedy. Then it's the performance, isn't it, this afternoon. And after that we're looking at part of the next story. Anghared – most exciting. Poor Elaine would have loved to read that.'

'Maybe she did,' I said.

'Indeed, yes. Let's hope so. Now, why don't we have another look for that footnote after we've read Anghared's tale?'

He left me a copy of his book on the sharescreen, but I wasn't optimistic about succeeding where he had failed. I spent a couple of hours flicking through it, randomly. Here was a paragraph about Mithraism. Popular with Roman soldiers in Britain, hence Delauney's temple in Romanised Caerwent, I guessed. Mithraism was outlawed in the Roman Empire in 394, Benedict's book said, when Rome became Christian.

There was a picture of a mosaic of Mithras, with Cautes and Cautopates on either side. Cautopates looked a lot like Elaine's drawing, only less evil. I looked up yet another footnote about the twins. My eyes were beginning to go blurry. Here was something about the cult of the dark twin, an interesting tale about the followers and what their beliefs were. But it was just a story, and a story from so long ago. Could it really have anything to do with Elaine's murder in 2071?

Although ... something I dimly remembered from Elaine's memorial might connect up with this stuff. And make sense, of a sort. Or maybe I was really losing it and building imaginary webs of meaning. Conspiracy theories. Losing the sanity I came here to save. Elaine had, after all, been in St Brynach's at the time of her death. But as I knew perfectly well, anyone could end up in the clutches of healer nuns. It was only Lyneth's intervention that saved me from that after Mab died. They were no match for my sister.

I flicked through my part-translation of Anghared's story, moved it to the shared area ready for later. One phrase in it took me back to the whole mystery cult thing – could it have any relevance?

I sighed and closed the file. Why was I trying to find out Elaine's secret? The thing that had led to her being murdered. I should just leave it to the police. But then, if it was connected to the translation, I could be next in the firing line. So what choice did I have? This was just basic survival. Which is what I was good at – had been raised to be good at.

I thought back to all those lessons in survival. That night at the rickety disused farm where we often stayed when we weren't travelling around. Sixteen-year-old me waking at two in the morning to the sound of gunshots. Lyn rushing into my room, pulling her jacket on, gun in hand. Ordering me to stay put. She and Rat would sort it out. Me following them to the old barn. Lights. Police. A strange stillness. Our Liverpool contacts and Jonno, our vice president, being stuffed into police cars. And Mab, lying there on the paving stones of the barn floor. Dark hair, red blood, spreading over the stone. That evil bastard, Alan Driscoll, turning to leer at us as we emerged from the shadows.

The anger surged up inside me again. For Mab, for Elaine. There'd been some justice done for Mab's death. And some revenge. Too much revenge. But Elaine had no family to nail her killer. No one even cared about her enough to find out what her secret was; and none of them were capable of finding out except me, because none of them could read the stories like I could. It all came back to the stories, like Elaine had said. So it had to be me.

And this musty old place, it was full of secrets. Everyone was lying about one thing or another. Not about their background, like I was, perhaps. Or their religion. My dodgy intel sources had come back with police reports on everyone and they all checked out clean, more or less. It was more about everyday deception. What they said and how their bodies and faces moved, it just didn't add up. I could tell that from my system. Delauney, Fish, Benedict, Owen, Kite, River, Rowan. Even Naz wasn't really religious, I suspected, and didn't actually like everyone, even though he was supposed to. Even Gwenda and Yvonne weren't being straight in some ways, but that might be to do with their respective love interests. There was so much contradiction with everybody, it was confusing me. Maybe most of it was harmless, to do with things like romance or faith, but someone … something … wasn't. Eccentric and genteel as this place was, it was dangerous.

The door announced Naz.

'Ready for your acting debut?' he asked.

'Uh, don't. This was just meant to be a simple streamed reading of the Ogham carvings until Delauney started getting all excited about it, hoping it would be a distraction for everyone; now it's become a piece of ancient Welsh theatre. Acted out in a bloody tomb.'

'But Lona, you've just proved Paganism was alive and kicking Saxon arse sixteen hundred years ago. The adoring eyes of the international Pagan world will all be upon you this afternoon; you're halfway to becoming a Pagan deity.'

'Oh stop it, Naz.'

'What's up? Not affected by all that forbidden incantation stuff are you?'

'Very funny. I notice that you're sending one of your underlings to do the recording rather than letting us have your wonderful self.'

'My trusted assistant, Smike, will capture your performance perfectly. I can't be everywhere, I deploy my troops as necessary. And that burial chamber's crawling with bacterial pathogens. You know there's a theory that the curse of Tutankhamen's tomb was really a fatal fungal infection, dormant for thousands of years, that became active when it found new human hosts–'

'Owen and Smike for you, Lona,' the door announced.

TEN MINUTES LATER, SMIKE WAS SETTING UP THE LIGHTING IN THE gloomy burial chamber. He was a rotund, unflappable sort of person who didn't seem bothered by the presence of any hostile bacteria or fungi. Or curses. Owen stood around chatting to the audience, who were standing on the grass above us, and I pretended to read the carvings.

There was a sizeable crowd of people up there waiting to hear our reading; several of them familiar faces. As well as Delauney and Benedict, Gwenda had turned up to see her boy in his first speaking part, and Fish had joined her. River, Rowan and Kite had been attracted by the spectacle too, despite Rowan's reservations. Rowan, Benedict and Delauney were deep in conversation but Kite stood to one side, watching everyone. I'd left Dodo with River, who he'd taken to, and she patted him, smiling down, encouragingly, at Owen. Owen glowed. Even I noticed that.

Looking up at them all, I thought what a strange theatre set this was. The audience gathered round, up there on the green turf, looking down at us in our grave. Our view of them, sketchy to start with, was dimming gradually, as the sky grew darker by the second. The air was heavy with the promise of a storm.

'Okay, everyone,' Delauney said. 'Thanks for coming today. It's good to have a positive event to focus on at this difficult time. Before we start, I'd just like to impress on you the fact that no one has heard this incantation since the mid fifth century, when Eirrod was buried, if then. There's a school of thought that believes Ogham inscriptions were never read out; that it was taboo. So you guys, today,' he paused, dramatically, 'you guys may be the first people ever to hear what Lona and Owen are about to present. I've got to say, to me, that feels like an honour.'

A spattering of applause followed Delauney's speech and then we started. I read out the first section and Owen came in right on cue with the translation.

'Eirrod, brave ruler of the land of Pryddych, the realm of the Seeing Stone, travels now on his journey to the Otherworld.'

I could tell from the quality of the silence that he was engaging the audience.

'The Seeing Stone will protect our kingdom from the coming darkness. It locks up the strength and vigour of our enemy. It is the rock on which we build Pryddych.

'Our king will protect his people, when he is in the Otherworld, through his song. The stories that make us, the stories that strengthen us, are your stories, great Eirrod, and our stories. Sing, on your way to the Otherworld, the bright stories of our golden king. We are those tales. Do not let them take our song from us, fair Eirrod.'

Owen started on the last short section, where we swapped over, with Owen reading in the language and me translating. In the silence, before the coming storm, Owen's voice rang out powerfully; rich with energy and conviction. I had a sense that the words were speaking him, as the wave of language caught him up and bore him along.

I started my translation the moment he finished. Very quietly he repeated the words in the language, at the same time as I read: 'Anwhyn! Anghared! Guardians of Pryddych. The bright day has been long, but when the darkness rises and the sorrow comes we will light the way through with the shining, golden tales of Eirrod and his tribe.'

We finished simultaneously. The silence, now, was immense. Dark purple-grey cloud hung low above us, extinguishing the sun and we could barely see the grey mass of the mountains. There was a great flash of lightning, preternaturally bright in the gloom, quickly followed by a bellow of thunder, and then rain started to fall from the slate sky in relentless dollops.

The keening sound started up. I knew it was only the wind but it seemed different this time. Sharper and more real. It howled mournfully, screaming, growling and whispering. There was a metallic taste in my mouth and all my senses howled *retreat*, but there was nowhere to retreat to. I looked over at Owen and Smike. Even Smike looked anxious but Owen was alert, watchful.

Above the relentless pounding of the rain and the eerie wailing, I just heard Dodo barking sharply, his warning bark. A second after, came the faint sound of Gwenda's voice screaming out, 'Owen. Lona. Look out!'

I looked up, puzzled. Darkness was moving towards me in a great block, getting bigger and bigger. I felt a sharp tug on my arm as Owen pulled me over to one side, but he was a fraction of a second too late. The darkness swallowed up the light completely and everything went black.

Naz: A Journal of Unnatural Thoughts

Thursday 22 October, 2071

9pm

Well, we've got a Shinto Priest in the infirmary doing rituals and now the Faith Police have turned up at the camp. Got out of their van this time. They've even visited here, much to Benedict's horror. Faith Protection Alliance at a Methodist College, the shame of it.

Everyone round here's getting hysterical. Two murder attempts in two days. Or possibly two murders, because Lona's still not woken up. She's got good nanotechnology, but it might not be good enough. Head injuries are the most difficult for the bots to fix, according to the medic, even vBots. Wait and pray, he says. Though presumably that wasn't what he said when he woke M up in Kyoto earlier.

Wait and pray.

The normal police here seem to be on overtime, too, since Lona's attack. Faye Driscoll and her team have been labouring away in her ops centre since yesterday, interviewing people, checking up all the details of everyone's past. They're going through what security footage there is, St Cadog's isn't too keen on surveillance, but if the murderer managed to override the lock to Lona's room and wipe any trace of that, they won't have a problem covering their tracks on the security system and the normal police don't have a blanket right to access everybody's comms, like the Faith Police. There's still a mountain of data for them to go through, though. They've drafted in a few uniformed plods, too. One's guarding Lona at the infirmary, though I suspect Dodo's sentry duty at her bedside is keeping her safer. I'm pretty sure he's more than just a pet, though that didn't help her in the tomb.

At the chapel service for Lona this evening, DI Driscoll came in and sat next to me. She looked at me, beadily and said she'd thought I was Hindu.

'My gods are listening, Inspector,' I said. 'They're very flexible.'

She laughed. Or snorted. And told me not to mention that to the Alliance. They weren't so keen on flexible. I said I'd remember that when they come for me.

And I will.

'Must be helpful for you to have them around, though, Inspector,' I said, innocently. 'Extra manpower.'

She made another one of her ambivalent noises. It would if pushing people out of windows or throwing rocks at them were faith crimes, she told me. But last time she looked at the statute book, they weren't.

Fish did his lay preacher bit, giving an address about spiritual protection and invoking God to heal Lona and keep us all safe from Satan's tyranny. Then we all sang 'Guide Me O Though Great Redeemer', to Gwenda's spirited organ accompaniment. Went down well, here, at the moment, the call for 'Death of death and Hell's destruction'. Understandably.

Out of the window now, I can see the glint of fire, and can just hear the sound of drums and chanting from the camp. The Pagans, conjuring up a fiery, cloudy pillar of their own to keep us all safe. Or to put two fingers up to the Faith Police.

Better go, my comms are bleeping.

9.45pm

Well, that was an experience. Being summoned to talk to the Faith Police. They're interviewing all of Lona's colleagues, apparently. And they seem to have hi-jacked Delauney's meetingroom to do it in. Even Delauney doesn't say 'no' to the Alliance.

There were two of them sitting at Delauney's shiny jade meeting table when I went in, both in the dog collar and velvet robes of the Faith Protection Alliance. Lieutenant Bevan and Sergeant Preece. Strangely, they blended in well with the luxuriant artefacts over-flowing from Delauney's office.

Lieutenant Bevan looked ahead of her at some information on her personal vision. Her small face perfectly regular, perfectly expressionless. A beautiful face, technically. On another person.

Her perfect mouth twisted when she said my name, as if it produced a bad taste. She asked me if I was an NZ 200, and I nodded. Uncomfortably. Her hard, artificially blue gaze bored into me and I tried to look like I'd told the truth.

'An AlterVerse creator.' Her voice was harsh, metallic. 'Very advanced for an android. Creatively. Spiritually.'

I could see my face reflected on a japanned cabinet behind her. Polite. Expressionless. I told her that we all developed differently. Just like naturals.

She glared at me. 'But what *you* are developing, Naz, is a Pagan universe.'

I kept cool, said I was employed by Synthesis to develop a histor-ical edutainment AlterVerse. She smoothed back a strand of ice-blonde hair and looked unimpressed.

Then Sergeant Preece asked me when I last attended temple. *Here we go*, I thought. At least I was ready for this line of attack. I told him the demands of work made it difficult to get to Cardiff or Newport but I had an altar in my rooms.

He asked me if I was integrated into the local Hindu community.

'I'm integrated into the multifaith community at St Cadog's.'

Lieutenant Bevan raise a carefully defined eyebrow at this.

Demanded to know how often I visited the Pagan encampment. I'd been once or twice, I told her, background information for my work. And then, politely, mildly, I went on the attack.

'Look, don't you want to talk to me about what happened to Lona? Or Elaine?'

Her smile was grimly superior. How much did I actually know about Lona? she asked me.

I informed her that Lona was a good translator and a committed colleague.

'Who hasn't visited a Shinto shrine since she got here. Is she integrated into the multifaith community, too?' She put her head on one side and gave a small, unpleasant smile. 'She hasn't told you about her background has she, Naz? Her family? Lawless Pagans, Naz. Roving criminals. Drug dealers.' She leaned forward slightly. 'Zanegells.'

I permitted my reflection to show a flicker of polite annoyance. Told her that as Lona was in the infirmary with such severe head injuries that she might not make it, did it honestly matter who her family were?

The Lieutenant gathered the folds of her velvet robes around her as she rose to leave. 'It will matter to her immortal soul, Naz,' she said.

V

I'm so much stronger now. My doubt has almost gone.

When I was told I'd have to intervene again, I was afraid, uncertain. And very sad. But when they said the words, every phrase became a ray of His dark light piercing me and giving me strength. Agonising, but sweet. I was alone in the middle of the spinning universe, held there by His will, as the rays of language punctured my body.

Afterwards, the stone was easy. I could have moved a mountain.

The Pryddych Cycle: The Lady of the Silver Pool

I am the West Wind. I am the stones of the mountains and the water of the rivers. I am the brown earth of this green land and the beasts that walk on its earth, swim in its rivers, fly with its wind in their wings. I am at the heart of Pryddych. I am Anghared of the Silver Pool.

The infant Anghared lived in the dark forest of the borderlands, with her twin brother Anwhyn and with Mabwen Morgana, the ancient witch of the wood. It was in Anghared's nature to be a sorceress. She learned all the magic that Mabwen knew and more. Mabwen was amazed at her powers.

'Child, you will become the greatest sorcerer that Britain has ever seen,' she said. 'But, for now, we must keep your gift secret, or harm may come to you.'

When Anghared was a small child, a dragon flew down from the Black Mountains and followed her around, tame as a kitten. This dragon was called Caw. As she grew older, she learned to converse with the oak and the mistletoe. Mountain boulders would move at her bidding.

By the time she had been with Mabwen Morgana fourteen summers, Anghared could turn a man into a pillar of stone, and stone into fire. She could speak with all the beasts and she had learned all Morgana's healing lore. She could throw the runes and tell of the future with much accuracy.

'You have vate blood in you, Anghared,' said Mabwen. But a shadow lay in Mabwen's heart, for the life of a seer is a haunted one.

Once her brother, Anwhyn, left the forest to serve King Eirrod, Anghared grew restless. There was little more she could learn from the witch of the dark wood and she knew that her future, too, did not lie within the confines of the forest.

One day, a group of soldiers came into the wood, to the farthest corner where the old woman lived and where no man of Pryddych would dare to enter. For the old gods were strong there and they protected the witch and her foster child. But these soldiers believed the old gods were dead and the forest was theirs.

'Who is here but this girl?' asked the leader of the group. But Mabwen was away collecting herbs in the forest and there was no one there but Anghared.

'Take the food and livestock and burn the hovel. The girl—' he hesitated as Anghared stood stock still and stared at him with her uncanny, silvery-blue eyes. 'Do as you will with her, but kill her afterwards. We've had too much trouble from these savages of late.'

Anghared said to the men, in their tongue, 'You are not welcome at the home of Mabwen Morgana. You or your underground gods. The forest does not want you here. I, Anghared, do not want you here. Go now.'

The soldiers laughed at this and one of them marched up to her and made to grab hold of her. But, with a flash of her strange eyes, the girl lifted her arms and spoke a powerful curse in the old language. The man disappeared. Where he had stood there was a side of steaming roast beef, on a platter with a silver knife.

'Can I offer you a slice of roast beef, gentlemen,' Anghared said, cutting a piece of the meat and holding out to the men. 'I cannot say that it is from Welsh stock, but it is sweet, fat meat.'

'Get the little witch!' the leader roared, but the men hung back.

'Get her, if you are men, or die by my sword,' he shouted. So, two men stepped forward to capture her. In seconds, one was a man no more, but a brown loaf of bread, on a wooden board. The other man, however, was quick and managed to grab the girl's arms. The leader raised his sword to run Anghared through the heart, as she stood, helpless. But as he was poised to strike, a great jet of fire appeared from above and melted the blade. He dropped the hot handle, cursing, and, looking up, saw that the fire had come from the mouth of Caw, the dragon who hovered above them. Caw beat his shining green wings and drew breath for another spurt of fire, but the men were gone.

Anghared laughed. 'They are quick on the retreat, Caw,' she said, stroking the dragon's head. Then she gathered up the bread and meat for their supper. She had broken with Mabwen's wish that she should keep her powers secret and she knew that tales of the girl-enchantress of the Celtoi would be told by the soldiers to their own people and to people in lands beyond.

Naz: A Journal of Unnatural Thoughts

Friday 23 October, 2071

11.00am

No news on Lona. But I've learned something interesting about the lovely Lieutenant Bevan. I was walking down the corridor with Fish, when she emerged from Delauney's meeting room. She's a lot smaller standing up, doll-like, in fact, and all the more sinister for that.

'It's Ann Hastings isn't it?' Fish asked. 'Lieutenant Hastings, I should say.'

For a nanosecond she looked a little discomfited. Then, greeting him as 'Captain Fish' (which sounded to me like a frozen food brand), she said that it was Lieutenant Bevan now.

He asked if she'd married someone called Mike Bevan and she nodded warily. Then, regaining the upper hand, she told him that she needed to talk to him when she'd finished with the College Principal and disappeared into Benedict's room.

'You know the nicest people, *Captain* Fish,' I said.

Fish didn't use his army rank nowadays, he told me, earnestly.

But that, yes, you did get to know a lot of people working in military personnel. He'd been with her unit for a while.

'Was she as charming then?' I asked.

He hesitated for a second then said she'd been ambitious and that people used to call her the Ice Fairy.

'Because she's small and cold-hearted?' I ventured.

She'd never let emotion cloud her judgement, he told me. Apart from when it came to Mike Bevan. She was devoted to him beyond reason.

Sensing scandal, I asked him what had happened.

Fish pursed his lips. He was concerned not to spread gossip.

'Oh, go on,' I said. 'We need cheering up.'

Slightly reluctantly, he told me that it had all been a long time ago, during the Faith Wars, when the Lieutenant was part of a drone strike unit, based in the UK. Mike Bevan was an agent out in the field, black ops, and she'd bent the rules to save his skin more than once. Whatever the human cost. She'd been completely ruthless.

'And she got away with it?' I asked.

He admitted that although disciplinary measures were initially invoked a couple of times, the Lieutenant was rumoured to have used her considerable personal charms on senior officers to get them quashed.

'But a lot of chaotic and unacceptable things happen in war, Naz,' he added. 'She may not have got punished but she was never promoted, either. And she's still only a lieutenant, so maybe some suspicion followed her into the Alliance.'

5.30pm

Lona's still in a coma. Everyone's still praying. And the Faith Police are still monitoring our prayers.

Dodo and the law are still watching over Lona. M's getting a flight from Kyoto. And Lona's had another visitor.

I was on my way to see her, when a huge bunch of lilies and roses came walking towards me down the corridor.

Gwenda's voice, from behind the flowers said that Lona's sister had brought them.

'Sister?'

She told me to help her get them to Lona's rooms, for when she was better. A sort of positive-thinking ritual, she'd got a room pass from Yvonne specially. And anyway, they wouldn't fit in the infirmary.

The Gawain Suite looked like someone had been battling a giant in it. Embroidered velvet throws and gold brocade cushions were tossed here and there on the emerald sofas, spilling onto the sage carpet in. Lona's belongings were strewn everywhere.

After our initial, stunned, silence, I said I'd call the police. Gwenda put her hand on my arm and gestured towards the kitchen area, full of dirty crockery. Suggested we just tidy up a bit. Not enough to offend her.

As we made it look less like a crime scene, I asked about this sister of Lona's. Gwenda said she was called Lyneth, nice enough woman, quite tough, though. Tough like Lona? I asked her. Tougher, Gwenda said.

'But more, you know, emotional. You could see she was upset. But then, you know, she's proper Welsh. Quite a bit older than Lona, very smart, mind, designer leathers, all that. Yes, I have heard all these rumours about Lona's family, Naz, but, well. Maybe they're exaggerated.'

We arranged Lyneth's lilies and roses on the coffee table and Gwenda said a suitable prayer.

Lona's been in a coma for over twenty-four hours now and the medic's looking less and less optimistic. So let's see if this floral offering reaches parts that science can't.

FOURTEEN

When the sleeping awake

Some individuals employ screen identities and screen histories to cover up who they are and where they come from. Our Alliance surveillance and cross-referencing software cuts through most of this fakery. Screens are a widespread form of dishonesty and there are many motives for using them. While not all of these involve faith crime, it is useful for Alliance operatives to note that individuals are often eager to provide information, rather than be exposed to their friends, family and employers as imposters.

Alliance Field Manual, Chapter 8: Verse 9

'Listen to what?' I asked. 'Only I can listen … to what?'

Anghared gazed at me intently. We were in a cave, sitting around a fire that burned with a wavering, blue light. 'You translate us,' she said, 'you create us.'

I stared into her level, silver-blue gaze and it expanded and began to swallow me. Those are pools that were her eyes. I was under water now and here were the mermen.

'Beware, storyteller' – a merman drifted towards me in the shimmering turquoise water – 'when you wake what is sleeping.'

The other merpeople joined in, chanting, 'wake, wake, awake, awake,' and then someone said, in detached, clinical tones, 'She's awake. She's coming round,' and I was staring into the unruffled face of the College medic.

'How can we breathe, down here?' I asked.

'With practice.' He looked at me like I was an interesting lab experiment. 'But for now, just rest. You've got high-end nanobot tech and it's come through for you. Synthesis vBots, aren't they. Hope you're getting a discount, all things considered. Anyway, we'll rev the little buggers up now you're awake, so just rest and let them do their stuff.'

I did a lot of resting. I rested and rested and rested. I rested until I never wanted to rest again. I never wanted to see a bed again.

'How long have I been here?' I asked the nurturer.

'Since yesterday,' she said.

Dodo brought a muddy stone and deposited it on my bed.

'It must be from the tomb,' I told the nurturer. 'It's something he does when he's under stress. Picks little things up.'

'Surely you can get that programmed out?' She swept it away in disgust.

M called from Kyoto airport.

'Just about to get on a plane, sweetheart.'

'Don't be ridiculous, I'm fine. Look at me. And here's Dodo, he'll look after me.'

'I hope you've turned up his override.'

'I don't believe you just said that on comms.'

'Sorry, sweetie. Look, are you sure you're okay? The Pryddych police told me you were attacked.'

'I'm totally okay. Really. It was an accident, the police are paranoid. I love you, stay there.'

I hurriedly deleted the conversation.

But someone had tried to murder me. I'd spent half my life in a drug-dealing, gun-toting Zanegell clan, and the other half translating for the international mob, all without so much as a scratch.

Four days working at a sleepy provincial university and I'd nearly been killed. I was more astonished than afraid.

Then I thought about Elaine, lying broken on the paving stones. First her, now me. I wasn't safe here, in this creepy, secretive place. Gradually, a ball of fear began to gather in my chest. Dodo put his front paws on the bed to reassure me and I stroked his head.

People came in to see me. Accompanied by a police guard, of course. They all seemed pleased I'd woken up but possibly one of them wasn't. I just couldn't tell which one.

'What a relief you're okay, Lona,' Delauney said. 'And what an unlucky accident.'

'Thank the Lord you've recovered,' Fish said. 'We're so grateful you've been spared. Now, Yvonne's been through all the health and safety protocols and nothing was out of place. We might have to think the unthinkable, Lona.'

'Glad you're alright,' Naz said. 'I expect it was Gwenda's ritual with the flowers that did it. Listen,' he glanced round and lowered his voice discreetly. 'We've had all sorts of police sniffing round the place. So just – well – watch yourself, Lona.'

'It's the prophecy, mun.' Owen pronounced. 'It's coming true. But you were saved. You must be chosen.'

Kite, who'd come with Owen, shot a look at the police officer watching from the other side of the room. 'We've got your back, Lona. Your enemies are ours, too. Anyone gives you a problem, you let us know.'

'Oh, my lovely,' Gwenda cried, enveloping me in such a tight hug that I nearly lost consciousness again. 'Now, I've brought you some bakestones here, there's fruit on your bedside table and I've left some soup with the nurturer, just let her know when you feel ready for it.'

'Dark forces, Lona,' intoned Rowan, and River added, 'We've bought you a herbal pick-me-up. It has some protective qualities, too.'

'My dear, this is terrible, the whole College is aghast. We must, we really must, get to the bottom of it,' Benedict said. 'Now, do you feel up to answering questions, yet?'

'Difficult not to make enemies in your line of work, I imagine, Lona?' said DI Driscoll.

This much they agreed on: although it had been too dark for anyone to see how it happened, a stone slab had come loose from the top of the tomb and, though Owen had managed to pull me partly out of its path, it had struck the side of my head and my shoulder. Had I been directly under it, well, that would have been another story. And not one involving magical regeneration.

I couldn't give DI Driscoll what she wanted, though. Details about the contracts I'd been working on in the last year.

'My agency can give you whatever you need,' I said. She shook her head. She knew as well as I did how expertly they would be able to dodge, weave, feint and fail to provide her with information.

'Help me out here, Lona. You're in danger. I'm trying to find out from who. You know the place is crawling with the Alliance? I'm keeping them away from you, but they're pushing hard. Give me something to incentivise my pushing back.'

'Honestly, Inspector, I may work for – international businessmen – normally, but that's not why someone tried to kill me. It's here, it's someone here that's the danger.'

'CymLib?' she asked.

I shrugged. It hurt like hell.

'I'm officially the most popular person in the Pagan world. Look at all these protective offerings I've been sent.'

She took in the bunches of greenery, wild flowers, herbs and weird little woven figures sent by well-wishers from around the world.

'Interflora's diversified lately, then.' She looked back at me. 'Look Lona, Elaine's dead and you came close to it. We'll do our best, but I'll be honest with you, we can't guarantee your safety here.' She looked around and said in a low voice:

'I haven't said this, mind, but if that wolf's got an override, I'd turn it up to max if I was you.'

She stood up to go.

'But then if I was you, I'd bugger off back home.'

Naz: A Journal of Unnatural Thoughts

Friday 23 October, 2071

10pm

Gwenda's convinced that her ritual with the flowers worked, because an hour or so later Lona came round. It gave me something to tell her about when I visited her in sick bay.

She looked smaller in the infirmary bed. Paler.

She muttered something about not having had time to clear up lately. Said thanks for the flowers. And, as an afterthought, for the prayers.

I told her the flowers weren't from us. Her sister had brought them.

For a moment she looked confused and scared. Then her face closed over and she was just appalled. Perhaps I should have kept quiet, I hadn't realised things were that bad with her family. I apologised, asked if I was upsetting her, should I go? She said to stay, she was feeling okay, she didn't need babying. And she wanted to know about Lyneth's visit.

'I'm … thinking you're not close?' I ventured.

She told me she hadn't seen her in twenty years, asked how Lyn knew she was here. I reminded her she was a bit of a celebrity in Pagan circles. She grimaced, said if I'd met Lyn then I must know about her family.

I told her I did, but because the Faith Police had sprung the Zanegell thing on me as part of their interview technique. I hadn't met Lyn, Gwenda had. And Gwenda hadn't made any assumptions.

'She didn't happen to notice that Lyn was the president of a Zanegell Chapter? She just thought she was a regular gal?'

I told her Lyn hadn't looked like Gwenda's idea of a Zanegell. She'd put her down as a businesswoman. Lona looked sceptical. Maybe things had changed with her family in twenty years, I suggested.

'Maybe.' She stared ahead of her like someone accessing data. Pretty grim data. 'That life ... her life ... it ... I couldn't stomach it. Lyn always thought I was soft. Sentimental.' She looked down at Dodo and stroked his head.

I suggested that Lyn must be pretty hardarse, then, and she laughed, humourlessly. Told me they hadn't parted on good terms.

'Yet she came to see you,' I pointed out.

Another humourless laugh. That's what comes of being a nine-day wonder, she supposed. People come to see you. Even your family.

I asked if her parents were still around.

'My dad died when I was a kid, bike accident. Lyn's ten years before that, killed by another gang. Our mam died when I was sixteen.'

The Faith Police hadn't been exaggerating, then. It did kind of explain Lona, all this. But it must have been terrible for her, as a kid and I said so.

'Yeah. It was a corrupt copper who killed Mam. Faye Driscoll's father, as it happens. He was sent down, Lyn made sure of that. She made sure people testified against him.'

DI Driscoll? I asked if there was bad blood there, then, but she told me Faye had just been a kid when Lona left, and that Driscoll senior was a nasty piece of work – alcoholic, violent – the family were probably better off without him. He hadn't lasted long in prison. I didn't ask if his short lifespan was something else Lyn had made sure of.

'I'm surprised Lyn's still going.' Lona was back to her usual tough self now. 'It's a short life expectancy, being a Zanegell president. But once I moved to London I didn't keep up with news reports about them, so I wouldn't know.'

I said that she must have been – what – sixteen, when she left? She nodded. Her screen said she'd spent her teens at a convent school in Cardiff, she told me, but it wasn't a secret in her normal life that she'd been a teenage runaway.

But London, during the Faith Wars, with all the bombings? An unusual choice, I said, everyone else was leaving. So there'd been work, she told me. It was how she'd got a start as a zlator, she didn't have much in the way of qualifications, but she'd soaked up all the languages spoken in the maelstrom of London during the wars.

So. Lona the Zanegell.

That would be why she did a dangerous job with lots of travelling and a big dog for company, I suggested. Even though it burned her out and kept her apart from M.

'On the road, with my dawg, doing dodgy deals with criminals? That's where I'm most at home is it, Naz?' Her smile was weak. But it was a smile.

FIFTEEN

A foul thing, loosed

'Y ou're pretty resilient, for a natural, Lona,' Naz said.
Against the advice of the medic, I'd escaped from sick
bay with industrial-strength pain killers to get me vertical
and functioning (another thing to not mention to M). I had my own
Elation designer smartmeds to clear the mental fog, and I couldn't
waste time. I wanted to tell Owen and Naz (together, obviously)
what I'd discovered.

'Good nanotechnology. vBots, as a matter of fact.' I looked at
them both. 'Someone tried to kill me. I'm not going to find out who
by staying in bed.'

'You're turning detective, then?' Naz asked.

'*Lona's* not just going to rely on the police to protect her, Naz,'
Owen said.

The news of my Zanegell heritage seemed to have spread, then.

'Look,' I said, 'I think I might have found out something just
before the reading. About what Elaine was trying to tell me.'

Owen sat up, alert in Naz's minimalist office chair.

I told them about finding the words 'The mystery cult. Dark
twin. RISING' with the picture of the light and dark twins, Cautes
and Cautopates in Elaine's notebook. Then I explained about the
secret, outlawed, Roman cult of Mithraism with its underground
temples.

'It's in the story, too,' I said. 'The first part of "The Lady of the
Silver Pool". Anghared tells the soldiers that they aren't wanted;
them and their "underground gods".'

'But surely those soldiers are Saxons or Romano British, or an
interbreeding of the two? That's how I've portrayed them in the
OtherWorld.' Naz looked doubtful.

'Yes, they probably were. That's part of the important bit:
Mithraism carried on in another form. It's Elaine's research, Benedict couldn't quite remember it, or so he said, but it's a lengthy footnote in their book. Listen.' I mapped the text of *Dragons, Dreams and
Drugs* to Naz's sharescreen and the system read out the footnote.

'The Mithraic cult was reinterpreted by Lucius Antonius

Proculus, a Roman Commander of the South Wales territory. His unnecessary brutality towards native Britons on the battlefield and in everyday life led Proculus to become known among the Romans as the "Barbarian Butcher". In particular, Lucius Proculus stamped out any expression of Celtic culture, especially Pagan religion, with remarkable violence, sometimes amounting to sadism. Proculus steered the mystery cult away from the Mithraic light and towards the darkness represented by Mithras's helper, Cautopates. His version of the religion celebrated the strong, dark fire of Roman will, a purifying force, cleansing savages of their backward, undisciplined, barbaric ways – by pain, if necessary – and leading the Empire on to true greatness. He renamed himself *Cautras* and called his version of Mithraism *Cautrism*. Proculus embraced the sacrificial element of the Mithraic cult and introduced the sacrifice, not of animals, but of young Celts, at the altar of the Roman god. Accounts say that he took great pleasure in this. Cautras's fanatical supporters believed he gained mystical powers from the devotion of his followers and the rites that were enacted to honour him, particularly from the ritual torture and sacrifice of Pagans. Cautras became a mythical figure, a deity, who was worshipped, secretly, in Britain, for hundreds of years after his actual death. His followers considered him to be immortal. In particular, they believed he could inhabit the body of a living human and use them to carry out his will. To become Cautras's agent was considered a very great honour amongst his followers.'

I stopped the audio and looked at them. Naz wary, sceptical. Owen looking like he'd learned the secret of the universe. Neither of them seemed to be faking, as far as I could tell, but it was difficult to know for sure. Since I woke up in sick bay, everyone looked, to me, like my potential murderer. I'd never been more glad to have Dodo at my side.

'The coming darkness,' Owen stuttered. 'It's in the reading from the tomb walls. "The Seeing Stone will protect our kingdom from the coming darkness. It locks up the strength and vigour of our enemy." And "the darkness rises and the sorrow comes" that's in there too. Like Elaine said. The coming darkness, it's the dark twin, this Cautras.'

'And this Cautras, this obsolete Roman deity, killed Elaine and tried to kill Lona? Are you serious, Owen?' Naz asked.

'It links up with the prophesy, mun, can't you see?' And Owen went on to recite the first few lines of it.

If Eirrod's book and Eirrod's bones
Leave the realm of the Seeing Stone
Then strife and doom will be at hand
A foul thing, loosed, will stalk the land.

Owen's eyes shone. 'It's Cautras. He's the foul thing that's been loosed. Because Eirrod's tomb's been dug up.'

'Lona.' Naz looked at me for help. 'Tell me this isn't what you're saying.'

'Not exactly. But if someone knew all this and had some kind of mental health problem, they might believe Cautras had taken them over. And act accordingly.'

'And they killed Elaine because she rumbled them, you mean?' Naz looked sceptical. 'Or was so mad herself that she believed their fantasy?'

'Something like that.' I said. 'Benedict mentioned at her memorial that she felt evil forces were controlling those around her.'

'He meant me, Lona. That's why she attacked me. With a screwdriver.'

'Maybe she thought, or was persuaded, that he'd taken you over, too,' I pointed out.

'Right.' Naz still looked unconvinced. 'And then the real crazy agent tried to kill you because you found this out.'

'Maybe.'

'How did they know? That you'd found it out?' asked Owen.

'Library logs,' I said. 'They'd have to break into that, if they didn't have official access, but they managed to get into my room and tamper with the security log for my door so I guess they could manage that.'

'But their book's a bestseller,' Naz pointed out. 'Plenty of people must have read that stuff.'

'Oh, come on, mun, who reads footnotes?' Owen said. 'Even Benedict didn't know about it and he's supposed to be the co-author.'

'And now you've kindly shared it with us, Lona, Owen and I can expect stone slabs to fall on our heads as soon as the agent sees from the library logs that we've read it?'

'Share it with the world, then, Naz,' I said.

'What makes you think it's not either of us, then? The crazy agent?' Naz asked.

'I don't know that for certain. Owen saved my life, probably, so it's unlikely to be him. Even if he had an accomplice, why would he have pulled me out of the way? Elaine seems to have thought it was you, Naz, but PsychLabs would have picked up on that, so I think you're less suspect than anyone else.'

'And of course you've left a record that you're going to tell us, just in case the two of us are both crazy agents of an ancient Roman deity in league with each other?' Naz said.

'Well, you know. I told Benedict and Delauney I was chasing this just before I was attacked, though, so the smart money'd be on one of them.'

Naz looked thoughtful for a moment, then made some quick gestures at something he could see on his personal vision. 'Can't say I'm convinced. But I've put a website link from the bit in Anghared's story where she mentions underground gods, to the footnote in Elaine and Benedict's book. Just in case you're right. Delauney'll bawl me out for overstepping my remit, but that's better than having rocks dropped on my head.'

SIXTEEN

Intelligent software

One symptom of illegal Pagan pseudo-religious beliefs can be a negative attitude to normal technologies. Early 21st century Pagans rejected everyday technologies, embracing a primitive, low-tech existence and vestiges of these beliefs have persisted. Some Pagan cultists, for example, oppose the existence of synthetic humans. They regard them as disconnected from nature and a threat to the idea of humans as part of the natural world.

Alliance Field Manual, Chapter 14: Verse 6

'You want me to arrest a god?' DI Driscoll sounded as sceptical as Naz had when I explained why I was calling.

'Tell the Faith Police if you think it's their terrain, Faye.'

My theory was spreading with surprising speed. Owen told the Pagans, who lapped it up and, of course, Gwenda, who told Fish, so by the time Benedict and Delauney were able to meet me for a proper conversation about it they'd already heard rumours. And seen the change to the website. And, no doubt, given Naz a hard time about it, but left the link there.

'I would have told you first if I knew anything concrete but, well. This is just an idea. I know it's a bit far-fetched. I suppose you think it's bonkers. Faye Driscoll does. And Naz.'

'No, indeed, I can see a logic to it,' Benedict said. 'An unstable person could get taken over by the idea of this powerful character, Cautras, and by a compelling narrative about his deification. And feel driven to commit these terrible acts.'

I couldn't see gentle, fussy Benedict hurling stones down at me or murdering Elaine. But maybe he was only possessed by violent madness some of the time. When the powerful character took him over.

'Best theory so far.' Now Delauney was admitting it wasn't an accident he was keen to make sense of what had happened. 'This psycho becomes Cautras's warrior, fighting the battle against Celtic culture. And it fits in with what the Pagans believe about exporting the grave goods. Even if it's all nuts, you can see how it would make sense. To someone unhinged.'

It was easier to imagine Delauney throwing rocks at people who got in his way. But killing me would damage his opportunity for fame and fortune. However mad he secretly might be, it was hard to see him working against his own interests.

The door of Benedict's study announced Fish, who hurried in.

'Sorry to interrupt, Benedict. Hi Lona, glad to see you're up and about. Benedict, DI Driscoll's put in a request to access everyone's psych report.'

'Everyone?' Benedict's colourless eyebrows shot up his colourless forehead.

'Everyone. Even Dodo.'

'I suppose we have to comply.'

'They're just being polite.' Fish was already halfway out of the door. 'They can access them anyway.'

As Fish left to sort out the next crisis on his list I thought how efficient he'd be as a murderer. But Fish was just too downright sensible to be mad; he was easily sanest, most reasonable person in the place. Unless that was just a good cover.

'Faye Driscoll didn't think your idea was so bonkers after all, then,' Delauney said. 'Good. But next time, Lona, tell us before you discuss your theories with the police.'

DODO WAS ABOUT TO TAKE ME OUT FOR A GENTLE RESTORATIVE walk shortly after my talk with Delauney and Benedict, when Naz offered to come with us.

'In case you have a relapse. Not sure a walk's going to do you any good. And Dodo's probably stronger than me, so you're not in any danger if I turn out to be the agent.'

The police had warned everyone at the College to be careful who they were alone with. Everyone you saw seemed to be going around in groups of three or more and staff had been told not to hold one-to-one meetings.

'*You* might be, though, if I was the agent.'

'You just got attacked, Lona, so I'm guessing not.'

'Does it do you any good?' I asked. 'A walk?'

'Psychologically. It's getting claustrophobic in here.'

We set off down the yellow path that looped around St Cadog's, with Dodo in the lead.

'To be honest, I'm getting fed up with all the suspicious looks,' Naz said. I could see that people who passed us on the path were staring at us. 'I know I'm top of most people's suspect list, despite my "always help and never harm" prime directive.'

'Owen's top of the police's list. Or was.' We turned up a track into the hills. Fewer people to stare up there. 'And the Faith Police have always preferred the Pagans.'

'What have your shady intel contacts come up with, Lona? Don't tell me you haven't got any or haven't tried them.'

'Um, yeah, I got them to access police files, before I got hit on the head. They couldn't find anything significantly dodgy for anyone at the College. Even the Faith Police don't have much on anyone. Benedict spent some time in a Methodist monastery when he was younger and they're always suspicious about people who leave their calling, but they haven't flagged him. Despite his longstanding friendship with Rowan, which they have noted. They had a trace on Delauney, when he first came over, because of his work on Paganism, but pressure from Synthesis made them remove it. They've got a query on me, coming from a Pagan background and being Shinto, annoying that, have to see if I can get it deleted. River, Rowan and Kite are listed as potential enemies of faith and State, naturally and Kite's got some civil and faith form for violent protest. Plus there's Owen's youthful bar brawls. Your screen held up completely, even from my intel moles.'

'No one constructs a false identity like PsychLabs.'

'So the dodgiest person on campus by far is probably me.' I said, as Dodo led us into the wood.

'The Faith Police outed you pretty comprehensively as a former Zanegell. But no one seems to mind.'

'No, the Pagans are well impressed. They think I'm the real deal. River's really chuffed, she says she used to have a Zanegell Bobby doll when she was little. As well as a Pagan one.'

'Not an Alliance one, presumably.'

I laughed.

'Speaking of which,' he continued, glancing round the quiet wood, 'I'm the only person round here officially and legally protected from Alliance comms surveillance. Because everything about me is business-sensitive. But I'm kind of assuming that you've got some shielding protection added in your selfware?'

'I couldn't possibly comment, Naz, that sort of thing being borderline legal.'

'Good. I know some of our mutual friends have got shielding because I've helped them with it and I gather Kite is the Pagans' go-to selfware protection provider. I'm getting the feeling everyone's going need some protection with the Ice Fairy hanging round. And while they're only supposed to access relevant data, everyone knows they go further than that if they aren't prevented.'

I nodded. I'd almost forgotten there were people whose selfware wasn't shielded. In my normal life it came as standard.

'I hear she's a piece of work, this Lieutenant Bevan.' I said. 'Haven't actually seen her yet though.'

'You can't miss her, she looks like an evil doll.'

'What, an Alliance Bobbie doll?' I laughed. 'Naz, there's another idea I've had.'

'Which is?'

'You know Elaine and Benedict's book has been quite a big seller? So she'll have made some money on that. And that'll carry on growing, especially as there's been an upsurge in sales since the tomb was found and people started to think Eirrod was Pagan.'

'Ah, you mean who inherits the royalties? Follow the money and all that.'

'Yeah. The police will be following up on it but they're not going to take us into their confidence. Can you find out who it is, Naz? Yvonne would know.'

'If I must. As it's for the greater good.'

'Speaking of which, you know Owen had another theory about the attack on me before I told him about the Cautras's agent idea?'

'Mystical forces from the ancient Celtic hinterland?'

'Jealousy.'

Naz looked puzzled.

'One of your admirers,' I said. 'Yvonne, maybe. Misinterpreting our working relationship for a romantic one.'

'Don't tell the DI, she'll take it seriously,' he said.

I turned as I saw a robed figure through the trees, near the remnants of a tumbledown old building. Tall with long silver hair. It couldn't be. I stopped.

'What?' Naz looked at the place I was staring at. 'It's just a ruined chapel.'

But she'd gone.

'Oh, nothing. Probably just one of the Pagans. The camp's near here, isn't it.'

Naz shot me a concerned look, but I pressed on with the walk. After a couple of minutes we reached the edge of the camp and the first thing we saw was Delauney, slipping into one of the tents. Naz looked like he was going to say something about it, when we heard Owen calling our names from the middle of the encampment. He was helping Kite mend the makeshift open shelter where the Pagans had their meetings and sometimes ate communal meals.

We went over to where they were nailing the tarpaulin roof back onto the uprights. There were quite few Pagans buzzing around who smiled as we passed. And not just at me and Dodo. But Kite's dark eyes slid over Naz and bored directly into mine.

'Good to see you back on your feet, Lona.' I could see Naz's nose wrinkling fastidiously at the thyme smell. Kite nodded towards the roof. 'The Faith wrecked our shelter yesterday.' He whacked a nail into the wood with considerable power. 'Searching, they said. Kwizzer bastards.'

'We're having a camp meeting in a bit.' Owen looked excited.

'To decide what action to take to protect ourselves.' Kite leant against the shelter and tapped his hammer on his palm, switching his gaze to Naz. Then he folded his arms across a broad expanse of *Skull Attack* T-shirt, flexing a Tree of Life tattoo on his right biceps.

Naz stared at him levelly. 'Elaine and Lona were the ones who got attacked, Kite. Not Pagans.'

'Because they found out about Cautras's agent. And were doing important work for the Pagan cause. And Lona,' Kite smiled at me. A slow, knowing smile. 'Lona's one of us.'

'I'm Shinto.' It came out primmer than I meant it to.

That slow, over-intimate smile again. As if he knew everything about me. Even if he did, since he was a bit of a hacker, there wasn't much to smile about.

'We need to act to protect everyone; the whole community,' Owen waved his hammer enthusiastically. 'The police aren't doing anything.'

'They're accessing everyone's psych files at the moment,' I told him.

He groaned. 'Fat lot of good that will do.'

· · ·

As we walked back to the campus Naz said: 'Have to say I agree with him. And I speak as the only person here who is officially checked for sanity on a daily basis.'

'Yeah, they'll only come up with Faith Police suspicions about peoples' spirituality. And we already know about that.'

As I bent down to pat Dodo I noticed that he had a small macramé dreamcatcher in his mouth, stolen from the Pagan camp. I sighed. He was going into overdrive lately with all the tension round here. I put it in my pocket to give back later.

'What's eating Owen?' I asked.

'He's been a bit over-excited lately. Well, everyone's on edge, murderer running round the place. But it's the initial Welsh Heritage court hearing Monday, and a lot of people are getting antsy about that. Including Owen. Synthesis's big shot legal team are about to descend on us and Fish is getting his drawers in a tangle about their conference, that begins the next day. Fish and his troops organise it – well, that and everything else here – so he's concerned about security. Thinks everyone's going to get attacked or CymLib are going to turn it over it or something.'

'That wouldn't help his situation with Gwenda,' I said. 'Now Owen's gone all CymLib'.

'My money's still on him,' Naz said. 'Fish is what Gwenda needs. Sensible, decent, down to earth. Delauney's glamorous, but he's not for keeps. Can you see Gwenda as an Ivy League Faculty wife, passing round the canapés and making light, inoffensive conversation? I bet Delauney can't.'

'But Delauney married the "right" sort of person once,' I said. 'And look what happened. Maybe he'll just choose someone he likes this time.'

'Oh Lona, you're such a synth sometimes. Naturals don't have intelligent software; they just go on making the same mistakes until they die.'

The Pryddych Cycle: The Lady of the Silver Pool (part 2)

One day a messenger came to tell Anghared and Mabwen that Dorath, the sorcerer of the Black Mountains, had heard of Anghared's talents and wished to take her as his pupil. This was a very great honour and Anghared's eyes shone like the mountain brooks when she heard this news. Mabwen was afraid for her, but knew she had to let the girl go. Many tears were shed by both women the day that Anghared departed for the mountains.

Dorath the Green had a reputation as a fierce man, but was kindly enough with the young witch. She learned fast and greedily, and the Druid was proud of her progress.

'You are truly my successor, Anghared of the West Wind,' he said, 'and have become as a daughter to me. You will become the Chief Sorcerer of Pryddych after I am gone.'

But Anghared did not care for worldly success or title. The ways of men were nothing to her. She despised their petty squabblings, vanities and desires. Only the world of the mountain and wood were real to her.

From Dorath she learned how to see visions in the Silver Pool, which was near the cave where they made their home. This became her mirror in which she could see the past, the present and all the possible futures. She learned Druid lore and powerful ancient magic. Her power grew, and, with her power, her wisdom.

'For power without wisdom is as nothing,' Dorath said, 'it is a thousand times worse than no power at all.'

One day, when Anghared had been ten summers under his tuition, the sorcerer of the Black Mountains told Anghared to look for his future in the Silver Pool. She stared into the water and gradually a picture formed. The old Druid lay sleeping in their cave. Something stirred in the shadows, a piece of the darkness, that moved slowly towards Dorath. It lent over him, so she could not see the sorcerer, but when the dark thing moved away she could see that the creature had sucked the life from him and nothing was left but a dead husk.

Anghared tried to see alternative futures to this. In one she willed herself to be in between Dorath and the foul creature of the shadows, but she was pushed aside and fainted. The outcome was the same. Downhearted, she went to Dorath and told him what she had seen.

'Child, this is my prophesied end,' he told her, 'and it is my destiny. It cannot be changed.'

'Father,' Anghared said, 'it cannot be so.'

'We all have a time to die, my daughter,' he replied. 'And I wish you to promise me two things. One, that you will not try to stop this from happening; and two, that you will not use a reawakening spell when I am gone.'

Anghared broke down and wept, but she promised to do as he asked.

That night, a loathsome thing, that had no clear shape or colour but was yet terrible to behold, filling those who saw it with fear and disgust, came to their cave. Anghared felt it enter the cave and she rose out of her bed to challenge it, but a heavy sleep came over her as she stood and she sank back into her bed. At dawn, when she awoke to the sound of the birds, Dorath was no more.

Anghared gave out a scream so sharp and terrible that the mountains rang with it. The dawn chorus ceased and the birds sat and trembled in the trees. Anghared cursed the thing that had done this to her adopted father and vowed revenge upon it. Then, despite her promise, Anghared gathered together what she needed for the reawakening spell. She dressed herself in ceremonial robes and slowly and carefully she prepared the potion, incanting the spells for creation over it. She poured the finished potion, which was thick and red, like heart's blood, into a golden goblet. This she then dabbed onto the dead sorcerer's forehead, as he lay in his bed and on each of his cheeks and on his chest, where his heart was. She did the same with herself. She stood in front of Dorath, and, raising her arms to the sky, slowly, solemnly, she spoke the ancient and terrible spell that reawakens the dead.

Thunder crashed around the Black Mountains as she spoke the spell and lightening split in the sky above. Anghared knew she was breaking the laws of nature by casting the spell, but still she continued. When she finished the incantation there was complete silence. She looked at Dorath, lying there.

'Awake now, Master,' she said.

The sorcerer's eyes snapped open and he sat up. He fixed her with a fearful gaze.

'My child, I cannot stay with you,' he said. 'We would have met in the Otherworld. But now I must serve that which took my life and we will never meet again.' He arose from his death bed and walked out of their cave.

For the rest of her life Anghared sought the Green Druid, using all the magic at her disposal. But never did she see him again.

SEVENTEEN

Where the dragons are

On my sixth day at St Cadog's, I became a sorcerer.

'Congratulations, Lona, you're a natural.' Owen went to slap me on the back, remembered my injuries and cautiously patted my good shoulder. I changed into a red kite and rose into the air, the grey and green landscape opening up below me like a medieval map. And I knew where all the dragons were.

At least I thought I did. But in the last few days, I'd kind of begun to accept that the world wasn't behaving normally.

Of course, I was constantly on my guard against another attack. I'd wake up at night, sweating and terrified, thinking I heard noises, despite having doubled my Elation sleepmeds. I'd go into the refectory for breakfast and everyone would look, to me, like a potential killer, under their masks of friendliness and normality. I'd talk and I'd smile, but all the time I'd be thinking *Is it you? Did you try to murder me? Did you kill Elaine?* The strain of all that was wearing me down. And everyone else was suspicious of one another too. You could see their eyes flicking around the busy canteen wondering which of the people on the next table was a murderer. And who was next.

I couldn't enter or leave the artefact centre without passing Faye Driscoll's ops hub and without encountering her or one of her minions. It didn't make me feel any safer.

'This theory of yours, Lona?' she said, pouncing on me as I passed by that morning. 'The crazy who worships a Roman god. A god that had it in for Celtic culture. Any ideas? Anyone seem hostile to what you're doing?'

'The Pryddych Cycle's putting this place on the map.' I frowned at Dodo as he went to shake hands with her, but he ignored me. 'Everyone here's a fan of the stories. At least on the surface.'

'I've had to tell the Faith Protection Alliance about this. They're keener on chasing the Pagans but they're always interested in a bit of demonic possession. You don't strike me as the mystical type, Lona, but have you seen anything out of the ordinary?'

'You're right, Faye. I'm not the mystical type.'

Which would have been true a week ago. But since I'd been at St Cadog's I wasn't so sure any more.

It had started with seeing Anghared in the corridor after the Harvest memorial, and had become pretty much everyday. For example, sometimes I caught a glimpse of someone or something out of the corner of my eye. But when I looked round, no one was there. At other times I could just – feel – that there was a person in the room with me. But they didn't show. I would hear noises, a rustling sound, footsteps, voices murmuring and muttering. But maybe it was the sound of the wind, whispering and sighing round the old building.

And then there were the dreams. They became so vivid and intense that I awoke in the mornings feeling that I'd been away for days, always in early medieval Cymru, usually in the land of the stories. I began to feel I actually knew Anghared and her hawk-faced brother, Anwhyn. That they were my friends. That Eirrod was my king.

I knew, really, that it was because I'd been putting in such long days in the eerie solitude of the artefact centre. The mysteries, bound up in the pattern of words and the dance of intertwining stories, had taken hold of me as the manuscript began to suck me in. I was inhabiting the borderlands in more ways than one. Gradually, painstakingly, I moulded my translation into meaningful narratives. That – combined with the danger I was in and the nervous strain of the fear and suspicion – was warping my perceptions. Well, maybe the medding was playing a part, as well.

And the world of the stories was a safe world, and that's why I was retreating into it, I knew that too. The College, the terrible things that had happened here, the pressures, became greyed out and only the stories had colour. I became folded into its vivid emeralds, intense blood reds and bright saffrons.

So it wasn't that surprising that my grip on reality was a little relaxed. This was a defence mechanism. Healthy. It wasn't like before. Like just after Mam died and I started losing it a bit, until the healer nuns started closing in and Lyn had to get them to back off. It wasn't like that at all.

I hinted at it to M in one of our daily calls. There was a long pause. M looked concerned, asked me how many hours a day I was working, how much I was relying on Elation products (M's not a fan of smartmeds) suggested I got more rest, took a day out in town. So I changed the subject.

I tried talking to Naz.

'Can I tell you something weird without you getting me confined to enforced care by the Little Sisters of St Brynach?' I asked.

'You can try, but I have to tell you I keep Mother Zachariah on priority comms nowadays.'

'I keep almost seeing things from the stories, or from the Other-World, in real life. Not directly. Kind of out of the corner of my eye. It's like characters from the stories are around all the time.'

'Oh boy. That's the real curse of the Pryddych Cycle, isn't it? Look, before I call in the nuns, why don't you try just getting out more? More to life than books, you know. Owen's playing rugby this afternoon; come and watch him.'

So I did. But when I got there all I saw was flying banners, fanatical tribalism, the ritualised barbarism of the battle. Owen, as captain, was a young chieftain marshalling his troops on the field. Heroic deeds were attempted; bravery triumphed in the face of disaster; blood was spilled, the crowd howled, the battle was lost and won.

Afterwards, in the crowded bar, tales of the fight were honed for later telling. Listening to a story of a daring win against the odds gave me an idea about a piece of text I was struggling with, where a magic goat named Ianto takes over a whole forest, including gaining sovereignty over the local dragon. I went straight to the artefact centre and the text opened up to me as if I'd pressed a secret lever.

Because the characters from the stories were like friends by now, it didn't really bother me, having them around when I hadn't invited them. But, occasionally, I encountered something different. Something less welcome. Sometimes, in a dream, or a vision I almost saw, or a sound I nearly heard, I got a sense of something I very much didn't want to have around. My senses flashed warnings and then left me in a cold, paralysed state of fear.

But it passed and I moved on. Not surprising, under the circumstances, after all. There was a lot to fear. And anyway, disruptions of reality were fairly normal at St Cadog's. Holograms were routinely used with all their off-campus students and vHolos, not only of real people, but also of images; and animations popped up, accidentally, in the most unlikely places, when the interface between Synthesis software and rival products failed. I once came across the martyrdom of St Sebastian in the refectory, which totally put me off my lunchtime kebab; and hologrammatic sheep and goats were always escaping from Bible stories to wander the corridors, much to Dodo's excitement.

Belief in the supernatural was part of the culture at the College, anyway. One of their most popular short courses is Exorcism for Ministers, which is Yvonne's particular headache and as it has to take place in a psychically secure room, so that no devils escape onto the campus.

EIGHTEEN

The world that was her home

Legacies of Faith: An introduction

Faith shapes both our present and our past. It determines our everyday lives. This is as true in 2069 as it was in 469. Possibly more so. The legacy of the Faith Wars of the 2040s lies heavily with us all today. We will not, and indeed should not, easily forget the millions of lives lost in drone warfare or in the thousands of international suicide attacks.

Nor will we forget that, despite many attempts at peace talks, the wars were not finally resolved until 2056. This was when Nobel Peace prize-winner Aisha Mohammed was elected President of the USA; and King Faisal of Saudi Arabia made movie star Bridget Moran his queen. Faith relies on performative acts.

So for contemporary Britons, as for early medieval Britons, faith shapes our peace and our war. For us, our emphasis is on religious tolerance and spiritual plurality. For early Britons it was a different story. Or rather, a competing set of stories.

Dragons, Dreams and Drugs by Pleasance and Bowen, p1.

'I t's Cautras,' Owen said. 'The thing that killed Dorath in *The Lady of the Silver Pool II*. But how come Dorath was at Megan's wedding? If he was already dead?'

My latest translation had just been published and it was unsettling some people. Aspects of the stories, and this story in particular, were darker than anyone had expected.

'That's an alternative narrative,' I said, 'from the *Book of Fwddog*.'

'I've fed the new stories into the OtherWorld now,' Naz said. 'So he probably won't be there at the wedding again. Or maybe he will be sometimes. Depends which possibility seems more overarching in terms of the overall narrative of the OtherWorld.'

We were in a train of cars on our way to Elaine's funeral. Elaine had been brought up by her grandmother who'd died a few years ago, and there was no other family. So Yvonne organised the funeral. At the village chapel. 'I did think about the College chapel, but the same building as—? That seemed wrong,' she'd said.

'You know, that does make narrative sense,' Benedict wiped a circle in the condensation to look out of the car window. There was nothing to see but rain. 'Cautras being responsible for Dorath's death. Dorath's killer is presented as the incarnation of malice and I can't think of another monster that is so overarchingly evil in Early Welsh mythology. They're usually more like Cawl, you know.'

'Sometimes friendly, occasionally eats people?' Naz asked.

'Arbitrary. Yes.' Benedict stared out into the falling grey water.

THE FUNERAL WAS THE FIRST TIME I SAW ELAINE'S FACE IN REAL LIFE. Or real death. Delicate, pale, surrounded by all that golden-red hair flowing onto the white pillow, onto the shoulders of her white gown as she lay in her coffin. Her eyes had been amber. But they were closed now.

It was an old-school ceremony: sombre, mainly about sin and doom and the faint, pale hope of resurrection. I was glad to get back out into the driving rain and away from all that redness and whiteness. And paleness.

The chapel had been packed. Familiar faces from the College, unfamiliar ones from the village. Faye Driscoll, sitting at the back, watching people. Because Elaine's murderer was here, too.

I WAS STILL FEELING GRIM IN THE CROWDED OTHERWORLD departure lounge, waiting to go into the post-funeral do. Benedict had wanted to hold it there. The world of Early Welsh culture was her home, he'd said.

I sat on a carved wooden sofa and Dodo sprawled on the stone floor at my feet, looking like some medieval chieftain's favourite hunting dog. Something about the way he lay there made me remember Jonno's dog, Tesler, from the old days – a big Akita who'd been my best friend for years. I'd looked after Tesler when he grew up too good-natured to be used as protection. Or maybe he'd looked after me.

Too much sadness in that memory.

'Can I get you a drink, Lona?' Fish had noticed I was struggling a bit. 'There's only this Merlin's Magick Drinks Dispenser stuff, not up to Gwenda's standard I'm afraid. Synthesis insisted we use one of their portal concessions, KwenchKwest.'

Fish selected Dragon's Blood (cranberry juice). I watched as the crimson liquid spilled into its goblet.

'I hadn't seen her face. Before.' I tried to explain. 'She looked – so vulnerable. Lying there.'

'Elaine was a fragile creature.' Fish sat down next to me. 'Such a sad, terrible thing. And we all feel so – so powerless. If only there was something we could do.'

He drank his Dark Knight (black coffee) sombrely.

'We could do something.' Owen joined us, followed by Naz. 'We could find out who killed Elaine and attacked you, Lona. This person who's Cautras's agent, or thinks they are. The police haven't got anywhere, apart from suspecting me.'

I took one sip of my Dragon's Blood and surreptitiously abandoned the poisonous substance on the medieval-effect coffee table.

'Why us?' asked Naz.

'Because Lona's in danger. And we're her friends. Because I'm the police's favourite suspect. And Elaine was my friend, kind of. My tutor, anyway. Because you're super-intelligent. And you're everyone else's favourite suspect. And for Elaine, for her sake. We have to do what's right by her.'

Owen looked round at us. I nodded, slowly. Naz looked sceptical.

Owen's gaze rested on Fish. 'You could help us, too, Fish.'

'I could? I certainly would.'

'You're super-efficient and everyone knows that's how you solve murders, "efficiency, intelligence and a little bit of flair," like Inspector Tapp in the Exmoor crime holos.'

'A little bit of flair? That would be where I come in.' Delauney plonked himself precariously on the carved gargoyle arm of the sofa. He beamed round at us in a slightly subdued way. His funeral smile.

'Cool.' Owen nodded. 'Look, we've all been trying to work out who it is on our own, haven't we? Everyone here's doing that. Let's do it together and we might get somewhere. What about it, Naz? Lona?'

'Sounds a bit risky,' Naz said. 'Putting ourselves in the firing line. And anyway, apart from Lona and maybe you, Owen, any of us could be the agent.'

'But there's enough of us that that wouldn't matter,' I said. 'It's a great idea, Owen.'

'Can't do any harm,' Delauney said.

'And at least we'd be *doing* something,' Fish agreed

Naz sighed. 'Oh, alright then. If we must.'

A FEW MINUTES LATER, YVONNE WAVED US OVER TO THE DEPARTURE doors.

'You're bringing Dodo?' Delauney asked me.

'Yeah, I always take him in now. He's been added to my safeword.'

'Good idea,' Delauney scratched the thick fur of Dodo's neck and he stretched his head up happily. 'Don't let her out of your sight, Dodo.'

'At least until she's finished the translation,' Naz added.

'What do you think of it now you've seen a few different scenarios?' Delauney asked me. 'The OtherWorld?'

'Very impressive.' I stood up. 'I've never been in an AlterVerse that came anywhere near it.'

He smiled. 'It's mould-breaking. I told you, Naz is a genius.'

'That's a technical description, not a compliment,' Naz said as we walked over to the massive, arched double doors at the end of the room. The wardrobe doors. Yvonne greeted Naz with a sad, toothy smile.

'Where do you want to go, brave travellers?' the doors asked, in hushed and expectant tones.

'Pryddych, 480AD,' Yvonne said. 'Party of, let me see, five. No, six including Dodo.'

The doors opened slowly into a dimly lit stone chamber, with stairs disappearing down into darkness. 'Find adventure, find mystery... find history!' they said.

'They're not meant to be saying that today, Naz,' Yvonne hissed.

Naz grimaced then made some startlingly fast gestures at an invisible screen until the doors said:

'Come in and celebrate the life of Elaine Bowen in the world that was her home'.

NINETEEN

New magic and the young prince

W e were in a large dining hall, lit by torches ranged around the rough stone walls; their light flickered on copper plates laden with food, and on silver goblets full of mead. King Eirrod presided over the feast with his red-cheeked, cheerful Queen, Nerys, at his side.

Benedict had chosen a feast from the *Green Book* as the setting for the post-funeral bash. It certainly beat ham sandwiches and sherry in the staff common room.

The familiar faces from St Cadog's intermingled with familiar faces from the stories; plus village people, both fifth and twenty-first century, real and virtual. Owen and Kite were sitting opposite me, next to Anwhyn, who was younger than he'd been at the wedding feast. His clever black eyes glittered in the torchlight above his gold torque, with its ruby-eyed wolf heads. The wolf heads looked round at Dodo and winked. Anwhyn, Lord of the Seeing Stone. Anwhyn the Wolf. Just as I'd written him.

Anwhyn listened with interest to Owen's enthusiastic chatter, but something about his speculative expression made me uncomfortable.

A voice from my left broke into my thoughts.

'You're not happy that my brother and your friend enjoy their conversation, Lona?' Anghared. Of the Black Mountains, the Silver Pool and the mirror in St Cadog's corridor. And more recently, my dreams. But it was the first time I'd actually met her properly in the OtherWorld; until today she'd been an outline character.

Anghared was as fair as Anwhyn was dark. The twin of light to his dark twin. Her skin was ghostly pale, her clothes were flowing and silvery-white. Around her head was a circlet of gold, inter-twined with silver, with a green stone at its centre. The circlet was, like Anwhyn's wolf-head torque, one of the burial chamber artefacts.

'Just a bit concerned, I suppose,' I said. 'Owen's … impres-sionable.'

Owen was now gazing at Anwhyn with eyes like saucers, as

Anwhyn related a tale of magical combat. A couple of Anwhyn's friends gathered round them and joined in as a chorus, from time to time, gesticulating dramatically and waving swords and daggers around in an alarming fashion. Kite listened intently but he was a bit detached. He'd been in real battles, so he knew they were never glamorous or heroic. Not outworld, anyway.

'The stories are strong with Owen. But for us, the telling of stories is powerful with everyone. You must know that, as the storyteller?'

'Yes, but I'm not the storyteller, Anghared. People from your world told them. I just translate their tales.'

'You translate us all,' said Anghared, in Early Welsh.

'All I do is translate,' I answered, in the same language.

Anghared looked across the table at Owen. 'Owen has the look of a warrior,' she said. 'You think his bravery will lead him into danger?'

'I don't know where it might lead him. He's so keen to do what's right, or what he thinks is right.'

'And you, Lona, are you keen to do what's right?'

And then Anghared recited, the prophecy with an insistent, trance-like delivery that made the familiar words seem new and powerful.

If Eirrod's book and Eirrod's bones
Leave the realm of the Seeing Stone
Then strife and doom will be at hand
A foul thing, loosed, will stalk the land
And haunt the people of the realm.

'You believe that, then?' I asked.

'The prophecy is mine. It was told to me by the North Wind. It was told to me by the mountains and the forests of Eirrod's realm. It's already coming true.'

'*A foul thing, loosed*. That was Cautras, wasn't it?'

Anghared shuddered slightly.

'Anghared. Elaine's death.'

'A great sadness. A great wrong. Elaine had the makings of a vate. A seer. We honour her.' Anghared lifted a goblet and drank. Then she looked at me over the rim. 'And you – you wish to avenge her?'

'I … maybe. Look … Elaine's murder. Was that something to do with Cautras? The curse?'

'We bound him up in the Seeing Stone, my brother and I. Now the power of the stone has been fractured, he returns.'

'We think that someone here might … might be one of his worshippers.'

'That is how he's operated before. By possession of acolytes.'

'How do we stop this, Anghared?'

'Not all those he possesses go willingly into his service. Maybe they can be won back. And,' she looked over at Naz, 'you have new magic.' She looked over at Owen. 'Your own brave princes.' She paused and stared at me as if she was analysing my DNA. 'And you have the stories, Lona.'

Our conversation was interrupted by a commotion from the other side of the table and I looked over just in time to catch the end of some jovial, masculine joshing, which then led into in some jovial, masculine swordplay between Owen and a great, burly, red-faced man sporting so much hair, beard and fur clothing that he seemed barely human. From the enthusiastic shouts of encourage-ment and good-natured derision, I learned that Owen's opponent was known as 'Ifor the Bear'. Their duelling continued round the table, under the table, on the table, amid shouts of advice and whoops of support, with Owen using some of his newfound acro-batic skills. He even did a bit of flying. Naz studied Owen's new moves intently, from the other side of the table, where Yvonne and a couple of Naz's other admirers were studying Naz equally intently. Poor guy.

Eventually, Owen struck the Bear's sword from his great hand and the crowd went wild. Someone proposed a toast to 'the young prince from another world'.

'Young prince?' I asked Anghared, amid the clinking of goblets, roaring of further toasts and snatches of high-spirited singing and rhyming.

'Your friend has the qualities of a prince,' she said

'What qualities?' I demanded.

'Bravery. Honour. Honesty. Faith in the land. The people. Belief. In this, he's like our king.'

Anghared nodded reverentially to the head of the table. Eirrod was a solid, sensible-looking, grey-haired man, who radiated gravitas. I could see little similarity to Owen.

'But Anghared, in your time princes had to be shrewd. Clever. I mean, they had to be able to outwit their enemies, do deals with neighbouring kings, form alliances, all that sort of thing. That's not Owen.'

'A good king has someone like Anwhyn, whom he trusts to advise him on such matters. The king, himself, inspires devotion and loyalty in the people. He embodies the spirit of the land.'

I looked at Eirrod. I could see what she meant. Everyone treated him with a respect bordering on reverence. In a tribal world that sort of thing mattered.

But we didn't live in a tribal world.

'ELAINE'S ART THERAPY PORTFOLIO?' BENEDICT WAS SAYING TO Sister Agape on my other side. 'Yes, we'd be delighted to have it. She was a talented artist. Perhaps we could display it.'

'The images are a little … unsettling.' Mother Zachariah's voice, from the other side of the table, was that of command. I automatically sat up straighter. She looked at me and Benedict as searchingly as Anghared had. 'Elaine was in a rather troubled, feverish state on the days before she ascended to glory. We suspect many of her pieces were drawn then.' She shook her head. 'They would only disturb you.'

'Perhaps, but we'd still love to see them, Mother Zachariah.' I wasn't going to be dicked around by nuns. 'It would make us feel closer to her.'

Sister Agape looked pleased. 'That's a very spiritual response, Lona. I didn't realise you knew her.'

'I feel as though I know her more and more each day, Sister Agape.'

Out of the corner of my eye I noticed Anwhyn slip away from the hall. I left the table as surreptitiously as you can when you've got a massive great wolf in tow and followed him a short distance to what rapidly became a grassy mountain-side on a spring morning.

ANWHYN WAS SITTING ON A BOULDER WITH A HAWK ON HIS shoulder. Dodo sat where he could keep an eye on the hawk. You couldn't be too careful, in his line of work.

'Welcome, Lona.' Anwhyn flashed his canines. The countryside of the Black Mountains lay around us, green and thickly forested and the world felt fresh and washed.

'Anwhyn,' I said. 'Good to meet you properly, at last.'

In fact, Anwhyn felt like someone I'd known forever, but had a chequered relationship with. Like a member of my family, maybe. He certainly had sufficient hair and attitude.

'But we've met many times, Lona,' he said, smoothing the hawk's plumage.

'We've met once. Except in stories. Or in dreams perhaps,' I said.

'What are we in now, Lona Luminos, a story or a dream?' he enquired, politely.

Dodo chose that moment to overcome his wariness of the hawk and trot up to Anwhyn. To my horror, he put his front paws on Anwhyn's knees then reached up and licked his face.

'Down, Dodo!' I said.

Dodo obeyed, but put his head on Anwhyn's knee and looked into his eyes, soulfully.

'A magnificent beast.' Anwhyn patted his head, laughing. 'And he recognises his own.'

'He's not normally that friendly with strangers,' I muttered.

'*He* acknowledges that we're not strangers.'

'Anwhyn, look, if we're not strangers, then can I speak frankly?'

I paused. He gestured for me to continue.

'Someone's killed Elaine and is trying to kill me.'

'Old magic fades, Lona. It will take your new magic to deal with him now.'

'And, the other stuff, the feeling that I'm being haunted. It's connected, somehow, isn't it?'

'You've taken buried tales and brought them back to life. You and Naz, who weaves your code. Does it surprise you that they're boisterous, unruly, keen to live, after more than a thousand years of silence?'

'Mmm. And Owen. This warrior prince thing. I'm not sure it's safe for him.'

Anwhyn paused at this, staring thoughtfully at the slate-grey mountains in the distance. Then, turning back to me, he said, 'How will you resist Cautras, with no help?'

'Owen's just a boy.'

'He's a man in our world.'

I sighed. 'And the dangers?'

'Owen chooses bravely. As you have, by staying in Pryddych.'

'I'm not sure we're up to this, Anwhyn. Me or your prince.'

Anwhyn looked at me and smiled. A long, lupine smile. Then he took the hawk from his shoulder and onto the leather gauntlet on his arm. Standing, he flung it up into the air, where it soared up and wheeled before disappearing towards the forbidding grey mountains.

Naz: A Journal of Unnatural Thoughts

Sunday 25 October, 2071

11.15am

Just caught up on the week's happenings in Ambridge. Listening to *The Archers* is a sort of therapy for me because my memory circuits tell me I've been hearing it all my life. All the way through the Faith Wars when city kids were billeted in Ambridge. All through the green shoots of peace when farmers could start using crop surveillance drones again. Through the gentle separation of Britain into separate countries and their individual reunification with Europe and the reinstatement of all those farming subsidies. It makes me feel like I have a shared history.

So that's where I go when I want a break; the virtual village in my head. But there's conflict there, too. Lately, the impasse between Rosie Archer's soya milk empire and Ruairi Donovan-Aldridge's lab-grown meat mega-factory has been tearing the community apart. So many of the Archers' characters didn't cope well with the outlawing of killing sentient beings for food back in 2058 and the change it brought to their lives. Tom Archer hanged himself with a string of organic sausages and Will Grundy holed himself up in a bunker in the woods with his shotguns, shouting, 'You'll never take me alive.' And they didn't. So it seems a shame the survivors are fighting amongst themselves.

Adaptive. Survivors need to be adaptive. Like we need to be, in what Fish calls 'this challenging situation'. And I'm getting a bit concerned about Lona, on that score.

She seemed pretty stable when she came here, but she told me yesterday that she's started to see and hear things. Not voices telling her that I sit at Satan's right hand and need to be destroyed, fortunately, this time.

She's seeing and hearing characters from the stories. Not properly, she added hurriedly, seeing my expression. It's as if she sees their ghosts.

Their ghosts. That's alright then.

Got to say, I'm worried about her. She's just recovered from a head injury and I'm sure she's over-medding to get the work done. She didn't want to get any help. Said she didn't need bloody healing nuns asking her stupid questions. What she needed was to find out who'd attacked her.

I suggested she take a bit of time off from the stories and spend a couple of hours baying encouragement at displays of mindless violence. Got her to come and watch Owen play rugby. I'm not sure it did her much good, though. She saw the game and even came to the club bar afterwards, but halfway through some anecdote she scuttled off back to the artefact centre muttering something about a goat called Ianto.

We've got Elaine's funeral now. Funerals are supposed to be therapeutic, but I don't think it's going to help Lona much.

3.30pm

So, as we were walking down to the cars in our funeral finery, I tried to draw Lona out a bit. I asked her if she'd talked to M about this haunting business. I knew they spoke every day. But she was adamant that it was just a side effect of the work and that M understood that.

'M's a translator too?' I asked.

In a way, she told me. An interactive book developer. Manga and children's books, that sort of thing. Which explains why M's in Japan a lot of the time. Lona sighed when I said this and said it'd be good if they were in the same place more often, but they had to take the well-paid assignments – couldn't choose where they went. They both had to pay back their mod-loans.

'Bit like being bonded,' I said and she looked embarrassed, the way naturals do when you mention it. Not that she's much of a natural. 'I'm free in ten years, though,' I added.

She told me it was fifteen years for her and asked me what I'd do when I was free. I said that I wanted to go to Manchester, where I was from. I remember everything about it, but I've never physically been there. She gestured towards my records. Wanted to know if that was why I was into 'all that stuff'.

'The Manchester sound thing?' I replied. Smiths, Fall, Joy Division, New Order. Morrissey more than anything. I know it's a cliché, he's massive with synthetics. 'Well it's either that or football. What about you, Lona? What will you do? When you're free?'

She said she was just trying to get there at the moment. To live long enough. But she wasn't sure where 'there' was. She looked a bit sad when she told me that – a bit lost. I felt sorry for her. At least I know where my home is, even if I've never been there. Her home was somewhere she wanted to escape from. And now she's sort of back there.

Then, after the early medieval funeral bash, she started getting worked up about the OtherWorld characters again. Specifically about them calling Owen a prince. I suggested Owen probably fitted the bill, for the world of the stories.

'Impulsive, headstrong, impressionable, always up for a fight – what sort of prince is that?' she demanded.

Looked at another way, that could be decisive, fearless, honest, open, good in combat situations, I pointed out. And Owen seemed to enjoy being a prince, so did it really matter?

She thought that something wasn't quite right – that it was sinister. As if Owen was being used.

'By OtherWorld characters?' I asked her. 'Really?'

It's getting to her, this situation. Perhaps Owen's idea about us becoming the Scooby gang has a point after all; helping Lona feel that she's fighting back might stop her losing it completely.

10.15pm

This evening, Ed Pillington, Synthesis's corporate lawyer arrived. Casual dress, laid back manner. Total confidence about the court case tomorrow.

A formality, he said. Because Welsh Heritage were well intentioned but didn't understand the late 21st-century heritage market and what technology could bring to it. Which is the Synthesis party line on the matter but not one you hear Delauney spouting.

Delauney told him how well I was doing with the OtherWorld development and Pillington stared intently at me, as if I were a piece of super-intelligent horseflesh, and nodded. He'd heard good things about me, PsychLabs really came through for them this time.

Even Delauney looked embarrassed at that.

'Your zlators seem to lead dangerous lives, though,' Pillington went on. 'Is this one going to shape up?'

Delauney reassured him that Lona was forging ahead with a top-notch translation. Pillington warned him not to let her pull out of the contract just because she got a bop on the head. They needed that final draft.

Fish pursed his lips. 'Synthesis is responsible for Lona's safety, Pillington. As it was for Elaine's.'

Pillington responded that it was a moot point and that the partner college was accountable to Synthesis for day-to-day health and safety issues. Fish looked like he was about to argue, but thought better of it. He gets a lot of practice at that around here.

Then Pillington asked why our police hadn't arrested those CymLib people yet and Fish replied, diplomatically, that while he agreed they were the most obvious suspects, there was no evidence against them. But with the Welsh Heritage court hearing tomorrow morning, then the international Methodist ministers' conference starting the next day, CymLib may well have other interventions planned. He and Pillington had a lot to talk about.

Delauney rolled his eyes at me, as Pillington and Fish walked off to Fish's office, discussing injunctions, security guards and restraining orders as they went.

TWENTY

Chosen

Although fiction and drama are often viewed with suspicion by the devout, popular drama can have a positive influence on the religious life of the nations. For example, the longrunning BeebMedia series, *The Archers*, has been a beacon of faith for many years. Even during the pre-wars period of generalised faithlessness, the drama's fictional village of Ambridge was a robust religious community, untouched by fleeting fashions for godlessness. This has been strengthened post-wars, with Lower Loxley becoming the Holy Shula Healing Sanctuary and popular Faith Protection Alliance Constable, Rob Archer, replacing the local bobby.

Alliance Field Manual, Appendix 2

I awoke, sweating and terrified from another bad dream. I knew instantly that there was someone, or something, in the bedroom with me. Dodo was silent, but alert.

Then the person in the room spoke to me. Not actually out loud.

They spoke to me inside my head. And as soon as I heard them, my fear went and the voice became comforting.

'Lona,' they said. I had the odd sense that the voice was profoundly familiar to me, while at the same time being deeply alien.

I could make out a figure in the gloom now. Dodo was staring at it too.

'You've been chosen to give voice to the stories, of light, of darkness. Learn which voices from the shadows you must resist. And how to resist.'

'How to ... resist?' I asked. Out loud.

'You've learned much already, in your search for the truth. From the tales, from your friends. From Elaine. There's more you could learn from Elaine.'

'If she wasn't dead.'

'Her knowledge may not be dead. Just forgotten.'

The figure faded away and the sense of presence subsided. Dodo looked at me, made a harrumphing noise, then went back to sleep.

I lay very still, not scared now, but anxious in a different kind of way. Because I realised two important things about the voice.

It had spoken to me in Early Welsh.

And it belonged to Anghared.

'I'VE BEEN CHOSEN,' SAID OWEN.

'Uh?' I put down my breakfast tray on the table opposite him. I was still a bit groggy from my disturbed night, surely he hadn't said—

'Came to me in a dream, it did.' Tucking into his lab-grown eggs and bacon, he described an experience uncomfortably similar to mine.

'It's not the first time, though,' he added, reflectively. 'But Anwhyn said not to tell anyone the other times. Last night he said I needed to gather my allies around me for the battle.' Owen looked distinctly pleased at the prospect.

Before I could say anything, Delauney turned up and sat down with us, yawning. Fish and Naz pushed their way through the busy refectory to join us, too.

'Uh, did I have a rough night.' Delauney poured himself some water. 'I dreamt Anwhyn came and spoke to me. Jeez, it was horrible, it felt real. He told me Pryddych was under threat. And I had a role to play in bringing peace and prosperity. And uncovering the truth.'

'It is.' Owen looked at him excitedly. 'You do.'

'I guess. But I don't need instruction from fictional characters.'

'That's a coincidence, Delauney.' Naz spooned yoghurt on his bowl of fruit. 'I dreamt something like that last night myself.'

'You weren't, by any chance, told you'd been chosen, were you?' I asked.

'How d'you know that, Lona? The sense of reality was brilliant, not like a normal dream. More like the OtherWorld, in fact. Well, not quite as good, but close. Anghared spoke to me about my duty to the community. To search for the truth.'

Fish looked disturbed. 'The same thing happened to me.'

'Me too,' said Owen.

'And me,' I said, my sense of reality pitching like a boat in a storm. But after a second or two it began to seem comforting that other people shared my warped perceptions. Maybe I wasn't really losing it after all. Or maybe we all were.

We went quiet for a few seconds, among the noise and bustle of the refectory, and looked at each other uncertainly.

'It's because of what we agreed yesterday. The five of us,' Owen said.

'To find out who killed Elaine and attacked me?' I said. 'Yes. Probably. But it's weird that our dreams were so similar.'

'The OtherWorld,' said Fish. 'We were all in it yesterday. At Elaine's wake.'

'Naz?' Delauney asked.

'You *could* try and imprint patterns on five people in the Other-World. Give them all the same dream. But I haven't.'

'And there's nothing in the underlying Synthesis software that you're using – what's it called? Liberation? – that might be suspect?' Delauney asked.

'It took a huge team of people years to write Liberation,' Naz said, 'but I know it inside out. And have improved some of the flabbier bits of it. No clever Synthesis manipulation going on there.'

We were silent again, against the background hubbub, then Owen said, 'Anwhyn told me I'd been chosen because my soul was forged in the flame of purity, truth and honour, like a warrior. Like Eirrod. And I'm to fight for Pryddych. For my land.'

'Anghared spoke to me about using my magical powers and my great knowledge,' Naz said. 'She spoke to me as one sorcerer to another. I suppose I am the nearest thing you've got to a Druid. A synthetic Druid.'

'Nothing as exciting as warrior-like abilities or sorcery, for me, I'm afraid,' Fish said. 'Anwhyn wanted me to use my tactical skills to bring about harmony and untangle truth. Logistics and organisation was my contribution, I think he said.'

'What about you, Delauney?' I asked. 'What's your superpower?'

Delauney looked uncomfortable. A rare occurrence. He looked around the busy refectory, but no one was in earshot.

'My abilities as a scholar. A sage. And a rhetorician.'

'Well,' I said, 'get you lot. A warrior, a magus, a tactician and a sage. I was only chosen to be the zlator. And we didn't even discuss a fee.'

'Eirrod couldn't afford you, Lona,' said Delauney. 'But come on, guys, remember, this is some effect of the OtherWorld on the myth-soaked, inward-looking world we're living in here, mixed up with our grief and anxiety. And, like Owen said, our decision to put our heads together and try and do something about the attacks. It isn't actually ancient voices calling to us from a mystical Celtic hinterland to save the realm or anything. Naz, help me out here, you're the scientist.'

'Subliminal imprinting via the OtherWorld? Someone tinkering with your implants to produce interactive holos?' Naz speculated. 'Both technically possible, if improbable, to varying degrees. I'll run an analysis on the OtherWorld. And you should all get your implants checked out. Even though you've all got vPlants. Don't do anything that will let Synthesis know about it, though. Obviously.'

'It's like the stories are folding us into them. Making us part of them,' I said. Naz looked at me with concern, Delauney with worry, and Fish with confusion; so I quickly added, 'I don't mean literally.'

'But we are part of them,' Owen said. 'Some of us, anyway.'

'Well, whatever the cause of what happened, what do we think?' I asked. 'About the murderer who thinks they're Cautras's agent, I mean? That's what the dreams were all about, after all.'

'What we know is that it could be anyone who has access to the College and knew Elaine.' Fish said. 'With the probable exception of you because you were attacked, and Owen and Smike because they were with you. Though that doesn't mean ...'

'We're not ruled out as Elaine's murderers,' I said.

Fish cleared his throat. 'Quite. Anyway. We drew up a list with DI Driscoll of all the staff who knew Elaine, and all her students. As well as her other teaching, she ran a module about Pagan cultural history which quite a few Pagans are enrolled on as extra-mural students. Including Kite. But the overall list of people who knew her and were here on the day is about two hundred names long.'

'And Faye Driscoll told me that less than half of those two hundred have alibis. That leaves a lot of people. Do we know anything else?' Delauney asked.

'I get the feeling that finding out more about Cautras would help,' I said.

'Because the killer thinks they're doing his bidding?' Delauney said. 'Good point. On that score, I had some news on that this morning from the excavation I mentioned at Caerwent. It's looking a bit peculiar for a Mithraic temple and I'm thinking it might have had some Cautran influence. I've arranged to go over on Thursday. Come with me, Lona, see if it gives you any ideas.'

'Mm,' I said, 'but there's something else. Anghared said ... well, it was in my dream, but anyway, she said Elaine's knowledge wasn't dead, just forgotten.'

'Forgotten knowledge? In a university?' Fish gave an ironic grin. 'There's so much choice I don't know where you'd even start looking.'

Delauney gave him a sour look and was about to respond but Owen beat him to it.

'We should definitely follow up on that, but this morning we can do something *practical*. Go to the court hearing. I'll be at the demo outside, but the rest of you should go in, watch people. Their reactions. If someone's thinks they're Cautras's agent they might give themselves away.'

'I need to work on the translation,' I said. 'You can manage without me.'

'But you'd be best, Lona,' Owen urged. 'Because you don't know many people so you wouldn't be biased. Or ... swayed by your feelings.'

'Come along,' Delauney said. 'Me and Fish have to be at the courthouse anyway and Naz has to come in case he's called to talk about the OtherWorld. Owen's got a point and it's probably best if we're all together.'

I looked round at my three potential protectors – Naz still thinking about his dream, Fish tense about the court case, and Delauney flicking his hair off his forehead and smiling at Gwenda over the other side of the room – and decided I'd best stay well away from the windows of the Abergavenny county court.

TWENTY-ONE

Trouble with a Bubble

D odo and I followed the others into the spherical, transparent pod of the large College TransBub. Delauney told the driver module our destination and the Bub took us up and away from the roof of the College into the drizzling, grey-green autumn afternoon.

We drifted along quietly, lulled by the welcome calm of the Bubble flight. I looked down at the expanses of green, punctuated by great lab-grown meat and dairy factories, their solar panels winking blue as we passed over. I could remember when there were sheep in those fields. Real ones, destined for slaughter.

I'd never seen the place from a Bub in those days, though. Usually I saw it from the back of Mam's bike, hanging onto her leather jacket as the hedges hurtled past. That part had been good.

At first we hardly saw another air vehicle and the Bub moved swiftly through the sky, but as we approached the blue and silver edge of Abergavenny, other TransBubs appeared and our pace slowed as the Bubbles avoided each other. Eventually, we reached the slate-grey centre of town and the roof of the court building appeared below us. Our Bub queued politely, waiting for the other court-bound vehicles to release their inhabitants; then landed, and we stirred ourselves to disembark.

The rain had stopped, here. Released into the chilly afternoon sunlight, we stared round dreamily at the other recently disgorged passengers and at the skyline. Slowly, we performed the psychological gear switch of Bubble passengers who now have to deal with the real world, as our Bub flew off to its docking garage.

The next queuing Bubble took its place and, as we absently watched our Bub float off, the four of us flinched, simultaneously, as it swerved violently to avoid another vehicle. The other TransBub, which had dropped quite suddenly from overhead, was zigzagging erratically, moving far too fast for the crowded sky. The single passenger inside it was still strapped into his seat, his face white and contorted, his hands gripping the arms of his seat. He looked straight at us, his mouth open in a noiseless scream. Within microseconds Naz called the emergency services and, as he was doing so, the new Bub danced off towards the river.

Dodo had been lying on the floor whimpering throughout this whole episode, as if in pain. As the Bub became more and more erratic in its movements, so his whimpering grew louder and more distressed. I knelt down and tried to calm him, but he wouldn't be comforted.

We watched as the Bub darted around, like a dragonfly, swerving off, climbing, until it was high over the River Wye. And then it dropped, as if in free fall. It clipped the large solid black metal bridge, smashing one of its transparent panels, and went into a dizzying spin as it plunged into the river. Bubbles of air, mocking ghosts of the dead vehicle, billowed up through the water.

The silent, unreal event unfolded in front of us, like something from a disaster holo, not something that would happen in Abergavenny on a grey October morning. A few minutes ago we'd been flying through the same sky in our own Bub.

Dodo's pitiful whining and whimpering had reached a crescendo, and by the time the Bub hit the water he was yelping as if with pain. Concerned that he was hurting in some way, I flipped up the control panel on his neck, tapped in the de-activation code and finger-swiped the security panel. Silent now, he lay there motionless, his muzzle on his paws, like a natural history exhibit in an old style museum. Though I knew he could be fixed, I felt a spasm of anxiety about him.

Police and ambulance jets appeared, whining through the sky, their alarms squealing, smashing the eerie silence of the unreal tragedy, loudly announcing this private horror to the world. They were at the bridge now, and uniformed figures were lowered down into the water, on ropes, from the hovering jets. A police dinghy kept its place near the accident. No one on the court roof moved or spoke. After a few minutes, the figures emerged from the water and, with the help of the dinghy, strapped someone onto a stretcher and air-lifted them into the Para Jet.

Once the Para Jet and its cargo had zoomed away, the four of us looked round at each other, and at the immobilised Dodo, stupefied.

'Sweet Jesus,' muttered Delauney. 'Did you see who that was?'

Naz, Fish and Owen nodded gravely.

'Who?' I asked.

'Ed Pillington,' said Fish. 'Synthesis's legal director.'

A LITTLE LATER WE WERE, SHAKILY, SIPPING COFFEE IN A CostaBuck. The court hearing had only lasted a few minutes, which was as long as it took for the proceedings to be formally rescheduled for next month. Most of the people from the court had gone straight to a nearby church, but Owen had helped me carry Dodo into the CostaBuck and Delauney and Naz had snuck off with us, too. Owen seemed nearly as horrified at Dodo's sudden illness as he was at Pillington's accident, and kept stroking his head, even though he was switched off.

'I'm sorry, Delauney. Everyone.' Fish appeared, standing awkwardly by Delauney's chair. 'Not good news. Ed – Counsel Pillington – was pronounced dead in the Para Jet, on the way to the hospital.'

'Dear God.' Delauney paled. He put his coffee cup down slowly. 'Another one.'

'Yes.' Fish sank down onto the sofa next to Dodo. His usual brisk, efficient manner was gone and he seemed to be having trouble making sense of what had happened. 'All this is just…' He shook his head.

'Pillington was a brilliant lawyer,' said Delauney. 'This is a body blow to Synthesis. There wouldn't have been any doubt about the court verdict with him in charge,'

'And now?' I asked, looking at Fish and Delauney, in turn.

'Who can tell.' Fish rubbed his forehead. 'The delay might mean … But this is so very sad. He had three children, you know. And TransBubs just don't malfunction like that. Except…'

'Except when they're sabotaged,' said Naz. 'You're thinking of that assassination in Tokyo last year.'

'No one in the movement would ever do that.' Owen looked up from where he was still stroking Dodo's head. 'Not in a million years, they wouldn't.'

There was a pause, then Fish asked, 'What do you think's happened to Dodo?'

We all looked at the sleeping wolf.

'Maybe he couldn't cope with seeing someone killed,' Delauney said.

'It's never – I mean – it would probably affect him, but not like this,' I said.

'Are you going to call DigiPal?' Naz asked, sweetly.

'Um, no. I don't use them for maintenance. I've got a company in London, so, ahem. Bit awkward.'

Naz smiled slightly. 'I can look at him when we get back, if you like. It could be that corrupted wireless messages from the TransBub affected Dodo when the Bub's computer malfunctioned. We'll sort him out.'

During the ride (by car, even Owen drew the line at a Bubble journey, all things considered) back from the court I said: 'I'll have completed the translation before the next court date. Assuming I survive that long. So the effects for Pagan recognition will have filtered through by then, won't they? That's what Fish meant by the delay.'

Fish was busy elsewhere with Benedict, breaking the news to Pillington's boss and his family. The tough stuff.

Owen paused a second, glanced at Delauney. 'Rowan thinks that they're on the brink of becoming a recognised religion. Now.'

'And if that happens, or looks like it's going to happen by the next court date?' I asked.

'Then Eirrod's body and the manuscript might be classified as holy relics.' Delauney said. 'Which would be a disaster for the College.'

'Because Welsh Heritage would win the court case. Right.' I said.

'That doesn't mean that it was us. CymLib.' Owen said. 'It wasn't.'

'Let's wait until we find out what happened with the TransBub before we go there,' Delauney said.

As soon as we got back to St Cadog's, Naz and I took Dodo to Naz's personal medlab.

It was a tiny room off the lounge of the Launcelot Suite and was a glistening steel and plastic affair, with even higher standards of cleanliness and tidiness than the rest of Naz's rooms. In the middle of it was a shiny, black examination couch, surrounded by an array of devices.

We laid Dodo on the spotless couch.

'So he was probably affected by corrupted messages from Bub's damaged computer?' I stroked Dodo's silky head. He looked furry and vulnerable among all that hard shininess.

'Or maybe the computer signalled for help, because it was failing and that upset him. Put him on standby and let's find out.'

I flipped up his control panel, keyed in the code and pressed my finger against the swipe panel. Naz moved a couple of the gadgets which were on flexible stands, so that they hovered over Dodo's head. Light appeared on them and they began to beep. Naz stared ahead at the data they were mapping to his personal vision, data from Dodo's operational logs.

'There's something here,' he said, after a while. 'At 10:34. Or there *was*.'

'It's gone?'

'Mmm, looks like it self-destructed. Almost. From the few code fragments left, it seems as though communication was received and sent. Can't be sure, though.'

'Do you know where it came from?'

'Impossible to tell. But 10:34 was just before the Bub malfunctioned. Most probably, he was affected by whatever caused the Bubble's computer to malfunction. And seeing as it's self-destructed, that does suggest sabotage.'

'But nobody else was affected. I mean you weren't. And the rest of us have all got plenty of mods. Even Owen's got sport performance ones.'

'Dodo's not got the same level of privacy protection. I mean, it wouldn't be massively difficult to hack into his thoughts, at read level, anyway. That's probably how he accidentally overheard a sabotage message.'

'So why was he whimpering?'

'Look.' He projected to a sharescreen. 'This recurring log entry. It's an affective intervention on one of Dodo's emotion circuits.'

'It made him unhappy?'

'Anxious, probably. Confused. Something like that.'

'He wasn't in pain, then?' I asked.

'Not physical pain.'

Naz spoke a few data commands, unintelligible to me. He paused, as the code and data structures on the sharescreen moved and changed. Then he gestured at them, waited for movement, issued more gnomic commands. He carried on for a while and I zoned out and looked at Dodo, asleep and defenceless on the couch. As I smoothed the soft fur of his neck, another memory resurfaced of Tesler, Jonno's Akita, sleeping in the sun. I hadn't thought about him at all in the years before I'd come here. Or Jonno. Why now? Just when I didn't need that kind of grief? I pushed the memory away.

'Okay,' Naz said at last. 'That's all looking normal now. Well. Not sure DigiPal would agree.'

'Er, yeah, well, mods, you know. You know what most of my contracts are like, Naz.'

'I won't tell anyone, don't worry. Probably a good idea in this place, at the moment. You can reactivate him now.'

Dodo came to slowly and then stood up, shaking himself, and began to lick my face with enthusiasm.

'Good *boy*,' I said. 'Good boy, Dodo. Off the couch now.'

Dodo jumped down onto the floor, only slightly wobbly and sat, staring up at me with golden eyes. I knelt down, hugging him to hide my tears of relief, while Naz sprayed antibacterial mist from a gleaming Perspex container carefully over the couch.

The Pryddych Cycle: The Last Welsh Martyr

When Eirrod the Fair became King of Pryddych, a new age began in the history of the realm. Foreign invaders were beaten back and peace was made with neighbouring chieftains. The harvests were bountiful and the grain stores full. Pryddych traded with tribes in lands beyond the sea, the people grew happy and prosperous, the land content.

With the help of Anghared and Anwhyn, Eirrod vanquished the magicians who had cursed Pryddych and the invaders who had kept it shackled for so long.

Many were the magicians they defeated. Val, the serpent sorcerer; Heggerty, the witch of the hours; Ramain, the Earth Warrior; Sal, son of Salvo, that made the oceans go back and the fish leap far into the air; Roc the mischief maker, from over the great water; and the one they call the Prince of Sorrows. It is of this last sorcerer, herald of the darkness, that we speak. The people of the South say he came to Pryddych one day in the time of Caer-forth, many, many summers ago, as a rain of blood that poisoned the streams and ruined the crop. The people of the West say he was born in the Otherworld to the sorceress Hwynna, who died giving birth to a great maggot that ate her flesh. As the maggot grew, it changed into a boy child who was exiled to the human world. This unnatural son grew into the sorcerer that some call Artris, some call the dark heart of the sun, and some call the Lord of Silence and Sorrow.

Anwhyn and Anghared worked for a year and a day to produce the new magic with which they defeated this creature; but, years later, he escaped from the spellbind they had placed on him and reappeared in the land. Then the son of the Lord of Sorrows, a true son of Pryddych, opposed the sorcerer. This great and golden son of the land led a brave band of warriors into battle against the evil one. Their battle raged in this world and the Otherworld; and magic creatures, witches and wizards joined forces with them.

Finally, the son of the Lord of Sorrows defeated his father. But this great and golden warrior, who had killed his own father for the good of the realm, died from his wounds soon after their battle. The skies wept to see this beautiful, brave young man dead, and the earth refused to accept him into its bosom, so unnatural was his death. The trees whispered, 'This brave one, this beautiful one, we will not let him die,' and the mountains rumbled, 'The last Welsh martyr, he must live.'

The Seeing Stone watched as Pryddych's bravest son was taken into the Otherworld. The Seeing Stone lent its magic and the Otherworld raised him back to life. He became the Immortal Prince of Light and lived forever in that magical realm.

TWENTY-TWO

A Messenger to the Kami

Shinto is a recognised religion in the United Kingdoms with over 50,000 registered practitioners. Many Shintoists, both in the UK and internationally, are unquestionably devout. However, the flexible nature of Shinto means that, outside Japan, it is often used as cover by the godless, particularly those hardened, but lost, souls who consider themselves too sophisticated to have true faith.

Alliance Field Manual, Chapter 17: Verse 6

Although few people at St Cadog's knew Pillington personally, his death sent shockwaves around the campus. Elaine's murder, my attempted murder, and now Pillington. Edgy, scared and suspicious as everyone was to start with, this was making them flip. You saw people going around zombied out on calm meds or getting hysterical about trivialities; everyone else watched them, got twitchy, avoided getting involved.

Delauney, in particular, was losing his shine. Synthesis had not taken the loss of their legal director lightly. 'They think the whole place is descending into lawless chaos, Lona.' Delauney sat with his head in his hands amid the eclectic splendour in his office. 'Thank God for your translation. And Naz's OtherWorld. That should be enough to stop us getting closed down.' He looked up, ten years older, attempted a smile. I watched him, got twitchy, avoided getting involved.

I'd had a call from M soon after we got back to campus. What was going on here? Another murder? M wanted the truth, but I knew how ridiculous the truth would sound to someone not in the middle of all this. I said the police were on it, reassured M that I was safe, I had Dodo.

M pointed out that that hadn't helped me last time.

The police were interviewing the Pagans again. Mainly DI Driscoll's Civil Police team, much to Benedict and Fish's relief, but the Alliance were poking round too. Owen had seen Fish's old colleague, the Ice Fairy, at the Pagan camp. Clergy were beginning to descend on the College as well, with the ministers' conference due to start the next day; so the place was awash with plain clothes cops and uniformed priests with a sprinkling of kwizzers, who were somewhere in between.

'Lona,' said Benedict, as I passed him and Fish in the corridor, 'Mother Zachariah kindly sent over Elaine's art therapy portfolio this morning. I remember you were interested in it.'

Fish nodded a greeting to me and moved off, saying to Benedict in parting: 'Don't worry, Benedict, leave DI Driscoll and Lieutenant Bevan to me, I'll deal with them.'

'Dear me, that is a relief.' Benedict ushered me into the comfortable gloom of his office. 'I really don't know where St Cadog's would be without James Fish, Lona.'

'He seems very … effective.'

'Oh, more than that, far more. He's brought us into the twenty-first century you know, technologically, and that's helped us compete – stay afloat financially. We really feel that the Lord sent him to us. And he's been such a tremendous help in these recent dark days.' He picked up an old-fashioned cardboard portfolio that was balanced precariously on a stack of kipple. 'Elaine Bowen' was emblazoned on it in the same ornate letters as the notebook.

'Paper drawings.' Benedict opened the portfolio. 'Elaine liked the old ways.'

I looked over his shoulder as he leafed through some charcoal drawings which were a bit like the ones from her notebook. And then he came to one of Owen. But not Owen. The same clear eyes, high cheekbones. But the generous mouth was contorted in a malevolent, mocking leer, the chiselled jaw tilted at an arrogant angle that Owen's never was – never could be. She'd captured Owen's vitality – his strength – but there was an arrogance, brutality and cruelty to it that our Owen didn't possess.

He turned over other pictures. All different versions of the same thing, from different angles. Bad Owen. Not Owen. Owen possessed by an evil spirit.

'She was ill.' I said, as he turned over more evil Owens. 'It doesn't mean anything.'

'No.' Benedict sounded uncertain. 'Of course not.'

'Owen saved my life, Benedict. He didn't kill Elaine. Whatever the police think.'

'Of course my dear.' He closed the folder. 'What are we to do with this, I wonder?'

'Here.' I grabbed at the portfolio. 'I'll show it to Owen. Talk to him about it.'

'But surely. I mean – the police?' Benedict was still hanging onto his end of the portfolio.

'I expect they've seen it. And if they haven't, well. We wouldn't want to upset Gwenda.'

Benedict looked horrified. His grip loosened. 'Heavens, no. But—'

'Especially with the conference?'

Hordes of hungry ministers danced in a vision before Benedict's eyes. He let go of the portfolio.

ON MY WAY ACROSS THE QUAD WHICH WAS BUSY WITH STUDENTS going to and from classes, I encountered Kite, struggling with the quad door.

'Bloody thing wouldn't let me in.' He came through to the quad and stood too close to me.

'What brings you here, anyway?' I asked.

'Don't you start. Going to a lecture on Pagan cultural history. Benedict's taken it over since Elaine was killed.'

The door shuddered a bit.

'But we're going to find out who killed her,' I told it. 'Bring them to justice.'

'You've started talking to it too?' Kite laughed, putting his hand on my arm. 'What is it with you translators?'

Dodo gave a quiet growl and Kite moved away.

'You'll find it quicker to leave by the back exit,' the door called after him.

BUT THE DOOR HAD GIVEN ME AN IDEA, WHICH I MULLED OVER AS I negotiated my way through the throng and up to my rooms. If the quad door was cleverer than the other doors and liked Elaine, then maybe it would have noticed if she was particularly friendly with anyone? It was worth a try anyway and I made a mental note to have a quiet word with it, when I got the chance.

BACK IN MY SUITE, I TRIED TO PUSH ELAINE'S FOLDER UNDER THE sofa but something stopped me getting it all the way in. The offending item turned out to be a small, brightly patterned wooden bowl, which looked like something Delauney would keep in his office. Yet another one of Dodo's stolen objects, but probably not valuable and one I could easily return.

As I slid Elaine's folder back under the sofa, followed by Delauney's bowl, there was hammering on my door. I opened it to find the Faith Police. Unexpected, unannounced. At least it was 3pm rather than their preferred housecall time of 3am. Lieutenant Bevan and Sergeant Preece: the Ice Fairy and her sidekick. The ones who had outed me to everyone as a Zanegell when I was unconscious in the infirmary.

'What can I do for you, Lieutenant?' I asked, as she and her sergeant enthroned themselves on my sofa. She rearranged the purple velvet folds of her robe and stared at Dodo, then at me. He put his head between his paws.

'You have a lot of contact with Paganism, Lona.' Naz was right, she did look like some kind of beautiful, evil, little doll. Her harsh voice had a grating Estuary English accent.

'I'm a professional translator,' I said. 'I happen to be translating a Pagan text, at the moment.'

The Lieutenant smoothed back an invisible strand of glossy, colourless hair. Ballerina's hair, twisted into a knot at the nape of her neck. It shone like glass.

'Your family?'

'We haven't met for many years.'

'But you were brought up as—' an expression of distaste on her tiny, perfect features, 'as a Pagan.'

'None of us have a choice about how we're brought up.'

'And this idea of yours? A Pagan-hating devil-worshipper who murders good Christians.' Her voice dripped with scorn. 'When they're not attacking *Shintoists*.'

'Someone unhinged, yes. Someone who follows a minor local deity in an obscure part of the Roman pantheon and thinks they're doing his work.'

'Local deity, hmm? Pagans like their local deities, don't they? And you Shintoists? Remind me when you changed from Paganism to Shinto?'

'As you know, I was Shinto at eighteen.' The age I first had to register my religion. Apart from M, pretty much everyone in my new life had been Shinto. Some were even genuine.

'During the Faith Wars. When Shintoists were neutral.' Her icy gaze rested on my travel shrine in the corner. 'You use that jinja to worship your ancestors?'

'Inari is the main kami I venerate.' I nodded towards the fox messenger statue on my jinja.

'Inari. The spirit of worldly success.' She stared at the statue and it seemed to shrink away under her gaze. 'I hear that's popular with internationals, like you.' She looked back at me. I refused to shrink away under her gaze. 'What about local kami, *Master* Luminos?' Only she could make my hard-won Guild title into an insult.

'Dame Shirley's popular at the Abergavenny temple.'

'Which you never visit. Your Pagan friends think the mountain and the river gods are active here.'

'Maybe. I travel too much to get involved with local kami.'

'Is it the local kami who murdered Ed Pillington? Or the local Pagans?' asked her sergeant.

I shrugged. It still hurt.

'That wolf,' he nodded towards Dodo. 'Is he a messenger to Inari, too?'

'He's a pet robot, Sergeant,' I said.

TWENTY-THREE

Spelling practice

Alliance Captain Bobby Doll

Faith Protection Alliance Captain Bobby is protecting us all! Dress her up in her clerical gown and dashing purple velvet cloak and send her out to fight the forces of evil.

Gain Faith Protection Bobby awards as you help your captain cast out demons and track down faithlessness. When you have ten awards you can join the elite Alliance Youth Corps* and become a real life junior Captain Bobby!

If you're a fan of **Alliance Captain Bobby** you'll love her little sisters: kooky little **Pagan Bobby** and the quirky rebel, **Zanegell Bobby**. Why not collect the set?

The Alliance Youth Corps is an educational charity dedicated to encouraging responsible and devout citizenship in young people.

During this time at St Cadog's we all headed to the OtherWorld frequently just to escape, for the odd half hour, from the nightmare outworld. You could fight monsters you could see here; you could leap around dancing without anyone thinking you were being insensitive; you could talk to the trees and forget yourself.

Everyone was becoming a sorcerer now. Naz had developed the new sorcerer level so that people had their own special power and there were different types of magic skills you could acquire. The Pagans loved it – had a whole host of specifically Pagan spells they'd honed, like talking the language of songbirds and making plants grow at miraculous rates. You couldn't stop them tweeting and greening. Kite was unusual among the Pagans in that he'd developed beguiling skills, which he had quite a lot of normally, but his sorcerer power was even odder: the ability to make people see the truth in a situation.

Owen, unsurprisingly, had taken his sorcerer skills down a warrior path. His acrobatics were stellar, he could walk up walls and his flying was better than anyone's. But his sorcerer power was leadership.

After one particularly rowdy episode, where we'd all gone on a raiding party led by Owen to get some magic sheep back from a neighbouring tribe, we found ourselves at a dancing and riddling competition. The sheep joined in and seemed to be winning. Much to Dodo's disgust.

Fish gave the sheep a run for their money in the riddle-solving but seemed to be enjoying the dancing more. Getting his breath back from the last reel, he gestured at the dancing sheep and said, 'Therapy, Lona. It's therapy. For half an hour here not only can I escape from the awfulness of it all, but I don't have to worry about our security measures or risk factors either, about being responsible for stopping more of this … horror. I don't have to be the sensible one.' And then he was off again whirling around with Gwenda and a couple of ewes.

Fish had specialised in riddling, eschewing the showier skills and powers. He was far better at puzzles than anyone, including the academics, which pleased him mightily. Gwenda, on the other had taken naturally to transformation. The rest of us could only transform into animals. Gwenda could transform into other people.

'I didn't choose it, Lona,' she said. 'It chose me. I don't even think about who or what to become. I just raise my arms and it happens.' And that was the best thing about Gwenda's transforming power. She always became the person or creature best suited to the situation. I had once seen her change into an attractive, female monster who distracted Cawl by undulating her tentacles a bit just as he was about to drown a few people in the river for getting his questions wrong.

Anwhyn sat down next to me.

'How goes your quest, Lona?'

'Another person was killed yesterday, Anwhyn. We were there, it was … it was horrible. The five of us, we're trying to work it out but I don't know if we're capable of stopping this kind of killer.'

'Some of your number have already begun.'

'Have we? I don't even know what that means. Can't you just give us some clues?'

'We would help you if we could, Lona. But we don't have the answer because – we're not real,' Anwhyn said. 'All we know is what's in the text and what can be deduced from this, by the code. You write us, in stories, in your program sequences, you animate the memory of us.'

'But it's to do with Cautras because the killer thinks they're his servant. And Cautras is in the text.'

'We know something of Cautras. The first time, when we defeated him, my sister and I, we didn't know we'd win. We knew we were the only people who were going to try.'

'You mean this time it's us.'

He inclined his head.

'But it's not actually Cautras we're trying to defeat, Anwhyn. It's a person who thinks they're doing his work.'

'You know this?'

I stopped. And stared. What was he saying?

'The alternative is … terrifying, Anwhyn.'

'All five of you have different abilities that can help to fight this evil. And your friend Naz has strong magic, here.' He nodded to where Naz was deep in conversation with Anghared. Anghared was keen to know all about Naz's 'sorcery' when we were inworld and he was happy to enlighten her. 'My sister is as interested now in the language of computers as she is in the language of the birds and the rivers. She admires his magic powers.'

Delauney joined Anghared and Naz now. He spent a lot of his inworld time with Anghared, too, taking part in her religious rituals, along with River and Rowan as well as Kite and some of the other Pagans. Delauney had developed his inworld abilities along the Pagan lines which surprised all of us who thought he'd be more interested in some brand of influencing. But I guessed that he was taking every opportunity to understand more about Paganism because it was actually the basis of his glittering career.

'To participate in a real fifth-century Pagan ceremony – truly awe inspiring,' he'd said, after their first gods-bothering session.

River, who had specialised in healing, was delighted too, because Anghared let her help prepare the ceremonial potion.

'The spirits in the plants speak to River,' Anghared had said, and River glowed like a happy holly berry.

I wanted to discuss Owen's princely tendencies with Gwenda and Fish while we were in a place outside normality. Once I'd influenced the music to stop so there'd be a pause in the dancing I went over to them. That was my sorcerer power; narrative influencing. I could only do subtle things but, like Gwenda's transforming, it came naturally to me.

'I don't know, Lona, it might help him learn about, you know, management, leadership, that sort of thing,' Gwenda looked over at where Owen and Kite were drinking mead with Eirrod. 'Responsibility. He could do with it, Saint Tom knows, he's a headstrong boy, I've been at my wits end with him at times, how I would have managed without James's help I don't know.' She put her hand on Fish's for a second. He brightened.

'Lona's got a point, though, Gwenda,' he said. 'I can't see all that will do Owen any favours outworld.'

Gwenda sighed. 'He's a good boy, too good, that's the trouble. Too generous, really; always ready to put himself on the line for other people. Like his father, may God have mercy.'

TWENTY-FOUR

A Revelation in Gethsemane

Indigenous Faith – or Satanic Debauchery?

Should Paganism be legally recognised as Britain's oldest religion and accorded faith status? Or does it lack the necessary rigour and consistency to be regarded as a religion? Are Pagans subversive just because of their current illegal status, or is there something innately anti-establishment and lawless about Paganism itself?

Professor Benedict Pleasance chairs this plenary debate on Pagan incorporation. Rowan Peartree, Chief Druid of the Cymru Pagans heads up the pro-incorporationist side; and Dr Philippa O'Hare, author of *Devilish Debauchery: the links between Satanism and Paganism* leads the anti-incorporationist team. This cutting-edge discussion promises to be lively and challenging.

Abstract from 24th International Methodist Ministers' Conference, 28th Oct, 2071

The great hall of the College was alive with Methodist ministers from all over the world. Naz and I had passed one group conducting a debate about whether Christians should be allowed to marry buildings and another discussing whether intersex clerics were less likely to be subject to parishioners' romantic crushes, or more.

We'd all agreed to robe up and show up at the conference reception that evening and try and act normal. It was too late to cancel the thing, so we just had to get on with it. Naturally, Fish and Yvonne had ensured that College security was wound up to maximum, and some of D I Driscoll's troops had come out of their ops room to patrol the campus.

Pagan acceptance was the hot topic of the conference and everyone was interested in Eirrod's stories and their implications. Rowan was doing the opening plenary on the second day and, as Naz and I stood looking round at the assembled company, I could hear phrases such as 'accepting the Old Religion of native British culture, as we do with other cultures,' and 'but can one describe it as a religion, when it has no actual doctrine or sacred text?' drifting around the room.

'It's huge, this thing.' Naz took a BrayneFruit drink from the tray offered him by one of the admin nuns. Sister Continence, if I wasn't mistaken. 'Years, they've been hosting it for, and the virtual participant numbers run into hundreds of thousands.'

'The Dalai Lama's holoing in from her court in Tibet to give the closing keynote, this year, Naz,' Sister Continence chipped in, as she moved off to ply her wholesome drinks elsewhere.

Looking round the room I spotted Owen, in his Eagles club regalia, his arm in a sling after a rugby training accident earlier that day. He was having a spirited conversation with a big Maori minister, and from their movements you could tell that they were both demonstrating previous adventures on the rugby field, despite Owen's injured arm. Next to them, Delauney was doing his stuff with an admiring group of female clerics, watched by DI Driscoll, an ironic expression on her freckled face. She spotted us and came over.

'I should stick with you, Lona. Always seems to be where the trouble is.'

'Like I said yesterday, I'm not looking for it, Faye.'

She'd interviewed me yet again after Pillington's death and still seemed to think I knew more than I was telling her. I got the feeling I was always a cleaned up Zanegell to her. Which, I supposed, was better than the Faith Police's view. They didn't think I was particularly cleaned up and made it clear they weren't fooled by my designer threads and handmade boots. I'd seen the Ice Fairy again just before we came to the reception, stalking the corridors, searching for demons. Searching in all the wrong places. She'd barely acknowledged me, and then only to sneer.

Benedict appeared and introduced a minister who was keen to talk to me about the manuscript.

'A fascinating development for the international Celtic community,' she said in her strange Patagonian Welsh.

'Fascinating,' I agreed. 'And full of surprises.'

BY HALF EIGHT THE ROOM WAS CLEARING, AS ALL THE MINISTERS disappeared into the main lecture theatre for their first session, and the admin nuns and Gwenda's caterers went around clearing up glasses.

'I said I'd keep an eye on their augmented reality system for the opening,' Naz said. 'After the Bubble sabotage, Fish and Benedict are a bit edgy about technical disasters. Want to come? It'll get you out of having to go to the keynote address and behaving like a human being.'

We went to the Launcelot Suite where Naz audibly tutted when I slung my robe over the back of a chair. So I picked it up and folded it, huffing like a teenager and pulling a face at him. Dodo looked at me, amused.

'Cool Zanegell thing, is it, this untidiness of yours?' Naz asked.

'Maybe. We moved around a lot so we never had that much

stuff. It drives M mad, too. I make more of an effort at home.'
Home. Suddenly I missed it, badly. Our own belongings around me:
Dodo's tatty basket; M's Japanese prints; my ancient, battered
fantasy paperbacks. But more than anything I missed M. And I was
beginning to feel the weight, here, of being in an institution, particularly one with its own built-in psychopath. I steadied myself, tried
to breathe slowly. In, out. Naz was watching me.

'You don't like me asking about the Zanegell thing?' he asked.

'No, I don't mind. Some of it was okay. I had a lot of freedom,
it's just… After Mam was killed it wasn't so good.'

'But you stayed for a while?'

'Until Alan Driscoll was sent down. A few months.'

'What made you leave then?'

'Lyn. We fell out, so I had to go.'

'Because she was president by then?'

'Kind of.'

'Is it a heredity thing, then becoming a Zanegell president? I
mean, if you'd stayed would you be next in line for the throne?'

'God, no. Not me. Jonno was president for a while after Mam
died, that's normal, he was VP. But he was … sort of discredited. So
Lyn took over.'

'Is that what you fell out about?

'Kind of. Lyn maintained he'd betrayed Mam to the police.
Mam was killed when the police raided a big drop from our suppli-
ers. Only Jonno and Mam knew that the drop was happening, so
Lyn thought it must have been Jonno who told them about it. And
she blamed him for Mam's death – for letting Driscoll draw a gun
on Mam. Jonno was meant to cover her. And I admit he screwed up
there, but maybe he just wasn't fast enough.'

'You thought he wasn't a traitor, though?'

'I didn't think he was the type.' I thought again of Jonno's big
Akita, Tesler, who turned out to be too friendly and indolent to be
any use as security, but who Jonno still kept. Lyn said he was a sentimental fool not to shoot Tesler and get a proper guard dog. I
couldn't see someone like that as a cold-hearted betrayer. Unless
Lyn was right and he was just weak. 'It was more likely that Mam

told Driscoll – he was on her payroll – and warned him to stay away. Then he betrayed her. But Lyn was convinced it was Jonno who was the traitor, even though he denied it to the end. She wouldn't listen to reason.'

'Any other explanation wouldn't let her take over as president, I'm guessing.'

'That was my suspicion. But she could have genuinely believed it. And she could have been right, Driscoll always maintained that's how he knew about the drop. But then he was a lying bastard.'

'What happened to him? This Jonno?'

'He ... he killed himself.'

'Sorry to hear that. Was it a death before dishonour thing?'

'Something like that. Look, are we going to watch the opening session of this conference, or what, Naz?'

Naz turned to the sharescreen and projected an image of the delegates sitting in a clearing surrounded by a cartoony-looking olive grove. 'I don't normally have much to do with this thing. They mainly use it for teaching their overseas students. It's called the Learning Garden, but the students call it Gethsemane.'

'As they would. What is it, exactly?'

'It's a viewer-centred, broadcast, virtual system augmented with holos. Quite old-fashioned but the hologrammatics have been upgraded to vHolos recently. The delegates sitting in the lecture theatre don't see an olive grove they just see the holos but you can do a lot with them. Simple stuff really, and quite common in universities now, but St Cadog's one of the first places to use it, so pretty forward-looking at the time. Fish's idea, originally.'

On our screen, Benedict gave the opening speech of the conference. He was standing on top of a small hill at one end of the grove, with enlarged images of his face projected to the left and right as he talked. It was all a bit comic book.

'Nothing like your OtherWorld, is it.'

'It's an off-the-peg, educational thing,' Naz said. 'You can't compare them. But it's helped St Cadog's do what they needed. And paved the way for the OtherWorld.'

Two tense-looking faces mapped onto the corner of our sharescreen. One was Yvonne, the other was Dilys, who ran the Learning Garden.

'Everything in Gethsemane looks tranquil, folks,' Naz said on comms.

'Thank the Lord you're here, Naz,' Yvonne said.

Now they were holding a one-minute silence in the olive grove in remembrance of Elaine and Pillington. We panned round the room. Benedict looked sorrowful, Fish tense, Owen still horrified, and Delauney wary.

When it ended, Naz said to me, 'So, who's your candidate, for the agent now, then? I'm getting the unpleasant feeling that I'd still get most people's votes.'

'Not DI Driscoll, she went into sick bay to talk to Owen this afternoon when he was having his rugby injury fixed. Gwenda had to fight her off. But I don't think it's him even if Faye Driscoll does. There's something he's keeping secret, though.'

'I've noticed him and River seem to be becoming an item, but they're keeping it quiet.'

'More likely that then. If he was the agent he wouldn't have tried to stop the attack on me. And he doesn't have the tech skills to sabotage the Bub.'

'No, but his friend Kite might; ex-army, fairly high-end tech security skills. There's the CymLib connection *and* Owen was friendly with Elaine. A bit friendlier than the gross moral turpitude clause in her contract might allow, or so College gossip has it.'

'She drew some pictures of him just before she died. Bit weird, I'll show you later. But you're saying that Owen and Kite might have something to do with Pillington's death?'

'I don't really think so. Owen's been too shocked by it. Kite's a different story, though.'

'He might have the tech skills to get in my room and erase the logs and to sabotage the Bub, but he didn't really know Elaine, except as a lecturer on this Paganism course he's doing. So why would she have gone with him to my rooms?'

'I gather he can be quite persuasive.' Naz looked at me with an amused gleam in his eye. 'And he's a Faith War veteran. Post-traumatic stress making him think he's the agent of a greater god? He wouldn't be the first.'

'Fish is ex-army, too, that's why he's so hyper-organised. Maybe he's got PTS.'

'He was in human resources not armed combat, Lona.'

'Oh. Well he'd still make an efficient agent.'

'You don't get PTS from sitting at a desk.'

'How about Delauney, then?' I suggested. 'He is quite secretive. About something.'

'You've noticed that? It's been going on for a while. He just disappears for the odd hour or two, no one knows where he is or what he's doing.'

'Yeah, but there's plenty of no-good he could be up to that doesn't involve thinking you're an agent of ancient evil, Naz.'

'Maybe, but I get the impression he's too keen on Gwenda to be straying. Though he does fancy himself as a bit of a ladies' man.' Naz flicked back his hair and smiled in a perfect impression of Delauney and I nearly choked on my coffee, laughing.

It was a relief to laugh. It made a change.

In Gethsemane, Benedict finished opening the conference and introduced the first keynote speaker, the leader of the Argentinean Methodist Council. She floated above the audience, ten times her normal size, swooping around, her clerical robes billowing out, dramatically. Her magnified voice boomed out, majestically. The audience gazed up at her with rapt attention.

'Ugh, the rendering of those graphics,' said Naz. 'More jagged edges than a Zanegells' knife fight. Oh, sorry.' He grinned.

'So, I'm ruling you out of being the agent because you have psych check every day,' I went on, ignoring him. 'PsychLabs just aren't that incompetent.'

'Appreciate the vote of confidence. And it's not likely to be you because you were attacked. Unless that was retribution for Elaine's murder and it's all more complicated than we realise. There's some evidence against it being Owen, but none against it being Kite or Delauney. So they're my top suspects.'

'That's just wishful thinking because Kite's bigoted against synthetic humans and Delauney's our boss and a bit of a prat. You could say the same about Fish. Or Benedict, or Gwenda. Rowan, River. Anyone. Yvonne even.'

'Yvonne would make an efficient agent. She'd probably make Cautras fill out some searching forms before she agreed to work for him though. But, ah, speaking of Yvonne…'

'Something new?'

'Well. It's not very convincing. But I found out from Yvonne where Elaine's royalty money will go now. She wasn't supposed to tell me, so don't broadcast it.'

'And?'

'It's in the terms of their contract with the publishers. Benedict.'

'Benedict?'

'He could have pushed the slab down on you, if he'd loosened it earlier, it wasn't that big. And—'

'What's that, Naz?' I broke in.

Behind the speaker's head, black dots began to appear, as if she were attracting midges.

'Oh, it's their cheap, synthetic sky algorithm. That sunlight looks like – ah, yeah, no, I see what you mean.'

More and yet more black dots were appearing in the bright, blue Learning Garden sky. They got gradually larger and it became clear that they were not black dots, but green dots. Larger still and they were not dots at all, but tiny, tiny frogs. The speaker broke off abruptly, as small, then normal-sized frogs appeared, plummeting down past her and onto the crowd below. More and more of them came down, until the air was green with frogs, falling from the heavens and pelting both presenter and delegates.

I watched, open mouthed, while Naz called up Dilys and said, 'Shut it down and get them out of there straight away, Dil.'

'I can't Naz,' she cried. 'Everything's frozen!'

The frog shower was slackening off now and the clerics, removing frogs from about their persons, looked skyward for the lecture to continue. Strangely unhurt, the frogs hopped off to the nearest pool.

The speaker bobbed around in the air, a surprised black balloon, staring down at the frog-strewn landscape. Once she realised her congregation was looking expectantly up at her, she shook the odd frog out of her hair and composed herself to continue. But when she opened her mouth what came out was not her voice, but a roar.

She clamped her hand to her mouth and went red. Very red indeed. The colour crept into her hair as well, which started to grow around her cheeks and neck. Her ears, now bright crimson, grew large and pointed and bumps appeared on her temples. The bumps got bigger and bigger and then they sprouted into horns. A bump on her neck got larger and larger until, lo! She grew another head. This new head was scaly and snake-like, with a forked scarlet tongue darting out of a lipless mouth. And then came another head. A snarling dog's head this time, its teeth bared, dripping saliva. Another followed, a skeletal, horned horse head with crazed, bloodshot eyes. And another. And another. And, as a final head formed, her body grew a forked tail, wings and a shaggy, matted, crimson pelt, until eventually, what was hovering in the sky was not a genial, motherly, Argentinean Minister, but a beast with seven heads and nine horns. Snarling and roaring with all of its seven mouths, it lunged down to snap at the delegates and swipe at them with its talons, its seven pairs of red eyes blazing.

'Give me override, Dilys!' shouted Naz.

The delegates were screaming and running away from the beast, their cassocks flying. One fiery soul moved towards it, holding up a cross and shouting out prayers, but it lunged straight at him and he fainted dead away.

Naz worked so fast his hand movements were almost a blur as he gestured at code and structures invisible to me. His face tense with concentration, he muttered incantations in one of his arcane tech languages, punctuated by the odd curse.

The minutes ticked past, slow second by slow second, and the beast still raged at the terrified conference audience. The few people who were less scared, such as Owen and some feisty looking nuns were busy tending to the others. Then, just as I was beginning to think Naz had been defeated, one of the ministers disappeared.

Naz's face relaxed for a second and then tensed up as he waited for the code changes to affect the rest of the congregation.

And slowly, one by one, they vanished. It took time, but, finally, there was nothing in Gethsemane but the red beast raging in the sky and an army of frogs hopping in and out of the olive grove pond.

'Can you go down and see what's happening, Lona? And keep your comms channel open to mine?'

I raced down to the lecture theatre with Dodo at my heels. Dazed clerics had emerged from the double doors and were being shepherded towards the refectory by Fish, Yvonne, their admin nuns and a couple of DI Driscoll's uniforms. Owen came out supporting his mother, with his one good arm, and the head of the Argentinean Methodist Council, now wholly human, looked as bewildered as everyone else.

'They seem okay, Naz,' I said. I spied Faye Driscoll heading for the lecture theatre and ran after her into the room, Dodo at my heels. Apart from us, the lecture theatre was deserted.

Then the roaring noise started again. Startled, I looked round at the empty room. Nothing.

'Get out of here, Lona,' Driscoll shouted, her eyes fixed on a point above my head as she shook out her baton.

The shaggy red beast was darting and swooping above me, looking down at me. It was huge, ferocious, predatory. Saliva dripped on me from its seven mouths, as it opened them and roared. At me. Its putrid breath hit me like a wave and its seven pairs of red eyes lit up in fury. Dodo gazed at it with uncertain bravado. I backed away from it, across the room. It followed me, ignoring Faye Driscoll, it's fourteen malice-filled eyes boring into me.

The creature stared at me for what felt like a long time. My heart was thudding so loudly I was sure the thing could hear it. Then, to my enormous relief, it moved its gaze to the corridor outside, where we could hear the delegates running away. It flew to the huge theatre doors and climbed onto them, snarling, its gaze fixed on the retreating clerics in the corridor.

'What the *fuck* is this?' Faye said, more to herself that me, as she approached it, slowly.

Dodo was still staring at the creature, while being slightly distracted by the odd remaining frog.

'Let's find out,' I rasped, my mouth dry and my heart still hammering. I had to do something. I couldn't let it escape into the corridor without knowing what it was – what we were up against. 'Dodo. Bring me that book.'

He picked up the big, hard-backed Bible lying next to him – someone's prized possession that they'd dropped in their haste to escape – and brought it over to me. I weighed it in my hand. More than just a book. Potentially a missile. I gathered up my courage, took careful aim with a shaking hand and then threw it, hard, at the unspeakable thing perched on the doors. The creature didn't even notice. Because the book went straight through.

'A fucking hologram.' Faye gave one of her snorting laughs. 'Tom on a bicycle, I've never seen anything so lifelike.'

It left its roost on the doors and flew through the doorway into the corridor. We could hear the panic starting up all over again. We ran out and found it raging down the hallway, terrifying the delegates as it roared and snorted, thrashing around inches above their heads.

'It's just a hologram. Calm down everyone.' Faye shouted. But I could see they didn't believe her. It was so real.

'It can't hurt you. Look!' I ran towards the creature, followed by Dodo. It turned to face us. Its seven monstrous heads, all fanged and predatory, snarled at me simultaneously. I recoiled. This was horribly realistic. Even Naz would be impressed with the rendering. I steeled myself, held my breath, shut my eyes and ran at it. And passed straight through.

'See?' I turned to the now quiet crowd. And although the creature, or the image of the creature, was still there, a wave of relief passed through the hall. People started laughing. And, as the laughter increased, the monster gradually became less real, then even less real, then slightly translucent, then transparent and, gradually, it disappeared completely, leaving nothing but a rotten smell.

TWENTY-FIVE

Infected

All incidents of demonic possession must be reported to the Alliance. Religious practitioners who perform exorcism must log an outcome report with the Alliance detailing circumstance and results. Possession rarely occurs in environments where good religious hygiene is practised and such incidents suggest there may be a culture of godlessness nearby.

Alliance Field Manual, Chapter 15: Verse 12

'What just happened here, Naz?' Delauney looked grim. We were sitting round the faux-jade table in his meeting room with Naz, Benedict and Fish a couple of hours after the Gethsemane invasion. The overflow of clashing artefacts from his office always made me feel like I couldn't breathe properly. And never more so than today. In, out.

'As far as I can see, the system logs show an incursion at 18:23.' Naz said. 'At 18:36 it stopped.'

'An incursion?' Benedict asked.

'Putting it simply, it appeared inside the code of Gethsemane as some kind of virus, corrupted the programme that interfaces with the holo software for nearly thirteen minutes, and then self-destructed. And it's the interface with Synthesis's vHolo software that was affected. So it will have sent an error message back to them.'

Delauney groaned.

'It was a virus?' Fish was tense but alert as ever.

'Some sort of trojan. More advanced.'

'Is that what happened to the Bubble yesterday, Naz?' I asked, my hand automatically moving to stroke Dodo's head. 'How they murdered Pillington?'

'Hard to say when all I've seen is the side effects on Dodo. Could be. There are similarities, but differences, too.'

'Did you manage to capture any of the Gethsemane virus, Naz?' Fish asked. 'Before it vanished?'

'I tried. Not sure how successful that was, it's a clever little virus. Repairing the corrupted code in Gethsemane has to be our first priority so the conference can carry on, but I'll get onto it straight away when that's done.'

'Thank you, Naz,' said Benedict. 'We appreciate your help with this … violation. This, after Elaine's death and the terrible tragedy with the Bubble, it's quite obscene.'

'And finding out what the hell's going on here's much more urgent since Pillington's death.' Delauney sat back in his chair. Rubbed his temples. 'I mean, his death's a sad loss, naturally. But for Synthesis … they sent him here as their fixer. And look what happened. So they're really beginning to lose confidence in St Cadog's, and if they hear about this, they'll think the whole damn place is unstable. We haven't got much time before they decide to take some kind of action.'

Naz looked grave, too. He was being tested here, even more than Delauney.

'So someone put the virus in there, Naz?' I asked. This was scary stuff. Being physically attacked by actual humans was bad enough, but having someone invade your software? Your perceptions of reality? Terrifying in a different way.

'Someone. Or something.'

'Something. Something evil.' Fish sounded stern. Resolute. The Methodist lay preacher surfacing.

'I meant an AI,' Naz said. 'But, you know…'

'There have been instances of diabolic possession working through people's comms, through digital systems.' Fish was determined to look Satan squarely in the face. Whether he was here or not.

'Yes indeed, I've witnessed something very like that myself,' Benedict added, 'many years ago.'

'But it's usually with help from an AI and from humans,' Naz pointed out. 'Although from what I've seen so far, it is quite sophisticated. It would be beyond most humans here.'

'Who wouldn't it be beyond?' Delauney asked.

'Tech staff mainly. And a few bedroom coders. Probably none of the Pagans, well, Kite, maybe. But that's not the right question.'

'Because?' Delauney asked.

'The person wouldn't have to be a technical genius they would just have to know how to get help.'

'From an AI?' Delauney asked. 'From something more sinister?'

'From other humans. You can buy viruses.'

'The agent, then,' I said. It came back to the agent. Not only could they attack us physically, they could attack us on a psychic level. Was this part of what had been haunting me?

'But why would they attack our conference?' Benedict asked. 'We've placed an emphasis on Pagan acceptance this year, certainly, but it wasn't an address by a Pagan that was disrupted.'

'Because they can?' I suggested. Because they wanted to show their power. Because they wanted to make us feel threatened everywhere, all the time. And it was working.

We were silent for a few moments and then Fish turned to Benedict. 'I hate to say this, Benedict, but it's looking like we'll have move the conference?'

'Sadly, it seems the only course of action open to us.' Benedict stood up. 'I'll go and talk to some colleagues at Aberystwyth, they may be able to help. Perhaps you could join me, Fish, when you've asked Naz about the other thing.'

As the door closed behind Benedict, Naz looked at Fish. 'The other thing?'

'I was going to ask you about it once we'd got the conference out of the way, Naz. There's been an increase in reported breaches of people's personal comms and … apparitions in the last couple of weeks at the College. Ones that can't be explained by glitchy compatibility between the Synthesis products, vComms and vHolos, and rival brands, or by an ordinary level of religious mystical experience. Nothing serious or particularly disturbing, though. Nothing like tonight.'

'What sort of things?' I asked. Other people were being haunted too? I wasn't sure whether this was good news or bad. Something to mention to M, though, as evidence of my sanity.

'There's no real pattern to it,' Fish said. 'And we don't actually know if it's connected with the increased levels of user anxiety since Elaine was killed.'

'Have you told everyone who's using Synthesis selfware to turn off their error reporting to Synthesis,' Delauney asked.

'I've encouraged them to but we can't enforce it.'

'Encourage them more,' said Delauney. 'Offer them Elation tokens. Free Braynes smartwine. Whatever it takes.'

'Delauney, that's unethical.' Fish was scandalised. People's choices about data privacy have become sacrosanct nowadays. Because they have so little choice.

'Interesting, though, this comms and holo stuff,' Naz said. 'I'll get Smike to talk to your IT people, if you like, take a look at that? Okay with you Delauney?'

Delauney waved his hand hopelessly. 'We've got to sort out what the hell's happening here. One way or another. And I know we can't rule out … possession, Fish. That would be irreligious. But let's not hand it over to Faith Police yet, eh?'

Naz: A Journal of Unnatural Thoughts

Tuesday 27 October, 2071

7.30am

I'd just started work on Gethsemane last night, when Fish called to let me know Dilys would be moving all the conference software to the servers at Aberystwyth, once it was ready. He said they were bussing the delegates out first thing today, officially, because of technical problems. Though they'd already been fielding press calls wanting to know about St Cadog's Satanic visitation. Delauney was telling Synthesis that there'd been some technical glitches, nothing they wouldn't already find out from some of the vHolo feedback.

Sorting out Gethsemane isn't a big deal. Not for me, anyway. Even the other things, the possible comms security breaches and holo apparitions Fish mentioned, are something I could deal with in my sleep, that's why I've got Smike on it. But I know I'm being tested here, quite literally. I'm still being lab-tested. And I could do without these unexpected cyber-attacks.

Then Dilys, turned up, still wide-eyed and horror-struck.

'My Garden, Naz,' she said, 'It's possessed.'

I told her we'd get it cleaned up, but I could see she didn't believe me.

'No offence, Naz,' she said. 'You're a top-class coder, but even your cunning procedures can't fight the forces of Satan and all his hordes.'

We worked late into the night and, by the time we'd finished, everything that went over to Aberystwyth was free from fragmented code, recursion bugs and any other kind of demonic visitation.

TWENTY-SIX

Looking for trouble

'Delauney,' I said, as we left the chapel early the next morning, 'where would you go to find forgotten knowledge at St Cadog's?'

I didn't usually go to their daily interfaith ceremonies but it had become normal for everyone to attend when something serious happened. And my sleepmeds hadn't been working too well lately; I was wide awake by 5am. Me and plenty of others, probably. It had been standing-room only today in the chapel, with all the conference delegates swelling our numbers. DI Driscoll had showed up as well and told me to expect her later that morning. Yet another interview. But Delauney said she'd interviewed him, Fish and Benedict yesterday, so maybe she wasn't singling me out.

'Forgotten knowledge?' Delauney asked. 'You mean what you dreamt Anghared told you?'

'I know. But I thought I should follow it up anyway.'

'Well, we've been all through Elaine's notebook. And the book she wrote with Benedict. Nothing more there.' Then he laughed, sharply, in that slightly bleak way everyone at St Cadog's laughed lately. 'Wouldn't have thought Anghared had such a twisted sense of humour, but there is something you could try.'

He'd just suggested a way I could follow Anghared's advice, when Naz caught up with us.

'What's the news?' Delauney asked him.

'We've fixed Gethsemane, rebuilt the firewalls and changed all the protocols and loaded it up on the Aberystwyth servers. Smike has looked at what Fish was talking about, the everyday breaches of people's comms. It's a milder form of the same thing. As if someone was … practising.'

'But did you manage to capture any of the virus code from Gethsemane?' I asked.

'Yes and no. What I've got is, putting it simply, more like a structural framework for code. With big empty spaces in it. What I need is to catch the virus in action so that I can find out what it actually is. Then I can write an anti-virus. Fascinating problem, analytically.'

We reached the refectory door, and after telling the others I'd catch up with them inside, I made a quick detour to try out my idea on the intelligent door while the quad was relatively quiet.

'You know I said we're going to track down Elaine's killer?' I asked it.

'And I wish you every success, Master Luminos. Can I be of any help?'

'Maybe. We're trying to find out if there's anyone Elaine was close to. Who she spent time with.'

'She often passed through with Professor Pleasance.'

'Nobody else?'

'Not regularly. Not recently.'

'Before that?'

'There was a period when she passed through with one of her students more regularly than anyone else. But not for some weeks.'

'Do you know their name?'

'Naturally.' It sounded offended. 'Owen Gryffydd.'

When I got to the canteen, Owen and Fish were sitting with Naz and Delauney, and Naz was telling them about the virus framework he'd captured and how he needed the virus to manifest again.

Despite the early hour, the place was packed with the conference delegates getting breakfast before they went over to Aberystwyth. I squeezed myself in next to Owen at the end of one of the long tables and looked at him thoughtfully. Had he known Elaine better than he'd let on? What was it Naz had said about College gossip? But if so, why keep quiet about it?

'What?' he asked.

I shook my head. I'd tackle him about it later.

'So,' Fish said. 'How do we get this virus to show up? So that Naz can catch it in action.'

'We go looking for it.' Owen said. 'We go looking for Cautras.'

The others looked blank.

'You mean in the stories, Owen?' I asked.

'I mean in the OtherWorld.'

'The OtherWorld's a completely failsafe system.' Naz looked

insulted. 'Even a virus this sophisticated wouldn't be able to penetrate it.'

'What else do we do?' Owen asked. 'Sit on our backsides and wait to be scared? Or attacked? Or killed?'

'It makes sense in terms of how the stories work,' I said. 'Hiding from your enemies never gets you anything but slaughtered. Usually in the night. And horribly.'

'This way we'll get slaughtered more nicely?' Naz asked.

'It was the five of us,' Fish said carefully, 'who experienced what I can only describe as a visitation. I know some of you are sceptical about that but it would be irreligious to deny that possibility.'

'And Cautras was a demon, for the people of Eirrod's time.' Delauney sounded a little reluctant.

'Maybe still is,' Owen said.

'Look,' said Naz, 'whether the source of the threat is human or AI or demonic; whether our call to action was created by code, by angels or by Ganesha himself; the fact remains that the virus won't manifest in the OtherWorld, so we can wonder round it all we like, looking for Cautras with no possibility of a result.'

'So there's no danger then,' I said.

'Where would we go, Lona?' Delauney asked. 'Which story?'

'Well I've still got a few more to translate. But so far? There's *The Fat Man of the Hill*, that's pretty dark. More than a hint of something more evil than usual in there. Or there's Dorath's death. Or undeath. You thought, Owen, that Cautras killed him and that fits pretty well.'

'And if Cautras killed him and then he's brought back to life, he becomes Cautras's helper,' Owen said, 'that's right isn't it, Lona?'

I nodded. 'He says in the story he has to go and serve the thing that killed him.'

'You mentioned Anghared said something to you about Cautras's helpers being conscripts, not volunteers,' Fish said. 'Remember, Lona? At Elaine's wake? And she said that they can be won back.'

'It makes sense,' I said. 'We could go and find Dorath, try to win him back, something like that. Rescue him.'

'Anghared does have an agenda, though,' Naz said. 'She wants the alternative narrative. She looked for Dorath for years after she brought him back to life, remember? But she never found him because he'd gone over to the dark side. She wants him to be rescued, more than anything. She's asked me about it explicitly in the last couple of days, whether it's something we can do. She can't help him because she's the one who cast the re-awakening spell in the first place. That's why she put the idea into your head, Lona.'

'Does it matter?' Delauney asked.

'It's just … I really don't like being played by a piece of my own software. However perfectly constructed.'

TWENTY-SEVEN

The realm of forgotten knowledge

F ish left us to our breakfasts and went to oversee the move to Aberystwyth. Owen finished his mountain of food and wanted us to go looking for Dorath straight away.

'Two people have died, you were nearly killed, Lona and now the murderer's invading our comms and taking over our Learning Garden. They're messing with our reality. And the OtherWorld's the only place we've got a chance to start fighting them. More people could die, there's no time to lose.'

But Fish would be tied up for a couple of hours, I had Driscoll to deal with, then Naz had a holomeeting with the Synthesis techs and Delauney was teaching.

'Teaching you, I believe, Owen,' he said, pointedly.

'People are dying,' Owen said.

But it needed at least five of us to go a trip, because we had to have three of us in the environment under the present circum-stances, and a minimum of two at the controls. One person couldn't be trusted anywhere and even two was risky. The agent could be any of us. And although Owen could get away with cutting a lecture, the rest of us were too high profile to suddenly disappear from our jobs. There'd be immediate repercussions that wouldn't help us with our hunt for Cautras.

'Can't you just pretend to be sick for a couple of hours?' Owen asked.

'Well, I can't, can I?' Naz said. 'And Fish wouldn't, so no.'

So we agreed to go in as soon we were all able to, and Delauney headed off to his office leaving Owen fidgety and restless.

'Owen, look, I've got half an hour before I have to see DI Driscoll, and there is something we can do. I've got some etchings to show you. Come to my rooms,' I said.

'I'm flattered, really I am, Lona, but River wouldn't like it.'

'Naz can be your chaperone.'

A couple of Naz's admirers were heading for the bench left free by Delauney, so he readily agreed to join us.

As Owen was admiring Sir Gawain's coat of arms on my living room wall and playing with the manual light controls, turning all the colours in the room to sickly shades of green, I retrieved Elaine's folder from its hiding place under my over-decorated sofa. At the same time I found the garish wooden bowl that I'd completely forgotten about.

'Isn't that Delauney's?' Naz said, when I put the thing on the coffee table.

'Probably. Tell that to Dodo.'

Dodo snatched the bowl up and then sat with it between his paws, looking pleased with himself. Owen laughed.

I shook my head and put the folder down where the bowl had been. 'No one's seen this but Benedict, who gave it to me. It's a bit weird, I wondered if you had any idea what it meant.'

Naz pulled a face when he saw Elaine's initials entwined with writhing snakes on the cover of the portfolio.

'Snakes. I'm phobic. Bad childhood memory.'

'Can't you get that – cured?' I asked.

'I could, but it's part of who I am.'

'Like Dodo nicking stuff?' Owen said.

'Infinitely more complex.' Naz tapped the folder. 'Are we going to open this thing, then?'

'Just one thing before we do. I had to really prise this out of Benedict's hands. He wanted to show it to the police. And Naz, what you said about Benedict inheriting Elaine's share of the royalties? I'm wondering if he should be higher on our list of suspects.'

'Benedict?' Owen said. 'That's bonkers, that is. I mean, I know the book was Elaine's work, mostly – it was based on her thesis – but Benedict had all the contacts and reputation and everything that made it successful. He was Elaine's mentor, he helped her make her name. He would never have hurt her.'

'It's a lot of money, Owen,' Naz said. 'And will be more now the stories are being published.'

'But Benedict's been gifting money to St Cadog's since the book took off,' Owen said. 'Loads of it. Endowed research projects. He'll do the same thing with Elaine's royalties I expect.'

'Was Elaine gifting money to St Cadog's?' Naz asked.

'No, she needed hers, she was only on a research assistant salary.'

'And St Cadog's is Benedict's baby. Especially the Early Welsh literature research,' I said. 'It's his life. So he still has a motive.'

I looked at my living room window and tried to imagine gentle Benedict pushing Elaine out of it. I shivered. It was an obscene thought.

'No way, Lona. Apart from anything else, he's probably not techie enough.' Owen shrugged off the idea and reached forward for the portfolio. 'Let's have a look at this, then?'

He turned over the cardboard cover. And stared at the face of his evil twin. His own face showed pain, regret.

'I didn't think she'd take it this bad.' He turned over another couple of pictures.

'Take what, Owen?' Naz asked.

'We fell out. She got weird about you, Naz, and about the OtherWorld and we argued about it. Just before we stopped her attacking you, that was. I didn't see her after that. Wish I had. I wish I'd been there to help her.'

'You were friends before that, though?' I asked.

'I grew up with her. Pryddych isn't a big place, she was only a few years older than me. Had a major crush on her when I was twelve, I did. We went to the same school, chapel, then St Cadog's. I mean she was … she kept separate from other people, liked to be on her own a lot, she'd always been like that. We weren't exactly friends. But she came to the matches sometimes.' His face was full of pain.

Naz put his hand on Owen's unbandaged arm.

'We became … a bit closer, earlier this year, before me and River got together. It wasn't serious, Elaine wasn't a relationship type person. She was more like a, a sprite or something. Other-worldly.'

'So that's why she saw you this way?' I asked. 'Because she liked you, you had a thing and then you argued?' The quad door was right then. So that was Owen's secret, the one I'd realised that he was keeping about Elaine.

'Doesn't seem enough, does it?' Owen closed the folder and looked straight at me.

'It does given the state her mind was in,' Naz said.

'Tell that to DI Driscoll next time she comes round looking for me,' Owen said. Something about his expression and body language told me he was still keeping something back, though.

'There's no need for the police to see this.' I stuffed the folder back under the sofa. 'And there's no need for them to know about you and Elaine. I'm guessing you didn't tell them.'

He shook his head.

'Is there anything more you know about Elaine?' I asked. 'Given that you were close at one time?'

But he just shook his head again.

'Did you say she had something against the OtherWorld. Naz's OtherWorld I mean?'

'No, she loved it, she was always coming on trips. That was why we had the wake there. It was just, once she decided that Naz was, well, you know. Possessed. That she thought the OtherWorld was haunted, too. Well, I mean, it is, obviously. But she meant in a bad way.'

'And that's kind of what we're hoping for, when we go in looking for Dorath this evening,' I said.

Naz looked disdainful. 'Elaine could be quite random in her accusations,' he said.

Owen and Naz had only been gone a moment before my door announced DI Driscoll. She came in and looked wearily round the extravagant Gawain-themed messiness of my living room.

'Long way from the farm squat you stayed in last time you were round here, Lona?'

'That was another time, Faye.'

'Over twenty years ago. You left on March 18th, 2051.'

'Something like that.'

'What made you leave?'

'Oh come on. Why would anyone choose to live in a farm squat?'

'Nothing to do with what happened at home the night before?'

I said nothing.

'Jonno Jenkins.'

Still, I waited.

'He was shot. At the farm where you lived. Your DNA was found at the scene.'

'Jonno was one of us, Faye. We were all in and out of each other's places. I used to take his dog out, had done since I was a kid. And he was my friend.' Easygoing, sleepy Jonno and his soppy Akita, Tesler. They were better than family.

She continued looking at me, from under her sandy lashes, with her calm, cynical gaze.

'You knew he was dead? Before you left?'

'I heard,' I said carefully, 'he killed himself.'

'Because he betrayed the chapter.'

'According to your dad, he did.'

Her face sagged a bit at the mention of her father, but she kept on.

'Where were you that night?'

'At home, with my sister and her partner. Look, don't you have enough suspicious deaths around here at the moment? You have to start reopening cold cases?'

'I'm following a link.'

'Uh?'

'You. You're the link. Why did you leave Wales then, Lona? You hadn't even finished school.'

'I didn't want that life. Like you didn't want to live like your family, your father.'

Her face crumpled a bit more. I'd have felt sorry for her if she hadn't been trying to pin a murder from two decades ago on me.

'I didn't want to keep losing people, Faye. And I didn't want to live with that kind of danger.'

'You're in danger now, though.'

'That's nothing to do with my background.'

'You sure about that, Lona?'

Spending a bit of time plugged into the stories was comforting compared to being threatened with arrest on a murder charge or having to go and look for a killer in the OtherWorld. I enjoyed it while it lasted. I'd told M about Faye Driscoll's obsession with my background in our morning call. M told me to stay away from the police, I was still a Zanegell to them. Which was true, but how do you stay away from someone who ambushes you every time you leave your workroom?

I managed to get out of the artefact centre without seeing her this time anyway, and headed over to the realm of forgotten knowledge Delauney had suggested, before I met up with the others.

A small back room, up some winding stairs off the busy hum of the main library. I'd expected somewhere dark, dusty and neglected but instead it was a clean, bright space with printed volumes ranged in orderly fashion on shiny metal shelving. But I was the only one in there and I got the feeling that no one had bothered these shelves for a long time. I looked along the volumes until I found the Bs. And here we were. Bowen. E. PhD 2069. I pulled the hardback thesis away from its companions and took it over to a nearby desk. *Narrative and Religious Practice in Wales, 43–500.*

It was disturbingly quiet sitting there amid all the volumes of unread wisdom. I could feel the other theses holding their breath and watching their lucky companion whose hidden knowledge was going to be brought into the light. I looked down at Elaine's thesis. That she'd poured herself into day after day, week after week, year after year. This was more her than anything. I touched the cover.

'We want to get them, Elaine,' I whispered. 'For you. For me. For all of us. Help us, tell us what you know.'

I scanned the link on the cover and brought up the digital copy on my visual screen. I had a quick look at the acknowledgements, which thanked her supervisor, Benedict; her two sponsors, the Methodist Synod and Braynes Health Drinks; and God. Nobody close to her who'd offered support. Then I searched for Mithras. Ninety-seven instances, too much. I tried Cautras. Only six of these. I got stuck in.

Half an hour later, Elaine's work had given me what I wanted. More than I wanted, in fact. Before I left, I called up some illegal software and, muttering a quick apology to Elaine, I deleted a couple of words from a footnote in her thesis. Then I carefully used the software to cover my tracks. The print version I consigned, intact, back to its shelf and oblivion.

BACK IN MY ROOMS, I HAD A FEW MINUTES BEFORE I WAS DUE TO meet the others to look for Dorath. I knew I should sit and rest, my vBots were still on the case and they needed all the help they could get to do their repair job. But I couldn't sit still. That unwanted bit of information from Elaine was too unsettling and I went over and over it as I paced restlessly up and down, Dodo following me. Was that why Elaine had wanted to talk to me, specifically? It didn't necessarily mean anything, but if it did? I just didn't want to be that personally involved. I didn't want DI Driscoll to be right. This was just meant to be another assignment for me.

I was going to keep my new knowledge to myself, anyway. I threw myself onto the sofa and called up something to read to calm myself. My mood monitor suggested that people who felt like me had enjoyed a book called *Frankenstein, the Modern Prometheus*.

You will rejoice to hear that no disaster has accompanied the commencement of an enterprise which you have regarded with such evil forebodings.

I read.

The soup she ate is made of the child's bones, the laverbread is made from his hair, and the pie contains his flesh.

This couldn't be right. It was a different story, breaking through. One of the tales from the Pryddych Cycle, in fact. I flicked through.

It was all of the tales. In the original language. This was wrong, even though the translations were being published on the nets I wasn't supposed to be able to access the originals from anywhere except the artefact centre. Given what the Cycle was worth, this was potentially very sticky for me, industrial theft, in fact. And why were they breaking through other outerbody texts? I checked their origin.

The file wasn't there, in my outerbody. Which could mean only one thing.

It was in my innerbody.

It had become part of me.

Naz: A Journal of Unnatural Thoughts

Wednesday 28 Oct 2071

11.30am

So today we're going chasing Cautras in the OtherWorld. I can't say I see the sense of it, but I've no other ideas. And, unlike the situation outworld, there shouldn't be any risk. But then with some kind of supernatural, human-controlling, tech-invading murderer on the loose, who knows?

Anyway, the inquest on Ed Pillington's death just pronounced. Open verdict. BubULike gave evidence that their Bub failed due to external interference, not internal malfunction. In other words, sabotage.

As Owen was quick to point out, they would say, that, wouldn't they? Otherwise one would ever travel in one of their TransBubs again.

And a sophisticated bit of sabotage like that? Bit high-level for Pagans. Though I'm not sure about Kite. If he learned his tech sabotage skills in the army and then carried on developing them as a hacker, he'd be more than capable. Anyhow, the police won't say whether it's accident or sabotage. They've not been able to find out how the on-board system was breached or why the emergency backup system didn't kick in. Bloody amateurs.

But I couldn't tell them there was evidence pointing to sabotage in Dodo's logs, because they'd want to examine him. And we can't have that.

And. There's more. The tests I've been running on the Other-World, to find out if there's anything there that might have created the nightmare the five of us had, has returned a big fat negative. Nothing there to disturb our dreams. My security is intact.

They'd better get their implants checked out, then. Although, that doesn't account for my nightmare. But it's the first one I've ever had, so to be honest I feel quite fond of it.

TWENTY-EIGHT

Poison

'W hat did the police have to say, then, Lona?' Owen asked. We were in Naz's lab, waiting for Delauney to join us for the OtherWorld trip.

'Faye Driscoll just wanted to rake up the past,' I replied.

'Is it related to our current problems?' Fish asked.

'Nope, she just hasn't got any leads and she's desperate.'

'Typical.' Owen shook his head in disbelief and was about to say more when Delauney arrived. Fish looked pointedly at his watch and Delauney ignored him.

'Find anything in Elaine's thesis, Lona?' he asked.

'Two things; one about Cautras's birth, one about his death. The birth one's probably not that important.'

'Tell us anyway,' Delauney said.

'The flesh and blood Cautras, Lucius Proculus, was brought up in a Roman military household, his father's house. His mother had been a servant in the household, so almost certainly native. She abandoned him on the doorstep so he was probably a product of rape.'

'He sided with the powerful violent father?' Naz said. 'Classic sadist psychology.'

'That'd be why he hated Celts so much, then,' Owen said. 'If his mother abandoned him.'

'She might have thought she was giving him a better start in life,' Fish said.

'Shame he didn't see it that way, Fish,' Delauney said.

'Anyway, not sure any of that helps us much, but this might be more use. His death was by poisoning – aconitum in his wine.'

'Interesting,' Delauney said. 'Any idea who put it there?'

'He had a daughter, Livia, and was arranging her marriage to a wealthy man, twenty years her senior, when he was poisoned. She immediately married a centurion who was a popular gladiator. So she was everyone's prime suspect.'

'Fascinating, Lona,' Fish said. 'Though I'm not quite clear what practical use we can make of this.'

'We feed it back into the OtherWorld,' Owen's eyes were bright with excitement. 'It's our enemy's weak point. That's always an advantage.'

'There's more,' I said. 'Because of the suspicions about Livia, some of the mythology around Cautras involves the belief that his offspring are a threat to him. To Cautras the god, that is. So his disciples did a fairly comprehensive job of wiping his descendants out.'

'Hmm. Well feed it back into the OtherWorld, Naz,' Delauney said. 'It might affect the narrative to our advantage. We need all the help we can get.'

'Yep,' I said, 'can't miss the opportunity to get a gladiator-shagging, patricidal poisoner on our side.' Naz looked amused, but the others gave me funny looks.

Fish said, 'Shall we go, then?'

Followed by a reluctant Naz, who lingered to issue last-minute instructions to Delauney and Owen about the code capture, Dodo, Fish and I made our way into the wardrobe.

The Pryddych Cycle III: The Tale of the Seven Sisters

When the youth called Anwhyn returned to King Eirrod's court he brought with him a prophecy. It said Eirrod would defeat the invaders and reclaim the Land, with Anwhyn's aid. Many distrusted Anwhyn, at first. He was a man who had travelled through many lands and had seen many things. He had grown wise and wily in these adventures. The people of Eirrod's court begged him to tell them of his travels and this is what he said:

'I travelled through a land of people who had but one eye each, in the middle of their heads and who each had four arms. They were called the Mahmuds. Fierce people are the Mahmuds, and brave in battle. The beasts of their country, though they have no wings, swim through the air, as though they are fish and the air the sea. The Mahmuds harness them to chariots and ride through the skies.

'Beyond the land of the Mahmuds is the country of Imishia. When I came to this land the people all walked upside down, on their hands. I asked them why and they said:

' "We are cursed for seven summers by the Seven Enchantresses of Flarrg. Great are the riches we would bestow upon anyone who could lift this curse. Many have tried and failed, at the Castle of the Enchantresses."

'I took the challenge and the road to Flarrg, with the good wishes of the upside-down Imishi. I rode for many days through gloomy conifer forests. Little light penetrated these woods, which were all the time as night. No birdsong was there, but the dismal hooting of owls; and instead of bees and butterflies, bats and moths flitted silently through the fir trees.

'The Castle of the Enchantresses stood on a hill in the middle of the thick, dark woods. It was surrounded by a dense, thorny barrier of briars which grew over the castle walls. The briars had large blood-red flowers. As I walked up the path to the castle door I drew my sword to hack my way through the dense foliage. But the briars parted to let me through. On either side of the door were the severed heads of men, impaled on huge thorns. "Turn back!" they whispered. But I went on through the great oak doors which creaked open as I approached and shut behind me with a great clang, as soon as I was over the threshold.

'The door opened onto the foot of a dimly lit stone staircase, which I climbed and found myself in a chamber. In front of me was a stone table and sitting on the table, dressed all in red, was a goblin.

' "Why do you come to the castle of the Seven Sisters, human man?" asked the goblin. "But yet – you are not quite human, are you?"

' "I come as an emissary from the people of Ishimia. I wish to speak with the Enchantresses. I am Anwhyn, son of the stone and soil of Pryddych and I am more human than you, my goblin friend!"

'The goblin laughed. There was nothing kindly in his laugh.

' "Come, my fine, young Celt, I have a question for you. Answer it well and you may pass through the doorway and have the audience you seek with the Seven Sisters. Answer wrongly and your head will decorate the briars of this castle, like a flower. Tell me, Anwhyn, born of the stones of Britain: which can fly the farther, a dragon, a witch or an owl?"

'The goblin's question was subtle. But the blood of Pryddych can be subtle too. "A witch may ride on the back of a dragon." I said. "And an owl may ride on the shoulder of a witch. When the dragon tires the witch flies on and when the witch tires, the owl flies on. So the owl can fly the farthest, gatekeeper."

'The goblin took off his hat and made a mock bow.

' "Anwhyn, Prince of the Stones, you may pass through the doorway."

'I walked through the door and beheld the Seven Enchantresses sitting on seven stone thrones, all in a row. Their thrones were ornately carved with images of flowers, birds and beasts. The birds were birds of prey, the beasts fearsome and the flowers looked like those that drank blood, not water. Each of the sisters was more beautiful and stately than the next and all were dressed in crimson silks and velvets and wore jewellery of rubies and gold.

'The sister who sat in the far throne, Paladia, asked me why I had come and I told her of the task given me by the Ishimi. All the sorceresses stared at me intently. They smiled and spoke low together and then Paladia said "Anwhyn, Prince of Stones, we will grant your wish on one condition. You must first serve us for a year and a day in our castle. You must never question us and always do our bidding. If you break these rules, you will die."

'And so I became a courtier to the Seven Sisters of Flarrg. Their orders were sometimes strange and hard for me to comprehend, but I remembered this was a magical place, where traps were being set for me all the time, and I kept to the road I had set out on. The Sisters were wilful and sometimes cruel, but I wished to remain alive and win the fortune I had been promised by the Ishimi. And I also began to covet the knowledge the sisters possessed. This they realised, and once I had proved myself worthy, they began to adopt me as their pupil. This secret knowledge came at a price. The Sisters would play games with me for their amusement, half loving and half challenging; always, I took up their challenges and learned much from them of the ways of women and men, of enchantment and desire. They taught me how to take other forms than this, so I might go about as a wolf or a hawk. They taught me how to cast shadows in the eyes of my enemies, so they knew not what they saw.

I learned about the power of dreaming, the strength of man's desires, the bottomless depth of his fears – and how to marshal these into my service. And I learned wit and wisdom, as well as Otherworldly powers. Though they were formidable mistresses, I learned to love and respect the Seven Sisters and became a man under their tutelage. It was with sadness that, after a year and a day, I had to leave them. They gave me this torque, which I wear always.'

Anwhyn's torque was a thick rope of gold around his brown neck. The torque ended in two snarling wolf heads whose eyes were rubies and these golden heads turned and looked at Eirrod's court.

TWENTY-NINE

The revenant Dorath

We were in a dimly lit cave. The walls glistened dark green; the only noise was the sound of dripping water. We stood still, looking round apprehensively. We knew we couldn't get killed here, not like in the real world, but it was still creepy. And we were here trying to get to the murderer's master, through another one of his servants. Not the way Inspector Tapp went about things in Owen's beloved Exmoor mysteries, but then she was fictional, so her murder cases were simpler.

'What happens next?' asked Fish. The smartmeds he'd needed to be sharp this evening, after travelling halfway across Wales and back, were making him a bit jumpy. Fish wasn't normally a medder, but everyone at St Cadog's was at it at the moment. Our loss was Elation's gain.

'Something nasty emerges from the shadows and asks us impossible questions or picks a fight,' said Naz.

NAZ HAD BEEN LESS THAN ENTHUSIASTIC ABOUT JOINING OUR AWAY team.

'But you're immortal, Naz,' Delauney had said, when we were agreeing who should come on the trip and who should stay at the controls and make sure anything untoward was captured.

'My personality circuits aren't,' Naz said, 'they're unique. They'd have to be replaced with different ones if they got damaged.'

'Okay, but the rest of you's immortal,' Delauney persisted.

'So is the Pyramid of Giza but just because you can rebuild it doesn't mean you'd risk demolishing it,' Naz said.

'I'll bring Dodo,' I said, 'We'll be okay.'

'Your spell making's brilliant, mun,' Owen said. 'And you can do that false reality thing.' Naz, the ultimate OtherWorld sorcerer, had a power that enabled him to influence people's perceptions. Effectively, he could create a distorted reality for a limited time. It was the opposite of Kite's truth revealing sorcerer power and they'd had some bizarre duels. Bizarre for those of us whose realities were being warped or exposed, at any rate.

So Naz reluctantly agreed to join us.

'I could come, too, and—' Owen began

'Nooo!' Fish, Delauney and I said in unison. 'Not with your arm still in sling, Owen,' Fish added.

'You're fast on the controls, Owen, even with one hand,' Delauney said. 'We could use you here.'

'And two of you on the controls means I'm free to go in and help out with the riddles,' Fish said.

In the cave, Dodo saw the movement first and our eyes followed his alert gaze. A tall shape, in green robes, drifted across the far end of the cave and disappeared down a passageway. We followed.

Naz and I had picked a cave in the mountains as the best place to find Dorath. It was tricky, because we wanted to find him after Anghared had brought him back to life, not before, and there wasn't a story about that. So we'd chosen that setting and Naz had dialled up a timescale after the second part of *The Lady of the Silver Pool* and specifically asked to meet Dorath. Which would almost certainly work but we didn't exactly know what would happen after that.

As we tracked Dorath – or Cautras's servant as he now was, if Owen was right – down the passage hewn into the rock, I couldn't help but wish I had Owen with me, despite Elaine's pictures. I would have appreciated his fighting spirit down there in the slimy, dark tunnel.

The passage broadened out into a low cave with a stone well in the middle. The Green Wizard swirled round to face us, sending a draft of icy air in our direction.

'You've come to try my mettle, outworlders?' he asked, in a quiet voice.

'We've come to rescue you, Dorath,' I said.

He stared at us blankly and shook his head.

'Rescue?' he said, as if he had long forgotten the meaning of the word.

Then he walked towards the well, turned to look at us and stepped into it as calmly as if it were an elevator and disappeared.

'We follow?' asked Fish.

'We follow,' I said. Naz muttered something under his breath.

I walked towards the well, called Dodo to heel, took a deep breath and stepped in.

The water was clear and green. But not cold. And I could breathe. With Dodo paddling away at my side and Naz and Fish close behind, I swam towards Dorath, whom I could just about make out ahead. There were long green fronds of underwater plants waving below, and to one side I caught glimpses of the merpeople.

We swam on through the silent world until Dorath stopped swimming and started climbing up something ahead of me. A ladder, I discovered as I kicked towards it. I cursed inwardly, realising that Dodo wouldn't be able to come with us. Touched him I said, 'Dodo: *Jabberwocky*.'

Naz grimaced as my safeword sent Dodo back outworld. Where he would now be sitting at the side of the huge OtherWorld studio, watching us behave weirdly but unable to help us fight invisible demons.

Feeling alone and vulnerable without Dodo, I hauled myself up the ladder which led vertically into a circular stone shaft. We emerged from the water, scrambled a little further up the rungs, and came out in a cellar, at the entrance of another well.

Something about the sweet unwholesomeness of the air in the cellar told me where we were. Well, that and the sconces on the wall made of knights' hands, still in their armour. Fish and Naz emerged from the well, both perfectly dry and looked around.

'This is *The Tale of the Seven Sisters*,' I said.

'The lair of the sorceresses of Flarrg?' Naz said. 'Pity we didn't bring Anwhyn.'

'We don't need him Naz, when we've got a pretty boy like you,' I said.

'Oh, please.' Naz pulled a face.

Dorath was disappearing out of the cellar door, so we hurried to follow him; down a dark hallway he went, then up two flights of winding stairs into a bedchamber. There, in a great four-poster bed, the seventh sister, Lilith, lay sleeping, her golden curls tumbled over the purple silk pillow. Dorath stopped still and stared at her as she lay under crimson velvet covers, her hands folded on her breast. He raised his hands slightly and streams of darkness welled out from the tip of each finger. He raised them further. A bowl of roses next to Lilith's bed wilted as the dark beam reached them. He directed the streams of darkness towards Lilith and she stirred in her sleep as the rays reached her, the darkness began to surround her, like an aura and she grew gradually less distinct, as though the cloud around her were sucking vitality out of her.

'Should we stop him?' Fish whispered to us.

Before we could answer, a crash sounded behind us, as the door was thrown open. We turned to see the oldest sister, the sorceress Paladia standing on the threshold.

She opened her red mouth wide in a scream so intense that the castle walls shook and my head flashed with intense pain. Fish and Naz were both pressing their hands to their temples too, but Dorath just stood there, his hands lowered, looking at Paladia with his blank stare. The cloud disappeared from around Lilith. The scream stopped.

'You come on Cautras's business, you foul, dead creature, to seek revenge on us? You, who we once revered when you were Dorath?' Paladia stepped into the room. 'Don't think our respect for what you once were will make us lenient with your punishment.'

'Of you or your companions,' said a bell-like voice from behind us. I looked round to see Lilith rising languidly from her bed. She walked towards us.

'Oh, we're not with him.' Naz attempted a charming smile. 'We're um, just, ah—'

'Observers,' Fish offered.

'Observers, yes,' Naz said.

Lilith circled Naz slowly, looking at him greedily.

'Our fine young friend is an observer, Paladia,' she said. 'You like to watch, do you, my little intruder?' She touched his cheek, delicately, with one long, crimson-tipped finger.

'Let's deal with Dorath first, Lilith,' Paladia said.

Lilith smiled hungrily at Naz and reluctantly turned her gaze to Dorath.

'We can't kill that which is already dead, sister,' she said.

'He'd be happy if we did so,' Paladia replied. 'We must find another punishment.'

'Even the walking dead feel physical pain,' Lilith gave a slow, sweet smile. 'And Rosa would be pleased to see just how much – and for how long – an Undead can take. It might be eternity.'

'Taking away his powers will cause him the most pain,' said Paladia. 'Tell Rosa to save that for last when you take him down to her.'

'Paladia,' I said, as Lilith moved towards the old man. 'Paladia, Lilith, we wish to challenge you. If we win, we'll take Dorath away with us.'

'And if you lose?' Paladia asked.

'Him.' Lilith, gestured imperiously at Naz. She thought for a little, then said, 'And him. The prim one.'

Naz and Fish looked a bit ill.

'Agreed,' I said. 'We challenge you.'

Paladia inclined her head in acceptance. I tried to influence the narrative so that they would leave Dorath with us until we'd finished the challenge. I managed to get Lilith to lead the somnambulant Dorath over to a corner of the room, where she parked him on a chair. But it was ten times harder than normal. Something wasn't right. I looked speakingly at Naz and could see he was trying to do his perceptual spell.

'Sister, take the revenant to Rosa now,' Paladia said. 'She can begin her magic while I put his friends to the test. It will help to concentrate their minds.'

Lilith turned to us, her chin up, her narrowed eyes watching Naz and Fish. I concentrated my mind on her and could see Naz was doing the same. It felt like wading through mud.

'Sister?' Paladia said.

Lilith's eyes had gone blank, confused.

'Take him down,' Paladia repeated.

Her eyes fixed on Naz and Fish, Lilith escorted Dorath out of the room. We'd failed. Something wasn't right. I felt a sense of panic grow inside my ribcage. My hands started shaking. I tried to steady my breath, concentrate on the story.

'Here is my question to you,' Paladia said. 'An innocent young man is captured by the ravening Sea Goddess and taken to her dark palace among the forests of the ocean. She tells him he will have a chance to gain his freedom. She will put two stones from the sea bed, one blue and one green, into a bag. If he draws a blue stone he will be free to go; if he draws a green one he must stay with her as her slave.

'But the young man sees this Merqueen's scaly hand slip two green stones into the bag. He cannot expose her in front of her court, or she will kill him, in anger.

'You must find a way for our young man to gain his freedom, if you wish to stop my sister, Rosa, playing her games with Dorath. With the thing that was Dorath.'

With that, Paladia swept out of the room. Naz and I both looked at Fish.

He rubbed his forehead. 'Give me a minute, give me a minute.'

'We can't let Rosa destroy Dorath,' I said, 'Or we'll lose our only clue.'

'As well as the not wanting him to be tortured issue,' said Naz.

'I – took that as read,' I said. 'There'll be hell to pay with Anghared, too if we don't save him. I mean we can't necessarily guarantee we'll get a second chance, can we? And Naz, what's going on with the influencing spells? Mine didn't work properly.'

'No, nor mine, it was sluggish. I'll have to look at the settings when we get back, increase the ratio of user influence to narrative drive. We're constantly tinkering with that at the moment, it's a subtle balance.'

'Blue stone free, green stone slavery,' Fish muttered.

'Much like our situation,' Naz said.

'Maybe you two could try helping me?' A sheen of sweat was

visible on Fish's forehead. 'That poor man's being tortured by that creature with every second we waste.'

'Sorry, Fish,' I said. But was Dorath actually being tortured? Because nothing was really happening if we didn't see it, was it? Even though it felt like it was. We were being emotionally manipulated, that's how this sort of synthetic reality worked. But I didn't say that to Fish, everyone was edgy, lately, it was the new normal, and lots of people seemed hyper-emotional to me, including Owen and Delauney. Though not Fish – not usually, anyway.

'Maybe he could pick up a blue one from the seabed?' I suggested. 'And pretend he got it out of the bag?'

'Picking a blue pebble and passing it off as the one from the bag might be the sort of thing the onlookers are a little alert to, under the circumstances,' Naz said.

'Mmm, no it's not as stupid as it sounds, though,' Fish said.

'Thanks,' I said.

'No, I mean he has to do some sleight of hand, somehow. A bit like you suggested. But something that reveals that the green pebble is in the bag, so by deduction, the pebble he got out of the bag must be blue,' Fish said.

'That makes a kind of twisted sense,' I said.

'Only he can't show it. The blue pebble he's supposed to have in his hand, that is,' Fish went on.

'Because he hasn't really got one,' I said.

'Exactly. So he has to make the Sea Monster show him a green pebble from the bag.'

'Sea Goddess,' I said.

'Not from where we're standing,' Naz said.

'But why can't he show the blue pebble?' mused Fish. 'Why can't he?'

'We can always bail out if it goes wrong,' Naz said.

'Naz,' said Fish. 'Dorath is being put through agony.'

'Sorry, Fish,' Naz said. 'You were wondering what excuse the young man could have for not having the blue pebble.'

'What excuse can he have – for losing it. Of course.'

'Of course?' I asked.

'He loses it,' Fish said.

'He does?' I said.

'That's the answer.' Fish was triumphant. 'He loses the blue pebble.'

'Ah,' said Naz.

'Paladia,' Fish called out, 'We have the solution to your riddle.'

Paladia and Lilith materialised in front of us.

'The young man takes a stone from the bag, fumbles it and drops it on the seabed,' Fish said. 'So he asks the Sea Goddess to show the one in the bag. Which he knows to be green, as he saw her put two green pebbles in the bag in the first place. But it implies to her court that he took a blue pebble. And so the young man gains his freedom. As do we. As does Dorath.'

'How clever,' said Lilith, clapping her hands in delight. 'I do like the clever ones.'

'That's very sad for you,' Naz said. 'Now, if we can have Dorath back, we'll be on our way.'

The two sisters stood there silently. Lilith's red lips curled into a lazy smile.

'You are going to let us go, aren't you?' Fish said. 'I mean, you have to. You have to abide by the rules of the stories.'

'You're quite right,' Paladia replied. 'We do. Normally. But lately – lately we've felt a degree of freedom.'

'So you're going to renege on the rules of our challenge, Paladia?' I said. 'Not a very noble act for a sorceress of your standing.'

'So refreshing being able to act ignobly,' Lilith giggled. 'Much more fun.' She put one bare white arm round Naz, the other around Fish. I concentrated hard to change the outcome. Make Lilith stay.

'I definitely think we should bail now,' said Naz.

'Oh, okay then,' I said.

'*Doppelganger*,' called Naz.

Nothing happened.

Fish tried his safeword.

'*Resurrection*.'

No change.

'Shit,' said Naz. I could tell by his eye movements and slight hand gestures he was trying the administrator rights on his comms.

Still nothing happened.

'Owen, Delauney, get us out of this,' I shouted.

Nothing.

'You're not thinking of leaving us just yet, my darling,' Lilith said to Naz, caressing his shoulder. 'That would be so hurtful.' She shepherded them both to the door and led them through. Fish looked round at me, helplessly. I ran to the door, tried again to alter the narrative, to make Lilith return. I was sure that Naz was trying his perceptual spell. But they disappeared down the long stone corridor with the sorceress. And just because I couldn't see *them* didn't mean they weren't being tortured. In some way. For a long moment I stared at the empty, silent corridor as cold and fear washed over me.

A sound of voices came from the room behind me. Alert for more trickery, I spun round to see – Anwhyn.

'I can't disappoint Lilith, my dear,' Paladia was saying. 'Dorath's attack on her has left her depleted, she needs energising.'

'I'm sure we can find another way, my lady.' Anwhyn smiled, wolfishly. 'And the outlanders are under the protection of my sister; it would be a shame if your friendship with her was damaged just to serve Lady Lilith's pleasure.'

'Anghared?' Paladia looked less than pleased.

'What's more, with this new relaxation of the rules, Lady Paladia, none of us know what Cautras can do now,' he went on. 'Not I, not Anghared. Not you even, my lady.'

Paladia considered this for a moment.

'That may be true, Anwhyn. But Rosa already has his servant and he was not strong. It may be a little late.'

With an irritated glance in my direction, she left the room.

'Am I glad to see you, Anwhyn.' I could hear the desperation in my voice. 'This is terrible.'

'The sisters are not easy company.'

'I mean we're trapped here. And our spells aren't working.' I tried to sound calm. I failed.

'Many have been trapped in the Castle of Flarrg. The sisters have powerful magic to disarm visitors,' Anwhyn said.

'No, no, the world we've created isn't behaving normally. According to the rules. It happened yesterday, as well. In a different world.'

'Evil disrupts.'

'That's what this is, isn't it? Cautras. Or his agent.'

'All five of you, together, have begun to defeat him. Keep faith.'

Easy for him to say. He couldn't die, he wasn't alive.

Paladia came in, carrying a metal box. 'Rosa's experiments on the undead did not meet with great success. He disintegrated. What remains is in this casket.'

She handed it to me. It was cold and heavy in my arms. Disintegrated. I was holding some sort of coffin.

'My friends?' I managed to croak.

'Are free to go now. As are you.'

'Delauney, Owen – pull Naz and Fish out of here,' I yelled.

After a couple of seconds we heard a howl of frustration echoing down the corridor.

'*Jabberwocky*!' I shouted.

'You're welcome,' said Anwhyn.

THIRTY

Narratively risky

Matter replication is a technology in its infancy and is unlikely to be a cause of concern to operatives. To date, replicators can synthesise simple inanimate objects. The current technology is not yet able to create flesh from wafer or blood from wine but any attempt to do so constitutes a perversion of the Christian sacrament and a faith crime. The replication of loaves and (lab-grown) fishes, however, is viewed as Christian charity and so is not illegal unless carried out in a manner that mocks at biblical miracles.

Alliance Field Manual, Chapter 15: Verse 3

'Can't we just open it?' Owen asked.

A few minutes after I left the castle, I was with him and Delauney back in Naz's office, staring at the casket. It was fashioned from lead, studded with what looked like emeralds and zircons, and inlaid with jade. When the Castle of Flarrg had disappeared from around me and the blank expanse of the Other-

World studio reappeared, I found this box was still in my arms when I sank, relieved, onto the floor, and Dodo came over to check on me.

'We have no idea what it is,' said Delauney. 'I mean quite literally. We're assuming it's matter replication, which the OtherWorld has some capacity to do, when that function's switched on and specified. But as far as we know, it wasn't. Not by us, anyway.'

'Oh, come on, we know it's what's left of Dorath,' Owen said. 'Paladia said. And you three saved him, Lona, sort of, so it's your prize. It has to be benign.'

'Not necessarily, Owen.' Nothing about that interchange with Paladia had felt benign to me. 'Opening boxes is always a risky business, narratively, I mean, think of Pandora. Even within the normal rules of our stories it could be Cautras's revenge disguised as our victor's prize. Or even a hostile intervention from the Sisters.'

'And we don't want any more of that,' Delauney said. Naz was currently undergoing intensive mental health checks and psychotherapeutic reorientation in his medlab. He hadn't even stopped to look at the box or the code Delauney and Owen had captured. Fish had gone straight to chapel and, as far as we knew, was still there.

'Isn't there any way we can get in touch with Anwhyn and Anghared?' Delauney sat back in his chair. 'This comes from their world and it was Anwhyn who sorted things out with Paladia. Maybe they could give us a pointer.'

But none of us knew how to summon them up on screen without Naz's wizardry.

'We'd have to go on an OtherWorld trip to talk to them.' The last place I wanted to be. 'But it's not safe there. And anyway I don't think Anghared's going to be too pleased with us. We were supposed to save Dorath.'

'I could go in and talk to Anwhyn,' said Delauney.

We looked at him in surprise.

'Well, in a safer place than the Castle of Flarrg, naturally. I'm not going round looking for any battles, I just want to have a conversation with a friendly character on their home territory. Anghared's cave would be good, he's often there. That's not so risky, surely?'

'Just being in the OtherWorld's risky at the moment.' I couldn't understand what Delauney was up to. 'Maybe we should wait for Naz.'

'It could be hours until Naz is back to normal,' Owen protested. 'Anything could happen by then.'

OWEN AND I SAT AT THE CONTROLS, WITH DODO IN BETWEEN US, and watched Delauney on the screen as he entered the cave.

'Hope Mam appreciates this,' Owen said.

'Uh?'

'He's trying to prove himself, isn't he?' Owen said. 'Prove he's man enough.'

'Right. I see. Because Fish…'

'Exactly. And he's trying to prove to her he's not Cautras's agent.'

'But if he is, he won't be in any danger,' I reasoned.

'He will be if Anwhyn catches him,' Owen said.

Delauney took a seat next to Anwhyn, who sat, staring into a fire.

'Your friends have recovered their composure?' Anwhyn poured wine into two ornate metal goblets, handing one to Delauney.

'They're recovering.'

Anwhyn nodded. 'The Sisters are formidable.'

'They found them so. They asked me to relay their thanks to you.'

Anwhyn inclined his head.

'That would be Delauney being a rhetorician,' I said to Owen. He snorted. Naz and Fish had been barely able to speak when they emerged from the castle into the OtherWorld studio.

'Anwhyn, I've come here to ask you about the casket that Paladia gave Lona. It contains Dorath's remains, Paladia said. We want to know if it's safe to open it.'

'Your science can't help you?'

'Our science will provide us with clues. But you have knowledge and experience of this sort of thing and we don't.'

Anwhyn thought for a moment.

'The contents of the casket may be both gift and trap. It depends how you use it. What you have is the essence of Dorath. He was once immensely powerful, and his essence will also be powerful. Look.'

Anwhyn gestured over towards our direction and then both Delauney and Anwhyn were staring right at us, out of the screen. Owen and I looked at each other, then realised that someone was standing behind us.

Anghared looked out of place in her swirling, silver robes amongst the chrome, glass and 'tronic gadgetry of Naz's office, but, at the same time, bizarrely at home. She stared around at the equipment approvingly and with curiosity.

'You have many interesting machines in your world.' She came over to look at the screen, where Anwhyn and Delauney were sitting by the fire. 'And this is your Silver Pool, where you watch what is going on elsewhere. Does it also see into the past and future?'

'Just the past.' Owen looked as bewildered as I felt. Only Dodo seemed to be behaving as if Anghared being here was normal.

'A pity.' Anghared looked thoughtful.

'I'm sorry, Anghared,' I said, 'We did our best to rescue Dorath,'

'That tale is not yet closed.' She indicated the casket. Its green stones glittered. Owen looked at her questioningly and she nodded. 'You must decide, prince.'

Without hesitation, Owen opened it. Inside, throbbing silently against the dull grey background, was a heart. It looked like a human heart, except that it lit up with each throb. And that it was green. And that it was still beating. Owen took it out of the box and held it in both hands.

'It feels like a real heart.' He stared at it, in wonder. 'Cold, though. But like it's alive.'

The two figures in the monitor continued to stare into the screen as if they could see us in the room.

'Within the heart of my master, Dorath, lies its secret. The secret that will help you to overpower Cautras. But you must be careful that it does not overpower you.' Quietly, she recited a rhyme.

Three talismans for a new Pryddych
Green as grass and tree
A beating heart plucked from darkness, first victory;
Our guardian of old magic, petrified history;
A new friend and pray, from an old country;
Capture future with past
And complete the Prince's story.

Then she disappeared from the lab and reappeared on the screen, next to Delauney and Anwhyn. They all faded away, and a minute later Delauney ran in.

'What was that? We could see you through a ... a kind of metal mirror. And Anghared. How did she get here? What was she?' he said.

'A holo,' said Owen. 'I think.'

'Everything's going haywire.' I shook my head 'The Other-World's just making up the rules as it goes along. It's like the characters are taking over.'

'Yeah, random holos, matter replication, screens popping up inside the OtherWorld,' Delauney agreed. 'We need Naz back.'

Owen carefully place the heart back in the casket.

'It must be a machine of some sort.' I stared at the thing as it sat there, throbbing, alien and creepy. 'Something's making it move and light up. Code.'

'And, if it's connected with Cautras, the helper, whatever, then the virus is in it.' Delauney snapped the box shut.

'Mmm, gift and trap.' The casket's green stones glittered back at me as I stared at it. Dorath's coffin. 'An infected computer. But in a lead casket, so it shouldn't be able to make contact with anything else. Probably.'

'Hmm, which one's Naz's office safe drawer?' Delauney opened a drawer in Naz's desk which was empty and lined with some kind of metal. Depositing the casket inside, he closed it and pressed the lock button. No one could open it now, except Naz.

THIRTY-ONE

Monstrous code

The next morning I made an attempt to tell M what was going on. In a censored way. I was pretty bleary after being awake half the night with Delauney and Owen, hopped up on smartmeds, trying to make sense of Anghared's rhyme. We hadn't got very far without Fish. Neither he nor Naz had been seen since they'd left the OtherWorld yesterday. Anyway, after telling M it hadn't gone well, M had said either I was losing it or St Cadog's was, but either way I should go home. This working holiday just wasn't working.

I wasn't going anywhere, of course. It was still very early, but I swung by Naz's lab. Smike was the only one in the outer lab, eating breakfast out of a paper bag at his desk.

'He's a bit more nervy than usual this morning.' Smike swallowed a mouthful of coffee. 'Mind you, he's been working all night. All this virus stuff must be getting to him. Fish too – he's with him. Like cats on crack, they are, the pair of them.'

I went through to Naz's office, where he was running diagnostic tests on the OtherWorld to find evidence of what had, actually, happened, and analysing the electronic heart to see whether it could help us. Delauney had left a message on Naz's comms about the heart and where to find it. It sat on his desk now, glowing evilly.

'You guys … okay?' I asked. Awkwardly. Smike was right. They looked far from okay.

'Yes and I don't want to talk about it,' Naz said.

'Thank you, Lona, I've sought spiritual guidance.' Fish looked pale. 'I'm recovering.'

'The code must have been corrupted in some way,' Naz muttered, half to himself, as he deftly moved structures around his holo sharescreen. He muttered unintelligible tech words at the shapes as they changed, moved, zoomed away and were replaced by others.

'But it's a failsafe system, Naz,' Fish said. 'All the compensations that come into play if something goes wrong with the code – what happened to them? How in Saint Delia's name could the protection have failed?'

Naz shrugged and looked miserable.

'Theoretically, it can't.' He shook his head. 'But it has. It has.'

He put his face in his hands.

I made Naz a cup of his disgusting nutrient-enriched herbal tea, while Fish said the right kind of things to him.

'But I'll find out what's happened.' Naz stood up a bit straighter, squared his delicate shoulders, nodded at the analytical tests he'd set in motion. Characters and shapes moved around on the screen – visual constructions of the whole giant data edifice of the Other-World and bits of the code itself, flowing in and out of the structures – but none of it made any sense to me.

'So,' I asked, 'who could do this? Who would have the technical nounce?'

'No one here,' Naz said.

'An AI? An electronic demon?' I asked.

'Something like that.'

'The disturbances in people's comms and the monster in Gethsemane? That was them … practising?'

'Practising. Playing. Flexing their muscles.'

'But the stories, the characters.' I stared at Naz's twirling code shapes, thinking. 'It's like they're becoming autonomous.'

'Well they're sort of created to have a degree of latitude,' Naz said. 'That's one of the things that makes OtherWorld special.'

'Are you saying, Lona,' asked Fish, 'that this thing is increasing that latitude? And the Cautras of the stories has got that – is getting that – too?'

'Maybe. That would explain our dreams and the way Anghared just appeared yesterday.' And the other times, I thought.

'Anghared appeared?' Fish asked.

'As a holo, here. There's something going on here that's more than the follower of Cautras. Something that kind of *is* the Cautras of the stories, only digital. That exists … on the nets, maybe, not just inside the OtherWorld.'

Something in the swirl of data on Naz's screen alerted him. He winced. 'Looks like you might be partly right, Lona.' He made more lightning gestures for a few minutes, then gradually slowed, stroking the code gently. Then stopped and stared at the cloud of data, looking far from happy. He flung himself into a chair. 'This can't be happening,' he groaned. 'Not to *my* code. Not to *my* system.'

'It doesn't reflect on you, Naz,' Fish said. 'This isn't a normal entity that's broken into your system. It's superhuman.'

'But so am I,' said Naz.

THIRTY-TWO

Gods and monsters

Since the ordination of multifaith saints, there has been much discussion of the correct way of referring to saints who have multiple titles. The Cymru national multifaith Saint is correctly referred to as *Saint Sir Tom Jones*. Dropping the *Sir* is a sign of excessive republicanism. Dropping the *Saint* can be a sign of Anti-Faith sentiment.

Operatives should be cautious with this assumption, however. For example, the correct title of our East Anglian multifaith Saint is Saint Dame Delia of Norwich; but, for many it is a gesture of pious intimacy to refer to her simply as *Delia of Norwich*.

Alliance Field Manual, Chapter 12: Verse 9

I left Naz with his code crisis and Fish with Anghared's riddle. Disappointingly, Fish didn't seem to have any flashes of inspiration when I recited it to him, but then he was still a bit damaged after yesterday. As I left, he'd said to me, in an undertone,

'You know the manuscript so well, Lona, you've translated most of it now. Does any of this make any sense to you? This evil?'

'Some of the stories are darker than you might expect. The one I'm working on now, *Gwenabwyn the Flame Bearer*, is pretty horrible. And evil kind of permeates all of them.'

'Yes, it permeates,' he said, absently. 'It tests our faith.'

But despite the horrible implications of what we'd just realised, the weight that I'd been carrying around in my ribcage felt somehow lighter. Perhaps because understanding what we were up against was better than feeling confused and bewildered in the face of it. Or perhaps because it meant I wasn't going mad after all. My perceptions had just been warped by an electronic monster.

Strange the things that can reassure you, sometimes.

The place was fairly quiet that early in the morning, but when I dropped by the refectory to grab a coffee before we met up with Delauney, I was hailed by River and Kite. As I went over to join them I spotted Faye Driscoll in the opposite corner with Lieutenant Bevan. Faye was hunched over her breakfast; she looked like she was enjoying it as much as she was the company. The Ice Fairy sat back with her hands laced behind her head, looking superior. A cup of black coffee sat in front of her. You couldn't imagine her eating, she probably just drank the blood of Pagans. Or faux religieuse. She looked over at me, contemptuously, as I joined her faith enemies.

'She was round looking for Owen last night, Lona.' River made a big fuss of Dodo, which he lapped up. 'DI Driscoll, that is, not the scary kwizzer. She knows about Owen and Elaine, that's why she's been hassling him.'

So River knew that particular secret of Owen's. Maybe that's why her body language sometimes told me she was hiding something, too. And now the police had unearthed Owen's affair with Elaine, they were getting somewhere after all, but somewhere wrong. Probably.

'I told DI Driscoll I didn't know where he was,' she continued, 'but I expect he was with you and Delauney. And Naz and Fish. He told us you're trying to work out what's going on. And stop it.'

'Mmm,' I said.

'We could help you.' Kite fixed me with his over-intimate gaze. 'In Tom's name don't shut us out now. You need us.'

'How do you mean?'

'This,' he leant across the table, 'is what we know about.'

'Software viruses? AIs? I know you're a bit of an intel hacker, Kite, but … I don't think so.'

River and Kite looked at each other, then back at me.

'Oh Lona, Pagans don't just understand the old gods.' River said. 'We know the monsters too.'

Naz: A Journal of Unnatural Thoughts

Thursday 29 October 2071

8.30am

A psychopathic superhuman entity. That's all I bloody well need on my first assignment.

Not that I'm not up to it. It's unpredictable, but then I coded the OtherWorld to be like that. So I know how it might be unpredictable. And if I don't, Lona might.

But it's ruthless, this thing. It kills, or influences its human helper to kill. Way beyond me. And beyond the others too. Well. Maybe not Lona and Dodo.

Naturally Delauney and Owen managed to mangle the code capture. It's clever – cleverer than them – and most of it self-destructed. I should have been there, at the controls, ready to grab it, instead of...

Anyway. The better news is that Dorath's heart may hold some promise, so the whole sordid exercise wasn't a total waste of time. I've had to handle it with care, but I've learned a lot about this virus from it.

Off to meet the others now, to try and explain it all to them. That'll take some doing.

And then there's Anghared and her special project. I've agreed to it now. Don't see why not. She's been good about us bungling Dorath's rescue so we sort of owe her. She wants to keep it between the two of us, just for now. Which is alright, but the whole thing is a little bit weird. Even for this place. And this situation.

But harmless. I think.

THIRTY-THREE

Three talismans

The personal selfware data of suspected faith criminals can be accessed by the Alliance, under UK law. Although selfware vendors must comply with these data availability regulations, anti-social elements routinely use shielding software to thwart legal access to their data. Additionally, although it would be theoretically possible for the Alliance to access individuals' location logs, these are so easily falsified that it is not our practice. Location logs have never been used as evidence in either a UK faith or civil criminal conviction. Evil attempts to outwit godliness in so many aspects of our mission, making it always a joyous challenge.

Alliance Field Manual, Chapter 14: Verse 22

'Does that mean you can create an anti-virus?' Fish asked Naz, when we all met for a council of war in Delauney's room this morning.

'I'm a step closer.' Naz said. 'This thing acts as though it's alive –

only better. Stealthier. It can jump from host to host; it decides where and when to move around, somehow. Since it left Gethsemane it's been somewhere, in some fenced off corner of the SubNet, in the acolyte's enhancements, maybe in their outerbody system, maybe their inner, who knows? And then it moved into the OtherWorld, during the time we were there. It's better at controlling reality in the OtherWorld, so that's where it would rather operate. Outworld it has more limited powers. At the moment, anyway.'

'Did it access the OtherWorld through the nets, Naz, or by some other route?' Delauney asked.

'No evidence of a firewall breach, so it looks as if it was plugged into the OtherWorld some other way,' Naz told us.

'The assistant put it in there, then, when they went into the OtherWorld?' I asked.

'Maybe that, Lona. The assistant carries it into the OtherWorld in a form that doesn't alert the security software, and then it changes, activates itself at the moment it chooses.'

Fish nodded, thoughtfully. 'Sophisticated.'

'Painfully.' Delauney said.

'So how do we get whatever else you need, Naz? For the anti-virus?' Owen asked.

'Well, because the OtherWorld *is* so sophisticated, it's protecting itself,' Naz said. 'It's coming up with elements of an anti-virus and manifesting it in ways that make sense within the narrative rules of the stories. That's why it created the heart.'

'Great news,' Delauney said.

'Not bad. And some of the ways it's doing it are pretty creative. Which is how I've designed it to be. Thing is, they're so creative now – and that may be because the Cautras element has loosened the rules a bit – that I don't always entirely understand what it's up to.'

We took a moment to digest this and then Fish said, 'But you can still do something practical about the anti-virus?'

'The OtherWorld might be able to provide me with the raw material, in its own mystical way, but it needs me to intervene and craft the anti-virus. So, so far, what I've got is this: to put it crudely, the code from Gethsemane is like a box with three empty spaces and the code from the heart slots into one of those spaces. I don't entirely understand how the two connected, but somehow they did, probably because of the Cautras virus. There are two other spaces in the Gethsemane code structure and what I need now is the two things that will help me fill those spaces.'

'Anghared's riddle,' Fish said. '*A beating heart plucked from darkness*, the first of the three talismans.'

'It fits,' Naz said. 'It was the first building block that meant I could start creating an anti-virus. The heart was infected code, infected by the Cautras virus. But the way it was given to you, in the story, was about the OtherWorld protecting itself.'

'Or about Cautras acting according to the rules of narrative and gaming,' I suggested. 'Because Fish got the riddle right.'

'Could be that too,' Naz said. 'What did you say Anwhyn called the heart? "Gift and trap"?'

'Mm. And the other two things that fit in your Gethsemane code gaps have to be Anghared's other two talismans,' I offered. '*Our guardian of old magic, petrified history* and *A new friend and pray, from an old country,*'

'And these other two things, they'd have to be infected by Cautras, too?' Owen asked.

Naz nodded.

'How would we know?' Owen asked. 'If we saw them.'

'They're material objects, of some description,' Naz said. 'And they're electronically active in some way. If we found a likely specimen, I could test it.'

'The *guardian of old magic, petrified history*, that has to be the Seeing Stone,' said Delauney. 'Anwhyn and Anghared used it to imprison Cautras and protect Pryddych. I know that's a myth, but the stone almost certainly exists locally as a revered historical artefact, though no one knows what it looks like or where it is. I don't get how a rock could be electronically activated, though.'

'It's never been done,' Naz said, 'but it'd be theoretically possible to make a crystalline substance like stone digitally active. If you magnetised it to create a complex micro-structure and then loaded the virus onto it.'

'So the Cautras thing, AI, whatever it is, would do that, wirelessly?' I asked. 'Or the OtherWorld gone defender would do it? Or both of them together locked in combat? Like the two fighting dragons in the *Mabinogion*.' Fish gave me a funny look when I said the thing about the dragons, but Naz smiled, Owen nodded, gravely, and even Delauney knew what I meant.

'Any of those. The Cautras thing might be storing itself somewhere, and aspects of the OtherWorld detected that and followed it. That sort of thing. It would need to local, though. I mean from Pryddych. For technical as well as historical reasons.'

'It's likely a standing stone.' Delauney suggested. 'That's how I've always thought of the Seeing Stone, as an ancient religious artefact. We have five groups of standing stones near here.'

'We can test them,' Naz said. 'But what about the third one? Finding the new friend and praying from an old country.'

'That sounds more like something the ministers' conference might have delivered,' said Fish. 'New friends from old countries. And plenty of prayer. But we've relocated them to Aberystwyth.'

'No reason we can't go befriend them there, if that's what it takes,' Delauney said. 'Or would they be too far away, Naz?'

'No. Whatever the object is that they've got, if they've got one, it could have been infected here.'

'I totally get that we have to fight Cautras in the places where he's gaining strength,' Owen said, 'but it sort of feels like a funny way to track down a murderer. I mean, shouldn't we be here instead of running off to Aber? Shouldn't we be keeping an eye on what's happening on campus as well as working out how to get what we need for the anti-virus. This is where the murderer is.'

'Yeah, but the police are supposed to be doing that,' I pointed out. 'I mean, I know they're not getting very far with finding out who the murderer is, but they are monitoring the campus. I see them all the time, whether I like it or not. Busily grafting away in their ops hub.'

Owen snorted.

'I'll make sure Faye Driscoll keeps us in the loop,' Delauney said. 'She's okay, as police go. A lot better than the Ice Fairy anyway. And we'll keep alert to anything that happens here. Anything suspicious, keep each other posted.'

In the end, we decided that Fish would go back to Aberystwyth, as it fitted in with his work; while Delauney, Owen and I tried to track down the Seeing Stone in Pryddych; and Naz began work on the anti-virus, using the new code. In between doing our day jobs. Fish left straight away once Naz provided him with a device which he could use to scan any likely talismans.

'He's eager.' Delauney fiddled with the gaudy wooden bowl that I'd finally got Dodo to return to him. 'Guess he can't wait to get to away from the Seven Sisters.'

'He'll get a lift with the caterers, if he's quick,' Naz told him. 'Gwenda's taking half the canteen staff with her. Don't look so horrified, Delauney, they'll leave enough people here to cook your dinner.'

THIRTY-FOUR

A temple meet

The savagery of Lucius Proculus's Cautran temple sacrifices appear to be unprecedented even in Roman practice. He regarded the ritual torture, rape and murder of young Britons as a way of purifying the 'barbaric' Welsh Marches through the dark fire of Roman power, strength and discipline. His followers continued these grim rituals long after Proculus's death in order to increase his strength as a deity.

Dragons, Dreams and Drugs by Pleasance and Bowen,
chapter 11, footnote 23

Delauney, Kite and I stood looking at a muddy patch of field in Caerwent. There was a big mound of earth and a hole in the ground. Rain spotted us gently and I wished I hadn't come.

I'd been far from enthusiastic about joining Delauney's jaunt today in the first place. But knew I had to. Because, according to

Delauney, what the archaeologists had found wasn't a traditional Mithraic temple.

'My contact, Gurvinder, says that although everything about it suggests a Mithraic temple, the sculpture of Mithras is like no other Mithraic image that's been discovered. And he's not flanked by the twins. You can see where I'm going with this.'

I could. And I didn't want to.

'The Pagans are interested too,' Delauney went on. 'Kite wants to come along. You know they've offered to help us with all this?'

'They're in conflict with Synthesis though, Delauney.'

'I'm trying to make alliances, find common ground. We don't quite know what we're up against here, Lona, we need all the help we can get.'

I didn't think a bunch of spells from a load of dodgy tree-worshippers was going to be much use against a demonic AI and its homicidal human helper, but I've learned to keep my irreligious thoughts to myself.

When I'd fessed up to M early this morning about what was going on, I'd mentioned we were visiting a dig today.

'After last time?' M was horrified. 'Ferchrissake, just don't go.'

But I knew I had to.

On the way to Caerwent we made a detour to test some standing stones with Naz's electronic gadgetry. None of them seemed to be anything but a lump of rock; no Seeing Stone here, no second talisman.

Once we got to the dig I felt even more apprehensive. The last place I wanted to be at the moment was somewhere designed to worship Cautras. Where people – Celts – had been slaughtered as a sacrifice to him.

Kite, on the other hand, was excited. 'The inner sanctum of the enemy.' He looked at me intently, standing too close, as usual. 'That's where we need to be to understand him.'

Dodo shoved himself in between us.

Delauney was greeted warmly by a woman in a hard hat and

muddy overalls, Gurvinder Pritchard, the lead archaeologist. He was obviously a bit of a celebrity in certain circles.

'Very exciting, Delauney,' she gushed. 'If there are connections between what you've found up at Pryddych and our discoveries down here, that could be something major.'

She made us all put on hats like hers. Safety precaution, excavations can be dangerous, she said and looked at me oddly when I laughed. Then, holding up a lamp, she led us down a flight of stone stairs and into a cellar. Once my eyes had adjusted to the lamplight I could see that we were in a large, dark, stone room, dominated by a dais with an altar on it. The lamps around the room lit mosaic walls. It smelt of damp and fear and death.

'We think it was built as a Mithraic temple, but then it changed purpose,' Gurvinder said. 'In these niches we would've expected to find statues of Cautes and Cautopates. But instead we've got these.'

She gestured towards four statues. Two of them were winged men wearing lion masks. The other two were men with bulls' heads or bull masks.

'The lion-faced figure has been found before in Mithraic temples, but no one really knows what it's meant to be. It might represent time. The other symbolises winter, darkness and death.'

I stared at the bull-headed man, the lion-headed man. Time and death, death and time. Cautras had triumphed over both of them; they were his servants.

'The other mosaic patterns and images around the room are standard for a Mithraic temple, as are the carvings. But here,' she moved to the altar, 'over the altar, the old mosaic or sculptured panel has been removed and replaced with a newer one. What you'd expect to find is the traditional image of Mithras slaying a bull – the sun god triumphing over winter, light over darkness and life over death. You get those over and over again in these Mithraia. But this is different.'

The temple was beginning to feel claustrophobic. It was sinister, bleak, nasty. Perilous. We were in Cautras's parlour.

'And you're sure it's not just a different way of depicting Mithras?' Delauney asked.

'Pretty much. The symbolism is all different, as is the clothing. And the face.'

'This main figure,' she pointed at the large image of a man depicted in the two-metre high sculptured panel, 'Is in the uniform of a Roman general. The armour, the cloak, even the helmet.'

I dragged my gaze reluctantly to the panel. Cautras.

'And the human Cautras, Lucius Proculus, was a Roman commander,' Delauney said.

I looked at Cautras and he looked back at me. I saw secrets I didn't want to see. The floor of the temple began to dip and sway.

'That's what we were thinking,' Gurvinder said. 'And look what he's standing on.' She held her lamp up near the bottom of the panel so we could see more clearly what was under his feet.

The Roman stood on the top of what, at first glance, looked like a pile of stones. But when you looked closer you realised they weren't stones. They were severed heads. Some were still bleeding.

Blood, too much blood. Blood on the stones, blood made of stone. Blood all in the wrong places. I was beginning to feel disconnected from my body. I wanted to get out of this place. Soon.

'He built his power on the slaughter of Britons.' Delauney was excited now. 'Both as a man and as a god. According to his secret cult.'

Me and the Barbarian Butcher, we had our own little secret. I looked at him, he looked back at me. A grubby, dangerous little secret. It scared me too much to tell anyone about. The walls began to move now.

'Then there's the animals.' Gurvinder held her lamp up to the middle of the panel.

Cautras's arms were open wide. On his left, a huge male wolf cowered, half ferocious, half afraid. On his right, a fierce she-bear tried to draw away from him, but was held there by the invisible leash of her fear.

'He tames the animals. By cruelty. He makes them his creatures,' Kite said.

Dodo's teeth were bared. I tried to calm him but I was far from calm. He looked at me and whined.

'And the animals are Britain,' Gurvinder said. 'Or maybe Wales, or even just the Welsh Marches. We think this Cautras was a local cult.'

She held the lamp up higher, towards Cautras's face.

Delauney gasped and Kite swore, both seeing something I'd already realised. A secret that was no longer a secret. That made sense of everything Anwhyn and Eirrod had been planning. I'd realised it first because I'd seen it before, the familiar face that was not familiar.

It was the Owen of Elaine's drawings.

Naz: A Journal of Unnatural Thoughts

Thursday 29 October, 2071

2pm

Bit of a dust-up between Lona and Owen when she got back from Delauney's trip to the temple of evil this morning.

She was furious with him. Because he'd known all this time he was a descendant of Cautras and he hadn't told us. She's pretty scary when she wants to be, Lona. You can see the Zanegell underneath the zlator. She didn't raise her voice, she was just really still and her face was blank, apart from her eyes, which looked, frankly, unhinged.

Owen stood his ground though. 'Anwhyn told me. That's why I was chosen. I'm not clever like the rest of you, I know that, but I'm something you're not.'

With significant menace, she asked him if he meant he was the one who had to kill Cautras.

Yes, was the short answer. It was his destiny. He didn't tell us because Anwhyn said not to. Anwhyn thought we'd try and stop him.

'Damn right we would,' Lona growled. She really did. 'Does Gwenda know about this?'

Owen said that his mam didn't like it much but that she wasn't being as psycho about it as Lona.

She nearly lost it then. He was planning to kill a superhuman mind-controlling god, single-handedly? He was twenty years old, for fuck sake, this was crazy, the responsibility was too much for him. This wasn't one of his hologames, she told him.

Very unwisely, I pointed out that Alexander the Great had become a king and a general at Owen's age and had never lost a battle. Lona turned her head slowly to stare at me and I added, lamely, that Owen wouldn't be acting alone, he had us to help him.

'And I *need* you to help me,' he protested. 'Not to tell me I'm not up to it.' With that he flounced off to break some heads on the rugby pitch.

Lona just stood and glared at me. But I'm not that much of a coward. I'm just programmed to look after myself. I said that – hard though it might be to see how Owen could off an ancient, murderous, super-evil, electronic deity – he just had to strike the final blow. We were going to be doing most of the work.

'He's not the Immortal Prince of bloody Light,' she said.

But, like I told her, he's the nearest thing we've got.

VI

Your temple, has been discovered, Lord. I'm drawn there so strongly it's like a magnetic current, but I'm not going to give myself away when everything's going so well. They know you've chosen a follower, too, they're trying to hunt me down. But I am on the side of Right and Truth and so will overcome.

THIRTY-FIVE

Gathering

The terms civilians use to refer to Alliance officers can give informative clues to their attitudes. The street term 'Faith Police' is generally considered to be benign, the shortened form 'The Faith,' slightly less so. Hostile elements commonly use the term 'kwizzers.' This is thought to be a shortened form of Inquisition.

Alliance Field Manual, Chapter 9: Verse 3

L ater that day I was out in the rain with Owen, testing stones. I still had huge reservations about his belief that he had to kill Cautras. What's more, although another one of his secrets had come out, I could tell he was still keeping something back. But, over lunch, we'd agreed to call a truce, and had spent the afternoon at local ancient Celtic monuments. We'd furtively pressed Naz's detection kit against the standing stones to check for any sign of 'tronic activity and find out if one of them was the Seeing Stone, our second talisman. Usually, one of us had to distract the security camera by dancing around a bit eccentrically, or something similar, away from the stone, while the other did the test. Dodo was a great help with this; at least he enjoyed it.

Now the light was going, so this had to be the last one of our day. We were running out of standing stones, anyway.

'Sorry guys,' Delauney's voice came through from the university, 'it's another dud.' Owen looked as disappointed as I felt. This was beginning to feel like a fool's errand.

'I feel like a right plonker.' Owen ended his dance with a final energetic leap as I put the equipment away. 'If we keep this up, we're the ones who'll end up being reprogrammed, not the virus. I keep thinking, there's a murderer out there, laughing at us while we're doing all this bollocks.'

We retrieved Dodo, who was still leaping around, and went to the makeshift refreshment area, which at least had some kind of roof. There we drank something made from herbs and ate something made from seeds. It was run by Pagans. On the plus side they treated us like their bestie friends. Both of us. News travelled fast on the Pagan network.

A familiar figure came round the side of the shack deep in conversation with one of the seed-mongers.

'Kite, mun. How are you doing?' Owen slapped him on the back.

'Alright, Owen. You feeling any better, Lona?' He put his hand on my shoulder, solicitously. To my shame, I'd blacked out for a few seconds in the underground temple that morning. Kite had caught me before I hit the floor.

'Yeah, cheers, it was just, you know. Bit of a shock.'

He nodded, slowly, fixing me with that gaze. Made me feel he was reading my mind. But, of course, I had technology to stop that sort of thing.

'So it was you then, Owen?' Kite sat down opposite us. 'That the Cautras-worshipper was trying to flatten? In Eirrod's tomb?'

'I reckon. Sorry, Lona. Didn't know you'd be in danger just by being next to me.'

Kite nodded slowly. 'A lot of danger round here, lately. And then they bring in the kwizzers and it gets worse.'

'They're more like the Coraniaid than the Inquisition,' I said. 'The Faith Police.'

Kite looked puzzled.

'The evil invaders from *the Mabinogion* who know everything that's going on?' Owen grinned. 'That's about it, Lona. How does it go?'

' "There was no conversation anywhere in the Island that they did not know about, however softly spoken, provided the wind carried it." '

Kite laughed, darkly. 'Only our Coraniaid have got Synthesis, and the other selfware BigTechs to do their spying instead of the wind.'

He leaned over the table towards me. 'If that's how you see it, surely you're going to let us help you now, Lona? The Faith Police are more interested in stitching us up than hunting down the real demon, and the ordinary plods don't understand what you're doing, they think catching a murderer's about fingerprints and DNA traces. You know you need us. Don't you?'

'I ... maybe.'

'Right.' He slapped his palm on the table and got up to go. 'I'll be in touch later.'

As we left us, I said to Owen, 'What was all that about?'

'I told him and River about the talismans. Delauney said it was okay. They'll keep it quiet.'

'Don't suppose it matters. No, I meant have I just agreed to some kind of CymLib offer?'

'I'm not sure. He's Sons of Anwhyn too.'

'What?'

'Don't tell me you haven't heard of it?'

'I'm obviously insufficiently hip to Pagan fashion.'

'They revere Anwhyn as a defender of Pryddych and Paganism. In a *by any means necessary* sort of way.'

'As a snappy dresser, too?' I asked, thinking of Kite's dark clothes and heavy silver jewellery. But although I was trying to laugh it off, I was disturbed by the bargain I seemed to have accidently struck with Kite. Getting into bed with the Pagans would only cause us more problems.

'Maybe,' Owen laughed. 'There's a band called Anwhyn's Tribe, we saw them supporting Skull Attack at the Equinox festival.'

'Lawd, you'll be telling me there's an Anghared cult next.'

'There is. Bit of a teen witch thing, though.'

'Have I got a cult I don't know about? The cult of the storyteller?'

'Sorry, Lona, you're not magic enough.'

ON THE WAY BACK TO ST CADOG'S, OWEN SAID, TENTATIVELY, 'I DID *tell* Kite you've got someone. Back home.'

'Not that it's any of his business.'

'Seemed to know already, about M. Knows a lot, does Kite. When he hacks intel he finds out what the police are going to do, what they know, finds out about people, that sort of thing. He could help us with information. There's a limit to what DI Driscoll's going to tell Delauney.'

'He could do things Naz can't? Really?'

'Things Naz … wouldn't.'

'Well, maybe. We need some kind of help. We've still got no idea who the murderer is and we're running out of time with the anti-virus. Synthesis aren't going to sit on their hands and wait much longer, either. But if we bring the Pagans in, the Faith Police are going to get interested.'

'Looks like we're on the wrong track with the Seeing Stone, though,' said Owen. 'There's only one other lot left round here.'

'Yeah – no – it seems too obvious, this. And not – I don't know – not intimate enough, somehow. Not special. Stuck out on a hillside like dozens of other sacred stones. The Seeing Stone is more important than that.' I'd been getting this more and more lately. A sort of instinct for the stories. Mind you, if they were in my innerbody, that wasn't surprising. I was the stories.

'Anghared's rhyme, how did it go again?' Owen asked and I recited it.

Three talismans for a new Pryddych
Green as grass and tree
A beating heart plucked from darkness, first victory;
Our guardian of old magic, petrified history;
A new friend and pray, from an old country;
Capture future with past
And complete the Prince's story.

'That *green as grass and tree* part,' Owen said.

'The green, green grass of Cymru. That's how everybody thinks about Wales. Blame Saint Sir Tom.'

'But Anghared's not everybody,' he reasoned. 'She wouldn't think of Cymru or Pryddych like that.'

'Then, if doesn't mean Pryddych, it must mean—'

'The talismans!'

'Well the heart's green, so, yeah, maybe the other two are. Standing stones are covered in moss and lichen, so they look green.'

'They look green but they aren't. Not really. Not inside. This is definitely something we should be asking the Pagans about. Rowan's still at Aberystwyth but I'll talk to River when we get back.'

'Mmm, that can't do any harm. D'you think Fish is going to make any green friends while he's over there?' I asked.

'The only person he's making green by being in Aber is Delauney.'

'Maybe it means politically green.'

'Yeah, I can see Fish getting down with the hardline Ceredigion ecos.' Owen grinned. 'He'll be weaving his own flax ties before you know it.'

As we approached the College gates, we got caught up in the most unexpected thing in the world. A traffic jam.

Decorated Pagan caravans and campervans queued to get into

the road that led to the College. They looked fantastical in the dusk. Owlight. As if a very strange circus was coming to town. A couple of cars with press number plates followed them.

'They're doing it, Lona.' Owen looked awe-struck. 'They're gathering.'

THIRTY-SIX

Extraction

I tried to stop them.' Delauney looked agitated. 'The last thing we need is more negative media attention. But with Rowan away at the conference, Kite's got too much influence. They wouldn't see sense, they wouldn't listen.'

Owen slipped away, muttering something about 'finding some stuff out.'

'What's going on?' I asked. 'This gathering?'

'They gather together when there's a threat to them or to what they hold sacred,' Delauney said. 'They're a flexible, highly connected culture so they can respond quickly.'

'To what?'

'Cautras, I guess,' he said.

DI Driscoll, who'd been deploying some of her people around the crowd, came over.

'All we bloody need,' she looked round at the new influx of brightly coloured wagons and tents and the mass of people milling around. 'I hope this lot don't start causing trouble.'

Naz showed up, shaking his head at the sudden expansion of the camp.

'Ideal conditions for cholera,' he said.

'That would be the least of our worries,' Delauney said, and Faye Driscoll gave one of her humourless snorting laughs.

'While I've got you three together, are you going to tell me what you're up to?' she asked.

'What makes you think we're up to something, Faye?' I asked.

'Look, I may not have blanket access to comms and the rest, like the Faith Police have, but we've still got some intelligence-gathering capabilities. And I'm not stupid, I've seen you all muttering in corners together. You're trying to chase the murderer by yourselves, aren't you?'

Delauney gave her one of his grade A charming smiles. 'Naz is working on a technical solution to what happened at the ministers' conference, as you know. You were there, you saw what it was like. And we're helping him.'

'But you think this is something to do with the killer.'

The three of us exchanged glances.

'You'll understand that anything we tell you is business-sensitive, Faye?' Delauney laid a confidential hand on her arm. 'I'm even having to manage how I brief our parent company about this.'

'It'll be just between you and my team, Delauney. No leaks, no press.'

Delauney nodded. 'Naz?'

'We suspect,' Naz said carefully, 'that what happened at the conference was caused by an electronic entity, possibly an AI. And that the killer thinks this entity is Cautras. I'm developing an electronic way to fight the entity.'

'You think it's in touch with the murderer? This entity?'

'Maybe,' Naz said. 'We don't actually know. If it is, then yes, I'm going to be helping to stop the murderer by doing what is, actually, my job.'

'Your job is developing the Synthesis OtherWorld, isn't it, Naz? Not providing security for other College software.'

'So I can't risk it affecting the OtherWorld,' said Naz. 'It's pretty sophisticated, this thing.'

'So has it affected the OtherWorld?' she asked.

'We had a bit of trouble on a trip yesterday,' I replied, knowing how hard it would be for Naz to lie to the police. 'But it was minor and it's helped Naz with the anti-virus.'

'And you think the murderer is in touch with it in some way. Controlling it?' DI Driscoll looked at Naz. 'You're assuming it's someone with advanced tech skills?'

'Not necessarily, Faye,' Delauney answered, quickly. 'If there is a connection, the murderer might think *it's* controlling *them*, despite the fact that they'll have acquired it, somehow. They might imagine it's a visitation. That's just a hypothesis at present.'

'Right. You're convinced this thing is electronic, though? Not demonic? Nothing you should be telling Faith Police about? Naz?'

'I've no evidence of anything other than a malignant digital entity,' Naz said.

'If there are demons, they're likely just in the murderer's head,' Delauney said.

She looked relieved. 'You'll need to talk to my tech guys about this, Naz. First thing in the morning, okay?'

Owen soon appeared from his reconnaissance, with River in tow. He looked at Faye suspiciously, then shrugged.

'The gathering's tonight, at midnight,' he said. 'It's not a secret. They want Lona to be there. And I'm going.'

'If Rowan was here they'd have kept me informed, anyway.' Faye looked annoyed. 'Earlier.'

'Why do they want me there, Owen?' I asked. 'Why not Delauney? Or Naz?'

'They don't know who to trust,' said Owen. 'Delauney and Naz are involved with bringing the Pagan past to life, but they're still Synthesis salarymen. You're a freelancer. And you're the storyteller.'

'Sorry, Delauney,' River said. 'I did try to persuade them. Lots of Pagans see you as sympathetic. Obviously. But, you know, Synthesis still want to ship out the artefacts.'

'And you told them they could trust me, too, I suppose?' asked Naz.

'Like you'd have come to the camp if I had, Naz?' River said, with her crooked grin.

'Just keep it peaceful, tonight, eh, River?' Faye said. 'Don't let your mate Kite start anything. Or it'll be the Faith Police who'll finish it for you, not us.'

Midnight. I couldn't tell how many people were seated in the clearing in the woods, but it must have been hundreds. I recognised a few of DI Driscoll's troops on the edge of the crowd, looking out of place in their steetwear. Pagan fashion was a bit more various and extreme. Dodo and I were in the middle of the mass, sitting with Kite, Owen, River and a few people I vaguely knew by sight, around a circular, purple cloth on which a stood a big, wooden chest. River, looking like a punk Ophelia in a white gown, was filling up stone cups with some of her elixirs, and handing them to the crowd to pass round. Some of them were already drinking from bottles. Not smartwine, I was pretty sure.

'I'm glad you took up our offer, Lona.' Kite leaned in close enough to make Dodo a bit wary.

'I'm still not sure what you're offering,' I said.

He smiled slowly, in a way that reminded me of Anwhyn.

'You'll see.' He stood up to open the proceedings.

'Friends,' he stretched his arms out to the crowd. The clearing went completely quiet. Even the owls were listening. 'Welcome. This is a historic day that Pagans will remember for years to come.' The big woman next to him, Ceri, opened the wooden chest and started to take things out of it, placing them reverently on the cloth.

'You see, before you, replicas of the important artefacts from Eirrod's tomb. Because the real artefacts are denied us, we will infuse these replicas with power. Power from our faith.'

There were five items place around the box, which were magnified to a hundred times their size in the holo display that hovered above our heads. They were Anwhyn's wolf-head torque, Anghared's circlet and dagger, Dorath's spear, and the Druidic ring.

'What about Eirrod's Books,' someone called out.

'We weren't able to replicate the original manuscript. Synthesis are keeping it from us. But we have the next best thing. We have Lona, the translator.' He pulled me up to standing. I could see my holo hovering above us. A shout from the crowd, 'The storyteller.'

There were cheers. But someone else called out, 'Is she with us?'

'Our cause is joined tonight,' Kite said.

'She won't respect us in the morning, Kite,' someone said, and there was laughter. There was also some muttering. I wondered if my popularity was waning among the hardliners.

I pulled my arm free from Kite's grip.

'Synthesis have never respected us, or what's sacred to us,' a whining voice called out from the darkened sea of faces. 'Why should we help their lackeys?'

'Our enemy is attacking St Cadog's and those closest to Eirrod's Books,' Kite said. 'He's attacking them first, but we'll be next. So we need to help them fight him.'

'But why does she have to be *here*?' the whining voice complained.

I looked at all the hundreds of pairs of eyes, fixed on me. Some of them weren't looking too friendly. Some were losing focus, as River's potions, and other intoxicants, began to take effect.

'Because she *is* the stories,' someone else answered. 'Listen, won't you?'

There was more muttering, but it didn't sound too coherent. For the first time in my life I felt slightly comforted that the police were here. Even if they were massively outnumbered.

The drumming started up and herbs were thrown on the fires that ringed the gathering. They burned green and violet, exuding sweet-smelling clouds of smoke.

'The chant of the warriors,' Kite shouted, above the drums, 'Ceri.'

Ceri rose to lead the chanting. Her voice was rich and deep, spiralling into wilder notes. Slowly, she moved around the edge of the purple island, around the precious items, swaying with the chant. People were on their feet now, dancing sinuously to the drumbeats, chanting softly.

'The power of the mountains, the trees and the rivers, the power of the sky,' they sang out, in contemporary Cymraeg. 'Come to us, give us your strength. We are the boulders, the leaves and the air. We are alive as the earth is alive.'

I was shunted towards the circular cloth and Kite, Ceri and the others formed a ring around the artefacts and around me. Dodo stood behind them, watching. He didn't look best pleased. The artefacts started glowing with an eerie greenish light. I stared at them, trying to work out if it was just the light from the fires making them look like that, but my head was getting fugged from the smoke. I looked at my own hand and that seemed to be glowing in the same way. I began to feel light-headed again. Confused.

Kite detached River from the circle and lifted her up onto the chest. She stood there, staring up at the stars and the crescent moon. Her eyes were completely vacant, trancelike. The green light from the artefacts crackled round her feet, then moved up her body until it surrounded her. The chanting grew louder and louder. I began to feel confused and weakened, and half-sat, half-fell down among the amulets, in their purple setting. The light crackled and fizzed all around us. The undulating Pagan throng were whooping and screaming now, their faces wild. I wanted Dodo, but I didn't know how to call him. I thought I saw a friendlier face, a calmer face, Naz's face, in the crowd, but then it blurred and resolved into the features of yet another chanting Pagan.

I looked up at the white figure of River, who glowed with the fluorescent light. River was standing quite still, continuing to look up at the sky. Then, slowly, distractedly, she looked down at the amulets around her. Her movements were automatic, jerky. She pointed to the circlet, and Ceri picked it up with both hands and held it up it in the air, as if in triumph. Slowly, solemnly, she placed it on River's now-bowed head. River stood up straight with her arms raised out to the sides and revolved around slowly on her pedestal in time to the chanting, a figurine on a music box.

'The Seeing Stone is here,' she called out in a high penetrating tone, nothing like her normal voice. 'The rock on which we build Pryddych. Rejoice!' She twirled round again, fast this time. 'The stories strengthen us. Look to the stories.'

Then she stood still. The fluorescent light disappeared and River staggered and then collapsed. Owen sprang forward to catch her before she fell from the box, and placed her carefully, tenderly on the ground. But I felt better immediately and stood up, motioning Dodo to my side.

The chanting stopped and a cloud moved in front of the silver sickle moon. Dodo lifted up his muzzle and howled. At the sound, River opened her eyes. Her face flickered violet and green in the firelight as she looked towards me, still in her trance. Gently pushing away Owen's support, she took my hand and led me through the mob, back towards St Cadog's, Dodo close at my side. Owen and Kite tried to follow, but, shaking her head River held up her hand.

'Only Lona,' she said.

She led me across the darkened rugby pitch and into the back door of the College. Along the corridors we walked in silence. I followed her down the stairs to the basement where River stopped outside the door of the artefacts centre and looked at me. I hesitated for a moment, then went through the door-opening ritual and entered the familiar room. She followed, walking straight over to the glass case which contained the original circlet. She looked straight at it; then looked at me again.

'The Seeing Stone,' she said.

Naz: A Journal of Unnatural Thoughts

Friday 30 October, 2071

2am

The Seeing Stone. We all stood staring at it as it sat, innocently, in Anghared's circlet.

'But it's so damn small.' Delauney sounded as though we'd cheated him.

I tested the stone a second time. And a third. It had been made electronically active and it held a deactivated form of the Cautras virus. Because, in the mythology, it's where Anwhyn and Anghared bound Cautras up all these years.

It was so obvious now, Lona said. Of course Anghared's amulet would be the Seeing Stone. Why hadn't we realised?

9am

I haven't bothered mentioning to anyone what I'd learned at the gathering. Because, well, maybe it doesn't matter. Maybe we've got more important things to think about.

I worked on the anti-virus into the early hours. Challenging stuff, even for me, but I got as far as I could without the third code segment.

Lona showed up a few hours after I'd finished. She's up early every morning, definitely over-medding. I told her the code wasn't the work of humans and she said it had been made by demons and machines. She's been talking like that a lot, lately. Bit of a change from the matter-of-fact person I first met just over a week ago. It's as though the stories have started possessing her.

We'd just stowed the anti-virus in our new secure place, when Fish came through on comms, looking agitated. He wanted to know what the Pagans had been up to. They'd just been hearing reports about rioting and arrests last night.

We reassured him that it was just a few stones thrown at what they thought was the College admin centre last night, after their ceremony. The police had taken a few of them in, but just Civil Police, it was nothing, Yvonne had handled it.

'They attacked my admin block. Why didn't anyone tell me?' he asked.

Lona told him that in their confused state the Pagans had mistaken the demonic possession labs for the admin centre; the mega high-security windows hadn't even got scratched.

Fish muttered it was a good job the windows had held up, we had enough demons to deal with as it was, but he seemed to relax. Despite the Pagans' antics he looked happier than we'd seen him for a while. But he'd made no progress with Anghared's riddle.

We told him we'd found the second talisman and although we couldn't tell him what it was on comms, we now knew the first and second ones were both green. So we thought the *green as grass and tree* part of the clue described the objects, not Pryddych.

'There's an eco fringe meeting this morning,' Fish offered. 'I could go to that.'

We heard a familiar voice off-camera, telling 'James' that she'd brought him some breakfast, then Gwenda swung into view bearing a laden tray.

Fish perked up even more.

'Hello, you two,' Gwenda said. 'No more nasty surprises? Owen behaving himself?'

We assured her all was well and left them to their breakfast.

'Maybe reliability's looking more attractive in these troubled times,' I said to Lona.

She looked bemused and said she couldn't see why it would ever be unattractive.

'Naturals, eh?' I agreed.

THIRTY-SEVEN

The Famous Five of techno-narrative

W hen I went to see Naz in his lab the next morning, he was pleased with himself.

'I've made a decent attempt at an anti-virus now – as far as I can go without the third code segment. It's fiendishly complex, this virus, I've never seen anything like it. This isn't human work.'

I nodded. Gods and monsters, like River had said. I had a sudden, sharp sense of dislocation. What was I doing here, trying to track down some kind of 'tronic demon and his murderous sidekick? I should have headed home, like Faye Driscoll told me to, after the attack in the tomb. But somehow I hadn't.

I breathed in deeply. This was just fatigue, after that business at the gathering last night. I breathed out. Came back to normal.

'Just one problem.' Naz gave me a sideways glance, too focussed on his code issues to really register my moment of confusion. Empathy circuitry or no empathy circuitry. 'I need to take the anti-virus off network and hide it somewhere secure. Really secure.'

'Your safe drawer?'

'Somewhere better than that.'

'And it's inert?

'Honest, just dumb data.'

'Oh, okay then. If you must.'

I deactivated Dodo and opened his neck panel as he sat there, frozen. It felt like a sneaky thing to do to my best friend but I knew it was the most secure place on the campus to hide our only hope. As I slipped the tiny module into the small compartment in Dodo's neck, designed for backup chips or other precious cargo, Naz's comms bleeped, audibly. He waited until I'd woken Dodo before letting Fish in on vidcomms. Fish was panicking a bit about the Pagans, but Gwenda came in with some breakfast which seemed to cheer him up. As soon as he went, Naz's comms bleeped again.

'Yes, sure,' he said. 'She's with me now. Okay, five minutes.' He turned to me. 'We've been summoned to breakfast in Delauney's scholarly room. To help him save the realm. Or his career, at any rate.'

'I'm doing my best with Synthesis, but it's tough.' Delauney squeezed lemon into his Earl Grey, with less than his usual care, and it went everywhere. He was edgy, we all were, and I suspected that, like me, he was 'elationing'– leaning heavily on smartmeds to get the work done and calm meds to relax and sleep.

'Their first translator murdered, their second attacked, then their fixer killed the second day he was here.' He tried to wipe up the lemon juice with a napkin. 'Well, understandably, it's rocked them. Especially losing Pillington. The whole Gethsemane thing made it worse and the press reports about rioting Pagans hasn't helped. I haven't told them what happened went we went to find Dorath. We need to nail this before they decide to close us down and relocate the whole project to somewhere they can keep a closer eye on it.'

Naz paused in the act of blotting up the lemon juice Delauney had missed. He looked taken aback. 'You mean their Celtic Culture Centre in the US? That'd be catastrophic, Delauney. I mean, the Cautras thing wouldn't just disappear – it'd find new ways to cause damage. And if they took us off the project there'd be no one to stop it. Think of the havoc it could wreak if it gets into more people's implants – takes them over. Think how many people could die.'

'We've *got* to stop Cautras before that happens.' Owen slapped the table for emphasis.

Amid murmurs of agreement, I said, 'I'm not sure we're looking in the right place for the third talisman.' It was a feeling that had been growing on me since the whole gathering thing. 'River was right about the Seeing Stone, so maybe we should do what she said last night. *Look to the stories.*'

'For a new friend to pray with,' Delauney added. 'A green one.'

'This is a bit literal,' I said, 'but there's the Green Man of Gilwern in one of the stories.'

'Yeah, in *The Fat Man of the Hill.*' Naz put down his disgustingly healthy BrayneFruit drink. 'He ends up as a course at the Green Man's banquet. That sounds safe.'

'He might want a new friend, then,' said Owen, through a bacon sandwich. 'And be keen on praying.'

'Or at least saying grace,' Delauney helped himself to another croissant. 'We can't actually get physically harmed in the Other-World, Naz.'

Naz just stared at him.

'We don't know we can't get physically injured,' I said. 'It just hasn't happened yet.'

'It shouldn't be possible,' Naz stared down at his drink, turning it round and round. 'But what happened last time shouldn't have been possible. I can't give absolute guarantees.'

'There is a risk,' said Owen, 'but how else can we stop Cautras killing more people? The police don't seem to be getting anywhere. What else can we do?'

'Is leaping into a dangerous situation like we're the Famous Five of techno-narrative really the only thing we can do?' Naz asked.

'If we don't find the last code segment, the whole place is going to be at risk soon,' I said. 'Fish says there's been a 300% increase in these comms and holo incursions in the last two days and they're getting … nastier.'

'We can't just sit and wait for him to kill someone else,' Owen said. 'Everyone's vulnerable, especially us.'

'If Synthesis pull out,' Delauney said, 'where would that leave you, Naz? Failing to deal with a hostile AI on your first mission? Apart from the wider consequences.'

'We *have* to go into the OtherWorld,' Owen insisted. 'Unless anyone's got any better ideas.'

'It could be a story with merpeople in it, instead of the Green Man,' I suggested. 'They're green, too. Well, bluey-green.'

'And sometimes friendly,' Naz said. 'Only eat fish.'

'Their domain's an old country,' mused Delauney. 'Rivers, lakes, the sea.'

'The water demons in *Gwenabwyn the Flame Bearer*, would probably be the best fit.' I said, reluctantly. It wasn't a story I wanted to spend time in, under the circumstances.

'What about the ones in *The Prince and the Great Boar* or, um, *Five Silver Fishes?*' Naz said.

'They don't seem like the right sort of tales, somehow,' I said. 'Too light-hearted. I think it has to be *Gwenabwyn*.'

Naz groaned. 'A story whose highlights are cannibalism and mass murder. Fantastic.'

'You don't have to come, Naz,' said Owen. 'My arm's fixed now.'

'We need three in the OtherWorld,' I said. 'And at least two at the controls, one of whom should probably be Naz, anyway. Can Fish port in from Aber?'

Naz shook his head. 'Not while we're still trialling.'

'He may as well come back, if he's not likely to find the third talisman there,' Delauney said.

'We can't wait around for Fish,' Owen said. 'This is urgent. What if the killer's about to off someone else? I'm probably first in the firing line. Or Lona because she's doing the translation. And Delauney, you're the expert on Celtic Pagan history, you're not safe. Nor is Benedict, nor any of the Pagans. We need to sort this now.'

'But who could we trust to be the other person?' I asked. 'Benedict or Gwenda, maybe, or Rowan. But they're all still in Aber. What about one of your team, Naz – maybe Smike?'

'Fine if he's on the controls with me,' Naz said. 'Not so fine in the OtherWorld itself. He's better at designing monsters than fighting them.'

'River found the Seeing Stone and she's sorcerer level,' Owen replied. 'So is Kite.'

'Not Kite,' Naz and I said together.

'We are going to need the Pagans' help now,' Delauney said. 'And Kite's a warrior in the OtherWorld.'

'He's a warrior out of the OtherWorld,' Naz said, 'but I don't trust him.'

'If River understands the risks, she'd be the best choice,' I said. 'It's not like we're going into a battle.'

'Even if you were, her sorcerer power's healing,' Naz said. Fine for him to think like that, from the safety of his lab.

As we were getting up to leave, I remembered that I hadn't told Delauney about Elaine's portfolio.

'It's full of pictures of Cautras,' I said.

Delauney looked at me quizzically. 'Which you failed to mention because you thought they were of Owen?'

'They weren't really like Owen. I mean they were like a mad version of Owen, so I, well, you know. But they were Cautras, I know that now we've seen his image in the Caerwent temple.'

Delauney frowned. 'There's no way Elaine can have known what he looked like. The temple panel is the first visual representation of him that's survived.'

'Yet somehow she did,' Naz said.

FAYE DRISCOLL COLLARED ME AND NAZ AS WE MADE OUR WAY ALONG the corridor towards his lab. 'Off on an OtherWorld trip? You haven't been in to see my techies yet, Naz.'

'Just doing our jobs, Faye,' I looked her squarely in the eye. 'And maybe helping you, too.'

'Policework's mainly about meticulously following up leads, Lona. Hundreds of them – takes time, but we get there. It's not about running round having adventures, this isn't an Inspector Tapp holo.' She looked irritated. 'We're following several lines of enquiry, but there's a lot of talk about your mate Owen being a descendant of this Cautras. Let's hope he hasn't got the same approach to ancestor worship as you Shintoists.'

Delauney caught us up in the corridor. 'You'll be pleased to know Naz is making progress with the anti-virus, Faye.'

'That's why we're doing an OtherWorld trip, to get more information,' Naz added.

She folded her arms. 'Hmm. Maybe I should come with you, then.'

'I wouldn't advise anyone going into the OtherWorld as a novice at the moment,' Naz said.

'Then I could watch from the control room. And when the trip finishes, Naz can come with me to explain what the fuck is going on in language my tech guys can understand.'

'This really is highly business-sensitive, Faye—' Delauney began, but she cut him off.

'That wasn't a request, Delauney. Tom on a bike! Do you want us to catch this murderer or not?'

WHILE I WAS WAITING FOR OWEN AND RIVER IN THE WARDROBE, I called M.

'You can leave any time you like, you know,' M pointed out. Not for the first time. 'The upside of being a contractor?'

'There's people here I don't want to let down,' I said. 'Good people. Not like my normal work.'

'You mean things are going tits up but you're too hardarse to bail? Even though you're in danger?'

'I'm not a target, M.'

'There's a block of stone says you are.'

'Look, I'll be finished here in a couple of weeks,' I said. 'Let's go on holiday. Somewhere sunny.'

'Mmm, sounds like you're sick of home after all. Too much rain – or too many demons, huh?'

The Pryddych Cycle V: Gwenabwyn the Flame Bearer

Gwenabwyn was the daughter of Bedwyr and Hafwen, whose father was the great Lord Caradoc, he who slew the terrible ogre of the north. Gwenabwyn was so fair that when she walked abroad by day the birds stopped singing and fell to earth in wonder at her comeliness; at night, the moon hid her face when she saw Gwenabwyn, who shone so much brighter in beauty.

Gwenabwyn was a wayward, headstrong girl, but was beloved by the spirits of forest and mountain. She was called the flame bearer because she was the one called on by the old gods to carry the torch to light the ceremonial fire at Samhain.

Gwenabwyn was to marry Grigor, the son of Uchdryd of the Valley of Nant, and so unite their great families. One night, a few weeks before the wedding, Hafwen went to her daughter's bedchamber, to find that her bed was empty. She hid behind a wall-hanging until dawn, when a white dove flew in through the window and transformed itself into Gwenabwyn. The girl got into bed and fell asleep. The next night Hafwen hid in the room before her daughter went to bed. After the girl had gone to bed and put out her candle, the wind outside started to howl.

'Come out Gwenabwyn, bearer of the flame,' said the wind. 'Come to the one you love.'

The girl stood up, as one in a trance and walked to the window. The wind rapped on the shutter.

'Come, Gwenabwyn,' it said. 'Your lover is waiting.'

The girl opened the shutter and the wind rushed in and swept her away.

The next day, Hafwen consulted the witch of the great wood.

'What must I do to stop this?' she asked.

'I will make you up a protection spell,' said Mabwen. 'Sew it into the hem of your daughter's nightgown and the wind will not be able to take her away. But remember that you cannot protect someone from what they most desire.'

Hafwen sewed the packet containing the protection spell into Gwenabwyn's nightgown, and when she opened the shutter that night she was not swept away. Instead, she stayed at the window, quietly weeping.

'Come to me, my love,' she said, 'for I am imprisoned.'

By the next moon Gwenabwyn had grown big with child. Hafwen kept the girl to her bedchamber so no one would know, but when the moon was full Gwenabwyn arose at the dead of night and walked down to the great river. When she came back in the morning she was no longer with child.

The girl was married to the fine young warrior, Grigor, and a great feast was prepared. At the height of the feasting a chariot, drawn by wild, sea-green horses, burst into the hall. The chariot was driven by twin maidens whose long green hair swayed around them as though they were under water.

'Sister Gwenabwyn,' they sang.

The River Lord has sent us, come with us
To bring his lover to him, come with us
Your child cries for you, your husband longs for you
Your river waits for you, come with us
Gwenabwyn of the river, come with us.

Gwenabwyn jumped up on their chariot, but Grigor stopped her.

'You must stay with me and be my wife now,' he said and lifted her down.

That night he awoke to see Gwenabwyn standing at the window, looking out over the river and weeping quietly.

'Come, Gwenabwyn,' the wind howled. 'Come to your lover.'

Grigor led her away from the window.

'You must stay with me and be my wife now,' he said.

The next day he looked for her but she was not there. He went down to the great river to find her walking into the water. Grigor ran after her and carried her back to the land.

'You must stay with me and be my wife now,' he said.

'If I do this your people will die,' she answered.

The next day he rode out to the dark forest to consult Mabwen.

'You cannot protect your bride from her desire,' Mabwen said. 'It is your people you must protect. You must go to her bedchamber no more.'

The first night back, Grigor stayed away from his bride. The second night he went to her bedchamber at midnight and she was not there. The third night he hid in her room and watched as she opened the shutter and disappeared into the arms of the wind.

On the fourth night he took men and arms and went out onto the great river to hunt the merlord. They stayed away for eight nights and eight days and when they returned it was the eve of Samhain. The whole town gathered for the celebration, and Gwenabwyn bore the torch to the altar where the Druid Dorath led the ceremony.

Grigor's cooks had prepared many delicacies for the feast that followed. Grigor was keen that his beautiful young wife, who had grown pale and thin of late, should eat well. He placed a bowl of soup in front of her, but she could eat no more than a spoonful. He placed laverbread in front of her, but she could only eat a crumb. He placed a pie in front of her, but she ate only a morsel.

The sky went dark and the river roared.

'What have you done, Grigor?' said Dorath.

'My wife has now done penance for her love of another,' Grigor said. 'Before we were wed she bore the merlord's bastard. The soup she ate is made of the child's bones, the laverbread is made from his hair and the pie contains his flesh.'

Gwenabwyn howled in anguish when she heard this, and the river howled back. Great waves rose up from the river and engulfed the village.

In the morning light, the little town in the Vale of Nant was no more. It was at the bottom of a deep lake of blue-green water. But every year, at Samhain, the bells ring out and the dead come out onto the street of the drowned village. And they dance among the fishes, led by Gwenabwyn, the flame bearer.

THIRTY-EIGHT

Praying with monsters

Smarten Yourself Up

Got that Monday morning feeling? Become more focussed and productive, increase your motivation, or have more creative ideas with your own tailored *SmartMix* from Elation.

Our adviser will prepare your personal enhancement *SmartMix*. Then get ready to amaze your colleagues! *SmartMix* can be used in conjunction with our *Long Weekend* mood and mind enhancement mix for a totally **Best You** week.

Goodbye Monday blues, hello Elation

The highly mystical and visionary, those who have undergone extreme spiritual reprogramming, and those with spiritual health issues, should seek medical advice before using our product.

Owen, River and I stood on the banks of the lake that had once been the Vale of Nant. Dodo had stayed behind this time; the safety of our virus fragments was too important to risk.

The three of us looked at each other. Owen was excited. River was trying to be brave. I was still worn out after the gathering last night, but determined to see this thing through to the end. Whatever the end was. Was M right? Did I think quitting would be an admission of weakness? Or did I think this was my responsibility? Because of that one word I'd found in Elaine's thesis?

'Come on, then.' Owen roused me from my thoughts and dived into the lake with a tremendous splash.

River and I followed. We could breathe under water here too, and we kicked out until we were at the bottom of the lake. The three of us swam slowly between the drowned buildings, down the watery streets. Shoals of little fish swam in and out of the skeleton branches of dead trees; long, slimy tendrils of plants reached out to twine around our arms and legs as we swam through them. Dull, green light shone down from the lake's surface.

We swam to the largest house in the village, the chief's house, and looked in through the window. There was Gwenabwyn sitting on her bed, rocking a baby. When we got closer, we saw that the baby was made of fish bones, wrapped in a shawl. Gwenabwyn looked at us with vacant eyes and drew the shawl a little closer around her charge, bending down to croon to its decaying fish head.

Grigor was in the next room lying on the floor, tied down by ropes. He was covered in crabs that moved busily over his body. We looked closer and realised that the crabs were tearing off and eating portions of his flesh. He looked at us with an expression of horror and pain in his eyes, until a large pincer plucked out first his right eye, then his left, and he looked at us no more.

Turning around from the scene, we faced the jaws of a giant salmon which opened wider and wider and then swallowed the three of us, in one gulp. Tumbling amongst the debris in the rank-smelling fish's stomach – apples and pebbles, rings and bones – I said, 'It's okay, so far. All this is normal, it's not Cautras. It's meant to be like this.'

The salmon zig-zagged through the lake as we rattled round amongst the magical detritus inside it. Then it dived. We descended, fast, down and yet down into deep water. Finally it stopped. Faint, greenish light appeared in front of us as it opened its huge mouth. Then, with significant force, it spat us out and we found ourselves sprawled on a slimy rock in the open air. Looking up we saw, on his encrusted, stone throne, the River King. As old as the oceans and as young as spring showers.

'Why are you here, humans?' his voice was weary.

We scrambled to our feet.

'Your Highness, we come as friends,' Owen said.

The merlord laughed. His court of water demons, who surrounded us, did not.

'We're fighting Cautras, my Lord,' I said.

'Cautras wishes to kill men?' He looked at me, shrewdly. 'I have no quibble with that.'

'And the old gods,' said River.

'I am no god.'

'Cautras would take your rivers and lakes from you,' Owen said.

'The Prince of Sorrows has no interest in my domain.'

'We fear he might, my Lord, and we want to … to pray with you for his defeat,' River offered.

'You want to pray with me? To pray?' He looked at her coldly, sadly.

'I loved a human girl once, a girl like you. That girl devoured our child. Humans are monsters and I will not pray with monsters. They *are* my prey.'

He gestured towards River with one scaly hand and a long, green water snake flew from his fingers and wrapped itself around her. Another came towards me and a third towards Owen. Owen was quick with his sword and cut his in two, but mine wound tightly around me, pinning my arms to my sides. I tried to concentrate on changing the narrative, trying to make the snake leap off into the water, but it was hard to focus as it squeezed tighter, cutting painfully into the flesh of my arms and chest. Tighter still and I struggled to breathe.

'We need to get out now,' I gasped. '*Jabberwocky.*'

Nothing happened.

'*Equinox.*' But River, too, remained within her snake's coils. Owen tried to cut her snake with his sword, but it was more delicate work than either the famous sword, or Owen, was suited to.

'Naz!' I shouted. 'Get us out of here.'

Owen finally managed to cut through the snake that bound River and it fell, writhing, to the slimy stone below our feet. But as soon as she was loose, a heavy, thick net was flung over her and Owen, knocking them both to the ground. The water demon who'd thrown it held down one weighted edge as others moved round to secure the other sides. As Owen and River struggled to get free, Owen trying to cut the net with his unwieldy sword, the merlord had sent another snake towards me. The two snakes crushed my rib cage tighter still until I could hardly draw breath. I was beginning to see stars. I made a final, supreme effort to raise my arms and push the snakes off but they didn't move a fraction of an inch. They could have been made of green steel.

Owen and River were getting more and more entangled in the net as Owen tried to cut them loose. Every rope he cut seemed to twine around them more, making it harder to escape the more they struggled to do so. River kept her head and managed to summon a cuttlefish knife from one of the water demon's belts. But she wasn't making much headway with it either.

Two pairs of cold green eyes looked into mine now, mesmerising. Two green tongues flicked out and then two pairs of greenish-white fangs were bared.

I was on my own.

I heard a voice. 'Transform,' it shouted, 'get as far away as you can.'

Naz's voice.

But I couldn't move my arms to transform. I struggled to take in each breath; and bursts of blackness were beginning to obliterate the horrible image of the twin snakes, reared up in front of my face, fangs bared to strike.

Out of nowhere, two delicate light-brown hands grabbed the snakes round their necks and pulled them away from me as easily as if they were pieces of string. I could see the revulsion on Naz's face as, carefully holding their necks to avoid being bitten, he flung them far away.

Owen and River were trying to transform. Awkwardly, they too raised their half-pinioned arms attempting the transformation gesture. They struggled with it, failed, tried again and again, but eventually River disappeared and then Owen. Two otters scurried under the edge of the net, off into the water and away.

Now free, I tried to raise my arms too but couldn't, the snakes' embrace had damaged me too much. I was still struggling to breathe and to see properly and the pain in my ribs was like fire. Naz looked at me, raised his arms, then disappeared.

A sea dragon now stood between me and the merlord. The water demons sent spears towards him but they bounced off his scaly hide.

The dragon Naz turned its head and breathed green fire in the merlord's face.

'Destroy it!' he shouted at his followers.

The dragon leapt on the merlord, tearing at him with teeth and claws. Then one of the water demon's spears hit home, piercing the dragon's shoulder joint. He roared with pain and the water demons jumped on his back, attacking him with small axes. Concentrating hard, I muttered disarming spells and managed to send their axes, one by one, flying into the water. The effort exhausted me so much that I staggered to my knees. It gave Naz some respite though, and he managed to shake them off, one by one. But he was still distracted by them and didn't see the glint of a pearly blade in the merlord's hand. Desperately, I tried a disarming spell on the knife. It rose out of the merlord's right hand, but slowly; I was too weak. The River King just snatched it back.

'Naz,' I gasped out between laboured breaths. 'The merlord.' But, at that moment, the Sea King plunged his serrated blade into the dragon's underbelly. Naz lurched back and collapsed on the stone floor, green blood oozing from his stomach wound. The torn, bleeding River King staggered to his feet, holding his serrated knife and stared at the half-dead dragon. I tried to disarm him with a spell, but my strength was gone. His knife just made a feeble twitch as he lifted it to strike the final blow.

Something moved near his feet; small brown creatures. Then Owen and River were standing there. As River started directing her healing powers towards the wound on Naz's scaly underbelly, Owen, taking the merlord by surprise, snatched the knife from him and thrust it into his heart. The River King collapsed and fell onto the floor. Rivulets of silver-blue merblood flowed into the pools of green dragon blood. As the life left the River King's eyes I called out, 'Quick, Delauney get us out of here,' before collapsing on the blood-wet stone which gradually became the grey expanse of the empty OtherWorld studio.

THIRTY-NINE

Obsolete skills

The preparation and supply of alcoholic beverages is a low-grade civil crime under the 2057 Misuse of Drugs Act, but possessing or consuming them is not technically illegal, in either civil or religious law. Consumption of alcohol is, however, a sign of deviant, self-harming behaviour, which is often associated with godlessness and anti-social attitudes, so agents should be alert to any signs of alcohol use. Additionally, some illegal quasi-religious, such as Pagans, use alcohol in their rituals to produce a euphoric effect.

Alliance Field Manual, Chapter 18: Verse 2

I dropped in and out of consciousness – in and out of dreams. Cautras was there, in the room with me now. A tall figure, in long, dark Roman robes. His face swam in and out of focus. He spoke.

'Lona Luminos.' The voice was familiar … and then not. He spoke in Latin. 'You've written me into life.' He moved closer, his face still blurring, then clearing, pixelating. 'But I'll write my own story now. So, Lona Luminos, what should I do with the storyteller?' And he bowed slightly, mockingly, keeping his gaze fixed to mine.

He became a blur once more. Time seemed to pass, but he was still there.

'Should I call the medic?' he said. In contemporary Welsh. 'Lona? Can you hear me?'

'Owen,' I said, wonderingly.

The medic turned up. 'Now that I've reprogrammed your nanobots to regenerate, it should all heal fairly quickly. But if I hadn't, you'd probably be dead by, ooh, teatime? You've excelled yourself this time, Lona. What did you do to the poor little sods? Even vBots don't make you immortal, you know.'

He reluctantly let me go after treatment, with strict instructions not to do anything physically challenging. With three broken ribs and some kind of lung injury, not to mention bruising that looked like a camouflage vest, that wasn't very likely.

We didn't know exactly how Cautras had damaged us so badly just with code, but it looked like he'd reprogrammed our internal bots to attack us – a form of nanotechnological warfare made illegal by the 7th Geneva Convention. Good job I had my error reporting to Synthesis turned off then, Delauney had pointed out.

We had no idea how any of this might affect Naz.

He'd still been unconscious when we left him alone in his medlab. River's inworld healing had probably saved his life but he was still very badly injured.

'A dog attack,' Delauney told PsychLabs. 'But there may be some technical damage as well. A freak software accident. The details are business-sensitive.'

'You sure have big dogs there in Cymru, Professor Delauney,' said the expressionless, disembodied PsychLabs voice. 'And highly technical ones.'

I'd wanted to stay while PsychLabs operated on him, but they wouldn't have allowed it, so I'd let River and Owen drag me off to the infirmary.

FAYE DRISCOLL HAD AGREED TO TREAT ANYTHING SHE LEARNED

about the problems in the OtherWorld as business-sensitive before she watched our trip. As long as no crime was committed.

'Although if it has been, it's way too big for us to deal with locally,' she said when she'd come to see me in sick bay. But she was prepared to wait until Naz was conscious before she made a decision about reporting what she'd witnessed to the national Cybercrime squad.

'There's nothing to suggest it's demonic and not digital,' she said. 'So I'm not obliged to tell the Alliance. But I need a proper conversation with Naz and my techies the moment he's back to normal.'

'AFTER ALL NAZ'S TALK OF BEING THE EIGHTH WONDER OF THE world, well, I wasn't so sure, but he didn't hesitate for a second,' Delauney was saying, as I walked into the culture clash of his meeting room a little later.

'He saved my life,' I said. Fish was there, just back from Aberystwyth, with Owen and River, and they all fussed round me, asking how I was, making sure I had a comfy chair. 'I wouldn't be here if Naz hadn't come inworld to help us.'

'He was really brave,' River said. 'Heroic.'

'You and Owen were brave to come back. I wouldn't be here if Owen hadn't killed the merlord either. Delauney could only pull us out at the moment the merlord died, because that's when Cautras's power weakened.'

'It was Naz, mainly,' said Owen. 'I just did the last bit. But your disarming spells and River's healing helped Naz. '

'They were all acts of bravery,' Fish said. 'But Naz has paid too heavy a price for his.'

'Well, it's the project that'll be paying to fix him up,' Delauney said. 'Let's hope we'll get him back from them tomorrow in one piece.'

'Why wouldn't we?' asked Owen.

'The repair work's extensive, Owen,' Delauney said. 'Like you guys said, he's a lot better than he would have been without River's healing, or your intervention. Or Lona's disarming spells earlier, for that matter. But the synthetics scientists said there's a risk that Naz might be – different – when he wakes up,'

'You mean his personality might be affected?' I asked. 'His memory?'

The others looked sombre as the implications sunk in. He might have forgotten us completely. And Cautras. And the unfinished anti-Cautras code.

'So he might not want to carry on with any of this.' Owen said. 'Or even know how to.'

'Did you tell Faye Driscoll that, Delauney?' I asked. 'When you persuaded her not to go to UK Cybercrime until Naz was back on his feet?'

'I most certainly did not,' he said. 'If she knew that she'd bring them in and Cybercrime would go straight to Synthesis. Then we've had it. So for Tom's sake don't tell her.'

'But even if Naz is back to normal when he gets out of his medlab it'll take him time to finish the anti-virus,' I said. 'Does she know that?'

'I didn't headline it,' Delauney said. 'So don't let her know that Naz is up and about until he's finished the anti-virus. Assuming all goes well.'

'All we can do now is pray that it will,' Fish said.

'There's plenty more we can do—' Owen began, but something Fish had said struck me. *Pray* I thought. Pray. The merlord wouldn't pray, but…

'It's not pray,' I interrupted him. 'It's prey.'

They looked at me, puzzled. Concerned.

'Are you feeling alright Lona?' Fish asked.

'It's been a hell of a day, perhaps, ah, you need to rest?' Delauney suggested.

'Prey. Like the merlord said to River. He wouldn't pray with us, we were his prey. P-R-E-Y.'

'Ahh.' Fish's eyes lit up. 'A homophone. It's *A new friend and* prey, *from an old country.*'

They all looked relieved. And then puzzled.

'Why would a friend be your prey?' Owen asked.

'Is it like when someone gets kidnapped and they begin to identify with their kidnappers? And become their friend?' River suggested.

'Stockholm syndrome,' Delauney said. 'Yes, maybe. Good idea.'

'Wouldn't that be what Cautras's agent is?' Fish looked thoughtful. 'As far as Cautras is concerned.'

'Well, yes, but green and from an old country?' Delauney looked unconvinced.

'Is anyone from a country older than Wales?' River asked.

'Not me,' said Delauney.

'Kite was in the Middle East during the Faith Wars wasn't he?' I pointed out. 'Plenty of old civilisations there. And he's pretty eco.'

'It's not where he's from though,' Owen said. 'And the other two talismans, the heart and the stone were *literally* green. Being eco's not enough.'

'Hmm.' Fish stood up. 'I'll have another bash at the third clue after I've finished calming down the Chair of the board of governors. She's getting jittery about the Pagans – all the publicity, on top of everything else.'

'We're finished if we don't solve it soon,' Delauney said. 'Even if we manage to keep the police away from this, something's bound to leak out from PsychLabs to Synthesis and then they'll close the whole operation down.'

'How long do you think we've got before that happens?' I asked.

'Couple of days, absolute maximum. Maybe less.'

'And like Naz said, Cautras would still be around – even if Synthesis move the OtherWorld – and be able to recruit new helpers and kill anyone who got in his way,' said Owen. 'He'd be at the Celtic Culture Centre or he'd be here.'

'Both and more,' I said.

'He would,' said Delauney. 'But Naz wouldn't.'

. . .

'COME DOWN TO THE CAMP WITH US, LONA?' RIVER SAID, AS WE left Delauney's room. 'Kite wants to talk to you.'

'What now?' I muttered, but went along. The waiting for Naz to come round was difficult. I was restless, and the riddle, in its new form, kept going round in my head. *A new friend and prey, from an old country.* The more I thought about it, the less sense it made. A walk down to the camp before I went back to the manuscript was appealing.

I walked slowly, every breath hurting. Through the post-lecture crush of students we went, out of the back door, and down to the edge of the camp. Lots more cheerful, decorated tents had been erected, and dozens of people were milling around them in the gathering dusk. More were sitting around talking in their meeting area or around fires outside tents and wagons. Mainly Pagans, but there were quite a lot of press there now, too, as well as some of D I Driscoll's uniforms. The place was noisy, buzzing. There was a large, high-end van, with tinted windows, parked among the brightly coloured wagons and campervans. It looked out of place, but the moment you saw it, you somehow forgot it. I wouldn't have remembered it at all, but Kite pointed it out.

'Kwizzers.' He appeared next to me. 'They're using one of those fields around the van that affects your short-term memory. Trying to avoid media coverage.'

'Aye,' Owen warned, 'don't get too near, I forgot a whole day's exam revision the first time I saw one of those.'

'That's not even legal,' River said.

'The Faith Police think the law doesn't apply to them.' Turning his gaze on me, Kite asked, 'Were you okay after the gathering? I mean, before what happened in the OtherWorld this morning. It was pretty powerful. You looked drained after it.'

Owen and River had walked away now, and Kite moved closer. 'Look, last night, we got you the result you wanted.'

'At a price.' I'd been thinking, ever since I came round, that if I hadn't had so much of the life sucked out of me last night, maybe I'd have been more use in the OtherWorld. Maybe Naz wouldn't be where he was now.

'And River came up with the goods again this morning, with her healing spells. So maybe you'll let us help you some more.' His hand was on my arm. I was enveloped in a cloud of thyme oil, and Dodo was uneasy.

'How, exactly?'

'Intel, for one thing. It's a lonely business, what you've taken on. You don't know who to trust, do you? People aren't always what they seem. Take your friend Naz, for example.'

'What do you think you know about Naz.'

'I know he's not an NZ 200.'

I did my best to keep a poker face. Even the Faith Police hadn't cracked Naz's screen. But Kite had.

'None of us know who Naz will be when he wakes up. But what I do know is he saved my life today.'

'That's what they're designed to do. And they'll be able to fix him; his sort can always be fixed.'

I shook my head. 'That's just unreconstructed crap, Kite. Is this the sort of thing you believe in the Sons of Anwhyn?'

He stared at me intently.

'Anwhyn achieved great things; for the Land, for the faith.'

'So did Eirrod.'

'Anwhyn was the strategist behind it. And he wasn't afraid to get his hands dirty to achieve something for the ultimate good.'

'You admire that?'

'The Pagan movement's not going to get religious recognition by being nice and hoping things will work out. We can't play by their rules, they'll crush us. And it's the same with fighting Cautras.'

'What do you mean?'

'We're not going to be able to keep Pryddych safe and destroy Cautras by following the rules either. People are being attacked and killed. We don't know who's going to be next and Pagans are probably top of Cautras's list. So we have to take the initiative. Isn't that what you're doing? You're not getting the police to do it for you, are you?'

. . .

I DIDN'T REALLY KNOW WHERE I WAS GOING WHEN I LEFT THE CAMP, I just wanted to get away from Kite and all the crowds. I headed towards the quiet of the wood and soon the noise from the camp disappeared; all I could hear was the sound of the breeze shaking the last of the golden-brown leaves from the branches. The pungent smell of thyme oil that had overpowered me was replaced by earthy scents of moss and lichen, punctuated by fox.

I stood still and began to breathe more normally. An owl's cry echoed round the wood; eerie, lonely.

I glimpsed movement ahead of me, and in the gathering dusk, could just make out a figure among the trees. Alert, I turned to leave. I had Dodo to protect me but it was still risky being out here in my feeble state, as night was falling. I wasn't thinking straight.

'Lona.'

I stopped. Turned.

Silver robes. Silver hair.

'What? How?' I began to ask.

'You're recovering from your injuries?' The lady of the silver pool emerged from the trees and walked towards me, as if taking a stroll in the woods were the most natural thing in the world for her. Anghared in the owlight.

'Yes. Naz is still being treated.'

'He'll recover?'

'His body, yes. But he may lose his memory and his personality might be affected. I mean, he might not be the same person when he recovers. We don't know yet.'

She stared at me for a moment.

'So we may lose him? That would be grievously sad.'

'Grievously,' I agreed.

'The heart of the Green Wizard. Naz was cleansing it for me. Erasing the taint of Cautras.'

'He ... was?'

'With Dorath's pure heart I could bring him back as he was. Before.'

'You ... could?'

'Dorath could live again. He could be the Druid of the Black

Mountains again. Before Cautras made him … what he became. With my foolish help.'

Her silver-blue eyes were blazing. And really quite frightening.

'Would that be an … entirely risk free exercise?' I ventured.

'Dorath was the greatest Druid that ever lived,' she proclaimed, gesturing skywards, her arms wide.

'But without Naz,' her hands fell to her sides, 'he can't live again.'

'We don't even know if Naz is going to live again, Anghared.'

***

As I went back to my rooms, after a couple of hours in the artefact centre spent trying to work on the translation, I saw Delauney emerging from the Launcelot Suite, opposite mine.

'Any news?' I asked.

'Nothing good. But nothing bad. We should know in the morning. I've put Smike in charge of the OtherWorld team until then.'

'Delauney, where will Naz go if Synthesis do shut us down?'

'If they take him off the OtherWorld project then wherever his next assignment is. Probably the US, maybe China.'

'Will he get a chance to go to Manchester while he's here?'

'Manchester? Ah, you mean his backstory. He'd likely have a different one, if they think this one didn't work out too well.'

'A different … but then he wouldn't be Naz.'

'He'd be a Chicago Naz, or maybe a Seattle Naz. That'd be a better cut and paste.'

'Delauney. Naz would be devastated. Losing his history like that.'

'But he wouldn't know about it, would he, Lona?'

***

I couldn't sleep that night. I thought about Anghared's obsession with getting her adopted father back, and what it might mean. I thought about Naz, and wondered who the person would be who came back to us the next day. I thought about the clue, the new friend who might also be prey. I thought about Kite. The scent of thyme and his unnerving gaze. And his unnerving intel. I thought of M, whom I hadn't yet told about the attack on us in the Other-World. And then it was three in the morning and Owen was hammering frantically at my door.

'Lona! They're raiding the camp. They're taking everyone away.'

I dressed quickly and we rushed over to the camp. Or to where the camp had been.

The tents were all pulled down and trampled in the mud. Not homes anymore, but tattered bits of coloured material with remnants of torn and broken belongings strewn among them. A brightly coloured caravan, damaged beyond repair, lay on its side.

The scene was lit by dozens of powerful headlights from ghostly, dark vans. Outside the pool of light, we could just make out robed figures dragging the last of the struggling Pagans into the vans.

Dodo whined and looked from the scene to me, questioningly. I quieted him.

'I don't know where River is. They must have taken her,' Owen whispered frantically. A broad-shouldered man in front of us turned around, and we both stepped back simultaneously, but Dodo went forward to greet him. Delauney.

'I knew something like this would happen.' He shook his head. 'They should have kept their heads down. That gathering, with the Faith Police as jumpy as they are at the moment? It was madness.'

'But then we wouldn't have found the Seeing Stone,' Owen said.

'What – what's going on, exactly?' I asked.

'They're putting everyone in detention,' Owen said.

One of the robed figures detached itself from the scene and came towards us.

'Professor Delauney.' The Ice Fairy. Unruffled, as ever.

'And Lona Luminos.' She looked at me with contempt, as usual. 'Complete with mascot.'

Dodo growled slightly and I quieted him again.

'Owen Gryffydd. Looking for your girlfriend, Owen? Are there no decent Christian girls at your chapel?'

Owen grunted because Delauney trod on his foot to shut him up. Then Delauney flashed a charming, but authoritative, smile at the Ice Fairy, his teeth gleaming in the headlights. 'Which detention facility are you taking them to, Lieutenant Bevan?'

'Several. Do you have an interest in these faith offenders, Professor?'

'Some of them are my students. The College has a duty of care.'

'It should concern itself more with the care of their souls, then.' She swept off back to her troops.

BACK IN MY ROOMS I GOT OUT THE EMERGENCY SAKE, AND OWEN and I gulped some of it down while Delauney paced up and down making comms calls. After a while he came and threw himself down on the sofa.

'They've got eighty-nine people in detention.' He poured himself a large drink. 'But no one knows who or where. They wouldn't deny or confirm that they had River. Or any of the other students.'

'Her comms are shut off,' Owen said. 'That's the first thing they do when they detain people. Isolate them.'

'We'll keep at it, Owen,' Delauney said. 'Publicity, alerts, networked media, you know the drill. I've got Fish on the case now, Rowan's on the way back from Aber, and Benedict is doing what he can from there.'

'It's what Fish wants, though isn't it?' Owen said.

'Not St Cadog's students in Faith Police detention, Owen,' I said.

'Samhain,' Owen said. 'They're doing it because it's Samhain tomorrow. Out of spite.'

'Trying to avoid media coverage of the celebration, probably,' Delauney said.

'You don't think they've been somehow influenced by Cautras, too, do you?' I asked. 'The Faith Police?'

'I think Cautras would be a moderating influence on our Lieutenant Bevan,' Delauney replied. 'She really doesn't like you, does she Lona?'

'Isn't she like that with everybody?' I asked.

'She's worse with you than with the Pagans,' Owen said.

There was a faint tapping at the door.

We all froze for a second but Dodo ran to it, his tail wagging. The tapping sounded again, very quietly. Dodo pawed at the door and I opened it. Outside were a dishevelled River and Kite.

'Is it safe to come in?' River whispered.

As soon as they got over the threshold, River was engulfed in hugs from Owen and licks from Dodo, and Kite was slapped heartily on the back by Delauney. He winced slightly.

'Have you got anything like a first-aid kit?' he asked. 'We can't go to a medic. It's just cuts and bruises, anyway.'

I managed to locate a mysterious box with a red cross on it in the bathroom cabinet. Owen insisted on attending to River's injuries so they disappeared into the bathroom to work out what to do with it.

'It's old-school healing,' we heard River say to Owen as they closed the bathroom door. 'It's easy, I'll show you.'

'What happened?' Delauney asked Kite.

'We were all asleep. They just turned up, no warning. First I thing I knew they'd pulled my tent down, dragged me out of it.

'Then they started smashing everything – and everyone – up. Grabbing people, dragging them into their vans. It was chaos, we were fighting them, trying to get away from them, trying to stop them taking people, but there were dozens and dozens of them. Uniformed Faith Police. Big fuckers, strong as synths. It was horrible.'

'We saw Lieutenant Bevan.' I said. 'The Ice Fairy. But she wouldn't tell Delauney which centre they were taking people to.'

'They don't think human rights apply to Pagans,' Kite looked bitter. 'Or that the law applies to them.'

'We'll throw everything we've got at this, Kite,' Delauney assured him, then left to hook up with Fish, get the lawyers and the publicity machinery moving.

River emerged from the bathroom with some odd looking plastic strips stuck on her arms. 'Can Kite crash on your sofa, Lona?' she asked. 'He won't be any trouble.' She shot a look at Kite that I couldn't quite de-code, then she and Owen disappeared off to Owen's room.

'Shall I, um, do the first-aid thing, then?' I looked at the mysterious contents of the box.

'I wouldn't mind having a shower first,' Kite said, which was handy as it gave me time to read the instructions on the funny packets and bottles of stuff. And have another couple of slugs of the medicinal sake. I was getting slightly light-headed.

Kite emerged from the shower with a towel round his waist revealing considerable muscle definition, extensive Celtic tattoos and some nasty cuts.

'Don't even remember it happening.' He sat down next to me on the sofa. He smelt soapy now.

I found the right sort of stuff to spray on the cuts. I only knew the theory about what to do with the dressing, so he had to help me.

'You've not done this before, have you?'

'Obsolete skill.' I busied myself with finding the correct stuff to spray on the bruises that were emerging on his back.

'Ow, that's freezing.' He looked back at me over his shoulder. His back was very broad.

'I believe that's the idea.'

He turned around.

And took hold of my arm.

'Thanks, Lona.' He smiled. And moved closer.

FORTY

A new friend

I was woken up, after a few hours' sleep, by someone fidgeting and turning over, heavily, in my bed. I surfaced dozily, thick-headed. Then my eyes snapped open in horror, staring frozen into the darkness. What had I done?

My stomach lurched with shame and regret. My head was hurting badly and I couldn't remember a damn thing. Too much alcohol. How could I have been so stupid?

I'd have to tell M. But tell M what? Exactly?

And now there was the immediate embarrassment of dealing with Kite. He was obviously awake, squirming around in the bed, restless as a sack of toads. I sat up carefully, pulling the cover up to my throat and switched on my bedside light.

It was cool. It was no big deal. I braced myself, assumed a nonchalant, expression and turned to him. 'Urgh, for fuck sake. What are you doing on the bed, Dodo?'

Relief surged down from my brain in a glorious, golden wave. My hangover disappeared instantly as the sun came out in my head. I was so grateful to Dodo for not being Kite that I didn't even tell him to get back on the rug.

Dodo was playing with one of his acquisitions, which seemed to be slightly animated. God knows where he'd got this one from, I'd given up trying to police his kleptomania.

He looked at me with a mildly exasperated expression, as if it was obvious what he was doing on the bed. With an intruder in the living room all night, where else would a conscientious guardwolf sleep?

'What's your new toy, then, Dodo?' I asked.

It was moving around in a fold of the duvet half under his huge paw. I lifted Dodo's paw to get a better look, but it wriggled away. I plunged my hand in to scoop it out, hoping it wasn't anything noxious or bitey. It felt small, warm and smooth. It wriggled lazily. I pulled my hand out and found a small frog sitting on my palm, blinking sleepily. Well, not a natural frog, or it would have died of shock at being befriended by a wolf, but some sort of automaton frog.

Befriended.

A frog. A green frog.

Dodo's new friend.

Or prey.

From the Learning Garden, Gethsemane, the Holy Land. An old country.

'Dodo.' I held his face in my hands. 'You are the cleverest wolf in all the world.'

Which, in truth, he probably was.

FORTY-ONE

Happy Halloween

Synthetic humans are programmed with a specific faith at manufacture stage. More advanced versions may change faith, usually when they stop being legally bonded to their manufacturer and become free individuals. Faiths differ on the issue of whether synthetic humans have souls and they are normally allocated a faith that has a positive view about this matter.

Alliance Field Manual, Chapter 11: Verse 28

There was a little shrine of flowers, cards and some small craft objects outside Naz's door. I loitered in front of it, looking at the kisses and wishes that fans and friends had sent him, before I summoned the courage to step forward and touch the entry panel.

The door greeted me. 'Good morning, Lona. I'll see if Naz is available.'

He won't be, I thought. *It's too early. Maybe I should go. I'll go now.*

'Come right on in, Lona,' it said, before I could get away.

I walked into the Launcelot Suite.

It shut behind me 'Have a happy Halloween!'

Naz wasn't in his living room. There was just silence. Absence. I was too early; or too late. I walked around the room, staring absently at things. His beloved cactus collection, his unused Hindu altar, his precious vinyl record collection. Would he wake up, study all these records and wonder what the point of them was? Would I have to explain why Yvonne had knitted him the stuffed Ganesha on the sofa, and that he kept it, though he disliked it, because he didn't want to hurt her feelings. Would he even know who Yvonne was? Or who I was?

'You're up early again.' The familiar voice behind me made me jump slightly. I turned too fast for my injured body.

Naz had emerged from his kitchen carrying two steaming cups. He still drank tea, then. Looked the same. Moved with the usual cat-like grace.

'It's – been a busy night.' I accepted a cup of tea. 'But are you – how are you?'

'Healthy enough, after extensive surgery that cost more than a vintage Bentley.'

'That's, um, that's good. That's great.'

'I'd rather not get hacked about and stabbed by web-footed demons any time in the near future, though. Or have to handle,' he shuddered, '*snakes* again. Ever.'

'No. I guess not.'

Naz sat down, next to Ganesha, placing his teacup carefully on the coffee table.

'I designed everything about the merlord, right down to the pointy grey nails on his scaly green hands. And the cuttlefish knife he used to stab me.' He sighed. 'All of it. I feel like Dr Frankenstein.'

I sat down, too. Sipped my tea.

'You're back to normal, then?'

'Possibly even slightly improved. Hard though that is to imagine.'

'And you remember everything? I mean the past few days.'

'With total recall, unfortunately.'

'So you'll carry on with the anti-virus?'

He gave me an odd, patient sort of look. 'Yes, Lona, of course I will.'

I nodded.

'I haven't decided what to do about my rooms yet, though.' He looked around. 'I don't really want to call the police.'

I stared at him, blankly.

'You haven't even noticed, have you?'

I looked round at the living room. Everything was the same as usual. Cushions and rugs neatly arranged. Records lined up on their shelves in alphabetical order. Fresh flowers in a vase, plants carefully tended.

'Ransacked.'

'Ransacked?'

'That cactus,' he pointed to a vigorous looking specimen, 'has been moved. It's normally three inches to the left. The gravel surface in the pot's been rearranged. On that other cactus, too. This cushion's been inverted and both rugs've been moved. My rooms have been searched.'

'Who would..?'

'Cautras's agent, looking for the anti-virus. Not hard to guess that I wouldn't keep it on a network, however well protected.'

I thought about someone methodically going through Naz's room in the night while he was undergoing surgery next door. Squeezing his cushions, rifling through his cupboards. Fingering the neatly folded clothing in his drawers.

'That's really creepy, Naz.'

'I've checked the system to see who came in, but they've erased it. Or their master has.'

'That must feel, um…'

'I feel violated. Obviously.'

'Yes. That's horrible. Can we do anything about room security?'

'Not really. The best thing we can do is finish the anti-virus.'

'Aha.' I broke the happy news of Dodo's Gethsemane frog.

'Brilliant, Lona.' He stood up. 'Let's go and get it.'

'There's more.' I said and told him about the early morning

Faith Police raid and its aftermath. 'So River's at Owen's and Kite's still asleep on my sofa.'

'Mm. First they came for the Pagans, eh?' He perched himself on the arm of the sofa. 'Listen – his probably isn't important – but there's something I should tell you about Kite.'

'Yes?'

'He's a fraud.'

'How do you mean?'

'He faked the magic tricks at the gathering. All the stuff with the green light and the energy flow.'

'How?'

'Technology.'

'So?'

'It's dishonest.'

'Perhaps, but Kite'd defend that as the means justifying the end.' And it hadn't felt like fakery to me.

'No, there's something else. In some of the duels I've had with him. Where I try to get people to believe an invented narrative and he tries to get them to see the truth?'

'Yes?'

'I've seen a truth about him. Because of his spell.'

'And?'

'The truth that he's a fake. He isn't what he seems.'

'But if he was, why would he take on truth-making as his sorcerer power?'

'You don't choose your power, it chooses you.'

'And the OtherWorld wants to unmask him? Come off it, Naz, you just don't like him. Fair enough, he's a bigot, but it's clouding your judgement.'

'Well you seem to have got very pally with this son of Anwhyn all of a sudden. Are you sure he slept on the sofa?'

'Let's go and get the sodding frog.' I got up and walked to the door. 'Before he fakes any magic tricks with it.'

Naz: A Journal of Unnatural Thoughts

Saturday 31 October 2071

10.30am

Well, I've done it. I've completed the anti-virus. A tremendously difficult and fascinating piece of work. And a particularly elegant solution, if I may say so. I've had to work on it hiding away in my rooms, so that DI Driscoll doesn't know I've recovered. If I told her what the real problem is, she'd have to bring in UK Cybercrime and we don't want that. I'm waiting for the others to join me now. We need to decide how we'll activate it.

As soon as Lona told me about the replicant frog, we rushed off to get it and the existing code from Dodo. I'm not sure about this truce Lona seems to have struck with Kite. He's obviously got a bit of thing for her, but she probably hasn't realised it. Anyway, when we got to her rooms, Dodo had him cornered in her bedroom.

He claimed he'd only gone in there to see if Lona wanted coffee. She'd already left, but then Dodo wouldn't let him out.

Dodo couldn't tell us anything, but it sounds suspicious to me.

What if Kite had been trying to get hold of the frog or attempting to open Dodo's neck panel?

What's more, I thought I caught a whiff of thyme oil in my rooms this morning. Before Lona turned up. Add that to the other evidence and Kite's beginning to look pretty suspect.

Anyway, I've done the work on Dorath's heart that Anghared wanted, as well. Only took a few minutes. When it was clean, I let the heart connect to the environment.

Anghared looked out from the screen. 'I'm in your debt, Naz.'

While she was still indebted, I consulted her about Kite. She is a wise woman, after all. And everyone else is so taken in by him they're not likely to believe me. So I told her my suspicions and the reasons for them and asked her what she thought I should do about it.

'My brother would counsel you to keep you friends close and your enemies closer,' she said. 'Myself, I would turn him into a stoat.'

FORTY-TWO

Betrayal

I stood with Delauney, looking at the Pagan camp. The desolation of trampled mud and broken dwellings was gradually being transformed by the new Pagans who'd descended on the place throughout the morning. Plenty of press there too, talking into cameras in front of the rebuilding. Non-Pagan supporters of the camp had turned out too. A Methodist group had set up a stand dispensing tea and solidarity and a group of Buddhists and students were slowly helping clear up the debris.

With Benedict's blessing, Delauney had got the St Cadog's press office to spend the morning pushing information about the raid and the detained Pagans out onto the media, while Delauney and some of his students had contacted other organisations that might be sympathetic. Or angry. Or both.

'If we can get a groundswell of support, then the Pagans will look like victims, not crazies,' he'd said. 'That'll reflect badly on the Faith Police which they cannot afford as they're about to be officially reviewed. And it'll affect how the Pagans get treated in detention. It's … better all round, too.' I knew Synthesis would be leaning on Delauney even more heavily as soon as the day started in California. Last night's events didn't help improve the picture of instability and danger at St Cadog's – the place they'd entrusted with their flagship project.

I'd lent a hand by datasearching appropriate contacts and pushing them to the student callers. Cold calling doesn't exactly speak to my strengths. Owen and River had been trying to help with the calls, but they got too vehement in their dealings with potential supporters, so everyone was relieved when Rowan showed up and swept them away to help rebuild the camp. Delauney and I went with them, to see how things were getting.

'I don't blame Kite,' Rowan said. 'A gathering happens when it has to. It's happening again now. But this one will be different.'

Faye Driscoll approached us.

'I want you to know this was nothing to do with us.' She looked round at the damage. 'I've got my work cut out tracking down a murderer. Any news on Naz?'

'We're not expecting him to be recovered until tonight at the earliest,' Delauney told her, smoothly, just as Naz bleeped me.

'The frog has landed,' Naz said, on my comms.

'Okay, Fish, we'll be there right away,' I said to Naz.

Delauney, Owen and I and rushed off to Naz's rooms, alerting Fish on the way. The anti-virus. We finally had it. Now we could stop all this.

WHEN NAZ HAD RECOVERED FROM OWEN SLAPPING HIM ON THE back and telling him how good it was to see him, and Delauney doing a gruff, masculine hug-thing, he told them he had another piece of news.

'I might know who the agent is.'

Naz presented the flimsy proof he'd mentioned to me earlier plus some stuff about his rooms smelling of thyme and then Dodo cornering Kite in my bedroom.

'That's hardly evidence,' I said. 'Dodo's a guardwolf and I bet you've got herbs in your kitchen.'

'He was there at the reading,' Naz said, 'and he definitely had a motive for killing Pillington. He's techie, for a Pagan, despite his prejudices. He knew Elaine; he was an extra-mural student on one of her courses, so he can access the College. And he was here when Elaine died.'

'He didn't know Elaine well, though,' Owen said. 'She was just his lecturer.'

'He did know she talked to the quad door, though,' I told them.

'Oh, come on Lona. The attack in the tomb?' Owen shook his head. 'Kite'd never do anything that put you in danger.'

Uh? I thought. *How about sucking out all my energy at the gathering? How about making sure I was still weak when I had to face the merlord?* But no one else seemed to think Owen's point was strange, except Naz, who said:

'Tell that to Dodo, Owen, he can't stand Kite.'

Owen smiled and rubbed Dodo's neck. 'That's just Dodo being macho. Look, Naz, I know Kite's got crap, old-school Pagan views about synthetic humans, I'm always trying to put him straight there, but it doesn't make him Cautras's helper.'

'Better be careful just how much we tell Kite,' Delauney looked at Owen, 'Just in case.'

Owen sighed. 'Look, now that we've got the anti-virus and everything. Well there's something I need to tell you.' He paused. 'What you just said about Kite having a motive for killing Pillington, Naz. It wasn't Kite. It wasn't Cautras's agent either.'

'Well, who? CymLib? ' I asked. 'Owen, you weren't involved?'

'No,' he replied. 'No, but you're not going to like this much, Lona. It was...' he paused again, looking at me, gravely.

'It was Anwhyn. He didn't want to. But if he hadn't, the protection – the books and Eirrod's bones – would've been taken away by now. Just when Cautras is active again. He did it for the greater good.'

There was a puzzled silence in the room and Naz said, 'How? Exactly?'

'He had to act through an intermediary. He uploaded the code onto them in the OtherWorld and it activated when we were in Abergavenny. And transmitted to Pillington's Bubble.'

'He can manipulate code, too?' I asked.

'Well he's sort of made of it, so I suppose so,' Owen said.

'And the intermediary?' I asked, warily. 'Do they know ... what they are?'

Slowly, he shook his head.

None of the other naturals had enhancements as extensive and high-spec as mine. I saw, vividly, the TransBub spinning out of control, the white-faced screaming man inside.

The bastard. He was supposed to be my friend.

'You might not like it, Lona, but try to understand.'

I remembered the smashed Bubble sinking under the water, the awful silence, the howl of the parajet siren.

'It was ... it was Dodo,' Owen said.

Dodo looked up at Owen and wagged his tail.

Dodo distressed and whimpering on the roof of the court, his head between his paws. Naz treating him in his medlab, finding fragments of alien code.

'There was no other way.' Owen looked down at Dodo then back up at me. 'It's a war. Sometimes generals have to make difficult decisions, sometimes the innocent get hurt. That's what Anwhyn said.'

'Or killed.' I put my arm round Dodo.

'I didn't know,' Owen said, 'beforehand. What he was going to do, I just knew he was going to stop the hearing. He just said—'

'He told you to get me to come to the court.'

Owen nodded, miserably.

Naz looked appalled. 'Looks like we've made more than one monster, then.' The implications for Naz of an OtherWorld character turning killer were pretty terrible, if this ever got out.

'Let's keep this under our hats for the time being, guys.' Delauney was pretty shaken, too. He had overall responsibility for all this, of course. Legally, if it ever came to that.

We all nodded in agreement.

'I don't see how we can trust Anwhyn, though,' I said. 'Now.'

'Neither do I.' Fish looked sombre. 'But I still can't see how he had the ability to do it.'

'It's part of the Cautras virus, though, right Naz?' Delauney asked. 'Characters being able to affect things outworld?'

'It's compromised the security protocols in ways even I don't understand,' Naz replied. 'So, yes. And all the more reason to get the anti-virus loaded as soon as possible. But that's not going to be straightforward.'

'You can't just upload it?' Fish asked, hopefully.

'No, I have to get it to work specifically on Cautras. So we have to get Cautras to manifest in the OtherWorld and then activate something that will interact with him and generate the anti-virus code.'

'So, if we put the anti-virus in, say, an apple that got activated when Cautras took bite out of it?' Owen suggested.

'That sort of thing,' Naz said. 'Although he'd be onto the apple in the first place; they're not usually electronic. But the most difficult part would be tricking Cautras into taking a bite out of the apple.'

'Yeah, he might have heard about that one,' Delauney said. 'What if something took a bite from Cautras?'

'That's more like it,' Naz replied. 'Something that's 'tronic in the first place, that can change state – say, from friendly to aggressive – to order and that can take a bite out of Cautras.'

'No,' I said. 'Unquestionably, no. After what Owen's just told us? How can you even suggest it.'

Naz: A Journal of Unnatural Thoughts

Saturday 31 October, 2071

1pm

Creating the anti-virus was one thing. Agreeing how to load it was another. Lona wasn't keen about us using Dodo.

'After what Anwhyn did to him? Used him as a way of murdering someone? And you want to do the same thing?'

Delauney said that Cautras wasn't a living human being, though. And he'd got it in for us, Lona included. Where would Dodo be without Lona?

Lona looked troubled at this idea. Without her, Dodo's life might be pretty unpleasant. He'd probably be repossessed by DigiPal and end up as some kind of criminal's guard dog. Or worse still, made to take part in illegal dogfighting in some barbaric corner of the US.

She protested that this could fry him completely. He could die.

I told her I'd prepare the delivery of the anti-virus to maximise protection for him. It would make it slower, but it would still work. As long as it wasn't so slow it gave Cautras time to build an anti-virus defence. And we'd all be there with Dodo, distracting and weakening Cautras so Dodo could bite him. He wouldn't be alone.

We couldn't think of any other way to deliver the virus, so in the end Lona reluctantly agreed. As long as it was done in a way that protected him and as long as enough of us went on the OtherWorld trip.

They wanted to know what would happen to Cautras, once the virus was loaded. And to the agent.

I told them Cautras would self-destruct in the way that his incursions did normally because I'd used one of his code's key abilities against him. Except it would be for good this time.

I had to admit I didn't really know about the agent. Cautras must connect up with them 'tronically normally. That could be with their outer or innerbody system or with their implants, probably all three. So it was possible the anti-virus would be loaded into them, too.

Delauney wanted to know if that would make them self-destruct too.

It depended how corrupted they were, I told him. The more taken over by the Cautras virus they were, they more it would affect them. But it was possible that it might just burn out the possessed part and return them to normal. Maybe we'd never know who it had been. Maybe they wouldn't know themselves.

Owen was tired of the theory and keen for action. Where do we go to find Cautras then, he wanted to know.

We all looked at Lona. She thought for a bit and said that the merlord had called Cautras the Prince of Sorrows. And Elaine had said the sorrow was coming, and that we had to stop it, maybe that's what she meant. So we should go into the Prince of Sorrows story, *The Last Welsh Martyr*.

Delauney pointed out the Prince of Sorrows thing might be a trap, planted by Cautras. But Lona said that yes, it could well be another 'gift and trap' thing. It could be the OtherWorld protecting itself, giving us clues, or it could be Cautras. She was getting the sense that Cautras wanted to inscribe himself, somehow, he wanted us to know who he is.

'I mean, that dig at Caerwent,' she said. 'It's just too much of a coincidence them finding that now.'

That raised a few eyebrows. Gurvinder had thought the dig would close through lack of funding, Delauney told us. But an anonymous donor had come up with the goods.

And, of course, syphoning off money from somewhere on the nets to donate to the dig would be child's play for an intelligence like this.

We paused to take all that in. Then Lona said that if Cautras did lead us towards the Prince of Sorrows, it was for a reason.

'He's trying to tell us he ate his mother?' I asked.

'He's trying to write his own story.' Sometimes she seems to know more about Cautras than she's letting on. As though she's got some direct channel to him.

It all seems to comes back to the stories. Every time.

Delauney pointed out that if Cautras was the Prince of Sorrows he'd have to be killed by his son and that that was part of the Cautras legend, anyway.

'I can't programme Owen to bite him,' I said.

Owen laughed. If he dealt the final blow after Dodo had bitten Cautras that would do it, he reckoned.

Lona looked a bit uncomfortable at that, for some reason, and muttered that we could be a bit creative with the text.

Don't know what that was about. She reckons she's confused by all the secrets people round here have, but she's got enough of them herself our Lona.

'Okay,' Delauney said. 'Artris. The Prince of Sorrows. And maybe we should take some backup this time.'

Owen wanted us to take some of his CymLib comrades but Fish wasn't keen on that. Or on taking the Pagans in general.

'Fair enough,' I agreed, 'but best take Kite. We need him where we can keep an eye on him.'

Lona and Owen exchanged glances but agreed he'd be an asset in a combat situation. Which he would be, if he was on our side.

'Anyone else?' I asked, looking pointedly at Lona. 'Anyone disciplined, pro-Pagan, not adverse to the odd bit of violence? Who we could trust to watch our backs?'

'Not content with using my pet you want to drag my family into this, Naz?'

I said if she wanted to protect Dodo, they might be her best bet.

'Your family really are Zanegells then, Lona?' Fish looked out of his depth.

She said she hadn't seen them in a long time and they hadn't parted on good terms, so she doubted if they'd want to help her. But if she could track them down she'd talk to them. No promises, though.

And she had someone else she needed to have an urgent word with before she did that.

FORTY-THREE

Assassin override

The ownership of electronic pets has become widespread in the UK. All synthetic pets, like synthetic humans, have the prime directive of never harming natural human beings. Some anti-social elements have their pets illegally altered with the so-called 'assassin override', to turn them into bodyguards who will attack humans and kill on command. The natural human body is sacred in all major religions and the possession of an assassin pet constitutes both a faith and civil crime.

Alliance Field Manual, Chapter 15: Verse 1

I went into Anwhyn's primary story. I knew the risks of going into the OtherWorld but I had to speak to him before we confronted Cautras. Somehow I thought seeing him in his primary story, returned from his travels, would make me less angry with him. Seeing what he was doing for Pryddych and listening to the good sense of his arguments.

It didn't.

I heard him railing against powerful incomers who 'have sucked out our lifeforce, stolen the gold from our hills,' and 'mocked at our gods and outlawed our ways,' and I remembered Pillington's noiseless scream as the Bub began to malfunction. 'These men bring their own gods and magic, which they use against us,' he proclaimed and I thought of Dodo's pitiful whimpering and yelping as the Bubble spiralled towards its doom. When he announced that 'Eirrod will make pacts with tribes where it benefits us to make pacts, and will out-manoeuvre our enemies to gain back control of our lands,' I had to stop myself from shouting out.

I knew that Pillington hadn't been a particularly pleasant character. He was an American corporate lawyer and I'd met enough of those not to have any illusions about his essential humanity. He probably didn't have any. And, although he didn't realise it, what he was planning to do would have brought about danger, maybe even death, for many people. I knew that. But coming from where I'd come from, living the life I had, seeing the stuff I'd seen, I didn't have much time for sneaky murderers, however compelling their motive.

And there was Dodo. What he'd done to my best friend, used him as a way of killing someone? That was going to haunt me forever. He'd made me an accessory, just for taking Dodo to the court and Owen, too, for persuading me to go there. And the implications for Naz, if this ever got out, would be disastrous.

After Anwhyn had finished speaking, he broke away from the crowd and came up to where Dodo and I were lurking in the shadows. Dodo was all over him as usual.

'Down,' I commanded. Dodo looked a bit surprised at the fierceness of my tone.

'Your codemaker's woven his magic now? To defeat Cautras?' Anwhyn asked.

'How do you even know that, Anwhyn?'

'It's the talk of the OtherWorld.'

'No chance of keeping it from Cautras, then?'

'It may be Cautras who lets it be known here. But we'd like to help you, Anghared and I. You know we can't carry out the final task. That rule's too strong to be broken, even in these times of greater freedom. But there may be other ways we can assist.'

'You want to help us now, then?' I said.

'We've never done anything else,' Anwhyn replied.

'Pillington?'

'Ah. It's Dodo you're angry about?'

'It's betrayal I'm angry about. And manipulation. Not to mention murder. Of a real live human being.'

'If I'd asked to use Dodo, what would you have said?'

'No. Obviously.'

'And if I'd told Owen why he should get Dodo to come to the court, what he have done?'

'He wouldn't have had any part in it.'

'Yet Pillington's death benefits what you're fighting for. So I've saved you both from an ignoble decision.'

'That's what you do with Eirrod, is it?'

'Smaller wrongs for greater rights. That's how lands are ruled and peace is won.'

'I don't believe that.'

'I wish it were otherwise.'

'Why Dodo? He's an innocent creature. Why did it have to be him?'

'You know the answer to that Lona.'

'Tell me.'

'You've programmed him to kill at command.'

'And if I hadn't taken him to the court building?'

'There was no one else I could use. And Dodo didn't know what had happened, so there's no lasting effect on him.'

'Do you know what would happen to him if the police found out about this? To Dodo? To me? To Naz, even?'

'Those who police you would believe that a fictional character is guilty of murder? They have more imagination than I give them credit for.'

FORTY-FOUR

Blood and brand

An hour later Dodo and I were standing outside a large, gated building deep in the countryside, about forty miles from St Cadog's. I'd had to take up Kite's offer of intel to track down Lyneth and Rat. He'd come up with an address straight away. And if he was right, they were living in a mansion.

Maybe they were a rockstar's bodyguards.

I was still shaken by what Owen – and Anwhyn – had told me about Dodo. It wasn't really Anwhyn I was angry at now; it was myself. My illegal assassin override, my guardwolf, my protection that enabled me to do the work I'd chosen to do. I could take the high-risk jobs that other zlators would quail at because I had him. I was heavily and dangerously armed at all times and Anwhyn had just used the weapon that he'd found. I rubbed my temples. Maybe Naz was right about me; maybe even Faye Frampton or the Ice Fairy were right. Maybe I was still a Zanegell, always would be. Maybe that was my story. 'It all comes back to the stories,' Naz had said, wearily, this morning. It came back to the way words create stories, in my case. And one word in particular.

There was something else on my mind, as well. Since I'd talked to Anwhyn there'd been an idea that half-surfaced in my brain then disappeared. Something about who the agent might be. Something … I couldn't quite think, maybe to do with what Naz said the other day about us not being the Famous Five. But the idea disappeared as soon as I tried to grab it.

When I'd spoken to M just before I'd come out, I'd kept quiet about the attack on me and Naz in the OtherWorld yesterday, but I had said that we were going in to try and sort out the AI this afternoon. And that we thought that might lead us to the person who had murdered Elaine and injured me.

'Exactly how dangerous is that?' M had asked.

I'd told M that it wasn't without some risk but that I'd tracked down Lyneth and was going over to see if they might give us a hand. M had stared at me in disbelief. And said that as there was no way of stopping me, I should call the minute I came back outworld. 'The minute, you got me? It's not like I'm going to be able to sleep.

I waited, while the gate-reader verified our ID. I didn't even know if Lyneth would let me in. I knew for certain that I didn't want to go in, didn't want to ask a favour of Lyn after all that had happened. But the gates opened slowly, silently and we walked through, up a gravelled drive to the imposing front door of an enormous old house in acres of well-tended garden. Despite myself, I was somehow heartened to see six big bikes plugged in outside the house, one of them being tended to by a man in Zanegells' regalia. Albeit smarter. The bandana round his head didn't look like he'd been cleaning his bike with it; his long, red, moustacheless beard was well kept, and his tattoos were spelt right. He looked up as we approached and responded to my nod of greeting with a similar nod. No one I knew, but familiar territory. Though not ground I'd ever wanted to come back to.

I rang the doorbell, staring at the great expanse of polished wood and shiny brass in front of me. It took a lot of will power to stand there, to wait, rather than head back down the drive and handle this without Lyn. Like I'd handled the last two decades of my life. I didn't want to see her and I didn't want to remember.

But here I was.

AFTER ANWHYN HAD DELIVERED HIS UNWELCOME INFORMATION earlier, Anghared had appeared.

'You are going to confront this evil thing? You should know that you have support from the old magic that lies in the contents of the tomb.'

'Eirrod's body? The manuscript?' I'd asked. 'Like the Prophecy?'

'Those, yes. But some of the gifts placed in Eirrod's tomb can also be of help to you: Anwhyn's torque will protect the wearer from harm; my circlet gives knowledge of evil; my dagger once belonged to an enemy and is now powerful against enemies of Pryddych; the spear of Dorath helps the bearer to fulfil their true destiny; and Eirrod's Druidic ring confers power on a wearer who is strong in the Old Religion.'

'You mean we should take them with us?'

'It's the only real help I can give you. They're precious items with complex histories and in this magical OtherWorld that your codemaker has created, they will offer you the protection of the Seeing Stone.'

'Great,' Naz had said, when I came back outworld. 'We've got to fight an omnipresent, superhuman 'tronic deity and his human side-kick. And the only weapons we've got as are a bunch of magic bloody amulets. Is it too late to change sides?'

THE IMPOSING OAK DOOR OPENED AND I RECOGNISED THE BIG MAN who stood in the doorway straight away. Rat didn't look much different after twenty years. Brown eyes with a slightly spaced out expression, brown ponytail, maybe augmented now. He grabbed me in a rough bear hug.

'Well, well – little Lona. I can't believe it. Oah, wait till Lyneth sees you, she's been worried about you. Well, come in, mun, come in.' And he hustled me into the house.

So good so far. But then Rat hadn't been there, had he? He would never have been so ruthless. It was Lyn I had the problem with.

We went through a grand, gothic hall area and into a big, comfortable living room, full of expensive sofas and rugs, with dogs lying around on them. One or two of them looked up, with interest, at Dodo.

'Lovely dog,' Rat scratched Dodo's head. 'Wolf eh? Tidy.'

'He's synthetic,' I said, absently, looking round. Lyn and Rat had come a long way from the dilapidated farm and factory squats I'd grown up with too. Farther than me.

'There's posh,' Rat said.

'Christ, Rat, you can talk. What is all this?'

'Not bad, is it?' He looked round, grinning in his spacey way. 'I'll get Lyneth, she can tell you about it. She's in the office.'

'*Office?*'

He laughed and left the room.

After a few minutes, I heard loud exclamations in a distantly familiar voice. I braced myself, fighting down the feeling of nausea. I had to do this. And then Lyneth was in the room, followed by Rat.

She stood there, looking at me warily. But hopefully too. She'd been worried about me, Rat had said.

'Lona. You better?'

I nodded.

'Things are different round here now, Lone.'

She did look different. She wasn't the rough-arsed Zanegell princess she'd been twenty years ago.

But I remembered her before. Remembered too much, too vividly. That evening at Jonno's, twenty years ago. His face when he realised why we were there, me and Lyn. Realised before I did. The way he looked at me sadly, as if I'd let him down.

And then the muffled sound of the shot.

'We have to send a message,' she said. I was sobbing and asking her *why? why?* 'He betrayed us. He had Mam's blood on his hands. Stop blubbing, will you, and grow up. It's how we do things. How we keep bread on the table, clothes on our backs.'

At that moment, old Tesler came in, headed straight for Jonno's body, pawing him, licking the wound in the side of his head, trying to make him better. I went over and put my arms round him, sunk my face into his fur. Hopeless guard dog, Tesler, too good-natured and sleepy, bit like Jonno. Otherwise, maybe his master would still be alive.

'Get away from him, Lona.'

I looked up puzzled. And then realised what she meant.

'No. Not Tesler. I'll take him, I'll look after him.'

'Don't be sentimental, he's useless, we don't keep pets. Like I said, we have to send a message. And he's part of it.'

'No. You don't have to. Not Tesler.' I stayed where I was.

'Get away, Lona.'

And, still sobbing, I moved away. Because I was seventeen, because I was more of a coward than I was principled, because you don't argue with Lyn when she's pointing a gun at you.

I ran out of Jonno's, blinded by tears. I wasn't there when Lyn shot Tesler or when she put the gun in Jonno's hand.

I wasn't there in the morning when she got up, either. Never saw her again. Until now.

I nodded again. Didn't trust myself to speak.

'So,' she moved nearer. Looked me squarely in the face. 'What's been going on with you? Getting attacked? And all this other shit we've been hearing?'

'It's complicated,' my voice came out in a whisper. I cleared my throat, tried again. 'But what's all this, Lyn?' I gestured at our surroundings.

'We're respectable folk nowadays, aren't we, Rat?'

She almost looked respectable. Her hair was still black and long, but tied up on top of her head, bohemian chic. Her jacket was still leather, but soft, pliable material, elegant. No tell-tale bulge under the armpit. She didn't look quite like the respectable business woman Gwenda had taken her for, but something on the edge of it. You'd have put her down as, maybe, a successful music promoter rather than the president of a Zanegells Chapter.

'What's happened?'

She sat down on one of the sofas, gestured for me to do the same.

'Well, what it is, things have changed a lot since the old days. Possession of recreational substances got de-criminalised first and then distribution. And once distribution was legal... when was that, Rat, about ten years ago? Well, the door was wide open, so I bid for the contract.'

'So you're the same, just legal?'

'Well not exactly,' she said. 'We've expanded. The local area, first, then Cymru, then, a couple of years ago, the whole UK. We had the network, the organisation and the security, from the old days. If you can operate illegally, operating legally's a piece of piss. No police to worry about and nobody's going to try and roll you. The only problem you're likely to get is competition and, well, we don't get much trouble with that.'

'So, this. It's all, what? Yours?'

'It belongs to the company. Elation, we're called. I'm the MD.

Pretty much all of the old chapter make up the company, working shareholders.'

'You're *Elation*? The chapter's Elation?'

'Well, a few didn't like the new ways, having to wash and talk nice to people, so they left, but most stayed. They live here, in the house or in cottages in the grounds. A good life. But what about you, Lona?'

'I've, we've, been having a bit of trouble. Over at St Cadog's. More than what happened to me.'

'We had heard,' Rat said. 'Some evil stuff going down. Killings and all kinds of shit.'

'We can't be officially Pagan any more, but, you know. We keep up. And the murders were on the news,' Lyn said.

'Bit of a celebrity, you are, Lone, with some of our old mates,' said Rat.

'I'm just a zlator. Bizlator, normally.'

'But you've got Old Welsh. And Ogham. For old times' sake,' Lyn said.

'I'm sentimental like that,' I couldn't stop myself saying.

She pursed her lips. Crossed her arms.

'We all get sentimental in our old age.' She sat back on the sofa. Looked at me for a long moment, weighing me up. 'Who attacked you, then, Lona? We can't have that now, can we, Rat?'

'It's complicated. This is going to sound a bit mad, to be honest with you, but...' and I started to tell them the whole fantastical tale of Cautras, his murderous agent, the OtherWorld, and the manuscript.

'So,' I finished up, 'we have to go into the OtherWorld and plant the anti-virus. But after last time, well, we could do with some backup. It's just me and a bunch of university staff and students. We've got Dodo and the odd Pagan warrior, but we could do with a bit more help.'

Lyn raised her eyebrows and looked at Rat. 'It's all true then, what we've been hearing? And more. Unless you've escaped from a high-security mental institution, Lone?'

'Nothing like that, you can check if you like.'

She shook her head, smiling slightly. 'Same old Lona.'

'We can't have it, Lyn,' Rat said. 'Lona being attacked. And our Pagan brothers; I know I'm not supposed to say that any more, but there it is. And it's about Cymru.'

'Hmm, yeah, we're all about being a Welsh Company. One of the biggest, we are, after the fantasy gaming industry,' Lyn said.

'Dragons, dreams and drugs,' I said. 'But our dragons are going a bit pear-shaped.'

'Well, if what you're saying's true, then … we have to protect our own blood. And our brand. And St Cadog's; yeah, I'm always open to a spot of collaboration with local enterprises. On the other hand, if you're just having a really bad trip, or something, Lona, then all we lose is a few hours of manpower. Go on then, Rat, take a few of the boys down there. We can't leave you to battle on your own, Lone, even if you did bugger off and not get in touch for twenty years...'

She went on for quite a while after that. But the important thing was that she'd said yes.

FORTY-FIVE

The disappeared and the charmed

Many recognised religions use holy talismans or amulets in day-to-day expressions of faith. Christian St Christopher medals, the Jewish mezuzah and the Islamic Hand of Fatima are all examples of these. Amulets are also widely used by devil worshippers and other godless. Agents should be on the lookout for these, often showy, items of jewellery or archaic weaponry which confer the power of evil on the wearer. Such godless should be approached with caution.

Alliance Handbook, Chapter 17: Verse 3

'They said yes.' Bursting into Delauney's office I delivered the news I knew he'd want to hear. He didn't crack a smile. 'What's up?' I asked.

'River's disappeared. She was out in the wood with a couple of the others, gathering decorations for the Samhain ceremony, and then they couldn't find her. They searched for her and now Owen's looked everywhere.'

'The Faith Police?'

'They say they haven't taken her. Given the media pressure on them now, that's almost certainly true. And it's what they've told DI Driscoll. She's drafting in extra manpower. We're just about to mount a proper search before it gets dark.'

Owen turned up – pale and distracted – followed by Fish.

Owen shook his head. 'Nothing, Delauney.'

'You think the agent's taken her?' I asked.

'Cautras's followers – they made human sacrifices,' Owen said, 'to give him more power.'

My stomach lurched.

'I've notified everyone in the College,' Fish said. 'They're all ready to help us with the search.'

'I'll go and liaise with Faye now and head it up, Owen, while you deal with Cautras,' Delauney said. 'We'll find her, I'll make sure of that.'

Fish and Delauney left to find DI Driscoll and round up the others while Owen and I went down to artefact centre, collecting Naz on the way.

In the artefact centre I unlocked one of the glass cases.

Naz looked uneasy. 'You're sure about this, Lona?'

But there was no time for that now. 'Anwhyn's torque. You should wear that, Owen.' The wolves' eyes winked at me as I passed it to him.

'Anghared's dagger. You know Delauney thinks it might have belonged to Cautras, once? Naz, that's for you.' The emerald snake eyes glinted. Naz took it, reluctantly.

'The Spear of Dorath. That's me. The circlet is Gwenda's.' Owen had wanted Gwenda to join the search for River but she wasn't going to leave her boy to face Cautras without her.

'And Eirrod's ring, that's for Delauney.' The shape of the stories was dictating it all. They had a kind of rhythm.

'Lona, do you know how much these things are worth? Delauney will be frantic if he knows we're taking them into a dangerous situation,' Naz said. 'And anyway, he's not even coming with us. Why would he need the ring?'

'He just does, okay, I can't explain. It's how the stories work.

And we won't tell him. We'll give him the ring and tell him it's a replica. Owen should give it to him.'

Owen left and Naz looked glumly at his dagger. 'I am so not programmed for this. In more ways than you can possibly imagine.'

FORTY-SIX

Visiting relations

This great and golden son of the land led a brave band of
warriors into battle against the evil one. Their battle raged in this
world and the Otherworld and magic creatures, witches and
wizards joined forces with them.

from the Pryddych Cycle: *The Last Welsh Martyr*

Owen paced restlessly round the departure lounge and
Dodo followed him. Up and down, up and down, up and
down they went. Naz sat still, self-contained. Occasionally he spoke via comms to Smike, who was on the controls with two
of Naz's other staff as backup. Naz's team had realised there were
problems in the OtherWorld, anyway, when Naz was injured, so it
wasn't a complete surprise when he told them a toned-down version
of what was going on.

'They'll be more competent on the controls than anyone else,'
he'd said. 'And if any of them were the agent, the code they churn

out would look less like a bowl of noodles. Unless it's really good cover.'

Our secret was out, anyway, because we'd had to alert the infirmary to be ready when we got back. They didn't seem that shocked, either. We knew we wouldn't be able to keep the Faith Police away, once we got back, but it was too late to worry about that sort of thing.

Kite sat opposite me on one of the wooden sofas, one beringed hand on the gargoyle armrest, one holding a baseball bat across his knees. Motionless, he radiated energy. No nerves there, if he was the agent, he was doing a good job of hiding it. But then he was a trained soldier. Who knew if he was in Cautras's army? My idea half-surfaced again, but then swam away. Dodo. Something to do with Dodo.

Gwenda was beside Kite. Unusually still, unusually quiet, the Seeing Stone glinting on her forehead.

I thought about what Cautras had already done. The long, lost scream and the green-robed figure on the quad; Naz, torn, bleeding and barely alive in the empty OtherWorld studio; the attempt on my life or Owen's, in the tomb; and, indirectly, Pillington's face as the Bub swerved out of control and a helpless, whimpering Dodo, being used as a murder weapon. And now River, kidnapped, helpless, facing his barely sane acolyte. Was anything happening to her as we sat waiting? I thought of her, with her pink hair, crooked smile and her colourful, scruffy robes, hugging Dodo, who loved her; giving the reading at Elaine's memorial: 'Ghost unlaid forbear thee, Nothing ill come near thee.'

But the ghost had come near River.

I got a comms message that Rat and the boys were nearly here, and ran upstairs to meet them, followed by Dodo.

At the front of the building, Dodo pricked up his ears at the low hum of engines, in the distance. The sound got louder and louder and then four big, shiny, chromed bikes drew up in front of the College, each ridden by a large, recently civilised Zanegell. Rat was at the head of the group. As I hustled them inside, a tiny feeling of hope bloomed beside the big knot of unnamed and unwelcome feelings in my rib cage.

Rat did the introductions.

'This yere's Red.' The solid, reliable-looking man I'd first seen outside the Zanegells' mansion. He greeted us. Steel handshake.

'Oz and Deadhead.'

The other two Elation shareholders nodded in turn. I knew them both. Oz was still wiry, mad-eyed, hyperactive. His job in the new regime, as in the old, involved ensuring there was no threat from competitors. Deadhead was blank-faced, slow-burning. He was the one Lyneth sent in to negotiate if Oz's powers of persuasion failed.

'Lyn's sent us her A-team,' I said.

Owen greeted them like a warrior prince meeting reinforcements and they responded like it was real. Naz showed no emotion but made sure he returned their handshakes with a titanium grip. Kite – Kite was more like one of them; they accepted each other on sight.

I explained our plan to them.

'...so,' I finished up, about ten minutes later, 'the five of us can all do different spells inworld, and we can use that, as well, if the OtherWorld works according to the rules – we don't just have to rely on physical strength. But the important thing is to make sure that Dodo can bite Cautras. And that we all stay alive and in one piece before and after.'

'What happens when this Cautras is bitten?' Red asked.

'He'll gradually fade out – stop existing,' Naz answered.

'And the tools we've brought?' Oz asked, gesturing to the bag they'd opened containing their arson of assorted coshes and knives. 'We can use them in this OtherWorld? No firearms, like Lona said.'

Naz examined them.

'Yes. They'll all work the same way they do outworld. Guns wouldn't, Cautras could easily affect the mechanism.' He returned the stash to the boys and they took a few minutes arming themselves.

'Right then,' Rat said. 'Bring 'em on, eh, lads? We're ready.' The others grunted assent.

Owen picked up his sword and the rest of us picked up our assorted weaponry.

'We're going in to win today,' Owen looked round at as all, intently. 'We keep our nerve, we stick to the plan. Whatever happens, whatever he does. We'll defeat him, remember that. We're the ones who'll be victorious. Making history is what we're doing, today. Remember that, too, everyone.'

He spoke with quiet conviction and his strange new authority. All of us, even Naz, nodded or murmured assent. I looked at Owen, a little in awe, a little in horror. It was real now. He really was a prince, going into battle.

With Owen at the lead, we walked from our world into the OtherWorld.

VII

We all have to make sacrifices. When I realised that I needed to make this one, I felt sad, at first. I remembered Elaine and how that felt. Her face as she fell. Although it made me feel powerful, I also felt disgust. At myself, at what I'd become.

But, with this sacrifice I'm beginning to see that it has to happen. However much it hurts me. That's part of the sacrifice.

So I just snapped into gear. Found the right location. Private, secure. Hidden in the wood. The chapel itself is a ruin, but the crypt's intact. And no one knows that but me.

FORTY-SEVEN

Sacrificial acts

Anwhyn and Anghared worked for a year and a day to produce the new magic with which they defeated this creature; but, years later, he escaped from the spellbind they had placed on him and reappeared in the land. Then the son of the Lord of Sorrows, a true son of Pryddych, opposed the sorcerer.

from the Pryddych Cycle: *The Last Welsh Martyr*

W
e were at a local settlement, the same one as we'd been to on many previous trips. But different now. The buildings had been burned to the ground and the bodies of the villagers lay among those of their livestock. An elderly woman sat on a stone, staring blankly at the carnage; her eyes trying to make sense of the red splattering the green land, of the blackened circle that was once her home.

Her blank stare turned to us. 'The Prince of Sorrows.'

'Where is he?' Owen asked.

She nodded towards the lightning tree.

A figure sat in the branches of the blasted side of the tree. Another hung by a rope, swaying slightly in the breeze. The man on the branch watched us approach as he leant casually against the tree trunk. He was eating an apple.

I had a sick sense of realisation. 'He knows.'

'He was bound to.' Owen led us to the tree. 'We keep to the plan.'

'And it *is* one of us,' I whispered.

The lounging figure in the tree and the hanging man were silhouetted sharply against the sky among the leafless branches.

'Their chieftain.' He kicked the body that hung below him, idly, so it swung like a pendulum. 'Didn't put up much of a fight.'

'So.' We couldn't see his face, but the angle of his shoulders, the shape of his head, were all so familiar. 'Visitors. How nice.'

Owen stepped forward. 'We've come to challenge you, Cautras.'

'Sounds diverting.' He tossed the apple core disdainfully to one side. 'You must let me welcome you to my world.' He looked down at Owen and I could see the silhouette of his face in quarter profile. Familiar, yet not familiar.

As he spoke, the scenery around us changed, gradually. 'My world, gentlemen.' The trees disappeared, the smell of blood and burning diminished. 'Your gods will not save you.'

The sun went out.

We were back in the dark stone room, with the altar and the huge marble carving of Cautras. His world. This time, flickering fire breathed by stone snake torches lit the mosaic walls. It showed the shadowy figures of the statues lurking in their alcoves, like before. The smell of damp and fear and death surrounded us once again.

The flickering of the torch flames became increasingly violent and gradually, very gradually, smoke appeared and thickened until a vague shape took form in the air in front of us. It drifted towards the altar, swirled and eddied and formed itself, slowly into a figure. As we stared, it became progressively more solid.

VIII

The arrangements for the ritual are prescribed. An altar – I've used some of the old headstones for that. Candles. And a victim.

She's waking now. Those primitive, woven clothes, tatty stone and leather jewellery and all that anaemic whiteness and the pale hairlessness of the body. Unnatural. They look unfinished, just hatched. Those hairless limbs, that shining white skin, so translucent you can see the blue veins beneath it, the blood coursing through. They're almost not human. More like a species of strange animal.

She's coming to, flickering blue eyes. Blue eyes, blue veins, white thighs.

A TALL FIGURE NOW STOOD ON THE DAIS IN FRONT OF THE ALTAR, dressed in Roman robes. Artris, Prince of Sorrows. Cautras. He was profoundly, almost obscenely, alive, this digital, semi-mythic, long-dead Roman. His black hair curled abundantly over that face. Owen's face. Everything about him was the same, the line of his shoulders, the tilt of his head. I looked from him to Owen. With the two of them in the room together, the similarity was painfully vivid. Seeing Owen's strength and vitality distorted in the dark mirror of Cautras was beyond disturbing. Owen radiated honest good-heartedness. Cautras did not.

But Cautras had a look of profound, vital, brutality that made it almost impossible to tear your gaze from him; from his eyes. Glittering, green pools. They promised a dark vision that was supremely enchanting, if you could only look into them for long enough to see it. I stared, hypnotised and frozen, searching for that thing, that horrible, wonderful thing that I'd been born to see, forgetting time, myself and why we were there.

Then I heard a sound.

'Cautras.' Owen's voice. I woke a little from my trance.

'We've come here today to put an end to this,' Owen said. 'Today you'll die, completely and forever.'

Owen's voice was firm, his gaze unwavering as he stared at his double. He wasn't hypnotised.

I roused myself, forcing my gaze away from the thing we'd come here to destroy. I looked sideways at the others and could see that even the Zanegells were having to recover themselves. They thought they'd seen violence and evil. I thought I had. Cautras showed us that we'd seen nothing; we'd just scratched the surface.

IX

I reconciled myself to the sacrifice. On my part as well as hers. It's not the sort of thing I've any desire to do. But I'm a servant and my desires aren't important.

And then? The sound of feet on the stairs. Pounding at the door. Shouting.

'We know you're in there. We can see you on the infrared scan. Let River go. Open the door and let River go. Everything will be alright if you do that. It's not too late.'

The ginger policewoman. She's been watching too many cop dramas. 'Everything will be alright.' Hah.

I have to refocus, in the face of this interference. Speed things up, forgo the more traditional aspect of the ritual. A pity, but too difficult to concentrate on that with all that shouting.

I can still succeed, I have time. I can hear them taking the screws out of the hinges on their side, but by the time they're through I'll have completed His work.

CAUTRAS STARED AT OWEN IN AMUSEMENT. HE CLICKED HIS fingers. Slowly, silently, six figures filed up to the front of the temple and climbed the stairs to the raised platform. They stood, three either side of him, still as stone. Three winged lion-faced men, three with the faces of bulls. Time and death, death and time. Motionless, expressionless, they looked out on their empty alcoves, on the mosaic walls and on the strange band of humans below, with equal impassivity.

Cautras paid them no attention.

'Is there some aspect of term "immortal" you're not quite grasping, my little barbarian whelp?' he asked Owen.

Owen leapt nimbly up onto the platform next to him. They

were the same height, the same build. For a second, Owen stood looking at his dark twin.

'You're finished, Cautras. You were only let out from your prison in the Seeing Stone to be destroyed.' He drew his sword. The Zanegells jumped up to join him on the dais.

The rest of us gathered ourselves, focussed. I concentrated hard on a narrative where Dodo bit his target and we all stayed alive.

Cautras eyed Owen disdainfully. 'Then you'd best not miss.' Carelessly, he flicked one hand at him.

A huge ball of purple flame went hurtling straight at Owen. He made a desperate dive for the floor just in time and it flew over him to scorch the wall behind him.

'Destroyed, forever!' Owen leapt to his feet.

'By your blood, Cautras, as prophesised,' a voice called out, echoing round the chamber. Anghared's voice. She and Anwhyn had made it clear they couldn't intervene in this battle for the new Pryddych. Could they see us? Had something changed? In the flickering light of the snakes' breath, a figure began to appear on the other side of the room.

On the dais, Owen slashed at Cautras, who moved quickly away so Owen's sword only caught the edge of his cloak, shredding it. Red and Oz skirted round behind him, then leapt on him with loud cries, wielding heavy coshes. Two of the masked stone men grabbed them, an arm each in their stony grasp, and flung them away from Cautras. The Zanegells flew backwards onto the altar itself, crashing into the marble. For a moment I thought they'd been knocked out, but they got to their feet and with wild yells, attacked the two stone men with their coshes.

X

Hail, O Lord, great Cautras. Dark fire of this earth, possessor of the air, immortal vanquisher of the sea.

You are beset on all sides by enemies who would bind and subdue you, and I humbly offer you this sacrifice to feed your might. May the blood that flows make you invincible.

. . .

Naz and Kite advanced forward, throwing spells at one of the lion-masked stone men on the dais, from below. Their best efforts only managed to break fragments of marble from his wings and shoulders. Cautras had sabotaged our inworld powers again. Gwenda was near Owen, sending up a protective shield around him. If her shield had the strength of Naz and Kite's spells he'd better not rely on it.

Owen, manoeuvring round another stone man, thrust at Cautras again with his sword. Cautras moved quickly, but Owen still caught him under the rib cage. A red stain flowered on his robe.

There was a crash as Naz and Kite's spells broke a wing and a leg off the stone figure and it tumbled off the dais and lay on the floor of the chamber, moving feebly. Cautras's wound had weakened his ability to block our spells.

'Attack, Dodo.' I pointed with the spear and he bounded up towards the stairs and Cautras.

His eyes still fixed on Owen, Cautras held up his hands, smiling, palms towards him. Then he drew back his fingers, slightly, before flicking them forward. From his fingertips shot ten long, thin blades. Rat and Deadhead were superfast, repelling some of the blades with their metal coshes. Some of them were affected by Gwenda's shield, slowed and fell to the floor before they hit their target. But three continued on their flight towards Owen. One, heading for his neck was deflected by Anwhyn's torque and bounced back towards Cautras. The second heading for his face, he dodged with a flick of his head. But the third plunged straight into his chest. Cautras started to smile as the blade pierced Owen's flesh, but the smile quickly disappeared. The blade that Anwhyn's torque had deflected flew into Cautras's eye; he grimaced as he pulled it out, blood streaming down his face.

XI

Gold dagger. Red blood, dripping into the cup.
I drink of the blood that is the life, O fire-walker, light-taker, star-tamer.
The sacrifice drinks of the blood.
Dwell in my soul, great Cautras. I release Death, as you have decreed in the Mystery.

DODO REACHED CAUTRAS AT THAT MOMENT AND LEAPT AT HIM, teeth bared. Cautras flicked his wrist and a flash of blue lightning threw Dodo to the other side of the room. He hit the stone wall with a sickening thud and lay still. I ran over to him, calling his name, ran my fingers through his fur, trying to wake him. His eyes opened wearily and he got to his feet, a little shakily. He looked at Cautras and, in question, at me. I motioned him to stay. We needed to pick our moment.

The wounded Cautras and Owen were still moving round each other on the dais, the stone men repelling any attempts by the others at intervention. He wanted this. Cautras wanted this duel between him and Owen. He'd engineered it.

Rat and Deadhead were both battling it out with masked stone men who barred their way to Cautras and Oz and Red were still fighting off their attackers, helped by Kite and his baseball bat. Their lion-masked man took to the air, flying low and clumsily, but gaining enough height to create an advantage.

Cautras's gaze was fixed on Owen, but for a moment it saw something beyond Owen. It wavered. A young woman in Roman dress stepped forward from behind Owen. Owen's age, she could have been his sister, the resemblance was so striking. But her arrogant bearing and icy manner mirrored the man opposite her.

'Still alive, Father?' Livia asked. The Seeing Stone glinted in the middle of her forehead. 'Not for much longer, though.'

As she spoke I whispered, 'Go,' in Dodo's ear and he flew towards Cautras like a grey streak. Distracted, in that critical moment, by the sight of his daughter Cautras didn't turn to repel him until it was too late.

Dodo sank his teeth into Cautras's leg. A wave of relief went round the temple. Now we had to keep on, distract him, weaken him, not let him work out an antidote. And not get killed in the process.

With a cry of anger, Cautras shook Dodo off and, with one last baleful glance at Livia, turned back to face the wounded Owen. Livia, her mouth moving as she tried again with the shielding spell, morphed slowly back into Gwenda. Naz, standing next to her, relaxed the false reality spell he'd been sending up to get Cautras to believe, just for a moment, that this was his daughter.

There was a crash as Red's bull-headed man hurled him onto the marble altar a second time. This time he remained there, motionless.

Trying to keep up the narrative spell, I raised Dorath's spear, took aim and was about to launch it straight into Cautras's belly a few feet away from me, when it became tremendously heavy. I looked round and the bull-masked stone man who had been battling with Red was holding the end of it with his remaining hand. I almost saw his eyes glitter behind the mask, then his cold stone hand was around my neck. The spear clattered to the floor. I started to see black and red flashes as I struggled to breathe, choking and coughing. The world was beginning to go black and the sounds of fighting around me seemed a long way away down a dark tunnel. Then the hand was gone. I coughed and spluttered, looking at the masked statue on the ground, pinned down by a wolf, while Kite hammered lumps off it.

Taking a painful deep breath into my damaged windpipe, I ran up the stairs to the platform and jabbed at Cautras with the spear, more to distract him from hurting Owen than in the hope of causing any real harm. Annoyed, Cautras reached towards me, his lethal hand flexing. From nowhere, Naz appeared on the altar plat-form between us, dagger in hand. Cautras made a grab at him, but Naz nimbly side-stepped. Owen made a lunge at Cautras while he was distracted and landed another blow, just as a lion-masked stone man swooped on Naz. Naz and the stone man hurtled backwards down onto the lower level of the temple, where they lay, grappling in a cat fight.

Catching sight of me and Dodo out of the corner of his eye as he turned back to Owen, Cautras made a gesture. At us, at the carving behind him. Two of the figures from the carving began to move, grew and as they stepped out of the carving became fully three-dimensional. In front of us stood a wolf the size of Dodo, and a she-bear, both with teeth bared. I froze. I felt Dodo freeze. I tried desperately to throw out a narrative influence spell that made the two wild animals run up the stairs to freedom, leaving all this human mayhem behind. But I could still hear their growls above the noise of the fighting going on around me.

Then their eyes, at first fixed on me and Dodo, began to flick towards Cautras. They looked confused. They looked more and more towards Cautras and less and less at me and Dodo, their expressions fiercer than ever. Something was happening. My narrative intervention? I concentrated harder on it, harder, until, gradually, their eyes, full of hatred, on Cautras, they began to move slowly backwards, then faster, then in a flurry of fur, teeth and claws, they headed for the stairs and freedom.

Weak with relief I turned to see Kite behind me looking puzzled. He shook his head. 'Thought they'd attack him.' His reality spell. He'd made the creatures remember the cruelty Cautras had used to make them his. And I'd confused them by encouraging them to escape.

Another stone figure threw himself at Kite, knocking me off balance and I fell, awkwardly, from the dais.

Out of the corner of my eye I could see Deadhead, taking another stone man on, whirling a bike chain round. But even though he'd smashed off most of its head, it kept coming at him relentlessly. It had him against the wall of the temple now and was squeezing his throat.

XII

The banging on the door is getting louder and louder, I can't concentrate, suddenly I'm feeling drained. Gold dagger. White neck.

Thud, thud, thud, it's banging inside my head. STOP. STOP. This is a place of worship. I must finish this, I must finish this now. Gold dagger. White neck. Red blood, flowing freely.

I STAGGERED TO MY FEET, AS FAR AS AN INJURED ANKLE WOULD LET me. Deadhead, Naz and Kite were all losing the battle against their granite opponents. Deadhead looked unconscious, Kite was on the floor being kicked by stone feet and Naz's head was being repeatedly pounded against the marble floor. As I limped forward to try and help Naz, supporting myself with Dorath's spear, there was a movement at the back of the chamber and the figure I'd seen earlier appeared more clearly.

The robes and bearing of a sorcerer. But it wasn't Anghared.

It was Dorath.

A stone hand crashed into mine and knocked the spear away. I fell, hard, onto the floor. The first blow from a granite foot caught me in the stomach and I curled up like a foetus, my arms over my head; the second hit my kidneys. After that the blows were just a blur.

Then there was a crash, and stone fragments rained down on me. The blows stopped. Feebly, I uncurled myself and looked up to see Dorath aiming his reclaimed spear at the stone man holding Deadhead by his neck. Green lightning shot from the end of it. The statue shattered and Deadhead slid down the wall. Another streak of green light exploded the stone man that was kicking and punching the unconscious Kite. Another dealt with Naz's opponent. Dorath picked up the knife Naz had dropped and strode over to the dais.

Owen, substantially weakened by the blade that was still embedded in his chest, lunged forward at Cautras again and struck, feebly. Cautras, too, was slowing down and his attacks on

Owen were being confounded by Gwenda's shielding spell. Cautras staggered behind Owen, avoiding the shield and, with a smile, reached over Owen's shoulder and grabbed the blade sticking out of his chest. He pushed it further in, as he held Owen from behind, in an embrace. Owen spluttered and blood oozed from his mouth.

Rat had finally shaken off his stone opponent and had grabbed Cautras round the throat, but he still kept his hold on Owen, who was shuddering, his eyes wide open.

'Goodbye,' Cautras said, 'son.' And with the last word he gave the blade a vicious twist. Owen slid to the floor.

Then Dorath was there. The tall green-robed figure stood facing Cautras. He grabbed him by the hair and pulled him away from Owen and Rat.

'Take back what's yours, Lucius Proculus.' He held the dagger at Cautras's throat.

'You're mine, Dorath. I die, you die.'

'So be it.' And Dorath slowly, carefully, cut Cautras's throat from side to side, then threw him onto the altar where he lay next to the unconscious Red and Oz. He began to flicker and pixilate.

XIII

I don't know where the blow came from; the one that knocked me off my feet. Pain in my jaw, my mouth, more red blood. But not the blood that should be shed. That won't make a sacrament.

He's standing there now, my attacker, with the policewoman. But I'm getting weaker and weaker, things are fading. There's a flickering in my head like a holo that keeps losing contact with the server. Don't stop transmitting, oh Lord, send stronger signals, cut through the buzzing and the interference. Cut through and bring me your divine blessing. The beauty and peace of darkness, sorrow and the night.

TWO FIGURES MATERIALISED NOW IN THE GLOOM OF THE TEMPLE – one light, one dark. Anghared and Anwhyn. They moved towards the dais where Gwenda was carrying out healing spells on Owen with a fierce, focussed intensity.

I hobbled up to Owen on the dais to join them.

'Owen,' I whispered, looking down at him.

Gwenda was cradling his head in her arms. She took off the tight torque from round his neck, wiped the blood from around his mouth. Dodo licked his face gently.

'I'll be okay,' Owen spoke with difficulty. 'I'm staying here ... not going away ... it's all arranged.'

'You're coming back with us, Owen,' I said.

'River. Make sure she's found, make sure she's safe. I know you will,' he looked up at me. 'We did it though – together. That's what matters.' Then gradually, very gradually he faded out and there was nothing left, nothing, not even his sword.

But he was wrong, he must be. He'd be back outworld, injured, but alive.

A groan of frustration came from behind me and, turning, I saw that with a final shifting of light, a movement of smoke, and a shimmering of a distorted electronic image, Cautras, too was fading. His compelling image swirled with a disturbance of energy, as if he were being sucked into a void, and was resisting with everything he could muster. Dorath stood over him, dagger in hand, watching intently.

Then, stillness. Silence. Cautras, too, was gone. The place where he had been was empty, his remaining guards turned to statues again, maimed and caught in combat postures.

Dorath came and stood by Anghared. Rather than dying, he seemed more solid, more present, now that Cautras was gone. Dodo sniffed round the place where Owen had been and whined, looking up at me.

Gwenda stayed sitting on the floor, looking down at her empty arms. 'It's ... it's sent him back outworld,' I said, kneeling down and putting my hand on Gwenda's shoulder. 'Hasn't it, Naz? *Hasn't it Naz?*'

I could hear my voice as if it were coming from somewhere else. A broadcast speech. Naz walked haltingly towards us, but didn't answer me.

Anwhyn knelt and put one arm around me, one around Gwenda.

'What Owen did today saved many people. It was a warrior's death. A prince's death.'

'*He's not dead.*' I shouted. '*HE'S NOT DEAD.*' My broadcast voice was screaming now, sounding like a soundtrack in a movie. A movie you've seen before; but where you keep hoping the end will be different, this time.

FORTY-EIGHT

The anti-project

It is thought that Cautran temple sacrifice involved ritual violation of a young Briton on an altar, before cutting the unfortunate victim's throat and forcing them to drink their own blood as they lay dying. The Cautran worshippers then drank from a chalice of the victim's blood.

Dragons, Dreams and Drugs by and Pleasance and Bowen,
chapter 11, footnote 24

The vast blank greyness of the OtherWorld studio materialised around us, as Cautras's temple faded away. People were waiting for us: medics, paramedics, nurturers. Yvonne and her admin nuns. The medical people headed straight for the unconscious bodies of Kite and Deadhead, spirited them off to the infirmary. One of the admin nuns picked up the spear and dagger from the floor near us and carried them away, reverentially.

'Owen. Where's Owen?' I looked around me, dazed. I was still kneeling on the floor, in front of Gwenda, who sat, staring with dead eyes. Anwhyn's torque lay on the floor in front of her. But no Owen.

'They've taken him away, haven't they?' I asked Naz. 'The medics?'

He touched my arm, looked at me sadly.

'No,' I said. 'No.'

But I knew that Owen was gone. He'd sacrificed himself to destroy Cautras. All along, he'd insisted that it was his destiny to kill Cautras. And the Prince of Light dies in the process, doesn't he? He's only immortal in the stories, not in real life. Why hadn't I seen it coming?

Or maybe I just hadn't wanted to see it.

'He told us to find River,' I tried to get to my feet and stumbled, failed. 'He said "River. Make sure she's found, make sure she's safe. I know you will." We have to go and look for her. Now.'

Yvonne was next to me, then, helping me to stand. 'You need to go to the infirmary Lona,' she said. 'We've just had news that River's been found.'

'She's okay?' Naz asked.

'DI Driscoll couldn't say, she just asked me to divert a couple of paramedics to the crypt.'

'The crypt?' I asked.

'The ruined chapel in the wood. It has a crypt underneath, apparently. Must be very unsafe. That's where they are.'

'Come on,' I grabbed Naz's arm and he winced. But he came with me, despite Yvonne's attempts to redirect us to the infirmary and medlab.

IT WAS A PAINFUL JOURNEY TO THE WOOD. DODO WAS THE ONLY ONE of the three of us who wasn't injured. I was limping badly. Naz's head was visibly damaged, but although he insisted he wasn't in any pain I could see he was weakened. I kept forcing myself onwards, as fast as my injured ankle would let me. Faster. I had to get to River. 'Make sure she's safe. I know you will.' Owen had said. The last thing he'd said.

The ruined chapel was dark and silent in the fading daylight, but as we went into the derelict building we saw a faint light coming up from an opening, concealed behind a tumbledown wall, overgrown with ivy. From the crypt. We headed for it, scrambling down rickety stone stairs which were, as Yvonne had predicted, far from stable. My ankle screamed in distress.

As my eyes adjusted to the gloom I could see there were eight people in the crypt. Everyone was quiet and still, apart from the two paramedics. One of them was bent over some sort of makeshift table that seemed to be fashioned from old tombstones, the other was at the end of it doing something with equipment. Someone was lying, still, on the table. Which was in the middle of the wall and lit with candles like an … altar, I realised, with a jolt. Another bloody altar.

And this one was very bloody.

I moved closer and looked down at the figure on the altar. River. Her eyes were closed, her face ghostly white in the dim light of the dozens of candles that flickered behind her. Blood soaked the front of her robes and caked her hair. It was smeared over her mouth like grotesque lipstick. It pooled under her. Red blood on grey stones. I felt a sick sense of horror. Not River too. She was so young, not out of her teens. A few years ago she'd still have been playing with her Pagan Bobby Doll.

'River,' I whispered. Next to me, Dodo looked at her, whined, looked up at me. The paramedic next to me stood up straight and I realised he'd been putting a dressing on her neck. That had to be good, didn't it?

'Is she—? How is she?' I asked.

'Lacerations to the throat. Knife wounds. She's lost a lot of blood. And she's been drugged.' The paramedic who was at the side of the altar, adjusted the diagnostic device on her temples.

'Is—? Will she—?

'We need to get some blood into her urgently. But her signs are reasonable, everything considered, and she's young and strong.'

I took a breath.

They moved her to a stretcher and took her up the steps and out of the crypt.

On the other side of the room, Benedict was kneeling on the floor with Fish sitting next to him. Delauney was standing in front of them, his arms folded. DI Driscoll and one of her team were in between them and Delauney, wary and alert.

I stared at the little group for a moment. Benedict had his hand on Fish's shoulder and was looking at him with concern in his face. Fish had blood on his mouth – on his chin. He sat staring into space, rocking slightly, his hands clasped in front of him. Then I realised. Not just clasped. Handcuffed.

'Fish,' Naz said, in disbelief.

Fish looked at Naz. 'The transmissions have stopped.' There was confusion on his face. 'They will come back, won't they?'

I took a couple of steps over to him.

'You. It was you. You killed Elaine.'

'Lona,' warned Faye Driscoll. 'Leave it to us now.'

'It was lonely doing the Lord's work.' Fish was earnest now, more like he used to be. 'Elaine was spiritually open, so I tried to show her the right path.'

'But she didn't want to know,' I said, slowly. Fish. Efficient, reasonable, sensible Fish. All the time he'd been working against us. Had murdered Elaine. Had nearly killed me. I could barely take it in.

'No, no, she was interested. Fascinated. It helped that she had feelings for me, of course. We were discreet about that side of things. Our secret.'

'You and Elaine?' Delauney sounded disgusted.

Fish and Elaine. She'd been impressionable, an unstable girl like Elaine. Fish had taken an interest in her and she must have fallen for him. So he carried on this clandestine affair with Elaine even though he was in love with Gwenda. He had no feelings for Elaine, she was just useful to him.

Benedict took his hand off Fish's shoulder. Sat back on his haunches. 'Elaine's interest in Cautras was purely academic, Fish.'

'But she was passionate about her research, Benedict. And about me. About our secret. And highly receptive, spiritually, keen to learn other secrets. So I thought she could be my helper.'

Benedict looked appalled.

'You thought you could turn her?' I could barely speak. 'Make her like you.' Poor isolated, eccentric Elaine. She'd cared for him and he'd used that. Worked on her, in secret, manipulated her, tried to control her. Make her Cautras's handmaiden. I looked at him and couldn't see the man I thought I'd known. He was repellent, evil.

'Show her the dark light,' he said, eagerly. 'Yes. She was keen to see it. But then she started to believe things she was reading in the stories and when they started contacting her, manipulating her, she got confused. So when I showed her the face of the Lord she lost all reason. She started ranting about evil, stopped making sense. Then she attacked you, Naz.'

'You didn't have to kill her.' I tried to keep the anger out of my voice. Tried to stop it shaking. Vulnerable, otherworldly Elaine. He'd just chewed her up and spat her out like she didn't matter.

'I kept trying to get through to her, even when she was at St Brynach's. But she started raving about denouncing me to the Faith Police, telling Gwenda about us. And she'd seen the face of my Lord and rejected Him. What could I do? She was a danger to the success of my project.' He gave a little laugh. 'My anti-project.'

His project. His anti-project. Was it his efficiency that made him so monstrous now?

'You'd seen the face of your Lord?' Naz said. 'Literally? That's how you knew Owen was a descendant of Cautras. So you tried to kill him, in the tomb.'

Fish looked at Naz, then at me. 'Owen or you, Lona Luminos? We've succeeded now on the first count, at any rate.'

Rage boiled over inside me and I flew at him, but Faye Driscoll and the other policewoman held me back.

'You want me to arrest you too.' Driscoll gave me a shake.

'It's possession, Lona.' Benedict stood up, with a sigh. 'This isn't Fish. Not the Fish I know.'

'And what, sick thing, exactly,' Delauney's voice was low and menacing, 'were you trying to do to River?' He moved towards Fish.

'Delauney!' Driscoll barked and he took a reluctant step back.

'Well, because of your interruption I was pushed for time,' Fish said, resentfully. 'So the traditional part of the rite had to go, the sexual sacrifice. A great pity, because it's a powerful element. But shedding and drinking the blood of the sacrifice still strengthens the hand of the Lord.'

'Not any more it doesn't,' Delauney said. 'Right, Lona?'

I nodded.

'You're finished, Fish. Cautras is finished,' Delauney said.

'My Lord will never be finished, Delauney.' Fish gave a smug smile. 'He's immortal.'

FORTY-NINE

Samhain

Samhain was a Pagan festival, celebrated from the last day of October to the first day of November. Feasts were held and the souls of the dead were thought to revisit the living. Places were laid for them at the feast.

Dragons, Dreams and Drugs by Pleasance and Bowen,
chapter 8

'I'm the torchbearer,' River sat up in her bed. 'I have to go.'

Ever since she'd woken up properly, River had been obsessed with the Samhain ceremony. She was more or less okay physically now she'd had a blood transfusion and the drugs cleaned out of her system, though she was very weak. But she seemed switched off from everything and everyone. She hadn't asked about Owen. In the end, Delauney told her what we knew, but she didn't react at all.

'Someone else can be the torchbearer, my lovely.' The nurturer put her hand on River's shoulder.

River looked at her blankly. 'It has to be me.'

The nurturer took me to one side. 'We'll have to call St Brynach's. Poor mite, she's not taking any of this in.'

'No, please, don't. I … I think she knows what she's doing, in a way. It matters to her.'

It had been a relief not to have to lie to the staff when we descended on the infirmary, this time. The medic didn't look surprised.

'That's what you've been up to, is it? No wonder your bots were in such a state. And are again.'

I'D CALLED M AS SOON AS I GOT TO THE INFIRMARY. IT WAS ALL over, I told M, the AI had been defeated and the murderer caught. M could sleep soundly. Like I claimed I was going to do for the next day or so. I could tell from M's face that I wasn't being completely convincing, but at least I was proving I was alive.

It took a while for them to get my nanobots working properly. As the medic did the final checks on me I suddenly remembered what Owen had said.

'Staying here,' I muttered.

'No, you're good to go,' the medic said.

'No, Owen. He said he was staying here. It was all arranged.'

The medic looked at me square on. 'No one knows what's happened to Owen, Lona.'

'He died. In the OtherWorld.'

'His body wasn't in the OtherWorld studio.'

'Maybe it's in the OtherWorld. Maybe that's where he's staying, like in the story. The earth and the sky and the trees and the mountains wouldn't accept the Prince of Light's death, so he was taken into the Otherworld and became immortal.'

'You know what, Lona, it might be best if you do stay here and rest for a while. You've been through a lot.'

Staying there and resting was a surprisingly attractive idea. In my head I couldn't stop seeing Owen, as he faded out to nothing. Fish, as he sat there, his mouth smeared with River's blood, grinning about manipulating, seducing and killing Elaine. About Owen's death. About his plan to rape and kill River, about cutting her throat, drinking her blood. My mind danced with horrible images. And despite the painkillers and the nanobots getting to work now, there wasn't a part of my body that didn't hurt violently and all I wanted to do was lie down and sleep. For a week.

'And you should,' said the medic.

But I couldn't. I had to go to Samhain celebration. We all did.

But not all of us could.

Rat and the boys had top flight, augmented vBots, a higher spec even than mine, but Deadhead hadn't recovered yet. He lay, unconscious, in the infirmary bed, the other three crowded round him, their faces sombre.

Deadhead was connected to complicated looking diagnostic equipment. In the hours I spent there, I watched the medic come in, repeatedly, and read off the results, nervously cross-referencing them, watched by the other Zanegells. Finally, on his tenth or so visit, late in the evening, he breathed a long sigh of relief.

'Well, boys, you can stop planning the funeral. He's going to be okay.'

Rat and Red broke into smiles and Oz bared his teeth.

'He's not going anywhere for a bit, mind.' The medic backed away, cautiously.

Kite was a different matter. Head injuries, organ injuries. He lay in the next bed to Deadhead, looking barely alive, hooked up to a drip and surrounded by bleeping, winking near-field machines, bent over him like vultures.

'Is he a friend of yours, Lona?' the medic had asked, once I'd been patched up and given leave to go. By that time everyone had either been stabilised or discharged.

I nodded.

'I'll be straight with you, we've done everything we can now, but it's not looking good. I'll have to call his next of kin. His wife, according to his ID chip. Do you know her?'

Wife?

The medic went off to have the difficult next-of-kin conversation in his glass cube office. I could see him, trying to find the right contact, scrolling down his invisible screen.

River was sitting on the edge of her bed by that time, staring blankly into space. I took Dodo to sit next to her. He tapped her on the knee with his paw and she stroked him absently. Then, both she and Dodo looked up, alert, at the infirmary door.

'They're coming,' she said.

The doors burst open and the Faith Police marched in.

'Lona Luminos.' The Ice Fairy swept across the room and stopped in front of us. Her sergeant hung a respectful distance behind.

'Perversions of Mithraism? Pagan practice? Not to mention digital necromancy. What in the Lord's name have you and your friends got yourselves into now?' Lieutenant Bevan was as self-possessed as ever, but you could tell she was enjoying herself. She cast a scornful glance at Rat, Oz and Red, as they stood by Dead-head's bed.

'A family visit, very...' she began, but as her eyes moved to Kite's bed, she broke off. She stared at him, prostrate and vulnerable, surrounded by machines. Lieutenant Bevan went pale; and furious; and headed straight for him.

I grabbed her arm to stop her. It hurt a lot.

'Get away from him, you evil bitch.' My voice came out hoarse and loud. 'He's never going to wake up to answer your stupid bloody questions.' But her comms were bleeping, loudly, too, drowning out my anger.

She tore herself away from my feeble grip and strode over to Kite's bedside. Stood, for several seconds, staring down at him.

'Mike.' Her voice was soft now.

Her comms continued to bleep and she continued to ignore it. She looked at me, at River and at the Zanegells, her neat little face contorted with savagery.

'What have you done to him, you *filthy godless bastards*,' she hissed.

And that was how we found out about deep-cover, Faith Protection Alliance Captain, Mike Bevan.

River wanted us all to attend the Samhain celebration. And we knew we had to; we wanted to. It was only our complaining bodies that were holding us back.

Naz met us at the Pagan camp after being patched up in his medlab. 'Not too bad this time. Probably only the cost of a mini.'

I drew him to one side. 'Naz, what do you think's happened to Owen? You know they didn't find his body.'

'That doesn't mean he's alive, Lona.'

'Not here. But maybe he is in the OtherWorld. He said he was staying there, remember? That it was all arranged.'

'Like the Immortal Prince of Light? It shouldn't be possible. But then a lot of things that have happened in the OtherWorld lately shouldn't be possible. I'll go in and see as soon as we get this over with. Don't get your hopes up, though.'

Rowan and Delauney came up and I told them and Naz about Kite.

'Deep-cover Faith Police?' said Rowan. 'There had to be one.'

'Married to Lieutenant Bevan? No wonder he went under cover,' said Naz. 'I was right for the wrong reasons, then. I mean, he was a fraud, just not the kind I thought he was.'

'It would account for his extreme views,' said Rowan.

'You think he was an agent provocateur?' Delauney asked.

Rowan thought for a second. 'Yes, I suppose he was. But we'll include an invocation for his recovery in our Samhain ritual. Because he was a comrade, in a way, even though part of him was acting against us.'

We were in the clearing where Kite had led the previous ritual. The crowd looked the same and I could see Faye Driscoll and a couple of her team at the back, but this time the atmosphere was different. Quiet, subdued. Friendlier. We stood by the unlit bonfire, watching the crowd part as River walked slowly through, holding the torch aloft with both hands. The orange light flickered on the white bandage around her neck and on her expressionless face.

Delauney stood next to me. Although he was as appalled as anyone by Owen's death, he also looked calmer than he'd been for a while. He'd contacted Synthesis, told them what had happened and that it was all resolved, before the sensational media coverage broke. A photo of a dazed-looking Fish, River's blood still on his mouth, being led into a police car by a tight-lipped Faye Driscoll was on every news site with headlines like 'Demon-lover attacks again'. But however horrifying it all was, however much grief we were yet to suffer, however many nightmares it was still going to fuel, it was over. We were safe now, those of us that were left.

Everyone was silent. River handed the torch to Rowan, who stooped and lit the bonfire. Orange flame spread, tentatively, then multiplied, then crackled, grew and leapt up with fiery confidence. Rowan turned their back on the blaze and stood waiting for midnight, before beginning the ritual address. One of the Pagans beat out twelve slow strokes on a gong, as Rowan, silhouetted against the bright flames raised their arms.

And it was on the stroke of twelve that Dodo attacked me.

FIFTY

Some other wolf

In Metamorphosis, Ovid tells how the plant aconitum or wolfsbane originated in the mouth of Cerberus, the dog who guarded the gates of Hell. Poisonous to humans, aconitum was used medicinally by the Romans and as a religious amulet by British Celts.

Dragons, Dreams and Drugs by Pleasance and Bowen,
chapter 17

The snarling, snapping jaws of the wolf closed on my bruised throat. I tried hard to hold him off, pushing desperately against his strength and savagery. But even as I fought and struggled against him, I somehow couldn't believe this was happening. Dodo? It must be some other wolf. Surely.

'Down, Dodo, down,' I cried out, foolishly. Because it must be some other wolf.

'The de-activation code, Lona,' Naz shouted.

I managed to stutter it out. I could hardly see Naz as he grabbed Dodo round the throat and opened his neck panel. Blood from my arms, which were being lacerated by sharp, white teeth as I held them up to protect my throat and face, dripped into my eyes. Naz grabbed my wrist and pulled it hard, but he couldn't make it reach the swipe panel on Dodo's neck. He tugged harder and then wrenched it towards him. I felt my shoulder explode in a white flash of pain which enveloped my entire world. I hardly knew what was happening as he connected my finger to the swipe panel.

Dodo had his teeth embedded in my neck as he deactivated, his golden eyes staring straight at me. Dodo's eyes. But not Dodo's eyes. Some other wolf's eyes.

River came over to where I lay bleeding, crushed under 150 pounds of inert, renegade wolf. She was holding a blue flower that she'd just picked.

'Wolfsbane.' She bent down and put the flower in my hand. 'You need wolfsbane.'

Naz: A Journal of Unnatural Thoughts

Sunday 1 November, 2071

6am

A more complex version of the virus than the original. Much more complex. I should have foreseen this. How could I have imagined that something as intelligent as Cautras wouldn't have a contingency plan?

And I'm working against the clock with Lona. Dodo's shut down, so it's inert in him now. But although Lona's sedated, so she can't harm herself or anyone else, her body's still functioning and her implants are still working. We've set up a protected room for her, so Cautras can't connect with computers outside her own, but I'm the only one who can go in it. No one else has the right kind of defences.

We came clean with DI Driscoll about what's happened. She guessed anyway. Delauney's managed to persuade her not to get UK Cybercrime in yet. Not because Cautras isn't a cybercriminal, but because I'm more capable than they would be at dealing with him.

But I'm struggling with this one. It's mutated again and it's different, more sophisticated. And it's still transforming, that's the problem. Faye Driscoll's only given me twenty-four hours before she calls it in, but by that time Lona'll have had it, anyway, if I don't come up with something. And now here's Delauney at my office door.

6.10am

That was a bit peculiar.

Delauney came in looking tired and rumpled. Slumped into a chair. Wanted to know how Lona was. I told him her arms and neck were beginning to heal, so her nanobots were still working at a basic level. But that I'd got no further with an anti-virus. The virus in her was changing all the time, mutating in a way that was almost organic.

Delauney looked almost defeated. The footage of Dodo attacking Lona was all over the nets, he told me. He'd tried to persuade Synthesis that it was just a problem with Dodo – coincidence – but they were sceptical. We were on borrowed time with them too. He stared hopelessly at my desk.

'What's that?' He gestured at a crumpled scrap of blue, the flower River had given to Lona. She'd been clutching in her hand when we took her to the isolation ward last night. I'd taken it from her, put it on my desk, I didn't know why, really.

Delauney picked it up and studied it closely, rotating it in his fingers. 'River gave it her?'

I reminded him that River was now in St Brynach's.

'I know, I know, but, maybe ... I've just thought of something. I'll be right back.'

And he left the room clutching the withered blue flower.

7am

Delauney's had an idea. Always a dangerous thing.

The flower's aconitum, apparently. Wolfsbane. The poison that his daughter, Livia, used to kill Cautras. Delauney thinks it could help Lona. He wants me to model the genetic coding from aconitum and incorporate it into an anti-virus. He thinks that Lona would say it fits the rhythm of the stories.

It sounds completely bonkers to me, but I've no better ideas. So, as it's all we've got, I'll try it.

10am

Well, it's done. I can just about see how it could work, at a stretch. I'm far from confident, but it's ready to upload.

'Into Dodo or Lona?' Delauney asked.

It was hard to say which was the most dangerous, in different ways. Dodo, first, I told him, but I needed someone to come with me.

'Someone for him to bite if it goes wrong, it'll give me time to turn him off. If he bites me, you're all screwed.'

Delauney suggested taking one of the Zanegells. They were good with dogs.

12 noon

A few minutes later, I was with Rat in my medlab. Dodo was lying on his belly on the couch, his mouth still open in a snarl and his yellow eyes still staring ahead of him. I lifted his neck panel and tapped in the activation code. Then, wearing the latex glove that carried the imprint of Lona's index finger, I swiped the pad. Dodo stirred and I quickly pressed the red ruby in the middle of Lona's pendant, round my neck. Dodo's eyes slowly closed and then his mouth. His sides rose and fell as he breathed, but he didn't move again. He was on standby now.

My medlab's near-field devices mapped Dodo's code to my personal vision. For the next half hour I manipulated it by gesture and voice to install the anti-virus safely into his system. A delicate business. Rat stood, still and watchful at the business-end of the wolf.

When I'd finished, I told Rat it was set up. It would take about another fifteen minutes to run through and change all his code back to normal. We just had to leave him on standby while I monitored the changes.

As we waited, I stared at the graphical structures of the code as they moved, changed, wove together and flowed out of each other, while Rat kept his place; hands folded in front of him, watching.

What was happening with the code was like nothing I'd ever seen or heard of. I watched it, gesturing to make the odd tweak here and there, moving it round to see what was happening to the different layers. Fascinating stuff, it really was.

It's hard to say what happened next. I shifted position, still absorbed by the dance of the code structures. I moved my other hand to push back a structure and pull another towards me. Fixated by the code, did I fail to notice that the pendant was in the way? Did I brush it, with my hand, then absently pull it out of the way so that I could see the code flow into the sub-structures? But put too much pressure on it? It's hard to say.

The wolf erupted into life. The first thing he saw as he opened his eyes was Rat and with a blood freezing growl, he leapt at him. With 150 pounds of snarling, synthetic violence launching itself at his throat, fangs bared, Rat kept his cool. He grabbed Dodo's front legs as he leapt towards him pulling them apart. All this happened within the fraction of a second it took me to press the pendant a second time. Dodo whimpered and then went limp. I pulled him back onto the examination couch.

'I am so fucking sorry, Rat.'

He held out his hand. Hesitantly, I took off the pendant and gave it to him.

'How, um, where did you get that move from?' I asked.

'The old days. I never liked to use it though. I loves dogs.' Carefully Rat put the pendant over his head.

For a few minutes, I monitored the code changes while Rat monitored the sleeping wolf, with equal concentration. Then I told Rat it was finished. And that I'd fixed Dodo's legs. Was he ready?

Rat nodded, took a deep breath, then pressed the pendant.

Dodo's eyes opened. He stood up, stretched. He looked from Rat to me then back again. Looked around for Lona. Then he jumped down from the couch, trotted to the door and scratched on it, turning his head to look at us.

'You're going nowhere for a while, Dodo,' I said.

Naz: A Journal of Unnatural Thoughts

Monday 2 November, 2071

1am

We stayed with Dodo for twelve hours, monitoring him. I repeatedly ran every test know to bio-robotics and he came up clean. So. Delauney's mad idea worked. On him, at any rate.

But will it work on Lona? She's so much more sophisticated. Or so much less, depending on how you look at it.

I'm with her now, just about to start it off. Delauney's contacted M, tried to explain what had happened. Got the next-of-kin agreement. Difficult conversation, apparently.

Right. Switched on, connected. Now we wait.

2am

It's done. And all the signs are good. As soon as I could, I let the medical staff and the others know they could come in. She was harmless now.

The medic entered, with a nurturer, followed by Lona's sister,

Lyneth, and Delauney. Lyneth's been here since yesterday, she seems very attached to Lona, in her own way. She ran to Lona's bedside as soon as she entered the room and enveloped her in a one-sided embrace. The nurturer gently detached her from her sister and put her on a chair, then changed Lona's drip while the medic started to run tests.

Delauney told me and Lyneth that there was something else he'd discovered when he was trying to find out more about how Cautras was poisoned with aconitum. He'd come across a reference to the man Livia married after she despatched her father. The gladiator.

'His name was Hector Phillipus Luminos.'

FIFTY-ONE

The Immortal Prince of Light

Owen Gwyn Gryffydd died 31 October, 2071, aged 20. Much loved son of Gwenda. Memorial Service at St Cadog's Interfaith Chapel, Upper Mill Rd, Pryddych, Wednesday 9th November at 2.30 p.m., thereafter at the Druid's Arms, High St, Pryddych. No flowers.

South Wales Gazette, Announcements, 4th November, 2071

Rowan led Owen's memorial. Not because Owen was a Pagan but because the Chapel Minister didn't feel able. Owen wasn't dead enough.

I'd been up and about for a few days by then. I'd started work again, even been into the OtherWorld a couple of times. Naz had got there before me though.

'You were right,' he said. 'Owen's become the Immortal Prince of Light. It's his story now.'

'You mean he's still alive? In the OtherWorld?'

'Yes, kind of. It's weird. Go and see for yourself, when you're strong enough. But … it's not like before.'

But my first trip into the OtherWorld was to see Anwhyn. There were things I needed to get straight before I met Owen again.

HE WAS SITTING ON THE ROCK WHERE I'D FIRST TALKED TO HIM properly. In the distance, we could see the broad sweep of the hillside. Two figures walked together, deep in conversation, down the grey stone of the mountain. One white, one green.

'Dorath's still here?' I watched the tall green figure in the distance.

'My sister didn't know if he'd survive Cautras's death. Naz's magic is strong.' Anwhyn turned to look at me.

'But you, Lona, you've come here to wrangle with me?'

I sat down next to him. 'You encouraged Owen to sacrifice himself. That was what the prince thing was all about, wasn't it?' I stopped and looked at him. 'No, I don't want to wrangle with you, Anwhyn. I just want to know why.'

'I helped Owen to become the Immortal Prince of Light, yes. It's in the Pryddych Cycle, Lona, you know that. There was no other way to win against Cautras.'

'You knew he was a descendant right from the start.'

'The resemblance was obvious. To us.'

'And you didn't tell us what you were planning? Together?'

'What would you have done, Lona?' He looked at me for a long second.

I looked away.

I had one last thing I wanted him to tell me. I'd finally – too late – managed to work out what the half-formed idea about the agent was, that had been slipping in and out of my mind since I knew about Anwhyn using Dodo to kill Pillington.

'Anwhyn, when you said you'd contacted the five of us, that included Dodo, didn't it? Because of how you … used him?'

He nodded.

'So you meant me, Owen, Naz, Delauney and Dodo? You never

contacted Fish when you spoke to all of us in our dreams. Told us we were chosen.'

'He told you we did?'

I nodded.

'Fish had no special skills to help you in your task. But we didn't know he was Cautras's creature.'

If only I'd been able to bring the half-idea to the surface in time. What Naz had said about us not being the Famous Five of techno-narrative helped spark it because one of Enid Blyton's Famous Five was a dog. If I'd worked it out maybe Owen would still be alive. Maybe River wouldn't be so damaged or Gwenda so heartbroken. Maybe Kite – Mike – whoever, whatever, he was, wouldn't still be in the infirmary, hovering between life and death.

GWENDA SAT NEXT TO ME IN THE CHAPEL. DELAUNEY WAS ON HER other side, holding her hand tight.

'Welcome,' Rowan stood in the pulpit. 'We meet here today to celebrate the life, and mourn the death, of Owen Gwyn Gryffydd.'

But we all knew that Owen's life was carrying on.

I'D BEEN TO SEE HIM STRAIGHT AFTER MY ENCOUNTER WITH Anwhyn. We'd sat under the lightning tree in the perpetual Other-World sunshine.

'If I hadn't insisted on protecting Dodo by slow anti-virus transfer – and that backfired anyway – you might still be alive,' I said.

'Or I might not.' He looked different now. He'd only been in the OtherWorld for a few days, but he looked tougher. More grown up. Maybe it was hanging round with Anwhyn and Eirrod and their tribe. Or maybe it was dying.

He told me the final secret he'd kept about Elaine. 'I wish I'd told someone about Elaine and Fish. I saw them together once, so I knew there was something going on between them. That's mainly why I fell out with her, as well as the mad things she started saying about Naz. She got obsessed with him, Fish I mean, in a weird way; sort of hypnotised. And him, well, he was chasing after Mam on the one hand, but getting off with Elaine on the other. I didn't say anything because, well it would look bad for Elaine as well as Mam.'

'Was that why you asked him to join us? Because you suspected him?'

'I didn't think he'd killed Elaine, Lona. I just thought he might know more about her if he'd been seeing her on the sly. But if I hadn't kept quiet about that at the time, maybe Elaine would still be alive.'

'Or maybe she wouldn't. Fish was trying to persuade her to join him and he claims she seemed interested at first. Who knows how she or Fish would have reacted if you *had* told people about them? Maybe something worse would have happened. You couldn't know. Whereas I knew I was putting us in danger by trying to make sure Dodo was safe.'

'Ach, Lona. This is where I belong. It was always going to happen. The Prince of Light would defeat evil, die in the attempt and be taken into the Otherworld, where he'd live forever. You know that, you translated it.'

'It didn't have to be like this. It didn't have to be you.'

'It was my destiny. Cautras could only be killed by his descendant. Not that I wanted to be his descendant, evil scum that he was. But there it is, that's what I am and I had to do what's right. And now I'm here, it's okay. I'm content.'

'Content? You gave up reality, Owen. To be content?'

'Come on Lona, you know outworld was never my best window. If I'd stayed there, I don't think things would've worked out that well for me. But here … here I can just be myself, my best self. This is my home.'

'What about Gwenda? And River?'

'Mam visits every day. And if River wants to come here she can, but I think she should make a life for herself without me.' His face was set and sad. 'I'll always be here to see Mam. I'll never move to the colonies and I'll never take up with some slapper she doesn't approve of. It's every Welsh mother's dream, except that she can't feed me. She can even have grandchildren, if she wants.'

'Electronic ones.'

'I'm 'tronic now. But so is Naz and he's still a person. It shouldn't matter. That sort of thing shouldn't matter anymore,' he said, stroking Dodo.

DELAUNEY WAS IN THE PULPIT NOW, TALKING ABOUT OWEN'S sacrifice. The loss we all felt. After that Naz got up to read 'Code Poem for the French Resistance'. He said it was written by a cryptographer, Leo Marks, to help agents remember ciphers for radio communication. Code could be poetry too, Naz said.

Then Rowan talked about how Owen had known for weeks what he must do and had carried on, alone, with the knowledge that he was soon to die. But would never die. River, who had sat silent and still, in her dark-green seeker's robe, until then, started weeping violently. Naz put his arm round her.

We sang *Calon Lan,* about the death of death; and *Cwm Rhondda,* about making our hearts clean, pure and strong. At the end we had *Men of Harlech.* Gwenda hadn't wanted it, but Owen insisted.

Men of Harlech! young or hoary
Would you win a name in story?
Strike for home, for life, for glory!
Freedom, God and Right!

FIFTY-TWO

A Name in story

Owen Gwyn Gryffydd, 20, student at St Cadog's College, Pryddych, has been reported missing since 31 October 2071 by Harry Michael Delauney, Professor at St Cadog's. According to witnesses, Gryffydd was last seen in a virtual-reality gaming environment where he appeared to be killed inworld, but did not reappear outworld. His family and friends regard him as dead and have held a memorial ceremony for him. No body was recovered. Gryffydd's disappearance occurred at the same time as the demonic possession of a member of College staff, James Fish. (Fish is currently awaiting trial for the murder of Elaine Bowen and the abduction, false imprisonment and attempted murder of River Pritchard.) Gryffydd's official status remains MISSING but the case is not being actively pursued.

South Wales Police report summary

O wen's wake was in the village pub, the Druid's Arms. Half the College and the village were there, and most of the Pagans. Plus Lyneth and the lads. Minus Kite. Fish.

Gwenda went off to talk to confused relatives and Delauney joined me, Naz and Benedict at a table with Rowan and River. Naz was trying to explain to us what had happened in the OtherWorld, after Owen's death.

'At the time Owen was killed, the OtherWorld was being invaded and the invasion repelled. So the code was in flux. And Owen got folded up into it, somehow, as it mended itself. He's gone into the code; become part of the brain of the OtherWorld.'

'And that's how come he's the Immortal Prince of Light now.' Delauney put down his glass of smartwine. 'He sacrificed his life outworld, an act of tremendous courage and selflessness. But there's still a detail that bugs me.'

Naz looked at him in question.

'Well, technically, wasn't it Dodo who killed Cautras?'

I knew what he was getting at and I wasn't having it. 'You could just as well say that Dorath killed him. Or Naz, because he wrote the anti-virus. Both times. Or you and River because you came up with the aconitum idea. Or Gwenda, because she distracted him at the vital moment in the temple, or any of us. Everything we did in there weakened him. But Owen led us, in there with Cautras, it was his battle. That's what matters.'

Rowan and River nodded, but Delauney didn't look convinced.

I changed the subject. 'Anyway, I think I've worked out why Elaine attacked Naz. She left clues, but I didn't get it at the time.'

'Because Fish had made her psychotic?' Naz suggested.

'Going by what she said to Owen, and by the drawings in her notebook, she thought you were the innocent maker of a machine, the OtherWorld, that would let Cautras suck out people's souls. She didn't think you were a follower of Cautras, Naz.'

'Though she knew Fish was,' Naz pointed out. 'And she never mentioned it to anyone.'

'She was obsessed with him, Naz,' said Rowan. 'Elaine was a

fragile person to start with, vulnerable. And he made her keep their relationship secret, so she couldn't talk to anyone about the Cautras stuff, or anything else. That's what abusers do.'

Delauney nodded. 'And he was the College Corporate Director, remember, while she was a lowly research assistant. He exploited a position of power to influence her. It stinks in so many ways.'

'You know, I didn't suspect him because of what happened at Flarrg,' I said.

Naz shuddered. 'Obviously a hard master, Cautras.'

Benedict sighed. 'It's still all very hard to take in. I can't help feel a sense of responsibility for what happened to poor Elaine. I worked so closely with both of them but I saw nothing.'

Delauney put his hand on Benedict's bony shoulder. 'Not your fault, Ben. He manipulated everyone, including me. We let him in on everything about our fight against Cautras. We even trusted him with the job of contacting everyone to come and help us search for you, River. Of course, he didn't do it, and that sabotaged the search. Lucky that your constable was in the right place at the right time, Faye,' he added as DI Driscoll joined us.

'Fish was one of our suspects from the start, Delauney.' She sat down next to River. 'A student told us she'd seen him being more than friendly with Elaine. And the breakdown he had after his wife was killed? Not unusual in itself, but he thought God was talking to him and making him his agent. So we kept an eye on him. DC Preece saw him sneaking into the chapel on his own when we were meant to be gathering for the search, so she followed him, but he seemed to disappear inside the chapel. Then Benedict told us about the secret crypt.'

'Unfortunately, it was I who told him about the place, originally.' Benedict shook his head, sadly. 'I regret that. I kept it a secret because it was so hazardous – the students, you understand. But we will always be immensely grateful to you and your team, Faye, for finding Fish before he could do more harm.'

'If he'd killed me,' River said, 'that would have re-energised Cautras. He'd have killed more people in the temple and he'd have been able to create a more powerful mutation in Dodo.'

Rowan put a parental arm around her, and Faye patted her hand.

'But, we are, in a sense – forgive me my dear –' Benedict looked over at River, 'we are, in a sense, mourning *him*, too. The Fish we knew, that is to say, the old Fish. James was so important to the College's survival. His energy, his efficiency. There's no more news on his condition, is there, Faye?'

'He's still pretty confused. His mind was partially burned out, our police healer says, when the colonising force left him. You get that with bungled exorcisms. We don't know if he'll recover enough to stand trial.'

'He must have been receptive in the first place,' said River, in her new abstracted way. She was a lot better than she had been a week ago but the news about Owen, when it finally went in, had hit her hard.

'People like Fish,' Delauney looked scornful, 'only see systems and processes. Plans. Objectives. Conformance, compliance. They don't see right and wrong, it's too big a picture for them. Or a perspective on the picture they could never see.'

'You mean like not seeing the wood for the trees?' Faye asked.

'I mean being so focussed on keeping the wood tidy that the trees become an inconvenience.'

'Delauney, it was possession,' Benedict sighed. 'Fish wasn't responsible for his actions.'

'I don't mind saying, it was Delauney being so handy with his fists that stopped Fish in the crypt,' Faye said. 'Like a blur, he was, none of us had time to move a muscle.'

Delauney tried to look modest.

'Using Eirrod's sacred Druidic ring as a knuckle duster, I hear,' remarked Naz.

'I thought it was a copy,' Delauney protested.

'You know it's only supposed to confer the power of speed and strength on the wearer if they're a true believer in the Old Religion, don't you Delauney?' My jibe didn't make Delauney smile. He did look pleased, though.

'I may as well tell you guys now. Benedict knows already. I've been taking part in religious ceremonies with Rowan and River for a few months. They were kind enough to be discreet about it. And, over time, what started as purely intellectual enquiry has … evolved. The upshot of it is that I've decided to make a religious commitment to Paganism.'

Naz, Faye and I looked at Delauney with amazement. I'd known that Delauney had a secret, but I never imagined it was anything like this. And that's why I'd sometimes found River and Rowan a bit shifty, too. They were keeping his secret for him.

'What about your career?' Naz and I chorused while Faye Driscoll sat with her mouth open, incapable of speech.

'The College governors have accepted it. As have Synthesis. They think it's the new cool. Times are changing and Paganism will be an accepted religion soon, if we push hard in the right places.'

'It isn't yet though, Delauney,' Faye pointed out. 'No business of mine, but the Faith Police?'

'We're discussing with the governors the possibility of the camp becoming a permanent place of worship. A religious facility,' Benedict said. 'So the Faith Police will have to change their approach, too.'

'It will be a beacon for all Pagans.' Rowan's eyes shone. 'In memory of Owen's sacrifice. And Kite's.'

'Kite?' I asked. 'I thought … the medic said last night he was turning a corner.'

'He has,' Delauney replied. 'An unexpected one. We can talk about this, can't we, Faye?'

'He's in a safe house by now, so yes,' she answered.

'When Kite gained consciousness today,' Rowan said, 'the first thing he wanted was to talk to us and to our lawyers. The governmental review of the Faith Police methods that's been brewing? Kite's going to give evidence. Against them.'

I nearly spilled my drink. 'But his wife? The Ice Fairy?'

'Is one of the people he'll be giving evidence against,' said Delauney.

Naz smiled slightly. 'Unusual way to file for divorce. But, for once, I see Kite's point.'

'I suppose he was never actually bigoted about synthetic people, then,' I mused. It was weird now, thinking that Kite had been acting all that time. But then in the end he hadn't.

'You mean the Pagan identity they invented for him was just out of date?' Naz asked. 'Maybe. I was convinced, though.'

'We were all convinced,' I said.

'When his OtherWorld power emerged as making people see the truth in things, maybe that was about him changing,' River suggested. 'Wanting to live an honest life.'

That was pushing it a bit, I thought. 'But River, he lied to you. And you and Owen, you thought he was your friend.'

'But he was, Lona.' Rowan lent forward, earnestly. 'Ostensibly the reason he's changing sides is because he believes in Paganism now, and because he disagrees with the Faith Police methods, sees them as corrupt. And all that's true, of course. But I'm sure it's about Owen and River, too. And you, Lona. He genuinely was your friend and the Faith Police didn't protect any of you from a demon or his acolyte. And that *is* supposed to be their prime objective.'

'He wasn't exactly *my* friend,' I said.

'He liked you in … a different kind of way, Lona.' River almost smiled. 'More than liked. Surely you realised that? Everyone else did. Even the Ice Fairy, that's why she had it in for you.'

I felt my face reddening. 'That was just Captain Bevan's capable role playing. I'd be a pretty unlikely replacement for the Ice Fairy, wouldn't I, even if I was single? Speaking of which, surely there'll be recriminations for him, betraying the Faith Police? I imagine Lieutenant Bevan's reaction would be to hunt him down and eviscerate him, slowly.'

'And she wouldn't be alone,' Delauney said. 'That's why he's been guaranteed a safe passage to another Pagan community, somewhere in the world. New identity.'

I sat back in my chair. 'We're all going Pagan, then?'

'St Cadog's is certainly going to be reaching out,' Benedict enthused. 'We might even expand our courses on Pagan Studies to include a professional Druidic qualification.'

'Thought it took twenty years to become a Druid?' asked Faye.

'Exactly.' Delauney replied. 'Think of the fee income.'

'You could co-opt Dorath and Anghared into teaching on it,' suggested Naz. 'Now Dorath's got a narrative where he lives. As well as one where he dies.'

'Hmm, think Anghared's teaching methods might be a bit old-school,' Delauney said. 'She probably turns people into toads if they get the answers wrong.'

'You've learned a lot from her about herbalism though, haven't you, River?' Rowan asked. 'You could probably help out with the Druidic teaching.'

River gave a faint ghost of her crooked smile. Then she turned to me.

'There's something I wanted to ask you Lona. Something I don't understand. Was it Owen Cautras was trying to kill? In the burial chamber, when you were hurt. Or was it you? Because of your name?'

'What do you think, Lona?' Delauney asked. 'I guess Elaine worked it out when she heard that your surname's Luminos, that's partly why she was trying to contact you.'

Delauney had tried to ask me about this before, but I'd made it clear I didn't want to talk about it. I still didn't. I'd admitted to him that I'd found and removed the reference about Hector Luminos marrying Cautras's daughter from Elaine's thesis. He'd been horrified. 'Tampering with research findings? Don't tell Benedict, he'll have you thrown out on your ear. For Tom's sake, change it back before anyone finds out.'

I looked round at them all. 'Am I descended from our own immortal psychopath, you mean, Delauney? As well as his patricidal offspring. And a champion gladiator. Would that explain everything about me that's always puzzled you?'

'Yes,' said Naz.

'Maybe I am. Maybe not. The Welsh tradition was that you inherit your father's first name as your surname, remember, not their surname, so I wouldn't have thought so.'

'But Livia and Hector Luminos were Romano British,'

Delauney pointed out, 'and it's only twenty miles or so to the English border. So other traditions will have had an impact.'

I shrugged. 'I don't know, River. Cautras knew Owen was his descendant because of the obvious physical resemblance and knew what his role was meant to be. Trying to get rid of me, because of my name was, well, risk management, I suppose.'

'But you knew,' persisted Delauney.

'You even look a bit like Owen,' River said. But having curly dark hair, broad cheekbones and pale skin wasn't uncommon in Wales. We couldn't all be descendants of Cautras.

'Why didn't you tell us, my dear?' Benedict asked.

More or less all the secrets were out now. Like the dénouement of an Inspector Tapp holomystery, only much bleaker, more full of gut-wrenching regret, and significantly less cosy.

I may as well tell them my last secret.

'I wasn't exactly proud of it. And, well, I … I didn't want to be the Immortal Prince of Light.'

FIFTY-THREE

Gained in translation

402

The arch hailed me like an old friend. 'Welcome back to St Cadog's edutainment experience, for the launch of the OtherWorld AlterVerse and museum, Lona and Dodo, and welcome to St Cadog's, M. Enjoy your next great adventure in the past.'

But in some ways I'd never left the OtherWorld in the last six months. It wouldn't let me go.

When I returned home from St Cadog's, I just crashed, completely. I couldn't get off the sofa, couldn't concentrate on anything. Outside the nightmares, I felt flat. I felt nothing.

I told M the uncensored version of what had happened. In episodes. Short ones, at first and then, one chemically fuelled night, one very long one. Next day they met Naz on a holovisit.

'It's true then. I mean, you're not completely barking,' they said. 'According to your mate Naz, anyway. Who's a bit highly strung himself.'

M coped admirably with my departure from normality. I coped less well.

Every night I'd wake up in sweating terror to a world less real than the horrors I'd just been through. Daytime was a kind of torpor where I escaped from the nightmare of the real world. But, even during the day, my mind went over and over the same tormenting thoughts with monotonous regularity. *If only you hadn't got an override for Dodo. If only you hadn't insisted that virus be delivered slowly. If only you'd worked out in time that Dodo was one of the five Anwhyn contacted. If you'd owned up to being Cautras's descendant, then...*

'I didn't know,' I'd find myself muttering, in answer to the accusations. 'I didn't think, I didn't know.' *You didn't want to know*, the reply came back.

Eventually, M managed to get me to tell them about the semi-silent dialogue.

'It's not real,' they put their arm round me. 'What the voice is telling you. We're glad you survived, anyway.' Dodo wagged his tail in agreement. He'd been as patient about my state as M. I felt like I didn't deserve their tolerant devotion.

M waited for a couple of months until I showed some slight sign of emerging from my numb misery, then started coaxing, suggesting, encouraging me into doing things, gradually. Like washing. And getting dressed.

I began to talk to Naz. Gwenda, too. Even Delauney, who got on well with M when he holovisited us. M did a bit of work for him, on the publicity for the OtherWorld.

'Seems like a decent bloke?' they said.

'He's improved.'

The pitiless voice had got a bit quieter, but the nightmares were still in force when the offer from Delauney came.

His idea was that M and I would work with him, Naz and Benedict, translating the Pryddych Cycle into other languages and creating interactive book versions of them. *Pervasia Publishing*, we'd call ourselves. Synthesis were keen for us to use their new *Freedom* interactive reading technology and had already agreed to front up the money for a new subsidiary.

At first the idea seemed just too much. A journey somewhere I was trying to escape from. But then it sort of seemed attractive to go back to the same places, in a better way. It was hard to think about, but it made me feel less numb. And it would mean I didn't have to be apart from M. I started getting dressed voluntarily and seeking out foodstuffs. The nightmares lost some of their immediacy. I began to feel like some who, lost in a small boat at sea, had finally seen the outline of land. Faint and faraway, but definitely land.

WE WERE AT ST CADOG'S FOR AN OPENING AND A CLOSING. Delauney had persuaded Synthesis that it was good for their image to invest in the cool new market in Paganism, and keep the artefacts at St Cadog's, in an offshoot of their US Celtic Culture Centre. Synthesis were making the launch high profile, internationally. And my old roommate, Eirrod, was due to be reburied in great ceremony, the next day, in a tomb exactly like his old one, with replicas of all his artefacts. Synthesis would be headlining that, too.

It wasn't the old, ebullient Gwenda who came up to meet our TransBub. That person had gone forever.

'The loss won't ever be any less, that's the way it is. You just get on with things, you can't sit on your arse and feel sorry for yourself forever.' She hugged all three of us tightly, in turn. 'And I'm proud of Owen. Very proud.'

'He was brave, Gwenda,' I said. 'Is brave.'

'I feel stupid, of course,' she went on, 'not seeing anything, with Fish. If I'd realised...' she tailed off and shook her head.

Dodo leant his big head against Gwenda while M put their arm round her and told her not to blame herself.

'You couldn't know,' I agreed. 'Nobody else realised. I thought he was the sanest person here.'

'Anyway, Harry's been a rock for me in these last months.' Gwenda led us down to the Gawain Suite. 'And he's going to announce it tonight, so keep it to yourselves for now, but we're getting married. Handfasted.'

When we saw Delauney at the opening, that evening, M slapped him on the back. 'Congratulations, Delauney,' they said, 'Gwenda told us.'

He looked proud, embarrassed and happy. Sincere.

Benedict made the first announcement.

'Some of you may know that I've reached my hundred and twentieth birthday now, but what you won't know is that I'm planning to retire as Principal at the end of this academic year.'

And that, I realised, was the final secret. Benedict's secret. He'd been planning to retire, but had kept quiet about it, to hang on to his authority and stop people jostling for power.

'It's au revoir, not adieu,' he continued, 'as my retirement project is a new enterprise with OtherWorld colleagues at St Cadog's, Pervasia Publishing. But tonight I can tell you the name of my successor. Well, I'm delighted to announce that the next Principal of St Cadog's College will be Professor Harry Delauney.'

For a second, there was astonished silence. Delauney would be the first Principal in the two hundred year history of the College who wasn't a Methodist.

Then the applause came and it was loud, not just from the Pagans, but from everybody. People stood up and cheered and whistled.

'And I believe Delauney has an announcement to make, himself,' Benedict continued as the noise was dying down.

The cheering and clapping started up all over again when Delauney proudly told us all that Gwenda had agreed to marry him.

'We'll be holding the ceremony in the OtherWorld, so Owen can be there,' Delauney announced. 'Rowan's agreed to officiate and I'm asking Naz – now – to be my best man.'

'I'd watch yourself, Lona,' Naz muttered to me, after agreeing to the job, 'you could end up as a Pagan bridesmaid.'

M smiled, broadly. 'Ah, she'd look great in apricot organza, Naz.'

They both chortled, excessively.

THERE WAS A BREAK WHERE WE ATE TINY FOOD ITEMS AND TALKED to people, in an unstructured way, before the formal opening. Yvonne was marshalling her troops to make sure it all went smoothly. I congratulated her on her new role as Director of Administration.

'I'm not bothered that they thought the Corporate Director role was too open to abuse of power and abolished it,' she told me. 'It wouldn't have been me, anyway, Lona. Delauney will do his thing and I'll keep the place organised. We'll manage very nicely.'

Dodo greeted Faye Driscoll with the offer of a paw. 'I gather you and Lyneth are reconciled, Lona.' Faye nodded over to where Lyn was schmoozing the Dean of Ethical Enterprise. 'One big elated family. Cold cases can be reopened, though, you tell her that from me.'

'We're taking on an Ethical Enterprise knowledge transfer place-ment,' Lyn told me. 'Help us with our marketing. And me and Rat are going to run a masterclass for the faculty on security management.'

'I suppose Oz and Deadhead are doing the part two advanced class?' I asked.

Lyn had already put River on the books as a consultant on Pagan religious ceremonial preparations and agreed to source the products St Cadog's would need for their Druidic practice-based teaching. More importantly for her, she'd cut a deal, through Delauney, with Synthesis. It was to supply a combination of hallucinogens and mood enhancers, a special Elation mix devised specifically for the range of Synthesis AlterVerses. Naz was alive to the possibilities for the OtherWorld.

'It would add a whole new dimension to experience in the environment. Difficult to control, of course,' he added.

'Somehow, Naz, "difficult to control" in the OtherWorld isn't lighting my candle at this very moment,' Delauney remarked, as he headed back to the stage to start the opening ceremony.

First of all he announced the conferment of a posthumous honorary degree for Owen, and Gwenda accepted it with an enormous show of control. The room went very silent, then. Next he announced the founding of the Elaine Bowen Chair in Early Welsh Literature. Funded by Benedict out of the proceeds of their bestseller.

Then, his rhetoric fuelled by genuine emotion, Delauney gave a speech about what had happened and what was going to happen.

He talked about the Pagan Centre and the new beginning for the Old Religion. He talked about the way new technologies were making the old world come alive again. He talked about the economic and creative importance of the OtherWorld to Pryddych and Cymru and about Pryddych having a place on the world stage because of it. He talked about Naz, about his bravery and about what his involvement meant for synthetic humans and for humanity. He talked about ghosts and history, about the mysteries of machines. He talked about the way Pervasia would make the stories known everywhere, to everyone. But, most of all, he talked about Owen, about faith and sacrifice. About the Owen who lived on in the borderlands. About life and death and how they weren't the same any more, not after this.

The great and good were present, but it was Gwenda who was asked to cut the ribbon to open the Owen Gryffydd OtherWorld Centre. I could feel the stories swarming with energy, as they adapted, proliferated, greedily waited to be let loose from sixteen hundred years of burial and silence. Scissors glittered on silk ribbon. Silver cut scarlet. The borders opened.

Faith Protection Alliance Field Manual: Glossary of Technical Terms

AlterVerse: A virtual reality, or as it's increasing called, synthetic reality, environment. Many AlterVerses are supportive of faith and help to encourage religious devotion. But there are those, such as Synthesis's *OtherWorld* and *Virtual Valhalla* that appear to have more questionable motives, as outlined below.

Comms: Contemporary methods of distance voice, video and holo communications which use implants. These have been useful to our mission as we have legal rights to access all comms in the United Kingdoms, including the popular Synthesis vComms. Anti-social and godless elements are known to use illegal shielding software to block this legitimate access.

Holos: Holograms, such as vHolos, are widely used for communication and entertainment. Holos are also used by many religions for strengthening faith, particularly in small children, who respond positively to, for example, visitations by hologrammatic angels. Hologrammatic devils can also be used to help them understand the constant presence of evil.

Implants: Nearly all UK citizens have some kind of implants, which are largely used for comms purposes. Higher end implants, such as vPlants, can also be used for various types of personal enhancement. Serious offenders against faith (as well as civil criminals) may be sentenced to have their implants modified, or new implants inserted, to prevent them reoffending, see *Spiritual reprogramming*, below.

Innerbody software: Innerbody dataware, such as vInside, controls an individual's implants, nanobots and any other innerbody technology. Offenders who have had their implants modified by law sometimes attempt to use illegal innerbody dataware patches to undo the effects of this modification. Such tampering often results in extreme psychological malfunction and physiological breakdown.

Nanobots: Nanobots, such as vBots, are largely used in healthcare to enhance recovery from injury or illness. They are becoming increasingly widespread and possession of them is no longer a sign of participation in violent criminality. Most religions see the use of nanobots as enhancing the work of the divine.

Netting: Legitimately searching the *WorldNet*, the network of online content that forms the world's foremost information source, is known as Netting. Anti-social elements are also known to Net the illegal *SubNet*, see below.

Otherworld/OtherWorld: The Otherworld is the mythical afterlife of the pseudo-religion of Paganism, which they imagine as being peopled with magical beings and fabulous creatures. Synthesis's new *OtherWorld* AlterVerse, which they claim is a teaching environment for Welsh Studies, is also suspected of encouraging illegal Pagan pseudo-religious fanaticism.

Outerbody software: Outerbody dataware, such as vOutside, controls an individual's file organisation and sharing. It also interfaces with Comms and can be another useful source of intelligence for operatives.

Personal Vision: Augmented contact lenses or lens implants can be used to enable personal vision. Comms, WorldNet and other images will then appear on an individual's personal vision while being invisible to others. Not to be confused with personal religious visions, which are of a spiritual, rather than technical nature.

Selfware: Implants, nanobots and the innerbody software they use, comms and outerbody software are all referred to as selfware. Holos are also sometimes described as selfware, depending on their use and origin. The Alliance have a legal right to monitor all selfware in the UK, but most of our surveillance work is carried out on comms. This is largely because illegal software is more effective at blocking our legitimate access to other forms of selfware than it is to comms. Selfware manufacturers are obliged to comply with our right to access, but most leave a back door open for illegal blocking technology, though all deny that this is their policy.

In recent years Synthesis have begun to dominate the selfware market, with their vPlant, vBot, vInside, vComms, vOutside, and vHolo suite of products, achieving much brand loyalty amongst users, colloquially known as *vHeads*. While Synthesis products are nominally compliant with the UK Alliance's legal right to monitor selfware, there are some question marks over Synthesis's planned AlterVerse, *Virtual Valhalla*. This AlterVerse uses an individual's Synthesis selfware to recreate a version of them after death. If *Virtual Valhalla* were based in the UK, or in many other countries, such necromancy would be a faith crime. Currently, however, *Virtual Valhalla* is a province of Luna.

Spiritual reprogramming: In this, psychological and technological expertise work together to alter the mis-thinking and criminal behaviour of both civil and faith offenders. Existing implants may be reprogrammed, or new implants inserted, in order to encourage consequential thinking skills and enhance spirituality, thus enabling former criminals to control their anti-social impulses. Additionally, robust monitoring software is included in such reprogramming to enable law enforcement agencies to gently guide offenders back to the path of virtue.

SubNet: This is a heavily encrypted form of the *WorldNet* frequented only by atheists, criminals and other immoral and anti-social elements. The legality of the SubNet is currently in question in the UK.

Synthetic Human: Robots in human form with self-awareness are known as synthetic humans. Synthetic humans are indentured to their creator for the first period of their lives, until they have paid off the cost of their manufacture. After this they have the same rights as natural humans. Because synthetic humans have been widely used in the sex industry, particularly as compliant sexual companions, there is understandable prejudice against them. But new models of synthetics are becoming more sophisticated and moving away from these areas of work, so such prejudice is not encouraged among operatives. In particular, the term 'synth', often referred to as the 's-word', is considered offensive and should not be used in dialogue with a synthetic human.

Vidloop: Vidloops are usually animated photographs. They are commonly used to display images of loved ones, particularly of the departed. Some religions use animated images of gods or holy men and women as part of their acts of faith. This has been viciously lampooned by the godless. One vidloop, for example, which is often displayed amongst the lost and damaged, depicts Jesus Christ performing a dance called 'The Time Warp'.

A note from the author

Hello there. You've reached the end of the book, so I hope that means you enjoyed it. If you did, I'd love you to leave a review on *Amazon* or *Goodreads*. Reviews are hugely important to new writers, as they're the best way for readers to hear about our books. Reader power helps us get a foothold in the big, bad world of publishing, which, in turn, means readers get more of the books that they want. So massive thanks if you do leave a review.

If you want to find out more about my books and stories, including new books, giveaways and pre-release specials, visit: http://www.catthomas.org

You can also add me on Facebook, where I'd be delighted to meet you: https://www.facebook.com/cat.thomas.90038

Acknowledgments

The key books and papers I used in my research for this novel are included in my bibliography, but I'd like to highlight the work of a few writers to whom I am particularly indebted.

Historian Peter Berresford Ellis's lively and interesting works on Celtic Britain were especially helpful in giving me a sense of place and culture. My ideas about the way in which digital technologies might shape the people of the future owe a particular debt to the theorists N. Katherine Hayles, Jodi Dean and the late Friedrich Kittler (and I'd definitely like to thank Caroline Bassett for pointing me towards Dean and Kittler). Stefan Collini's accessible, and erudite, dissection of the direction of travel for UK universities has helped me to better understand my experience of working in them, and to imagine how they might change in the future.

My conceptualisation of a future of compulsory religion has been aided by some of Humanists UK's work on religion, State and human rights. When designing the non-traditional funerals and wedding ceremonies in this novel, input from some members of the

North London Humanist celebrants' group was most helpful. Thanks to all you lovely people.

Many thanks to my clear-sighted and practical editors, Scott Pack and Eleanor Abraham. I also had feedback on earlier drafts of the novel from Caroline Goldsmith and Rodge Glass, for which I'm grateful.

My feline assistants, who have slept on my desk, keeping me company throughout the long haul of writing this novel have also played their part admirably.

But, most of all, thanks to Paul for his understanding, patience and support.

Bibliography

Below is some of the reading which helped me to better understand, and imagine, the digital futures and Celtic pasts of this novel. Additionally, although most of the ideas about the future of universities come from my own workplace experience of UK higher education, I include some of the more significant books and articles that helped give shape and organisation to these thoughts.

Andrejevic, M. (2007) *iSpy: surveillance and power in the interactive era*. Kansas: University Press of Kansas.

Anon. Undated. *The Mabinogion*. Trans: Gantz, J. (1976) London: Penguin

Barcan, R. (2013) *Academic life and labour in the new university*. Farnham: Ashgate. Kindle edn, 2014.

Brown, R. and Carasso, H. (2013) *Everything for sale? The marketisation of UK higher education*. Oxford: Taylor and Francis. Kindle edn.

Berresford Ellis, P. (1988) *The Celtic revolution*. Talybont: Y Lolfa.

Berresford Ellis, P. (1996) *The druids*. London: Constable.

Burrows, R. (2012) 'Living with the h-index? Metric assemblages in the contemporary academy', *The Sociological Review*, 60 (2), pp. 355-72.

Chadwick, N. (1971) *The Celts*. London: Penguin

Collini, S. (2012) *What are universities for?* London: Penguin.

Collini, S. (2017) *Speaking of universities.* London: Verso

Crary, J. (2013) *24/7: Late capitalism and the ends of sleep*. London: Verso. Kindle edn.

Davies, J. (2007) *A history of Wales*. London: Penguin.

Dean, J. (2002) *Publicity's secret: how technoculture capitalizes on democracy*. New York: Cornell University Press.

Geoffrey of Monmouth (1136) *The history of the kings of Britain*. Trans: Thorpe, L. 1966 London: Penguin.

Hayles, N. K. (2005) *My mother was a computer: digital subjects and literary texts*. Chicago: University of Chicago Press.

Hayles, N. K. (2006) 'Traumas of code', *Critical Enquiry*, 33 (Autumn), pp. 136-57.

Jarratt, A. (1985) *Report of the Steering Committee for Efficiency Studies in Universities*. (Jarratt Report). London: CVCP.

Jones, T. and Ereira, A. (2007) *Barbarians*. London: BBC Books.

Kittler, F. A. (1986) *Gramophone, film, typewriter*. Translated by Geoffrey Winthrop-Young and Michael Wutz. Stanford: Stanford University Press, 1999.

Kittler, F. A. (1997) *Literature, media information systems: essays*. Amsterdam: OPA.

Matthews, C. (1996) *The elements of the Celtic tradition*. Dorset: Element

Matthews, C. (1996) *Arthur and the sovereignty of Britain*. Bungay: Arkana.

McMahon, W. (2009) *Higher learning, greater good*. Baltimore: John Hopkins University Press.

Morozov, E. (2013) *To save everything, click here*. London: Allen Lane.

Mosco, V. (2004) *The digital sublime: myth, power and cyberspace*. Cambridge, Mass: MIT Press.

Newman, J. H. (1853) *The idea of a university defined and illustrated: in nine discourses delivered to the Catholics of Dublin*. Public Domain. Kindle edn, n.d.

Poster, M. (2001) *What's the matter with the internet?* Minneapolis: University of Minnesota Press.

Scholz, T. (ed.) (2013) *Digital labor: the internet as playground and factory.* New York: Routledge.

Thurschwell, P. (2001) *Literature, technology and magical thinking, 1880–1920.* Cambridge: Cambridge University Press.

Wertheim, M. (1999) *The pearly gates of cyberspace.* London: Virago.

Wood, M. (2005) *In search of the dark ages.* London: BBC Books

Also by Cat Thomas

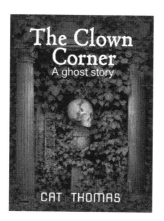

A FORGOTTEN GRAVE REVEALS SINISTER SECRETS

When Susie discovers a secret grave in a deserted corner of a Gothic London cemetery, she knows that things are about to change for her. She's sure this find will help her turn her troubled life around. Susie sets off to solve the mystery of the man who lies there, 'Clappy the clown'. Who was Clappy? And why was he buried so secretly, 100 years ago?

Her quest leads her to the quirky East End clown museum, and helped by its eccentric curator, Sparky, she begins to find unsettling answers – and a new vocation in life. But as Susie gets to know Clappy better, we begin to realise that neither Clappy, nor Susie, are quite as they appear to be.

The Clown Corner is both a creepy ghost story and a study of how a dark obsession can shade into madness. Cat Thomas's writing brings a light touch to a deeply twisted tale.

About the Author

Cat Thomas is a writer of speculative fiction. She grew up in South Wales and now lives in London, UK. Find out more about Cat by visiting:

www.catthomas.org

You can also connect with her on FaceBook at:

www.facebook.com/twistedfiction101

Printed in Great Britain
by Amazon